THE
JOURNEYMAN

....

THE COMMONS: BOOK 1

MICHAEL ALAN PECK

Dinuhos Arts, LLC
CHICAGO, ILLINOIS

Dinuhos Arts, LLC
5315 North Clark Street
#230
Chicago, Illinois 60640
www.dinuhos.com

Publisher's Note: This is a work of fiction. Names, characters, places, and incidents are a product of the author's imagination. Locales and public names are sometimes used for atmospheric purposes. Any resemblance to actual people, living or dead, or to businesses, companies, events, institutions, or locales is completely coincidental.

Book Layout ©2013 BookDesignTemplates.com

The Commons: Book 1: The Journeyman/Michael Alan Peck. -- 1st ed.
ISBN 978-0-9860823-2-0

*To Ira J. Peck, who gave me dreams of flying—and
to Renée, who keeps me on course*

PART ONE:
NEW BEGINNINGS

....

ONE

THE ALL-SEEING EYES

P aul Reid died in the snow at seventeen. The day of his death, he told a lie—and for the rest of his life, he wondered if that was what killed him.

"Don't worry," he said to Mike Hibbets, the only adult in New York City who'd ever cared about him. "I'm coming back."

Pop Mike ran the New Beginnings group home, where Paul lived. He didn't believe the lie. And Paul told himself that it didn't matter.

"Does your face hurt?" The old man leaned on his desk in the New Beginnings main office.

Paul twisted his pewter ring, a habit that announced when something was bothering him. His face did hurt—especially his swollen eye.

As did the ribs he hadn't been able to protect two days earlier, when he hit the ground, balled up, in a Hell's Kitchen alley while four guys stomped him until they tired of it. He'd tried to shield his face, where damage might show forever. But he fared just as poorly at that as the afternoon sun cast a beat-down shadow show on a brick wall and a girl stood nearby and cried.

Paul had little to say, and no one worked a silence like Pop Mike. His nickname had once been "Father Mike" due to a talent for sniffing out guilt that rivaled any priest's. He asked the New Beginnings kids to drop that name so potential donors wouldn't confuse his shelter with a religious operation. There's no God to lift us up—we rise or fall together, he taught them. So they compromised and shortened it.

"Five foster homes, three group homes, some street life in between," Pop Mike said.

"So?" Paul couldn't look him in the eye.

"So no one makes it through that without survival skills, which you have. And you've found a place here for four years, and now you're just up and leaving."

The desk was a relic of the building's days as a school, a general hospital, and before that, a mental hospital. Its round wood edge was uneven and worn, as if the many kids trapped in this chair over the years had stared it away, varnish and all.

Paul shifted in the chair, his side one big ache. He hated hearing his life recited as if it were recorded and filed somewhere, which it was.

The winter wind forced its way through the gaps between the cockeyed window sash and its frame. A storm was due.

Outside, the fading daylight illuminated the wall of the adjacent building. A cartoon-ad peacock, its paint battling to hang onto the decaying brick, peddled a variety of Pavo fruit juices.

"New Beginnings matters to you." Rumor was, Pop Mike could go weeks without blinking. "Look how you tried to save Gonzales."

"I told him to run for help. He just ran." Paul had practiced this conversation—how it would play out. Pop Mike wouldn't mind that he was leaving. If he did, Paul wouldn't sweat it.

Yet he was unable to face the man.

The painted peacock smiled despite its sentence of death-by-crumbling. Its tail, gathered in one fist, bent outward in offering. The feathers ended in a once-vibrant assortment of bottles spread above the Pavo slogan like leaves on a branch of a shade tree: "Wake up to the rainbow! Wake up to your life!"

Decades of sun and rain had rendered the flavors unidentifiable in the grime and washed-out hues. Paul could only guess at grape, apple, orange, and watermelon.

"You could apply for our Next Steps program— work your way to an equivalency credential."

Paul didn't bother to refuse that one again.

Pop Mike followed his gaze. "The all-seeing eyes."

"What?"

"The peacock. In some Asian faiths, it's a symbol of mercy and empathy. In others, it's the all-seeing eyes of the Almighty. What that one sees, of course, is a customer."

"It's time for me to go." Paul touched his fingers to his eye, which flared in protest. "This is how New York chose to tell me." He prodded the bruise to see if he could make it hurt more. He succeeded.

Pop Mike reached across the desk, took hold of Paul's wrist, and gently pulled his hand away from his face. He didn't let go until he was convinced Paul wouldn't do it again. That was the only way he could keep Paul safe from himself.

"Please," he said. "That's the one word I have left. It won't work, but I'm saying it. Please."

Paul twisted his ring.

Pop Mike took in the beaten-up backpack at Paul's feet, the military-surplus coat thrown over the back of the chair. "Where are you going?"

"Away. I'll let you know when I get there."

Wake up to your life, said the peacock.

THE THREE-BLOCK walk to Port Authority seemed to triple in the stinging wind. Paul's military-surplus coat was suitable only for motivating the troops wearing it to prevail before winter. It came from a pallet of stuff donated to New Beginnings as a tax write-off. He'd thought the coat would keep him warm and make him look tougher. The bite of the air and the beating in the alley proved him twice wrong.

A radio, its volume cranked up to the point of distortion, hung from a nail on a newsstand, dangling over piles of papers and magazines draped with clear plastic tarps. A weather-on-the-ones update milked the conditions of the approaching storm for drama, as did several headlines. "Blizzardämmerung!" screamed the *Daily News*. "Snowmageddon!" warned the *Post*.

The stand's owner, his face framed by graphic novels and tabloids binder-clipped around the window of a dual-pane Plexiglass wall, sung about how he'd just dropped in to see what condition the conditions were in. Commuters trying to beat the weather home paid him no mind.

By now, the meteorologist was more reporter than forecaster. Rounding the corner at Forty-second and Eighth, Paul had to blink away hard-blown flakes.

A feral-looking girl pulled one of the terminal's heavy glass doors open against the wind and held it for Paul as he swept into the stream of business-people headed for the buses within. She shook a jingling paper cup at him, but neither he nor his fellow travelers dropped anything in.

Paul was relieved that he didn't know the girl, but as he angled through the rush of commuters, he chided himself for ignoring her. He'd worked those doors in more desperate times. He knew what it meant when people were kind enough to part with a few coins—and what it meant when they weren't.

Getting past the beggars meant going head-down at a steady pace. Paul was holding money, so he didn't want to see anyone who knew him. The big ones wouldn't try to take it from him in a public place, but the smaller ones could talk him out of some.

"One way to San Francisco, please," he told the woman behind the ticket-counter glass after waiting his turn. She laughed at something the man working the adjacent line said.

He couldn't hear either of them through the barrier. That was the way of Port Authority and the world beyond for the children of the streets—for the concrete kids. The people with something to smile about did it in a world built to keep you out.

She slid Paul's ticket and change through the gap under the glass. He counted the bills against his chest to see how much was left, keeping his cash out of view.

There wasn't much to hide. He was nearly broke.

TWO

....

TRINA AND THE
TRAVELIN' SHOES

A nnie Brucker sat on the floor of the Port Authority basement, waiting in line for gate two. Leaning against the wall, she read aloud to her five-year-old son, Zach. She held the book, *Trina and the Travelin' Shoes,* with one hand. With the other, she kept a cat's-eye marble rolling back and forth across the backs of her fingers.

She'd been doing this for forty-five minutes, flexing her knee to keep it from going stiff. Her throat burned from speaking. Her fingers ached. But she kept it up for him.

Success with the marble meant Zach watched it instead of withdrawing to his inner place. If he didn't withdraw, then he might listen. Keeping him engaged was worth the discomfort, and Annie chose to believe he was paying attention because she had no proof that he wasn't.

Their matching red hair marked them as mother and son to anyone who might have noticed them waiting in line. And whoever did notice would have been shocked to know how much sitting cost her—that a thirty-something mom suffered from advanced osteoarthritis.

That was because they wouldn't have imagined this pleasant-looking woman held down on a table by three men working hard to keep her there while she screamed, her leg filled with nails, ball bearings, and other shrapnel too tiny and blown out to identify.

"Trina took one step and was gone from her little bedroom—gone from her little house," Annie read. Zach watched the marble. "With the next step, she left the town of Jarrett, where she knew everyone and everyone knew her." The legs of the passing commuters flickered light and shadow across the pages. "The shoes didn't tell Trina where they were going, and they never asked permission to take her there."

The H.M.O. doctors in Newark said Zach suffered from autism. The V.A. doctors wouldn't go that far because they weren't equipped to deal with children, and certainly not kids like him. The experts in San Francisco would tell her more.

Annie didn't want to know about autism. She wanted to know about Zach. Did he suffer? Was he happy, or was he lost? Was he truly autistic, or was that the easy answer for doctors chasing a goal of how many patients to see in a day?

"Trina watched the trees flow beneath her, step by step," she read. "Up and over, over and up, she and the travelin' shoes went." The marble traveled along with Trina—west to Annie's little finger, east to her thumb.

The flickering of the moving legs was a distraction. So was the knee, which didn't approve of her choice of seating. When the two tag-teamed Annie, that was all it took.

The marble went rogue, clacking to the floor and rolling away. She reached for it and missed, and Trina and her travels piled on. The book slipped from her hand, her place in it lost. Cursing to herself, she fought her way to her feet.

A fast-moving commuter, lost in his texting, kicked the marble. It bonged off of a recycling bin and fled into the shadows of a vacant bus gate.

Annie limped across the terminal floor, dodging people, and ventured into the murk. Bending to grope the floor in the dim light near the empty gate, she looked back to check on Zach.

He gazed into the air to his left—already gone.

She needed that marble. No other would do. To hold her son's attention, it had to be a certain mix of blue, green, and white. It had to be a cat's-eye.

Zach knew when it was a replacement, and it took him days to adjust. Until he did, she lost him.

Annie walked her hands across the tile, through candy wrappers and empty corn-chip bags. A few feet in, she clipped the marble with her pinky. It escaped and clicked off a wall.

Further into the gloom she went, patting the varying textures of the floor. She was damned thankful for the hand sanitizer back in her purse, assuming that hadn't already been stolen.

This was New York City. She should have taken it with her.

The noises of the concourse were transformed in the blackness. Voices came not from behind her but from the dark ahead.

"I'm trying!" an old woman cried. "I'm trying!"

Annie conjured an image of a frail figure somewhere off in the terminal. Back bent, cocooned in donated blankets, the poor lost creature was having an argument from years and years before. It was a plea to no one—an attempt to convince some greater force—or maybe just a battle with herself.

Pistachio shells.

A penny, a dime—if what she felt was U.S. currency.

An empty box of some gum or candy called Gifu, its label hardly legible in the bad light.

And there, at last, was the marble, which allowed itself to be captured fair and square. She stood to return to Zach.

The victory fell away from her.

More commuters had entered the concourse. Many more. Flowing four-deep, they blocked her view entirely.

She pressed into the current of people, the tide of sharp-cornered briefcases and interfering backpacks, trying to catch a glimpse of her son. "Excuse me, please." It was just something she said—a talisman. It had no measurable effect.

"Zach?" A sidestep. "Pardon." A dodge. She caught sight of their bags.

He was gone.

"Zach?" The voice was nothing like hers. "Zach!"

One of a pair of teenage girls looked up from her smartphone and pointed down the line of ticket-holders. Zach stood alone at the bend, where the queue folded in upon itself like a millipede.

He watched a skinny kid in an army jacket who used a pack as a cushion. The boy, a teen from the looks of him, was up against the wall, eyes closed, unaware that he had an audience.

Annie calmed herself. If she allowed Zach to see her upset, he would be frightened, too. Despite all of the things he screened out, he was quick to adopt her moods and slow to lose them, even after she moved on. Freaking out would make the long ride ahead of them that much longer.

She took a breath and held it for a count of three.

"Zach?"

The voice ended Paul's attempt to doze through the wait for the bus. Napping was impossible in Port Authority. Faking it could stop people from bothering you, but not often enough.

A pretty red-haired woman stood behind a little kid who was staring at him.

"Whatcha doing?" she asked the boy, who Paul figured was hers. She smiled in greeting.

Paul replied with a stiff nod. Cute girls threw him off his game. Women were even worse. He knew it, and so did they.

"Who's that, Zach?" she said. "Did you make a new friend?"

"Hello, Zach," Paul said. The kid regarded him with the most serious of expressions. "What's going on, buddy?"

The woman's smile fell a little. Maybe she didn't like nicknames.

The kid turned to his mother and held his hand out, beckoning. She hesitated, unsure, but then placed something into his palm.

He offered it to Paul—a marble.

Paul liked to keep to himself on the road. Other people meant complications—delays. But this was kind of interesting. "That for me?"

No reply. The kid just kept holding out the marble.

Paul took it from his hand.

The boy looked back up at his mother, who seemed as flummoxed by her son's behavior as Paul was by her. Something important was going on, but Paul had no idea what.

The mother didn't, either. She glanced from Paul to the kid, as if there were some secret they kept from her.

He tried to hand the marble back. "He'll miss it," he told her.

The kid wouldn't accept it.

Paul gave it another try, but no. "You sure? I have to give you something, then."

The kid pointed at his ring.

"Not that." He went into his pack, pulled out his notebook and pen, and wrote "I.O.U. one gift" on a page. Tearing it out, he handed it over to the boy, who studied it.

"He doesn't do this," the mom said.

"I work with little kids at this place I live—lived. Worked. Sometimes they give me stuff."

"No. He doesn't do this. With anyone."

Paul was so terrible at reading girls—at figuring out what they meant when they said things to him. "I'm sorry," he said, because he couldn't think of anything else to say, and because maybe he'd done something wrong.

Zach held his arms out to his mother. He appeared to be satisfied with the trade.

She picked the boy up.

"I'm sorry," Paul said.

....

THREE

BUMP-DI-DI-BUMP

"How fast are you going?" June Medill asked the bus driver, leaning sideways to check the speedometer.

"Fast enough to get there, slow enough to get there alive," he said.

June Medill had asked the driver about his speed many times in the hours since the bus commenced braving the storm. Paul figured the driver would ignore her at some point—or tell her to shut up. But June Medill was tough to tune out, and she didn't seem the type to listen to others anyway.

Paul, Annie, Zach, and everyone else knew June Medill's name because when she'd boarded, she told the man sitting behind the driver that he was in the seat reserved for Medill, June. She'd told him loudly, and she'd upped the volume when the driver said that the bus line didn't issue assigned seats.

She'd been just as audible when pulling out her cell phone and threatening to call Port Authority and New Jersey Transit to complain.

The driver had pointed out that they were not on a New Jersey Transit bus, but the man in the seat got up and moved in order to keep the peace. That freed June Medill to hector the driver as he guided the motor coach through curtains of snow at a safe crawl, though not a crawl safe enough for June Medill.

Near the middle of the bus, Paul watched the storm stream across his window. Passing headlights illuminated veins of ice on the glass, lighting up a tag someone had scratched into it: "IMUURS."

Another tagger had claimed the back of the seat in front of Annie, across the aisle, in silver-paint marker. Paul tried to read it, but couldn't make out the words as the headlights washed across them. Maybe it was the bad angle. Maybe it was June Medill.

Annie had given up trying to read to Zach over June Medill's interrogation about a half-hour in. Instead, she leaned close and murmured to him while he stared at the graffiti on the seat back as if he were able to read it.

"Normally, I wouldn't make such a big deal," June Medill said. Paul was certain that wasn't so.

"But it's coming down so hard. Don't you think it's hard?"

"Everything's hard with you yammering," the driver said, angling forward to peer through the powdered arcs cleared by his wipers.

Paul switched on his overhead light and rummaged through his pack for his iPod, last year's holiday donation. He pulled out socks, snacks, rolled-up shirts, his notebook, and other items, and piled them on the seat next to him. He'd packed in a hurry. Nothing was where he remembered putting it.

He wanted to listen to something other than the chatter up front, and he was sorry that Annie had quit reading. Her soft voice and the tale of the traveling girl reminded him of story hours with his mother—a long, long time ago and far, far away. He couldn't recall much about Jeanne Reid other than the yarns she spun, which starred heroes named Paul who always succeeded in doing right.

"Are you going to the Gaia festival?"

Paul stopped digging.

Annie held his notebook, which had fallen off the adjacent seat, along with a pamphlet and a photo from its pages.

"Not until summer," he said.

"You're going to San Francisco to see family, then, or is this your girlfriend?" She studied the worn snapshot.

"That's my mother."

"Now I'm prying. Never mind. It's just that I like to sneak into the world of boys so I can be prepared for when he's older." She ruffled her son's hair.

Zach scrutinized the tag on the seat back. From what Paul had seen of him, he might never be like other boys. Which might not be the worst thing, given what boys were capable of.

For instance, they abruptly left behind those who helped them. But that didn't matter, right?

"It's okay." Paul didn't like anyone handling the photo, which he'd examined so often and for so long that he could see it in his own mind with little effort. A young woman in a crowd, her hair the same shade of red as Annie's, looked back over her shoulder, caught before she could pose, as if someone had spoken her name. On her left hand was the ring Paul wore now.

"Very pretty. When was this?"

"Ninety-six."

"Are you staying with her?"

"No. She's not—" He didn't want Annie to feel bad or, worse, feel sorry for him.

"I ask way too many questions," she said.

If it had been June Medill, it would have been too many. But Paul was pleased that Annie wanted to know even one thing about him.

She handed him the photo and the notebook, then switched on Zach's light and gave the boy a few crayons. The process required some negotiating before he had colors he liked, but he soon settled into drawing on the page from Paul's notebook.

Paul steered the subject back to Gaia, an arts-and-culture festival held in the Nevada desert every year. He hoped that Annie might understand why he'd want to go to it, unlike most of the other New Beginnings kids, who didn't.

"This was taken at the very first one," he said of the snapshot, holding it like a charm to ward off the danger of him saying something stupid. "She told me it was one of the happiest times of her life."

"That was nineteen ninety-six?"

"Yes."

"You're what—sixteen, seventeen?"

"Seventeen."

"So she tried to explore a little bit before settling in with a baby."

"I don't think she had a plan. She was there to find one. That's where she met my dad."

"And he wants you to go there now?"

"No. That was the only time they ... I never—"

Her eyes shone when she smiled. "Sorry. Too many questions."

She did understand. Paul was sure of it. "I'm closing the circle," he said. "I need to go there to figure out who I am."

Up front, June Medill demanded to know how it was possible that they hadn't yet passed the Delaware Water Gap. The driver said he thought the problem was going too fast, not too slow. June Medill told him that too many people drove while talking on the phone.

"This is already some trip," Annie said, listening to them. "I'm guessing we both know about traveling, Paul."

He agreed.

Later—much later—he would wonder why he had.

They hadn't known a thing.

BOMP-BOMP-BOMP-BOMP. The thud of Paul's earbuds provided a backbeat to the bus's plodding progress through the landscape of otherworldly white.

Outside, a man stood by a snow-carpeted car that looked like it had slid off the interstate. He watched the bus as it passed. Paul blinked, his eyes heavy. The car's trunk was angled up higher than its hood; it wouldn't be going anywhere without a tow.

A blast of wind coated the window with powder. By the time it cleared, the man was gone. After that, Paul couldn't be certain he'd been there at all.

BUMP-DI-DI-BUMP. *Bump-di-di-bump. Bump-di-di-bump.*

"Watch it. Watch it!"

"Dammit! I told you to sit down!"

June Medill and the driver invaded the rhythm, cracking through it, waking Paul. He hadn't felt himself falling asleep.

Across from him, Zach and Annie dozed, the boy's head in his mother's lap. The notebook page and the crayons lay in the aisle.

Paul picked them up and turned Zach's drawing over. It wasn't a drawing.

It took effort to read the boy's scrawl—the letters were more like shapes than language—but it was the tagged phrase from the seat back: "Unus pro omnibus, omnes pro uno." What was weirder: that someone tagged a bus seat with such a thing— or that a five-year-old worked so hard to copy it down?

Paul tucked the paper and crayon into Annie's bag. She didn't budge.

Bump-di-di-bump. Bump-di-di-bump. Bump-di-di-bump.

Taillights passed the bus on the left—way too fast for the conditions. The veins of window ice flashed red, like lightning, flagging the recklessness. So did the scratched-in tag. IMUURS.

"I'm only trying to help," June Medill told the driver.

"Look, you leave me alone from here on out, and maybe I won't have you arrested when we get there, all right?"

Bump-di-di-bump. Bump-di-di-bump. Bump-di-di-bump.

"Can I just—"

He turned around to glare at her. "What?" He'd reached his limit.

The windshield glowed with the red of the passing car, framing the driver in crimson frost as he turned his attention back to the wheel. Then the red went sideways, replaced by the blue-white of headlights as the car spun out in front of them. The lines and shadows of the bus's windshield wipers swept through the glare.

"Hey." June Medill's voice was soft, her surprise barely audible through the earbud beats.

The light grew brighter. The driver stomped on the brake pedal.

The bus fishtailed.

Bump-di-di-bump. Bump-di-di-bump. Bump-di-di-bump.

Everything slowed.

Something hit Paul very, very hard as shapes filled the white. A flash of a question. When had the fight started?

It hit him again. Cries from all around. Bang.

Bump-di-di-bump.

Some trip, Annie had said. But he didn't care, right?

A thing broke. A thing tore. A thing howled.

Bright, bright light. Too much.

All was light as the snowy windshield blazed at him in lines of hot stars.

The bus imploded into white.

Bump-di-di-bump.

FOUR

....

THAT NO LONGER APPLIES

Jonas Porter sat at a desk in the Central Assignment Department of the Envoy Corps home office. The desk was the size of a dining-room table, and it was not his.

Porter's desk was in cubicle 814, near a window with good light. He'd earned that spot decades before, when Corps management rewarded his century of service with an enviable new location and a leaded-crystal paperweight containing a hologram that resembled him if tipped just right.

He'd commandeered the team director's office, which was closer to the message-relay tubes. If something came in, he would hear it. His assigned desk was out of earshot. That was why, when the office was busy, he received his assignments there only when a courier was on duty to deliver them.

There were no couriers left now. The office was silent. Porter was the only person in the building, which claimed a full city block, and his solitude was a circumstance to which he'd long since adjusted.

He clocked his days watching dust float in sunlight focused through thick windows. He wondered if he should again try to stop drinking diet soda.

When the tubes began delivering fewer assignments, the couriers stopped coming to work, so the Envoys monitored the tubes themselves. When the Envoys stopped coming to work, the director asked Porter to use a cubicle closer in. When the director failed to show up, Porter claimed her space. And when the vending machines ran out of caffeinated bubbles, he brought his own.

The relay tubes were pneumatic and noisy. Long before, when the office was filled with the din of Envoys coming and going with their assignees, typing reports, and giving counsel, the hiss and thunk of the steel capsules hitting the tubes' intake doors was difficult to hear. When there had still been some hold-out Envoys left, they'd listen hard and race to the tubes at the sound of the rare capsule. Porter's seniority gave him dibs on assignments, but he doled them out fairly to keep up morale.

Then the assignments ceased to mean anything. Then they ceased altogether.

Now there were no capsules and only one Envoy. The tubes could be heard anywhere if they bothered to clunk—even in the empty waiting room, which Porter paced to keep his legs from falling asleep.

The last of the Envoys checked the director's desk clock, which no longer kept time. He drew a line through the current day on the blotter calendar—which had multiple lines through its days—and drank the last of his soda. He didn't like ending the day early but allowed himself that lapse in professional rigor.

In the hallway outside, he turned the deadbolt and realized he'd forgotten his walking staff. He went back inside, retrieved it, and was locking up again when he swore he heard the hiss-thunk of a capsule through the door.

He did this to himself every day—this and the diet soda. Determined to make headway on at least one bad habit, he yanked his key from the lock.

Pocketing it, he walked to the elevators at a brisk pace. The heel-strikes of his wing-tips echoed down the hall.

They echoed up it, too, when he hurried back to the door and inserted his key for the fourth time that day, ignoring his inner voice's scolding. The voice was winning as he inspected the relay tubes, which held only dust, their signal flags all down.

The voice shut up when he opened the door to the second-to-last tube in the rear-facing bank—the one with the flag that hadn't worked in years.

EVERY FIGHT PAUL ever lost mattered, and he'd lost a lot. Pop Mike said he had a talent for being out-numbered and overmatched—a Captain Marvel heart in a Rick Jones body.

Paul Googled the reference. Pop Mike had a point.

The afternoon he happened upon the gang bangers bothering Victor Gonzales and his girl-friend mattered. They were targeted because she was white, or because Victor wasn't, or just because the two of them were there and so were the guys.

After Victor ran off and the thing got started, Paul landed some respectable shots. He tried to protect the girl before the numbers had their say. But he went down hard into the gravel and glass while she screamed.

He needn't have worried. They never touched her.

When the kicking was over, the guys moved on. Gonzales wasn't coming back. The sobbing girl tried to help him.

It wasn't clear whether she cried for Paul or for herself. Or maybe because her new boyfriend bailed on her. It didn't matter. Paul just wanted her to let go of his wrists and stop trying to pull him up.

He couldn't breathe. He was too hurt to stand, and her tears burned his burst knuckles.

Drip. Drip. He opened his eyes. This wasn't the alley.

A crying peacock sat on a branch above, watching him. Paul blinked water away. The drops weren't the bird's tears.

He was on his back on a snowy hill. The peacock, lit by the undulating tangerine glow of nearby flames, peered down at him as ice melted from the tree's limbs.

Paul took a breath, sending a crack of hurt from hip to shoulder. The next was a little better and the one after better still.

Cold wet splatted across his face. He wiped it off, and the back of his hand came away streaked with flecks of red. His nose had been bleeding. An icy rain followed as the peacock pushed off from the branch and flapped up into the sky, which was lightening into a gray dawn.

He sat up with care. To his left, a hunk of the bus was on its side, twisted. It had plowed a trench into the snow and earth, seats jutting from the floor at a right angle to the ground. Yards away, a woman's shoe sat upright in the snow, as if its owner had jumped out of it in a trick performed for her child.

Beyond the shoe was Annie. A trough of pink on white marked where she'd dragged herself over to cradle Zach.

Both were still. Both were dead.

It was a tableau of awful serenity. Bodies, some still belted into their seats, marked the path of the motor coach. The bus's remains were scattered—a few of the pieces burning—all the way down the hill.

Paul hurt inside. The hand he leaned on was numb. The cold was too much.

Annie and Zach were dead, as were many others. The trees wept into the snow.

Standing, the grind of his ankle and the jolt across his body were audible in his head, a pulse of their own. Then came louder sounds: the rhythmic thrum of helicopters, the growl of trucks. Help.

Paul wanted Annie and Zach to know, as if they could still be told—and might be saved. But that wasn't so.

It all arrived fast. Black military choppers descended toward the hillside in the gray—hovering, surveying. Black trucks and black-uniformed soldiers in helmets and goggles boiled up from the woods at the bottom of the hill.

Paul waved his arms to get their attention, his shouts hoarse and unheard over the din. He looked to Annie and Zach again, maintained his fool's notion. This could be changed for them.

Then the elements of the picture became questions, and the questions had answers. As Pop Mike said, Paul possessed survival skills. Why soldiers and not medical personnel? And who wore helmets and body armor for a rescue operation?

He stopped waving.

The soldiers ignored the living—the few on the ground who moved, the handful who sat up or tried to stand—and dealt first with the dead. The troops on foot worked in tandem with those in the covered trucks who handed down stretchers and bags.

Fast and not at all gentle, they zipped up the bodies, rolled them onto the stretchers, and hefted them up and into the backs of the trucks. Paul couldn't see into the dark interiors. It looked like the bodies were fed into hungry mouths.

They were not here to help. This was not a rescue.

One man was able to get up on his own, waving an approaching soldier away and pointing him toward a woman lying nearby. He was clubbed down with a rifle butt and bagged. Other soldiers dealt with the woman in a similar fashion.

Paul didn't want to register what was plain to see. June Medill shook him out of that.

One moment she wasn't there, the next she appeared from behind one of the bus pieces to come at a soldier from his blind side, yelling. He didn't notice until his partner pointed to her. The soldier pulled a long baton from a holster on his leg.

A truck passed, blocking Paul's view. When it was gone, June Medill was on the ground, her hand reaching up, as if trying to tell the soldier she was sorry or begging for understanding.

Another truck passed. June Medill lay face-down in the snow, arms out to embrace it. The soldier unzipped a bag.

Paul was exposed against the white.

Down below, a trooper spotted him and spoke into a shoulder microphone. Others turned to look up the hill. Some headed in Paul's direction.

Move. Move and hide.

The bad ankle brought him down in one step, and he slid and crawled as fast as he was able. He bit down against the pain, fighting his way through the snow to the nearest piece of the bus—the one he'd been sitting in, judging by the trail Annie left. He threw himself into it and rolled his back up against the now-vertical floor.

He chanced a look over the sideways seats. Soldiers made their way up the hill, some stopping to bag bodies or club the living. Choppers beat the skies overhead.

The bus piece rocked as Paul grabbed the seat and pulled himself to his feet. He shouldered aside something hanging from the arm rest, and it fell to the ground.

His pack. In the snow next to it was his coat. He wriggled into the coat, grabbed the pack, and limped around the end of the bus piece.

Keeping the fragment between him and the soldiers, he made it to a nearby tree. His ankle threatened to give out again, but he clung to the bark and worked his way over the snow-covered roots to the far side. From behind the bus came a radio's crackle and the sound of a man bludgeoned into submission.

The helicopter grew louder.

At the next tree, Paul could only hope that the chopper wouldn't spot him—that the soldiers were too busy with the other bodies to target him.

Annie and Zach. He pushed that thought away.

He was a dozen long yards from a stand of trees, and a clump of woods beyond those offered the chance to hide. He looked back. Hope faded.

A trail of footprints and drag marks in the snow pointed the way right to him. His only chance was to run and pray.

Now came what Pop Mike called a moment of true seeing. They came along in various situations, but Paul had only ever experienced them just before a fight. It didn't matter if you were smaller, outnumbered, slower, or scared. The thing started, and you were in it. You swung for the soft spots. You moved.

He crossed the snowy clearing, lurching and hopping. It wasn't his fastest, but it was enough.

Passing a clump of shrubs, he brushed against the white-covered branches, spooking some birds hiding within. They flew up and out in a burst of flapping and chattering—a stream of winged alarm bells. Even if they weren't heard over the choppers, they'd be seen.

A shout from close behind. A trooper by the bus piece pointed at him, talking into his shoulder mike.

Paul flat-out ran, agony and all. A good way across the clearing, a hole hidden by the snow took him out. He fell on his pack and rolled, grunting and holding his ankle.

He was done. Caught. Maybe the soldiers would be merciful enough to knock him out, and he wouldn't have to feel anything for a while.

"You have to stand up, Paul." A voice from above.

A curse came to his lips as he prepared to tell this idiot that he would be carried, or he wasn't going anywhere. But the man looking down at him wasn't a soldier. He was upper-middle-aged, gray-bearded, and dressed like a civilian—here in the snow in a patch-elbowed jacket and dress shoes.

The man glanced in the soldiers' direction, frowned, and offered Paul the end of a thick carved-wood-and-brass walking stick. "Grab hold."

"I can't."

"There's no choice being offered here. I cannot do your standing for you."

Paul gripped the brass foot of the stick. The man leaned back with the weight and pulled him to his feet. A spear of hurt pierced Paul's ankle, and he hissed.

The man reached around and grabbed him by the back of the neck, pulling him in until their foreheads nearly touched. "Listen to me," the man said. "Your mind remembers what happened to you in the wreck. That no longer applies."

With a measuring look, he shoved Paul backwards.

Paul stumbled, catching himself on his bad ankle. An echo of the expected pain flared, faded, and was gone. He shifted the weight to the good leg, then back. Nothing. It no longer hurt.

The man picked up Paul's pack and handed it to him.

The soldiers allowed them no time for explanation. The *whup-whup-whup* of the chopper grew.

The man looked over Paul's shoulder at a spot behind him. His eyes narrowed, and he raised his walking stick, as if testing the air.

Paul turned to see a black-helmeted trooper, rifle to shoulder, taking aim. The shot was a crack in the beat of the helicopter.

The man twisted his staff. The soldier's back arched, chest thrust out like he'd been struck from behind. He dropped his gun and sank to his knees, flailing for the fallen rifle, then trying to stand. He pitched forward into the snow.

"Let's go," the gray man said. Hitching the shoulder bag he wore higher, he made for the next stand of trees. The sound of the chopper above pounded through them. Paul followed.

Emerging on the other side of the trees, they trotted through tall snow-powdered grass—and right into a half-ring of soldiers who rose up from the cover around them.

They looked back. There were more troopers coming through the woods behind. They were surrounded.

The chopper descended. Speakers in the machine's belly emitted an unintelligible squawk.

"You won't like this!" the man said over the noise. He was strangely calm, given their predicament.

"What?"

The man raised his staff. "This," he said, giving it a twist, "might feel a bit—"

The clearing, trees, and sky spun. Paul's vision went fuzzy, and his balance deserted him. In the next instant, the soldiers, the helicopter, and the noises were gone.

"Odd," the man finished. His voice was softer now.

Around them, all was silent. They stood in a field of grass, feet immersed in anemone-like dandelions. The man took a deep breath.

Paul celebrated their escape by easing himself down into the green and yellow.

The man sucked in more air, then dropped to one knee beside him. "You all right?"

It was all Paul could do not to pass out.

"I'm sorry," the man said. "A jump that big costs you." He took another deep breath and let it out. "And costs me even more these days."

Paul was able to get to his feet with help. The man shouldered his bag, tucked his stick up under his arm, and strode away.

"Wait," Paul said. "Where are you going?"

"Wherever you are." He moved fast and didn't look back. "But first, away."

"Hold up."

He didn't.

Paul understood that this was not a person to lose. "Please."

The man stopped.

"How did you get away from the bus?" Paul said. "Where are we?"

"The Commons. Now, I could tell you about it while we stand here, and then we could see if our friends in the black helmets find us again."

"I just—"

"I've never seen that kind of Ravager commitment at a drop zone," the man said. "We were lucky to make it clear of them, and that's probably because they weren't expecting me. Now they know I'm with you, and they'll be prepared. We will not be here in the open when they arrive."

He walked away again, covering an impressive amount of ground without appearing to hurry.

Paul ran after him. His ankle still felt fine. "How did you know my name?"

"Paul Benjamin Reid. Born April tenth."

"How do you know that?"

"I'm Jonas. Friends call me by my surname, Porter, and I've never convinced them to stop."

"Where did you—"

"All right, that's not true. I have no friends. They're all gone."

"You know my name."

Porter increased his stride. Paul struggled to keep up.

"I have a sad habit of showing up at the office even though there is, for all intents and purposes, no functioning office to speak of," Porter said. "Every day I wait for an assignment and none comes. Today, that changed. No one ever escapes the Ravagers. Today, that changed. Let's see what we can make of that."

Paul tried to shake off his fog. "Wait."

"No."

"We have to go back for the people on the bus."

"No, we have to keep moving—for you. You'll keep up. You'll do what I tell you. And if we have more luck than I've enjoyed in a very long time, we may make it through the afternoon."

Paul was sweating in his heavy coat. It was no longer winter, and they hurried along under a warm sun. "Where's the snow?"

Porter stopped, leaned on his stick, and watched Paul try to sort out his situation. Birdsong echoed across the grass.

"I don't understand," Paul said. "I'm in a bad place here."

"Yes. You are."

"Those people on the bus need help."

"Yes," Porter said with a note of sadness. "They do."

Then he turned, swung his stick back up under his arm, and walked off across the field.

....

FIVE

MUCH TO DO, MUCH TO RUE

r. Brill examined the red-haired woman, and Gerald Truitt watched. Truitt enjoyed nothing about the process, but Mr. Brill drew satisfaction from reviewing new arrivals in detail, as if he were going over acquisitions for an investment portfolio.

Which he was.

The big man was thorough in all things, especially those related to equity. He expected the same of his personnel.

It was not advisable for those in Mr. Brill's employ, which was anyone not hanging from a rack or soaking in a vat somewhere, to disappoint him. Employment was far preferable to the alternative.

Much to do, much to rue.

The woman, immobile and insensate, was suspended upside-down by her feet in a web cocoon that covered all but her head. Wisps hung from her hair like pulled strands of cotton batting. Webbing filled her open mouth and was stitched from lip to lip.

No seamstress had done the work. In the dim light of the warehouse, the web's creators were visible only in shadows crawling up and down the threads and in fist-sized lumps scuttling under the batting, which stretched across the floor like malignant moss.

Mr. Brill stood in front of the hanging woman, studying her inverted face. He leaned forward for a closer look. "Interesting."

Steady as a surgeon, he reached for her eye. Truitt feared he might blind her. Instead, he brushed strands of webbing from her lashes.

No response.

He lightly tapped his finger on her pupil, as if testing a microphone.

Nothing.

Truitt blinked.

Much to do, much to rue.

Mr. Brill straightened, his suit stretching over his muscles like snakeskin. He thumbed some notes into a digital tablet, frowning. "This is how they manifest the process."

"Yes, sir."

Truitt surveyed the room. He knew from years of service to avoid viewing the numbers while Mr. Brill was evaluating them. Some believed that Mr. Brill left his screen unguarded to see who was unwise enough to read it, and that was why certain people enjoyed only a brief career before vanishing. Truitt had never known anyone to test that theory, nor had he ever considered doing so himself, which was probably another reason for his length of service.

The new arrivals, all of them cocooned, hung in rows stretching off into the reaches of the industrial space. Mr. Brill, for whom efficiency was paramount, said that his storage facilities were no larger than necessary. That may have been true; Truitt had never seen the end of one.

Already, many of the new faces were veiled in webbing. Farther down the rows, the veils were full shrouds, the cocoons much thicker. With the older ones, it was difficult to discern a human form.

The weavers worked fast. The red-haired woman would be covered within hours.

Next to her, unnoticed by Mr. Brill, a small boy whose hair was the same shade as the woman's was being similarly wrapped into a chrysalis. Something about him was different, though Truitt couldn't say precisely what.

Much to do, much to rue.

He couldn't remember when that rhyme became his mantra, but it helped see him through the execution of his duties. Which was a personal detail he never shared with Mr. Brill.

"It doesn't have to go this way for them," Mr. Brill said.

Truitt couldn't imagine it going any other way but kept that to himself, too. "No, it does not, sir."

"They could be in soft beds, meditation rooms, lying on a beach. Instead they conjure up webs, bloodletting facilities. Do I look like an insect to you? A vampire?"

"It is unfair, sir."

Mr. Brill glanced up from his screen to see if Truitt was being sarcastic.

At the edge of Truitt's vision, the boy turned his head to regard them. Years of practice were all that kept him from looking back at the boy.

"Repeat that?" Mr. Brill said.

Truitt didn't dare break eye contact to see if he was imagining the boy's movement. Mr. Brill would interpret that as fear. The big man was a predator weighing a strike.

"It is unfair, sir." This time he sounded more aggrieved. "But as you know, they remain somewhat aware of what's being done to them, even if the resulting expression of that is unjustly harsh." He waited for an appropriate amount of time, then averted his eyes in deference.

The boy hadn't moved after all.

"This one," Mr. Brill said, nodding toward the red-haired woman. "Brucker, Ann Elizabeth Thomas." His screen zoomed into her specifics. "Two tours, Army database administration. Civilian contractor in the green zone after that. Top-secret clearance." He closed her record. "Pull her."

"Yes, sir."

Mr. Brill began to walk away, swiping the glass of his tablet with his fingers.

"Sir?"

The big man stopped, still reading.

"What about her son, sir?"

"What about him? He's of no consequence."

"It will mean fewer resources to maintain her focus if we keep them together."

"Fine. Him, too."

Much to do, much to rue.

MR. BRILL PROCEEDED down the path between the rows of cocoons. Truitt maintained his customary position a few steps back—close enough for service, far enough for protocol.

They moved from the warehouse portion of the storage facility to a section Truitt found even more unsettling: The Fen. Their footfalls now thumped along the spongy planks of a floating walkway that crossed an expanse of foul water black as tar.

Orderly rows of former people—now charges, in Mr. Brill's parlance—floated upright and naked in the murk. Heads tipped back, they were like patients awaiting sustenance or a dose of medicine. Their faces were losing features, as if rotting, or being consumed. The odor, thick and obscene, invaded his nose and mouth.

"Sir, I have an update on this last harvest. The bus accident," Truitt said. "It seems that there was a problem at the drop zone."

"What kind of problem?"

"There was a boy."

Mr. Brill stopped, opened the tablet's cover, and tapped the screen. "A boy."

"A youth."

A river of numbers flowed over the tablet as Mr. Brill swiped his fingers across it. His brow furrowed more deeply with each pass.

"There was some small resistance reported." Truitt didn't have Mr. Brill's full attention. "The boy managed to clear the zone. And we lost a man."

"We lost a man?"

He had it now. "Yes, sir."

Mr. Brill closed the tablet cover and began walking again. Truitt followed.

"The new acquisitions I just reviewed," Mr. Brill said. "The priority lot."

"Yes, sir."

They made their way into a new environment, footsteps muffled by office carpet as they walked down a long row of bleak clay-colored office cubicles. The cubes were filled with fatigued workers in matching white and gray who stared at screens filled with line graphs, bar graphs, tables, and scatter plots.

All of them avoided eye contact with Mr. Brill and Truitt.

"I thought we went in heavy."

"We did, sir."

"Not heavy enough. This is why we have safeguards, Truitt. Redundancies."

"I understand, sir."

Truitt had delayed delivering the news as long as possible, certain that Mr. Brill would be looking for someone to punish. Timing was everything in such circumstances.

Instead, the big man appeared to have taken the news in stride. That might change once he gave the matter further thought.

They arrived at a massive door of polished mahogany. A glance from Mr. Brill brought a muted click from within it. He waited for Truitt to step up and open it for him.

Sometimes the door opened itself. When Mr. Brill wanted to remind Truitt of his place and standing, he made him do it.

On the other side of the door, which was as thick as a bank vault's, was Mr. Brill's personal office. It was a palatial space of robber-baron opulence, from its rugs, trim, and appointments to its furnishings.

Mr. Brill took his place behind the room's centerpiece—an altar-sized, ornately carved antique desk. An assortment of floating video monitors, all positioned to give him the perfect viewing angle, provided most of the light in the otherwise shadowy office.

As Mr. Brill moved, so did the screens. Some displayed views of rooms similar to the one they'd just left, with rows of workers toiling listlessly. Others showed training camps from on high, with black-clad Ravagers drilling and practicing combat maneuvers. Still others trickled out flowing lines of data in a painter's dream-palette of color.

Mr. Brill scanned a bank of smaller monitors floating over his desk. He swiped his fingers through the air in front of him, cycling through screen after screen of numbers.

"Circumstances change, Truitt. We change with them, or cracks become fractures—and fractures become fissures. I want to know why this nit wasn't picked."

"Well, that's just it, sir. We know something of why." Truitt adopted a collegial tone. They were in this together and would address it as a team, though only one of them would find himself floating in The Fen if the other chose to abandon the cooperative approach. "He had help. From an Envoy."

Mr. Brill fixed him with the predator's stare for the second time that day. "There are no more Envoys."

"It would seem that there's one," Truitt said. "Sir."

SIX

THE VAN-TASTA

J onas Porter knew this about beliefs: the more faith you fed them, the more they spit it back at you. When he believed that the Envoys would survive, he found himself alone in the office. When he was certain he would never again receive a Journey assignment, the tube brought him one.

Undependable, these beliefs.

Porter believed this about knowledge: the more sure you were, the more likely you were to be wrong. With that belief in mind, Porter easily rendered an accurate assessment of the current Journey and his worthiness as a guide.

He knew almost nothing.

The last of the Envoys stood in the middle of a narrow country road, feet planted on either side of its double yellow line. He gazed into the distance and risked the betrayal of another belief—that a ride would appear because they needed one.

"Can't you just jump us where we need to go?" The boy sat on the roots of a sugar maple, his back against its trunk. They'd been here for a while—a generous stretch of tedium on top of Paul's traumatic arrival in The Commons. And there were only two choices for a place to rest: roadside gravel or nearby hardwood.

"Too soon. No more jumps until you're used to them. Anyway, we haven't identified our destination."

The boy sighed. He wanted better answers than Porter could give him.

In his lap was a book-sized video gadget meant to be an icebreaker—an introduction to his situation. Envoy best practices called for a crisis counselor to handle intake duties in the office, but there were no counselors here or anywhere. It was a field situation, so Porter was stuck with the portable solution—a device he'd never used playing a video he'd never seen.

"Welcome to The Commons," a man in the video said. "Right about now, you have a lot of questions. That's normal. As a Journeyman, you're free to ask your Envoy as many as you like."

Paul sighed again.

"Your Journey through The Commons is a big adjustment, so be patient. You have the full strength of the Envoy Corps on your side. We're here for you, and we know what you're going through."

Half-true, that. The boy did have the full strength of the Corps on his side: Porter. But as for knowing what they faced, his years of dusty desk duty meant The Commons was a black box. He would have felt guilty, but his time stuck in the office was unavoidable.

The administrative infrastructure of The Commons—what remained of it—operated under the disuse protocol, better known as the "use it or lose it" or "into thin air" rule. Someone had to be in the Envoy office every day even if there were no Journeys in progress. Otherwise, the office would cease to exist. Sustaining its presence required a great deal of Essence. Essence was everything, and The Commons would reassign the office to something more useful if ever the Envoys stopped using it.

When there had been thousands of Envoys and Journeys, there was no risk of that happening. When it was just Porter and no Journeys at all, disuse was his biggest worry. Thus, he had a spotless attendance record—one which, documented on blotter calendars, would have stacked up high enough to hide a tall man standing.

Bravo for him. Tough luck for Paul Reid.

Porter was rusty. He'd only just managed to change the bullet's course, as his inner judge reminded him.

You nearly missed.

I did not miss.

But you nearly did.

Belief. The power of an Envoy ran on it. Belief in one's strength, in the integrity of the calling, in The Commons itself. The power remained while one served, and it faded the longer one went without an assignment.

Every Envoy enjoyed a unique ability, and it was up to each one to make the most of what he or she had. Carl Levy could change attitudes at will. It seemed a silly talent early on, but Carl's file was a perfect record of success. Porter never heard what had become of Carl. He, like many, failed to report for work one day and was never seen again.

The attitude around the office suffered.

Audra Farrelly warmed things, which also didn't sound like much. Yet it made the difference on many a Journey. A woman who looked to be in her seventies—age was slippery in The Commons—Audra never revealed to anyone what temperatures she was capable of attaining. "Hot enough," she'd say.

When they came for Audra, she burned two square miles and took dozens of them with her. Believe that.

"Fear is not your friend," said the man in the video. "It's understandable to be afraid. As a Journeyman, you're here to determine your fate, and that can be frightening. But you have powerful friends in your corner."

And more powerful foes in the other guy's, Porter wanted to add. "Who is that?" he said instead, walking over to the boy.

"Mister Desmond—a life coach who volunteered at New Beginnings. But he didn't dress like this."

Paul paused the video, freezing the black-and-white image of a chubby man who sported slicked-back hair and an argyle sweater vest. He sat stiffly on the edge of a blonde-wood table in a 1950s-era school classroom.

"These intros are a mish-mash of your memories," Porter said. "Some real, some seen only in dreams, like The Commons itself. Memory and imaginings are its clay."

The boy pressed play. The fifties Mr. Desmond went to great lengths to assure Paul that his Journey, tailored to his needs and his alone, would be a hard challenge but a fair one.

Porter longed for an intake counselor. Experience taught him you couldn't get someone to believe their situation until they'd learned the particulars for themselves.

Beliefs. Knowledge.

After a string of pleasantries, the screen went blank. Paul hit the play button several times, to no effect.

Porter took the device from him but had no idea how to fix it beyond staring at its logo. It really had been a very long time. "What's a Newton?"

The boy shrugged.

Porter handed the gadget back, and Paul tossed it over his shoulder, disgusted. It landed in the rushes.

"I'm a Journeyman."

"Yes."

"I'm here to determine my fate."

"Yes."

Paul plucked a tall piece of curled grass from the roots of his tree and chewed the end of it. "I'm dead."

"Not necessarily. Not yet."

HOURS LATER, Porter and Paul still had no ride. They couldn't tell how many hours, as tracking time hadn't worked since—well, Porter didn't know. He was back in the center of the road, trying to will a car to appear.

The boy sat in his spot under the tree, twisting his ring and occasionally pulling up a piece of grass. "I don't need your help," he said.

At least, that's what it sounded like. "I'm sorry?"

"I don't know you. So I don't need you."

Porter's old director referred to that as "Ar" in her periodic table of Journeyman reactions: angry rejection. It was common, especially in the younger ones. Recognizing their situation, they tried to gain control over it. Many rejected the only people who could help them, thinking that was a route to independence.

"Where are you from, Paul?"

"You know."

"Humor me."

He considered his answer with a dark look and executed another grass stalk. "Nowhere. All over."

"Well, in your hometown of Allover, did you ever see a man get shot in the back with his own bullet?"

The boy hesitated, then shook his head.

"Ever blink and wind up somewhere else? Were you ever told that a fresh injury was gone—and just like that, it was?"

Paul prodded the area around his eye.

"Doubting me is a luxury you can't afford." Porter peered down the road again. "It's already difficult enough to reach Journey's End."

"Where am I going?"

"That's up to you."

Paul sighed and pulled up another piece of grass.

"Jonas."

A woman's voice—one Porter knew well. He turned and saw only Paul, who was dozing. "Audra?"

The boy opened his eyes and blinked his sleep away. Before he remembered to don his street veil of toughness, he was but a child waking in a strange place. "Anything coming?" he said.

Porter shook his head and resisted the urge to shush him. Was it really her? If so, had Paul heard? He hadn't woken up until Porter spoke.

"Audra?" Porter said in a stage whisper, facing the road again.

"Return me from the wilderness, Jonas. Unless you don't want my help." If it was Audra, she was having a jolly time at his expense—which had been a favorite hobby of hers. "You always were the loner. And you were never careful with Corps property."

The Newton.

Porter checked Paul again. He was oblivious. He couldn't hear her.

"Don't let the boy see," she said. "I mean it. That's as important as anything else you do."

Porter concentrated on the device, picturing it in his mind where it lay in the rushes. He gave his walking staff a twitch, and the Newton appeared in his free hand. He curled it under his sleeve, blocking the device from Paul's view, and dropped it into his coat pocket.

Is it really you, Audra?

"If you're trying to ask me something, I can't hear you think."

"Is it you?"

"Is it *you*?" She giggled—the only person he'd ever known who could laugh like that and still maintain the dignity of a head of state. "There's only one Jonas, and I'm assigned to him. In truth, I volunteered. The Envoy's Envoy, if you will. How are you? I've missed you. I've missed working with you."

Porter was dumbstruck.

"This is some trip you're on," she said. "Some Journey."

"The boy, you mean. I'm on no Journey."

"No?" Audra Farrelly's laugh was a blend of distortion and mirth. "Oh, Jonas." More static in the mix. "Aren't we all?"

"WE CAN SAY GOODBYE NOW," the boy said.

Porter thought he saw something approaching in the distance, a gnat drawn in on a double-yellow tether, but wasn't sure of it. He no longer trusted his eyes. "Where were you going on that bus?"

"Did you hear me? I said we can say goodbye."

Porter said nothing.

Paul sighed. He had a talent for that. "Why do you keep asking me stuff you already know?"

Porter waited for his answer.

"Gaia," Paul said, finally.

"Say again?"

"Out in the desert. Gaia. The earth mother. It's a festival. A place to—never mind." He stirred the grass with his foot. "You wouldn't get it."

Now Porter was certain he saw something coming. "I know who Gaia is. Greek myth. A friend of mine met her once—and you'd be surprised by what I get." Yes, definitely something. "This is a place? The place you want to go?"

The boy nodded.

"Then that's where we're headed."

"I'm going by myself. You're not getting us anywhere."

The sound of an engine now.

Paul got up and joined him. "You don't know anything about me."

A seventies-era custom van came over the rise, bearing down on them with an eight-cylinder growl.

Paul stepped back to the side of the road. Porter remained in its center.

The van closed in without slowing, its driver unseen behind the tint of the windshield.

Porter raised his staff.

The purple hood grew larger with alarming speed. On it, a painted werewolf tore its way through a bleeding full moon.

"You think I haven't traveled on my own?" Paul strained to make himself heard over the engine. "I know the world."

Porter adjusted his grip but didn't budge.

At the point where the driver had to choose between stopping or running Porter down, the van squealed to a halt. Its front end pitched forward, nearly kissing him on the chin, then rocked back. The transmission shifted into park.

The Envoy walked around to the passenger side, which twinkled with violet-glitter lacquer and bubble letters identifying the vehicle as the "Van-Tasta." Its motto hung below its name: "No prisoners. No mercy."

"Your world, perhaps," he told Paul as the window lowered with a hum, revealing a bulky man whose face was divided down the middle. The right side was a sea of scarred flesh with a milky eye floating in it, the left pocked steel, circuit boards, and a glowing red lens where the left eye should have been. "Not this one."

PART TWO:
THE JOURNEY

SEVEN

··

PINKIES

The knee was a whisper, not a scream, thanks to the pinkies. The Minute Clinic doctor who prescribed the painkiller at the company's Wednesday Wellness Wing told Annie that the pink capsules were formulated for subtle benefit. She'd be sharp, her pain dull.

They did make the throb tolerable, but Annie was most definitely not sharp. She focused well enough to be competent. Excellence was out of range.

It didn't help that the Metrics team was burst-tasking again, launching fusillades of data requests into the project-management queue. Numbers. Now.

If Annie had to write queries in the bathroom in order to turn them around faster, that was just gin-chy with Chez Metrics. In fact, if she was dumb enough to mention the idea to them, they'd make it a stretch goal.

Comfort was not a priority, the woman assigning the requests noted in the comments field, because it didn't matter to Mr. Truitt or Mr. Brill. The two men required twice-a-day updates on resource throughput as an assurance that system integrity was bulletproof. If those updates were late, productivity inquiries were launched, and the subjects of said inquiries might find themselves on the firing line.

Yes, the woman used the phrase "firing line."

Annie wondered how much the lady who typed these things meant them. And what, if a damn thing, did she know about being shot at?

The job was as good as others Annie had worked, and better than some, but that made her concern over losing it even worse. She was good with data—very good—which should have granted her some modicum of employment security.

It didn't.

Annie's cubicle was housed in Distributed Common Ground System Unit Thirteen. Monitors and resource graphs claimed eighty percent of its surface area. She felt most engaged with the world when lit by the glow of realtime data. Her gift for analysis had been burnished by years of wrestling mammoth volumes of information.

She had Operation Iraqi Freedom and two in-country stints to thank for that. She also had it to thank for the steel-packed bomb, hidden in a rotting dog in the middle of a Mosul road, that gave her the gift of career transition just in time for Operation New Dawn. It robbed her of enjoyable walks, but moved her to a new line of work: processing surveillance-drone video at a desk instead of watching friends die in the field.

Her skills landed her in Brill's organization, which paid her enough for a two-bedroom apartment, food, and a life. And if she were ever able to live it free from the pinky-blown mists, she might even enjoy it.

But she didn't feel at home. At all.

There was too much unease. Her team monitored the stability of Brill's colossal data infrastructure, and she was one of the key point people for the data about that data. It made for sleepless nights worrying about the tiers of backup systems and whether or not they could be relied on in a sprinkler malfunction or sector failure.

Even when she did sleep for a few hours, it meant dreaming. And all of the dreams were bad. She suspected the pinkies on that front, too.

Dreams about things that had happened, like the bomb and the screws. Dreams about things that hadn't but seemed real at three in the morning, like the snow and the bus.

Still, on balance, the pinkies and their fog were partners of a sort. They allowed her to get her work done—just not as well as she would have when clear-headed.

The other data jocks had their crutches and saviors, too. Tara was a texter. At lunch every day, her thumbs worked the glass of her smartphone like a massage therapist. Her colleagues had to remind her to eat. For Melissa and Sinead, it was the cafeteria TV. They sat at the break-room table closest to the hanging screen, the twenty-four–hour newscast their lover for the hour. But if you asked them what was happening out in the world, they couldn't say. They didn't much want to know, either. Watching was the thing, not the thing they watched.

The chief concern for all was the data and the warehouses each of them tended. Annie worked the flow like it was her child, or, in drier terms, a reactor core always on the verge of overheating. Those were the visuals the pills delivered while she toiled: a tangle of sweating pipes about to blow, a beehive unable to contain its colony, a school of fish tacking in unison, invariably threatening to break ranks and scatter.

The data was an entity unto itself. The jocks and analysts didn't know what it represented, ultimately. They weren't meant to. But it was needy, and they were needed. That was the job.

"Are last night's performance numbers ready?"

The voice would have been startling, but the pinkies slowed its trip from ear to brain. The meds were on guard, subjecting all auditory input to a full-body scan before allowing it through the gates.

A short, solid woman with a man's jawline stood at the entrance to Annie's cubicle.

"I'm working on them now," Annie said. "You can add yourself as a watcher to the request if you like. Then you'll know when I upload."

The woman stepped over the threshold. She didn't require permission to be in Annie's space. There was something familiar about that.

"No need to watch," she told Annie. "It's my request. They all are." She waited for that to sink in. "But I asked the wrong question. I know the numbers aren't ready, so I'll rephrase. When?"

"An hour. I'm sorry I'm not as quick as some people would like, but I prefer to check and make sure they're right rather than right on time."

The woman sucked her teeth, registering the push-back. "I'll expect them in an hour. As will Mister Truitt."

"I understand. And please, if you have any other concerns, don't trouble yourself with coming over. You can continue to tell me about the firing line by email."

The woman tilted her head, as if seeing Annie in a new light. There definitely was something familiar about her. "I prefer correspondence to be tracked in the system. That way, there's no after-the-fact editing."

"I understand. But what's your address, in case I need to avoid system lag?"

"If there's system lag, you need to report it." She stepped back out of the cubicle. "And my address is on every request I log. June-dot-Medill."

....

EIGHT

SHE SHIFTED HER GUN
IN HER LAP

The Van-Tasta roared down the highway, hidden speakers assailing its occupants with shredded-guitar salvos from all directions. The wine-grape shag carpet covering every surface but the leather of the twin captain's chairs up front quivered along like cilia. On the built-in refrigerator, the fibers danced. Even the wings of a jellybean-sized housefly trapped in the vehicle bounced with the noise when it landed on the front of the mini-bar.

Paul had hitched many rides with those eager to show off their audio. Usually, they were generous with transportation but not conversation. This driver, Vizzie, was happy to be an exception.

There were five people in the car, assuming the two in front were human. Vizzie, in a tuxedo and stovepipe hat, looked like he'd been buried a number of years before—a mortician who didn't yet realize he'd joined his customers in the Hereafter. His ash-gray skin was pulled tight over a skull that was all angles. A hard sneeze would split his face like an old bed sheet.

Vizzie didn't sneeze. He was too caught up in asking questions. Porter, in the seat behind him, kept just as busy with evasive replies.

Vizzie's partner Deck, the half-man, half-machine, said little. He mostly glared with his robot eye or ogled the girl sharing the rear-most seat of the van with Paul.

Paul guessed that Rain was about his age. She sported sleeves of tattoos on her slim arms—an iridescent koi on her shoulder, a leafless tree on one forearm, and a disquietingly realistic black widow spider in a web on the other.

She wore her raven hair long and free, and her beauty was such that Paul's heart hurt whenever he stole a look. Her second-most striking aspect was the short-barreled shotgun in a custom holster resting on her thighs.

"Where'd you say you're coming from again?" Vizzie said over the shrieking strings.

Porter hadn't. And Vizzie knew it.

"North," the Envoy said.

"Yeah? Whereabouts?"

"Montreal. Or what passes for it."

Deck glowered at Paul as if his robot half enjoyed lie-detector functionality. That being the case, it would have had no time to rest. Porter hadn't uttered a word of truth since climbing in.

The fly headed toward the glow of Deck's eye but thought better of it. It buzzed Paul instead, then set a course for the rear cargo area.

"Where are you guys going?" Vizzie asked.

"West."

"Or what passes for it?"

Porter nodded.

"You don't sound like a Canuck." Deck's tone was all steel-edged suspicion.

"No."

"That's more talk than we get out of our cutie back there," Vizzie said, eye-checking Rain in the rear-view. "She won't give us a blue clue—will you, little friend?"

She shifted her gun in her lap.

"Warm, ain't she?" Vizzie said.

Paul struggled to keep his eyes off the girl, fearing he wouldn't be able to stop if he gave in. At the edge of his vision, a flurry of moving colors defeated his efforts. Her tattoos.

The koi was now on her lower arm. It had swum downstream from her shoulder, and the formerly skeletal tree was bursting with lustrous green.

"She swore you guys were pals," Vizzie said. "Insisted we stop for you when Deck wanted to run you down." He hooted. Neither Porter nor Deck reacted. "How could I refuse the most beautiful thing to ever crawl into our cart?"

Pals? In the window's reflection, Rain met Paul's eyes with her own, then looked back out at the passing landscape.

It was simple hitchhiker's math: a girl on a ride with bad players added a couple of strangers to the equation. If she was lucky, it meant a layer of protection, provided the new guys weren't worse. Even if they were, more people in the mix forced slower decisions, and a loaded gun in plain view was usually a solid persuader.

"You hear any of the action?" Vizzie said.

Porter remained silent.

"You didn't hear? New meat in at first light. A load of them."

"One got away," Deck said. He kept his robot eye on Paul.

"Oh?" Porter was almost effusive in his ignorance. "A Journey's afoot?"

"What vacuum do you live in?" Vizzie said. "Yeah, man. A rabbit on a bus. I don't know how he skated, but a trucker told us the Ravs brought in a hell of a welcome committee. Air cavalry, shock troops. Something's up. They don't burn that hard for just anyone. Not right off. This was someone they wanted."

"Isn't that something?" Porter said.

"This rabbit died under a bad sign, right?" Vizzie grinned. His face didn't rupture, to Paul's disappointment. "Must have, if he drew that hot a fire. All-out heart of darkness, man. They'll get him, too."

Porter looked out the window. All that had nothing to do with him. Paul attempted to do the same while Deck studied him.

Rain watched The Commons go by as if she were alone on a train. The tattooed spider on her forearm now had a finely detailed something caught and bundled in its web.

Paul's stomach fluttered. That was new.

He looked around for the fly.

NINE

....

IED

A nnie finished dressing for work and checked on Zach. He was in his bedroom at the closet-door mirror again.

It bothered her that he spent most of his time looking at himself in the glass. It was also unsettling that when he wasn't doing that, he was playing with an old cassette recorder he found in his night-table drawer soon after they moved into their apartment.

Hour after hour, day or night, he murmured into the handheld microphone in a voice so low she couldn't hear a word. With the lunchbox-sized recorder in one hand and the mike in the other, he looked like he was taking sustenance from the machine rather than speaking to it.

It should have bothered her more. She felt like she'd long ago battled to keep her son from losing himself to whatever bewitched him, though those memories never seemed all that solid.

That's what the pinkies were for. Why fight what you can fog?

Did the pinkies keep her old feelings at bay, or did they cause her to invent remembrance of things that never happened—places in their lives that never existed? Did the pill numb emotions or create false ones? She didn't care.

That, too, should have disturbed her. It did not.

When she managed to sleep, she dreamt of made-up apartments that she and Zach had never inhabited, even if the details of them felt genuine, seemed real. Hardwood floors were scuffed ruination. Battered steam radiators arced jets of scalding water from faulty valves. Cockeyed bathroom doors sagged under dense layers of paint, the wood of their frames gone soft from decades of shower steam.

So real. But Annie and Zach had never so much as visited New York.

There was no rest. She closed her eyes and thought of sleep, observing the ritual out of loyalty to the routine.

It was the same for Zach. She got up in the night to find him at the mirror, staring at the glass in the dark. She no longer pretended to want him to go to bed. He could do what he pleased.

That was the pinkies' gift. Her knee hurt less; her worries fell silent.

Days before, she'd snuck into Zach's room to play one of the tapes he'd recorded—a rare bout of curiosity amidst her chronic apathy. The old Annie might have felt guilty about the invasion. Not Annie of the Pinkies.

She listened to the first tape, and then another and another to make sure she hadn't grabbed an outlier.

She hadn't.

Tape after tape held nothing but hiss.

AT THE OFFICE, the pinkies came up short. It started with the data, as did most everything.

During a differential backup, while Annie had a double-sized mug of loose-leaf English breakfast in hand, the visions hit again. It was one of the usual visitors: the nautilus. He showed up whenever she got to contemplating data concepts during boring maintenance tasks.

She was considering the Catalan numbers before jumping to a logarithmic spiral, which prompted the little guy to come calling. Annie thought of it as a friend, unlike the wayward school of fish who always signaled a bad sector.

Then things turned.

The nautilus came to a stop on a reef, probing with its tentacles, and began to spin. Gaining speed, it blurred into a vision of a shifting ball and drilled into the coral. The whirling creature then vanished and was replaced by some sort of portal in the water.

On the other side was Charlene Moseley.

Annie's knee throbbed. Her numbing pal, the pink mist, was overmatched.

Char's flawless skin, the color of tea. The nearly shaved head, a style few women who weren't fashion models could pull off. The ever-present smirk, like she already knew your good news but was too generous to say anything until you'd had a chance to tell her.

Charlene.

Here was the comrade who'd been in the M-113 with Annie when it rolled over the IED in Mosul. Here was Char, the friend laid out on the adjacent table while they worked on Annie's knee without painkillers—who died as Annie watched the light fade from her eyes, her face only a foot or two away.

The pinkies couldn't stop Annie's shaking when she realized Char was working in a cubicle much like hers—one nearby, perhaps. And they couldn't stop her from dropping her pen when Charlene looked up from her monitor screen, through the window in the water—and right at her.

TEN

....

BOOM

Paul lost it at the highway rest stop. He'd been losing it all along, but had thus far convinced himself that he was in an extended dream. He'd wanted to see how the situation developed before really and truly freaking.

It wasn't much of a plan. So the state of things overwhelmed him while he and Porter were eating at an outdoor picnic table near some bathrooms.

An assortment of travelers filled the other tables, which were scattered around the concession stand where Porter picked up lunch. Paul thought it was lunch, anyway. He'd lost all sense of time. Regardless, having cheeseburgers for breakfast wasn't anywhere near as strange as the display of creatures around them.

A life-sized astronaut action figure with a Ronald Reagan haircut enjoyed some yellow goop from a regulation NASA squeeze-tube. Across from him, a black-and-white projection of a television housewife winked in and out—invisible, then there again. Interference and vertical-hold lines traveled down her form as she dug into a TV dinner in a foil tray.

Vizzie and Deck sat a distance away. They watched Rain, who kept to herself at her own table. Her holstered shotgun was strapped diagonally across her back, stock up. Paul doubted that Vizzie and Deck would steal her lunch with the weapon so close at hand. Then again, they probably weren't after her Philly cheesesteak.

After a long stretch of staring, Vizzie got something in his eye. He leaned back and pulled at his lid, trying to dislodge it. When that didn't work, he dug his eye out and popped it into his mouth. Paul used to do the same gag for the younger kids at New Beginnings, the key difference being, of course, that he'd faked it. Vizzie swirled his eyeball in his mouth, giving it a thorough wash, and smacked it back into his empty socket, blinking to orient it in his skull.

Paul's gut made a fist of itself. He fought to swallow a bite of his burger and pushed the rest of it away.

"You should finish that," Porter said. "We don't know when we'll eat next."

"I'm in Hell."

Porter swallowed. "No."

"I'm dead, and this is Hell."

"Nothing's been decided. We're only starting."

"Oh, my God."

"No." Porter grabbed Paul's arm. "Hear that. No. That's why you're in The Commons. Your fate will be determined here. By you."

The past couple of days went on playback in Paul's head. Pop Mike. Port Authority. The rolling miles in the van.

Porter looked around them at the TV housewife, Vizzie and Deck, Rain. "I haven't done this in a long time."

"Where am I, Porter?"

"The Commons is its widely used designation. Others call it Sojourn, The Roundhouse, The Way Station. It's Purgatory to the Catholics, but their model's a bit off. It's named in thousands of other languages, not all of them spoken aloud."

"I died on the bus."

"Some did, to be certain, but not necessarily you. What you do here decides where you go next—back to your life or forward to the next stop. Reward and punishment may come into play, but that's never been proven. Your fate is yours alone, and no one can predict it. Nor does it profit us to try. The world you left squanders its time on the mystery of what's ahead. We've learned not to."

The astronaut took the TV housewife's hand. She smiled, changing from grayscale to Technicolor.

"When do I find out?"

"At this Gaia festival, I believe. You're a Journeyman. A Traveler, a Wayfarer, a Seeker. Again, many names. You'll face a challenge unique to you, just as the version of The Commons you travel is unique and adapts to..." Porter thought for a moment.

Paul let the Envoy's words gestate, trying to get a fix.

Porter watched Vizzie and Deck study Rain. "The Sioux said it was a spirit journey. A person's ni—their spirit—enters the world beyond the pines to make a difficult trek. They called it crossing a river on a very narrow tree, and it is. Other cultures and thinkers expressed the idea of The Commons, too—the Akasha, Jung's collective unconscious." He pushed Paul's food back toward him. "And you really should eat. This is all difficult enough without traveling on an empty belly."

Paul picked at the food. At another table, a fat man covered in porcupine quills tapped away at a portable typewriter. "Then who are these ... people?"

"Some come from you. The Commons remakes itself according to each Journeyman's memories and imaginings."

"I don't recognize any of this."

"There are stragglers—more, it seems, than when I was last out here. They are contributions from everyone who's ever Journeyed. Stories of remnants abound. I never saw her myself, but someone conjured up Mothra in the sixties. She flew around at night, smashing stadiums and airports and anything else that was lit up. Then, poof—gone."

Porter watched Vizzie and Deck, chewing his lip. "Think of The Commons as a hard drive that's never defragmented. There are stray memories scattered around it, wandering about." His face darkened. "It wasn't always like that."

"What about the Ravagers?"

"All too real, I'm afraid."

Rain stood up from her table, stretched, and headed for the bathrooms. Vizzie and Deck watched her go.

"What about Rain?"

"Hers is a story we'll need to hear, if circumstance keeps us together," Porter said. "She should watch her back. But she's aware of that."

"Her tattoos are alive."

"I know."

She went into the women's room, the door shutting behind her.

Vizzie stood and made for the bathrooms, too.

"How many times have you done this?"

"Too many to count, which doesn't mean I don't know the exact number. I've led Journeys across everything The Commons can cook up. A pitch-black trip with a blind Journeyman, a trek across Antarctica—which was a misery of frostbite. You're American, so we get America. Or your version of it."

"How hard will this be?"

Vizzie entered the women's room. Deck got up, made his way to the bathroom, and joined him, pulling the self-closing door shut.

Porter stood. "If that girl isn't out of there in five seconds, stay here while I see to this. How much TV do you watch?"

"A lot."

"Comic books? Video games?"

"Yes."

"Then we're in for a violent mess."

"I read books, too."

Porter started for the bathrooms. "Jolly good. That's not my point."

"Then what—"

The boom of Rain's shotgun echoed from within the bathroom's cinder-block walls, blowing Vizzie through the door and onto his back on the ground outside. Then *boom* again.

Rain burst through the door, hopped over the unmoving Vizzie, and headed their way, Vizzie's keys jingling in her hand. She cradled her shotgun, wisps of smoke trailing from its barrel.

"You're American, so everyone's packing," Porter said. He raised his staff, gauging her intentions.

She sprinted past, straight for the Van-Tasta. Unlocking the driver's-side door, she jumped in.

Porter and Paul ran for the van as its engine cranked.

Rain saw them coming. They reached the doors, and the lock buttons popped up. Porter got into the shotgun seat, aptly named given the firearm he had to move before sitting. Paul pulled the side door open and climbed into the back.

She cursed. Deck emerged from the women's room, blackened wires flashing and sparking in a shot-out portion of his electronic half.

The motor turned over and she gunned it. The side door slid open the rest of the way, smacking hard into its stop.

Deck moved fast considering the extent of the damage done to him. His eye glared redder than ever. Then the engine revved, and he lost the race.

The Van-Tasta fishtailed out of the parking lot, gravel flying in a wave. Rain straightened it out, and they rumbled up the picnic area's exit road.

"He told me it was time for fun," she said, reaching for the shotgun and stowing it between her and the driver-side door. "It wasn't. What did he think the gun was for?" She shook her head.

Once they reached the road proper, she gave the engine even more gas. "You two have any fun in mind?"

Porter kept his eyes on the speedometer as the needle passed eighty. "I'm no fun at all," he said.

....

ELEVEN

ITS DISTANT OCEAN

After dinner, Annie threw the leftovers away. Once again, neither she nor Zach had eaten much of their microwave meals.

She went upstairs to see what he was up to. Like so many other things that had to do with her son, this was a checklist item rather than a task in which she felt invested.

At the mirror again. And again, Annie was thankful because the closet door was a reliable sitter.

"Hey, buddy." She called him nicknames more and more lately, though she suspected she hadn't always. "Ready for bed?"

He ignored her. It didn't matter what she called him. She was a non-entity.

Annie went to the closet door and stood in front of it, blocking his view. No reaction. "Time for all little guys to sleep so their mommies can, too."

Her son looked right through her.

She stepped aside. His eyes didn't follow. She slid the door open, revealing the emptiness of the closet's interior. He scooted sideways to stare into the other mirror.

There was a crinkling sound to his shifting. She bent to take his hand in hers. He let her.

That hand was empty, but the other held a carefully folded, tattered page from a notebook, its edge stubbornly retaining shreds and chads from where it had been torn out.

Scrawled on it in crayon was a phrase that Annie guessed was Latin: "Unus pro omnibus, omnes pro uno." The letters were nearly illegible.

She closed the closet door and moved out of the way. He slid back to his original spot.

With the notebook page in hand, she headed for the door. She'd search the Web for a translation. The scrawl piqued her interest—a novel feeling these days.

Zach stood to face her, his hand out for the paper.

She knew that look. If she tried to leave without giving it back, she'd have an episode to deal with. "What?" she said, though she already knew.

He stayed as he was.

"Okay." She handed it over.

He folded the page and tucked it into his pocket with care. Then he returned to his post.

"Good night, buddy," she said.

Nothing. She was nothing to him. And maybe she deserved it.

ANNIE DREAMT of dinner basted with love—a meal she'd have thrown out in her waking hours. It was a five-hour pot roast.

She lowered the meat into a Dutch oven filled with tomatoes, onions, celery, red wine, water, and spices, and left it at 300 degrees. Then she and Zach went walking in the snow so that their kitchen—again, a kitchen in New York, where they'd never lived—greeted them with a wondrous aroma when they came back in from the cold.

The Annie of Mr. Brill's working world couldn't imagine bothering with that level of preparation, given her schedule and lack of appetite. But it was real in the dream, as was the sense that Zach was calling her.

She awoke and rolled over to see his silhouette next to her bed in the dark. The smell of the cooking roast and the dream bond with her son waned. She turned on her night-table lamp, squinting with the click.

"Hey, buddy. What's wrong?"

The boy, holding his cassette recorder, said nothing. She suspected he'd been standing there for some time, but the sudden light didn't bother him.

"Can't sleep?"

He licked his lips.

She couldn't remember him ever uttering a word, but it was so hard to find him in her memories at all. The Annie of dreams, who sang as she brought her little boy in from the winter outside to breathe in the meal she'd prepared, would have been stricken at that.

This Annie could only wonder what such caring felt like.

He held the recorder out. She reached for it, but he kept it away from her, clicking the play button. The cassette's white plastic wheels turned. He watched her listen.

Hiss. Like faraway breakers or a summer shower.

"Is there something you want me to hear?"

His chin tipped down as he waited for a reaction. The recorder continued its distant ocean.

"I'm sorry, buddy. I don't hear anything." Then it hit her. "Do you?"

He maintained his silence. After a while, he pushed stop. It was a harsher click than the play button had delivered.

"Do you want some water?" She swung her legs over the side of the bed to stand, but he held his hand up, stopping her.

Zach wiggled his fingers, the way he had as a baby, when he first learned that they were attached, and he had the power to move them. As an infant, he'd stared at them for hours, but now he regarded her instead, keeping the motion going like a little parade-float veteran. When she didn't respond, he waved his hand from side to side.

"Oh." She smiled. "Hi." And waved back at him. "Hey there, buddy."

He lowered his hand.

"Hi," she said. "Right?"

TWELVE

....

A COLONY OF
THUMB-SIZED MEN

A Journey of unknowns required clothes ready for anything. So Porter and Paul hunted for outdoor gear in a big-box store off the highway.

If Paul had ever tried to imagine what death would be like, a shopping trip wouldn't have been part of it. Yet here he was, holding quick-drying pants, wicking shirts of varying sleeve-lengths, and a pair of mid-weight hiking boots.

Porter emerged from a dressing room fully out-fitted in similar gear and dropped his blazer, pants, and dress shoes on the floor. He clapped his hands once, with finality. "I've been wearing that get-up for several multiples of your lifetime. It looks like long days and smells of tedium. I shall not miss it."

The gray man cut a formidable figure in his new clothing and boots, which were a better visual fit for his large walking staff. The worn leather riding hat on his head completed the picture.

"Where'd you get the lid?"

Porter grabbed the wide brim and adjusted it. "It's a Kodiak. Australian. I jumped it here from the office. Taxing at such a distance, but necessary. I couldn't remember where I'd left it until now."

The Envoy went off to find a trash can for his old suit and shoes. When he returned, Paul asked him for his thoughts on Rain, trying to make it sound like conversation meant only to fill the void.

"How old would you guess she is?" Porter replied. "Your age? A year younger?"

"Maybe."

"She's seventeen at the oldest, but it's difficult to say because she's done more living than that. She carries a shotgun, which she fired twice today. Her targets weren't human, and they probably can't be killed with an ordinary weapon. I believe she'd be disappointed to know that. So what do you think I think of her?"

Paul's face grew hot. Porter was supposed to be the leader but had kept them waiting hours for a ride. Rain freed them from two dangerous players who attacked her, and she'd gained them a vehicle as a bonus. And Porter didn't trust her.

"She has the keys to the van, doesn't she?" Paul said, the question edged.

"True. And if it's still there when we walk outside, we'll know what kind of person we're traveling with. If she and the van are gone? Well, we'll still know—and will be better off with that knowledge and her absence."

The possibility of Rain taking off on them hadn't occurred to Paul.

"Go see while I pay," Porter said. "But do not get in that van with her under any circumstances. And if she's with someone, come back inside and find me. Do you understand?"

Paul dropped his new clothes and boots on his way out.

THE VAN SAT at one of the fuel islands in front of the store. The windshield gleamed, and Rain was filling the tank when Paul arrived. He leaned against the driver's side and hoped she didn't notice how relieved he was to see her. To give himself cover, he made conversation and asked where she was from.

"Philadelphia born and bred. If you call how I grew up breeding." The gas pump clicked off. She tapped the nozzle against the edge of the intake, knocking the last drops into it.

"How'd you end up in this van?"

She returned the hose to its hook, pausing long enough to let him know he wasn't owed an answer—giving him one was her choice. "Bad decision on a bad day. Usually that means someone trying to convert me or a guy who's only going as far as the next bed. Those I can handle." She looked to her shotgun, which rested against the dashboard. "This was a bigger oops."

"Why are you here—in The Commons? What happened to you?"

Her smile was meant to look forced—and did. "We usually build up to that one."

Chastised, Paul surveyed the other motorists gassing up. Two pumps over, a man sprayed the windows of a beat-up Humvee with blue fluid. He was actually a colony of thumb-sized men clinging together to form a larger version of themselves. They moved with flawless precision.

Flawless, that is, until they stepped back and tripped on a water hose. The men forming the arm dropped and scattered on the ground. They scurried up a leg composed of their brethren and reformed the limb, chattering in squeaks that were dog-whistle high.

"Everyone brings things in," she said, watching them. "Everyone leaves things behind. I wonder if somewhere the pony I wanted as a kid is running around. Only it probably has a duck for a head. Or a steam shovel."

Across the lot, Porter approached. He was once again dressed in his old suit and shoes and was empty-handed. Passing under a sign with gas prices on it, he looked up at the digits and scowled.

"Why'd you tell those guys we were your friends?" Paul said.

"I needed a way out in case I couldn't handle it." She waited until Porter was close enough to hear her. "I figured your Envoy would take care of them if I didn't."

Porter put on an impressive show of confusion. It didn't fool her.

"I've been here long enough to read you," she said. "Both of you. I know."

The gray man dropped the pretense. "I understand that there are bona fides out and about, but you don't see many traveling alone," he said. "At least, you never used to. You are bona fide, correct?"

"Bona fide means real," she told Paul. "He wants to know why the Ravagers haven't gotten me yet." She studied Porter. "You're a man. Between a girl's gun and other things, there are ways to survive when your Envoy leaves you without a word or a prayer. Want to hear them? I'll give you a second to think it over."

Porter softened. "If that happened to you, I am sorry."

"Do I get a question now?" she said.

He nodded.

"Does Paul understand what he's up against, or did you pull the what-he-doesn't-know-yet-can't-hurt-him Envoy crap?"

Paul looked from Rain to Porter. Where was this going?

"Did you tell him about Brill?" she said.

Porter straightened the lapels of his jacket. "They rejected my Corps credit card, but agreed to put everything on layaway," he said to Paul. Then he bounced his staff on the asphalt, thinking. "The amount of money available to an Envoy is usually based on how his Journeyman behaved in life. I've seen dirt-poor people arrive with flush accounts and filthy-rich vulture investors forced to survive on roots and rain water. Given the current situation, we count on nothing." He shot Rain a look.

"I'm not dodging your question. I'd planned to ease him into it."

The Envoy focused on the side wall of the big-box store, which had an ATM near its corner. "Anyway," he said, "since you know." He closed his eyes in concentration, took a small breath, and gave his staff a flick. His free hand filled with as many twenty-dollar bills as it could hold.

"We're robbing the bank?" Paul said. "Why not just steal the clothes?"

"At first, I thought that a working economy out here boded well for your Journey. I assumed it meant a formal structure. But I don't see any structure. Everything's in flux. I don't like that the Corps card doesn't work, and now I wish I hadn't tried it." Porter riffled the cash, counting. "I'll keep track of this. It will be repaid."

"Can they tell where we are because of the card?" Paul said.

"Perhaps. I don't know."

"What do you mean you don't know? What else don't you know?"

Porter ignored him and headed for the store again, his fist packed with cash.

Paul looked to Rain, but she merely watched the Envoy walk away.

....

THIRTEEN

THE GREAT EIGHT'S
FAVORITE BARBER

After the nautilus showed Charlene Moseley to Annie, the visions were no longer a by-product of the data-examination process. They were the process itself—its focus, not a distraction. If she allowed them to find her rather than running traditional queries to access the information, her job was easier. What she sought would seek her.

She loved nature. Maybe that was why the visions took its form. Like attracted like, which was, perhaps, why she'd been shown Charlene. They had a history together, so their data clustered. Information wanted efficiency.

Some of the things that sought her attention were awful, however. She periodically found herself on the Plain of Ghosts when she got lost in her work and couldn't find a host creature to guide her out. At a distance, it appeared to be a pocked moonscape. But what looked like divots from afar were upturned faces—so many that she couldn't see where they stopped. Those farthest from her were missing eyes and tongues.

Buzzards wheeled overhead, now and then landing to claim a prize. Cries followed—some in familiar voices.

Like attracted like. She knew some of those people.

Good thing the pinkies were there to take her away, even if the off-feelings sometimes hit not when she was deep in the data but simply moving about the office. In the women's room, where her reflection was slow to appear in the mirror, like a lamp on a delayed switch. Or in the far stairwell, where she heard a baby crying.

And the spider webs. They were rare at first, but lately when she arrived in the morning, her keyboard and monitor were covered in them. One day, she'd been afraid to approach her desk until she was certain that the lump under the off-white mat of threads was her mouse and not something that would attack if she touched it.

The creepy webbing greeted her daily, and she got in early to clean it up before her colleagues saw it. She never noticed it in anyone else's cubicle. That wouldn't reflect well on her, and she needed this job.

Even so, Annie was unprepared for the afternoon she walked into the break room to find a criss-cross of blue masking tape over the clogged sink. A taped-up notice informed her and her coworkers that management was sorry for the inconvenience, but they would have to use the eleventh-floor sink instead.

No surprise there. People were forever dumping coffee grounds down the drain, despite the prominent sign asking them not to. Every other week, the resulting brown cement sealed off the drain.

The surprise came when she climbed the steps to eleven, which she did because of a bad vibe from the building's elevators—a feeling that their doors might open on a floor from which there was no return. In the lounge area, a woman sat alone at a corner table, pecking away at a laptop.

Annie forgot about the tea she was there to make.

"Char?" She wanted the woman to keep typing, to not respond, so that she could laugh at how some people looked so much like others and at how the mind was tricky that way. Then she could pretend she hadn't said anything, head back downstairs, and bang out more work while her whole-leaf steeped for the recommended five minutes.

"I'm sorry," the woman said. "I'm terrible with names. We've been in meetings together?"

"You know me, Charlene." Annie approached the table, but left five feet of space. Less than that, and anyone with training stopped listening and concentrated only on the hands. "And I know you."

Char's eyes betrayed an inner struggle, but there was no recognition in them.

"In bars, you never tell men you're from Ohio because you're afraid they'll think you're too boring to buy you a drink," Annie said. "Your dad was the Great Eight's favorite barber. You have a picture of him with them in your wallet, but it's only with seven. You're an amazing standing shot with a twenty-two, but you didn't join the rifle team in college because the competition would have ruined it for you."

She crossed the five-foot line. Charlene watched only her face.

"Your sister doesn't speak to you anymore," Annie said. "You don't know why."

Annie was back on the table in Mosul, watching her friend's breathing stop. Tears blurred her vision.

Charlene's eyes glistened, too. She leaned over her laptop to take a closer look at Annie. "I'm sorry," she said. "I know I should remember. But I don't." A tear slipped down her cheek. She wiped it away.

"Where are we, Char?"

"You don't know?"

A harsh clearing of a throat at the lounge entrance brought the moment to an end. June Medill's face was a portrait of displeasure. "I've been trying to find you," she told Annie. "Are the throughputs ready?"

"Almost."

June Medill gave them the up-and-down. She was not happy to see two workers sharing anything. "Annie, why are you up here?"

"The sink downstairs isn't working."

The sour little woman's frown deepened.

BACK ON THE TENTH FLOOR, June Medill walked Annie to the break room. The sign and tape over the sink were gone.

She walked to the faucet and turned it on. The water swirled down the drain, unimpeded.

June Medill watched Annie for a reaction. "This isn't why I was looking for you," she said, turning the water off. "Do you know my real reason?"

Annie had no answer for her.

"No?"

They walked back to Annie's cubicle. June Medill's reason was apparent before they got there.

The walls were draped in webbing. Annie's computer and desk were nearly unrecognizable, the floor below them covered in a wispy white carpet. Something—several somethings—scurried beneath it.

"Might you explain?" June Medill said.

FOURTEEN

....

THIS WILL NOT GO
WELL FOR YOU

The Van-Tasta rolled through the night with Porter behind the wheel and Paul beside him. Rain slept in the very back.

Paul counted the dashes of the highway's center line as they dripped through the headlights. "I'm being hunted by Satan," he said.

"Brill is not Satan."

"He takes everyone who comes through here and eats their soul, right?"

"No. He leeches Essence, the soul's energy, which cannot be destroyed. It merely changes form. He's a parasite, not a devil."

Paul twisted his ring and watched the landscape slide by, the untended cornfields lit by the blue of the undercarriage lamps. Once at speed, the van ran quiet. "How long's he been doing that?"

"Unknown."

"Hundreds of years?"

"We really don't know. Long enough to attain the level of power he now enjoys, which is considerable. He did it in secret at first, preying on those whose absence wasn't noticed. He had influence, and his victims' assignments never made it to us. We only realized what was happening when he no longer needed to hide it. Many came to him willingly. And soon he didn't need to convince anyone anymore. He was too strong. He took what he wanted."

They passed a sign for exit twenty-four. It didn't say what one would find there.

"How far is twenty-five?" Paul said.

"There's no guarantee that there is one. When you were in New York, what street came after Forty-second?"

"Depends on which way you're going. North, Forty-third."

"Not here. Not even if it was there the day before. What comes next might not even be a street at all. The landscape forms itself for your Journey."

Glowing animal eyes reflected the lights back at Paul through gaps in the corn. "Why is he after me?"

"Because he's after everyone and everything."

Really, Paul had no idea if they were animals at all. And it was probably safer to assume that they weren't friendly. "Why is he so strong?"

"There are only guesses, and he's not about to tell anyone, certainly. But the real answer probably lies somewhere between Newtonian conservation of energy and Gödel's incompleteness theorems."

"What?"

"He exploits the contradictory state of The Commons. Everyone here is in-between. They are—and are not. It's about the Journeys that never happen. The energy doesn't know where to go, and Brill captures it. The universe doesn't care, ultimately, so long as the energy exists somewhere. But it matters to us."

The universe didn't care. That Paul understood. One kid gets stomped in an alley while another plays tennis in his back yard. The first has only a picture of his mom; the second has only bad things to say about his.

"The Commons exists in paradox," Porter said. "This sentence is false. If that's true, then it's also not true. That's what Brill exploits."

"Vizzie said I was a rabbit who died under a bad sign."

"Rabbit's not a term I use. Neither should you. Believe, and trust your belief. We might get lucky and catch Brill with his attention elsewhere."

"He said they went all-out heart of darkness on me."

"On someone. Take this in the spirit in which it's meant: I doubt Brill is losing sleep over a skinny kid in a van. Whomever he wanted on that bus, let's hope he found them. Not because we wish such a fate on anyone else, but because we wish a better one for you."

"At least this skinny kid wanted to go back and help the others. According to Rain, the Envoys aren't big on that lately."

He couldn't see Porter's jaw tighten, but he swore he heard it. The gray man turned to him in the low light of the dashboard. "You've made it this far because of me. Don't you think that I would have taken everyone on that hill with us?" He turned back to the road. "I look old to you. I'm older. I do what I am able to do. And I am alone."

Paul let his head fall back against the headrest and looked up. Stars floated past overhead, their light dimmed by the moon roof's tinted glass. "Does that include helping her?"

"If Rain's Envoy abandoned her, as she says, then she must find the end of her Journey on her own—if it even remains viable. But she knows how to handle herself. We have a vehicle because of her, and we need all the friends and firepower we can find." He paused. "And since you can't take your eyes off her, I'll help where I can."

Paul started to protest, but Porter waved it off. "People decide their fates here. Do you believe there's no room for human feelings—that we forget how to love?"

"It's not love."

Porter drove on in amused silence. Suddenly, the only thing Paul had to worry about was whether Rain was really asleep.

AT DAYBREAK, Porter turned off the highway and into the parking lot of a truck-stop diner.

Across the asphalt, a phalanx of tractor-trailers in a range of colors, customization, and road-worthiness surrounded a cargo scale. A painted sign, a veteran of many cycles of fading and touch-ups, advertised coffee, beer, ammo, and fireworks.

"If this place is built on my thoughts, then maybe my world's pretty scary after all," Paul said, reading the sign.

"As long as nobody's using those simultaneously," said Porter.

Inside, the Envoy bought them breakfast. Paul polished off both his and Rain's bacon after he was unable to convince her to eat more than a few bites.

He finished his toast while Porter went to the men's room. Around the diner, their fellow patrons ordered and ate.

At the counter, a truck driver used his one good arm to mop the yolk from his plate with a piece of pumpernickel. His other arm was a slot-machine handle.

Periodically, customers and even a waitress or two approached him and apologized for interrupting his meal. They gave him some change, waited while he swallowed it, and pulled his handle.

Amusement-park sounds blared from a speaker in his back. His eyes flashed rolling patterns of red, blue, and yellow as the players gazed into them with hope. When the eyes stopped, some of the players yipped or cheered and walked away happy. Others were upset by what they saw.

One man accused the trucker of cheating and had to be led away by the manager. A woman with a mass of tangled power cords for hair returned to her table in tears, sparks flying from her plugs as they collided.

At the adjacent table, a man-sized pillbug dined solo.

In a booth sat a wooden robot made of matchsticks. He'd wanted another spot, but the waitress insisted on seating him as far from the entrance to the fireworks store as possible.

In two big booths closer to Paul and Rain sat a gang of skinheads in matching leather jackets. They appeared to be human. Certainly, their mean streak was all too familiar.

They alternated between finishing their omelets and taunting two customers sitting a couple of tables away. A few of them gave up on eating altogether and focused only on the harassment.

One of the targets of the abuse had his back to Paul and the skinheads. Because he was wearing a fedora and a trench coat with the collar up, it was difficult to tell much about him. He may have been blind; Paul could make out a large pair of what looked to be Wayfarers on him. He also, perhaps, had been in an accident. He was extensively bandaged—and large.

With him was a compact, bald Asian man in sandals and a saffron hooded robe. Paul figured him for some sort of monk.

"Hey, scrap," one of the skinheads said to the little man, his tone as unfriendly as he could make it.

The monk ignored him and peered into his soup with fierce intensity.

"Scrap. You know I'm talking to you."

"Here, scrappy, scrappy," said another skinhead. It was the call of someone luring a cat within boot range.

The two men tried to act like the skinheads weren't speaking to them, but only the bandaged one succeeded. He dipped his sandwich into a gravy boat that looked comically tiny next to his sizable hands. The monk just kept glaring at his soup, as if warning its alphabet noodles to spell out a different message—or else.

Paul knew the scenario well. He'd been in the monk's place too many times.

Anything the monk said would hasten what was coming, and he was a slightly built man up against bad odds. The bandaged one was big enough that anyone taking him on would only do it with numbers on their side. There were fifteen or twenty skinheads at the tables—more than enough to offset the size advantage.

"Scrap!" the first skinhead screeched. His eyes closed to slits when he bared his teeth, like the mongoose in a documentary Paul had watched in the New Beginnings TV room.

The skinhead flung one of his fries. It landed in the monk's soup, spraying his face with broth. The little man didn't blink.

A third skinhead—all arms, chest, and shoulders and the size of an offensive lineman—guffawed.

That was how the set-up worked. Mr. Little starts the fight; Mr. Big has an excuse to finish it. The one with the mouth never throws a punch.

Paul knew it. And hated it.

Soup running down his cheek, the monk seethed, but wouldn't wipe it away. He said something in sign language to the bandaged man, who shook his head.

Paul gave the skinheads the hard stare.

"Don't," Rain told him.

The second skinhead dredged a fry through a puddle of ketchup and launched it. It arced through the air—red and sloppy, splattering patrons who knew enough to stay quiet—and hit the monk's chest with a blot like a silenced gunshot.

Following suit, the first skinhead grabbed a whole handful of fries, swirling them in the ketchup until they dripped like they'd been gutted.

"Hey," Paul said.

The skinhead looked over at him and Rain, pleased to have additional victims for the next round.

"Leave them alone."

"Paul," said Rain.

All of the skinheads turned their attention to Paul except the big one, who had eyes only for the bandaged man and the monk.

"Better listen to your mommy, Paul," said the skinhead with the bloody fries. He gave Rain a quick up-and-down.

The diner grew quiet.

The one-armed-bandit trucker drained his coffee cup and left without paying, the sleigh bells on the door a shrill announcement of his departure.

The manager made a visual note of the lack of cash on the counter, frowning.

The matchstick robot left a handful of bills on his table and headed for the fireworks store, which was his closest exit. No one moved to stop him.

The big skinhead swatted the girl sitting next to him on the shoulder, his eyes never leaving his two targets. She grabbed her coat from the seat and slid out of the booth, unleashing him.

Standing and removing his jacket, he limbered his neck up and stretched, flexing his fingers and letting everyone get a good look. He was steroid huge—a cartoon.

The mongoose skinhead got up, too. They marched toward the monk.

The bandaged man stood to greet them, fast and smooth for someone so big.

The two skinheads slowed. The muscleman skinhead was huge, but the man in the bandages was a head taller and wider still in his trench coat.

And not fat wide. Big wide.

The bandaged man was no burn victim. He was a mummy—a giant mummy.

The big skinhead hung back, studying his opponent. His friend stepped forward.

Paul had seen the big-skinhead type before, too. Strength and mass won him all of his fights, but he'd probably never gone up against someone his own size—or the mummy's. Still, his eyes showed no doubt; he was sure of himself.

"Easy, Tut," the wiry skinhead told the mummy. "We just want to commune with the Lama, here."

The monk pondered his soup, alone at the table. Paul half-expected the liquid to boil.

"What is it you wish to tell him?" the mummy said. "I will relay it."

"Is he deaf?"

The mummy didn't answer.

"Well, whatever he is, he's more my size."

"You're better off with me."

The little skinhead appraised the monk, snickering. "Aren't those guys supposed to be all about peace and love? He looks like he's gonna blow his radiator cap."

"We're working on that."

The temperature in the diner rose ten degrees. There was a swift, though by no means tidy, exodus as others got up and left. Not all of them bothered to pay.

The wait staff left with the customers. The manager, who had bigger problems now, slipped a cell phone from his pocket and crept into the kitchen.

The skinheads piled out of their booths to stand behind their cohorts.

Paul and Rain stayed put. Porter was still in the men's room. What was taking him so long?

"I'll ask you to reconsider," the mummy told the little skinhead. "This will not go well for you."

"You can leave," the skinhead replied. "Tight-eyes stays."

The mummy turned to Paul and Rain. "You two go outside."

"We can help," Paul said.

Rain gave him a look. Could they?

There was no time for anything else.

The little skinhead grabbed a plate and swung it at the mummy's head.

The monk sprang up and out of the booth. His fist shattered the skinhead's plate on its way through it, striking the mongoose's forehead with gunshot force. Then it was back down at his side. There'd hardly been a blur.

Flecks of plate adorning his head and face, the little skinhead wobbled stupidly. A scarlet line appeared on his forehead, as if by magic. It split open. He dropped.

The big skinhead picked up a fork and stabbed at the mummy's face. The mummy caught it with one of his enormous mitts, both flatware and hand vanishing into his grip.

The skinhead swung with his other fist. That, too, was halted and trapped.

The mummy squeezed. The moist crack and the skinhead's scream came in unison.

"Go," the mummy told Paul and Rain. "Now."

The room erupted in skinhead rage. Leather jackets rushed the mummy and monk.

The big skinhead's bulk may not have helped him any, but the mummy made good use of it. He effortlessly picked the muscleman up over his head like a bundle of bubble wrap and lofted him into his friends, who toppled under the weight of their champion.

The ones who chose to rush the monk were even less fortunate. The slight man in the robe couldn't match his friend's raw strength, but his adversaries' defeat was much more viciously accomplished.

An orange dust devil of hands and feet, he was in his element when outnumbered. The air filled with the smack of knuckles and sandal leather on skin and bone, the *thwap* of tissue under assault, and cries of pain.

It all blended together, too rapid to register as discrete sounds. Blood and spit flew. Wrecked joints popped.

The monk knew what his attackers would do before they did. It was as if he'd been shown a preview of the brawl in his soup while being pelted with food.

The fight wrapped up faster than any Paul had ever seen or been in. The skinheads almost didn't deserve what was done to them. They hadn't understood what they were setting in motion.

There were only two left standing. One of them reached into his jacket and came out with a pistol.

Rain was impressive in her own right. Paul heard her chamber a round before he even realized what he was seeing.

Still, she had nothing on the monk, who threw a coffee cup and saucer in succession. The first disarmed the gunman. The second shattered his teeth.

The skinhead wailed and clutched his mouth, as if trying to keep something from escaping. He ran from the diner, his pain lingering in the air.

There was but one of the bad guys still upright—the girl who'd let the big skinhead out of the booth. She ran a petite hand over her buzz cut and took an inventory of her pals, who ranged from moaning to unconscious.

The fallen were blood brothers now. And a good deal of that blood would have to be mopped up.

The sound of an approaching siren grew louder. The manager had made his call.

Porter came out of the kitchen, not the men's room.

The monk turned to face him, still in battle mode.

The Envoy surveyed the carnage without a flinch.

"Where were you?" Paul said. He didn't try to conceal his annoyance.

"Shall we?" The gray man ignored Paul's question and motioned toward the door.

Paul and Rain got up to go.

Porter stepped over the fallen skinheads and made his way to his plate. He left a wad of bills under it—clearly more than what was owed for the meal and tip.

The mummy looked from skinhead to skinhead with sadness, then turned to the buzz-cut girl. He appeared to be prepping a fatherly lecture, perhaps one about her taste in friends.

Paul would try to pry his answer from Porter later. "Come with us," he told the mummy.

The Envoy and the monk both looked at him, equally puzzled.

"They didn't start it," he explained. "And those guys would've been on us next."

Porter shrugged. They all headed for the door.

Except for the mummy, who stayed put. He waited for the manager and his staff to reappear, along with the customers who hadn't had a chance to escape before war broke out.

"My apologies," the mummy told them. "Breakfast should be savored, not feared." He tipped his hat to the shellshocked group. "There is always tomorrow."

PAUL INTENDED to grill Porter as they left, but they stepped outside to face a Sheriff's Department car in the parking lot. Its blue lights flashed, its siren drowning out any such attempt.

A rangy deputy got out, all badge, hat, and holster. He spotted Rain's shotgun, still in her hands, and promptly pulled his sidearm. Ducking behind his car, he took aim at her across the hood.

"Freeze!" he yelled, difficult to hear over the siren. "Drop it!"

Paul didn't think the guy was much older than him.

Rain half-obeyed. She stopped walking.

The mummy, bringing up the rear, moved closer to her, preparing to block a shot in either direction.

The monk eyed a golf-ball-sized stone at his feet and scrutinized the deputy, calculating.

Porter raised his staff.

The deputy was a raw nerve in a uniform. He might have lost his grip on his pistol had the car not been there to steady him.

They waited for him to realize that the siren killed all hope of conversation. They waited even longer for him to maneuver around the open door to turn it off, all the while struggling to keep his service revolver aimed in Rain's general direction.

The siren faded.

"I'm sorry, Deputy," Porter said. "We are not in the wrong here—and we're leaving."

"I'll know who's wrong and who's not after I talk to Ira and Bonnie. You best not have hurt them."

"Is Ira the proprietor?" the mummy said. "He is well, but I presume he is upset about the mess and his frightened customers. I've apologized, but please do pass along my additional regrets. I am not certain that Bonnie is inside."

"Miss, I'm counting to five," the deputy told Rain. "When I get there, you drop your weapon. I mean it."

He made it as far as four.

Porter flicked his staff in a compact circle. The deputy's bullets clattered out of his gun and onto the hood, where they rolled around in tight arcs before going overboard and bouncing off the asphalt.

The Envoy headed for the van.

The deputy scrambled to grab some of his ammo and reload. His gun disappeared. "Hold on!" he said. "You—"

"Your holster," said Porter.

Sure enough, the pistol was at his side. Flummoxed, he went for the riot gun in his car, but couldn't get to it. He was handcuffed to the side-view mirror with his own cuffs.

Checking his duty belt for the key, he came up empty. His face turned red.

"It's on the number-three gas pump," Porter said. "Ira will retrieve it for you, I'm sure." He motioned for Paul and Rain to get into the van.

The mummy and monk made their decision wordlessly. Leaving the fuming lawman behind, they waited for Paul and Rain to get settled and climbed in back.

"I'll follow you," the deputy said.

Halfway into the driver's seat, Porter leaned out and moved the top of his staff in another fast loop.

Liquid splashed out from under the police car. The deputy looked down at an alarmingly large puddle of motor oil pooling around his uniform shoes.

"Don't," the gray man said. "You have a job to do. But so do I."

Porter started the van's engine. They pulled away.

Paul watched the deputy shake oil from his feet as the growing distance shrunk him in the frame of the van's rear windows.

The monk, in the seat beside Paul, watched, too.

When the deputy was out of view, Paul spotted an eyetooth, edged in red at its root, on the leather seat. It must have fallen from a fold in the monk's robe.

The monk saw the tooth and offered Paul a full, reassuring grin. It was not his.

How could this little man with the pleasant face be capable of such damage? Paul had known some hard cases, to be sure, but the fight in the diner had reached a whole different level. Then again, the skinheads would have done just as bad or worse to their intended victims, who were only trying to enjoy a meal to start their day.

The monk rolled his window down a crack and tossed the tooth out. After closing the window, he reached over to give Paul's shoulder a friendly squeeze.

As soon as he made contact, his expression shifted to one of confusion, then concern. He tilted his head, viewing Paul through a different lens. He let go slowly, as if disengaging from something unstable.

"What?" Paul said.

The monk offered no answer. But he appeared to have questions of his own now.

....

FIFTEEN

TELL HER GOODBYE AGAIN

Zach's mother went to bed before dark. She did not say goodnight.

She'd never done that before. Not in New York, in 624 East Seventieth Street's apartment 14, where his bed had been in the tiny arched front room, and Zach's mother's bed had been a fold-out sofa on the other side of the curved entrance, next to the part of the floor that gave him a splinter in his foot one Christmas morning.

Not in their basement apartment at 1351 West Seventeenth Street, where the roaches were bigger than two fingers put together and flew if you knocked them off the wall, and the neighbor, Sean Hulce, cried because his gecko escaped and ate the roaches until there weren't any left, and Zach's mom found it dead, dried, and crunchy when she pulled the refrigerator out to clean behind it.

The pink pills Zach's mother swallowed a lot made her sleep. She took them because her knee hurt. Zach knew that because when he talked into his tape recorder and played it back, the taped version of himself told him so.

Everything the tape recorder said to him turned out to be true. Zach was afraid for his mother, but his tape-recorder self said she would be okay if he did what it told him to do and tried his hardest. Well, it didn't know for sure, but Zach and the directions he had to follow were their best chance.

That was why Zach practiced in the mirror. He knew he wasn't supposed to, and that Zach's mother would have been upset to see him practicing if she weren't taking the pink pills. That was why he couldn't think about her knee hurting. Because he had to get good at the mirror.

His tape-recorder self said that. So when Zach's mother was at work or asleep late at night, he tested himself—to prove to his tape-recorder self how good he was getting.

His tape-recorder self wouldn't let him stop practicing. It wouldn't let him be not good at the mirror game. Because it was time to play for keeps.

For keeps wasn't how his tape-recorder self wanted him to think about it. It wanted him to see it as an adventure. Only not a game. It wasn't something he could mess up and start over. It was a very hard thing Zach was supposed to do.

It was about Zach's mother. And Paul, the boy on the bus.

Now Zach's trick counted. It hadn't before. Now it did.

He stared at himself, eyes on eyes, until the only thing he saw were the pupils of the Zach in the mirror. His tape-recorder self told him what to do. How to do it. The way it would work.

Why it must.

He had to bring all three of his selves together—the Zach in the bedroom, the Zach in the mirror, the Zach in the tape recorder—and then pull them apart again. He also knew what his tape-recorder self hadn't told him: if he did it wrong, all three would go away and not come back. The trick was to know it was dangerous, know it was hard, and then use that knowing to erase everything but doing it right.

He raised his right hand, like the teachers always asked him to do, though he never did it when they wanted it. He'd raise his left for them instead, which always made them write in their notebooks. They never realized that for him, it was about having the power to make them scribble.

But he raised his right hand now in order to receive other, more important powers. Mirror Zach raised his hand, too.

Zach lowered his hand. So did Mirror Zach.

He listened to Tape Recorder Zach once more. He wanted to make sure he got the next part right.

He raised his hand again. Mirror Zach did, too. But this time, when he put his hand back down, Mirror Zach kept his up.

Tape Recorder Zach spoke. Zach stared into Mirror Zach's eyes until the room was nothing but pupils again, until the pupils made black tunnels through the glass.

The room changed and changed again. Zach was aware of it in steps: Tape Recorder Zach's voice no longer came from the machine Zach held; it came from the recorder in the mirror. Tape Recorder Zach spoke faster, saying that Zach had to finish and finish now. So he did.

Zach—real Zach—was now in the mirror version of the room, hand down, and Mirror Zach was in the real bedroom, his hand still up. The windows in the room and in its mirror version brightened as nighttime left and morning arrived.

Tape Recorder Zach said to go deeper into the glass. Zach obeyed, leaving the apartment, the pink-dream home of Zach's mother, behind.

Before he left, he looked back at Mirror Zach, who'd traded places with him and was now stranded there in the real bedroom, hand in the air. Mirror Zach looked disappointed, like he'd just realized no one would ever call on him.

Zach wished he could step back through, say he was sorry to Mirror Zach for tricking him, and then go down the hall to wake Zach's mother up one more time.

He wanted to tell her goodbye again.

SIXTEEN

....

BAD METRICS

Truitt knew what was coming when Mr. Brill ordered him to bring Carol Laird to his office. She, of course, had no warning. So she went.

Carol Laird had caught Mr. Brill's attention when he was returning from a Ravager review. He happened to deviate from his habitual route to his office and caught a glimpse of her at her desk.

Poor Carol Laird.

She was the kind of pretty that Mr. Brill preferred. The most beautiful girl in her suburban high school, she was middle-of-the-pack in Los Angeles or New York. Her discovery of her low rank after moving to one of those places—her wretched heartbreak—was the kind of pain that got his attention.

Mr. Brill liked a girl who knew she wasn't going any further. He lived for her dejection—for when she forgot to keep it off her face.

He loved nothing more than a broken spirit.

Carol Laird showed up in an interview suit that was probably the only good outfit she'd ever owned. After all, she had no idea what he had in mind. Don't blow an opportunity, right?

She didn't know what Truitt knew.

Mr. Brill was at his desk, surrounded by rings of floating graphs of all sorts. The bad metrics were trending up, the good ones in the opposite direction.

The crossing of the lines in a negative manner explained the flat light in Mr. Brill's eyes as he reviewed them. It also informed the worry emanating from Carol as she sat, ignored, at the conference table.

By this time, she recognized that she'd been summoned for a so not-good reason, as Truitt imagined she was likely to phrase it. She was a mouse in the pet-store tank with a python. The sole survivor of the dozen dropped in, she was free to wander the glass box only because the big snake's hunger had been sated by number eleven.

For now.

"Sir?" Truitt said.

"I know." The big man didn't bother to look away from his data. `

"Of course, sir. Would Ms. Laird like anything?" Truitt wouldn't risk asking her directly.

She prepared an answer, but was cut off.

"Ms. Laird wants a glass of whatever burns," Mr. Brill said. "In exchange for my considering her brother for an opportunity in our organization, she's agreed to be my close personal assistant. Is that not generous, Truitt?"

"Very, sir." Truitt was unable to tell whose generosity the big man meant.

"Indeed. She says he's in a place right now where—what was the phrasing again?" He didn't wait for her to speak. "Oh—where the heights steal his breath."

Reminding Mr. Brill of a fellow charge's suffering was no way to garner mercy, even if it was her sibling. Especially if it was her sibling. She'd given up on saying anything more, but that was wisdom acquired too late.

"You have an update?"

"Yes, sir. We're monitoring the adjacency of the Brucker woman in her duties. It appears to be even better than expected."

Neither Mr. Brill nor Truitt bothered to explain to Carol Laird the concept of adjacency. When seeking a target's Essence, it was advantageous to use a data admin with some relationship to said target. And when measuring such an effort to ensure that the admin performed well, it was also best if the person doing that measuring was connected.

"Not better than I expected," Mr. Brill said. "I knew it would work. The data admin was on the bus with the orphan kid. That's why she has that job."

"Of course, sir."

"Who's on top of that again?"

"The Medill woman, sir. She's an exemplary project manager and has shown quite an aptitude for dosage. In this case, the amounts required to limit Brucker's memory are high enough that her concentration can be an issue. But again, adjacency should more than compensate."

That Mr. Brill allowed Truitt to discuss all of this in front of Carol Laird did not bode well for her. He wasn't worried about her telling anyone.

"Make Ms. Laird's drink a double," Mr. Brill said.

He never once called her by her first name.

THE SNAKE TANK in which Carol Laird was trapped had plenty of room for Truitt. He'd long understood that. And while he had no intention of finding himself cowering in the corner and waiting for his time to come, his fate was not under his control. The countless years of service to Mr. Brill, of staying in his good graces, meant not a thing.

His fate relied on the acquisition and exploitation of Essence, which, in turn, depended on many people who were not named Gerald Truitt. He had plenty of say in who reported to him and what their duties were, but right now his future state and welfare were in the hands of June Medill and, through her, Annie Brucker.

Which meant that Truitt had to spend more time than he would have liked with the Medill woman. And by more, he meant any.

Much to do, much to rue.

June had her own office, a wasteful use of Essence that Mr. Brill did not know of. But Truitt wanted to keep her happy—or, rather, as happy as she was capable of being. Brought from the web-covered warehouse space and placed in a larger cubicle than anyone else enjoyed, she'd asked for an office with a door to keep anything from crawling on her. That was her chief memory of the warehouse—the weavers. Morale having its worth, Truitt granted the request.

Truitt noted that June once again had her door open, which brought the veracity of her stated fears into question. She sat at her desk, a sensible steel affair that suited her nature, poring over three large ledgers.

Earlier in her tenure, Truitt had been mildly interested when the monitors she'd been given disappeared and were replaced by leather-bound paper—a reflection of her identity and preference. Earlier. Right now, he didn't care a whit.

"I know, Mister Truitt," she said when she saw him. "I'm aware of our performance issues. I prepare the reports, and they disappoint me even more than they disappoint you or Mister Brill, I promise you."

"I doubt that." He sat in her guest chair and made a mental note of two more areas of waste— its ample cushioning and a lone iris in a glass vase on her desk. From the angle his seat afforded, the flower appeared to hang from her left nostril.

"I want you to know that I'm up to our current challenge, sir."

"Do you understand the challenge?"

She nodded and smiled, showing little white teeth made for grinding.

Truitt tried to guess at how vividly, if at all, she recalled having those lips sewn together. "Impress me."

"Essence is who we are and what we do. Its trust is earned, its care paramount."

"Is that from the manual?"

"Verbatim."

The iris was a distraction. He picked up the vase and set it down to the side with a solid clunk. "Memorization is not helpful if you don't comprehend the words' import. Do you understand the challenge?"

"I can summarize."

"By all means."

She leaned forward, eager to please. She understood, at least, that she needed to get this right. "Before Mister Brill, The Commons was an unjust and inefficient place. It molded itself to each person and Journey. People entered with Essence, and when their Journey was complete, their Essence left with them. It was a waste of resources and chaotic as well. No one had control over their fate until Mister Brill stepped in."

Truitt nodded her on. He would have preferred to avoid enduring this beginner's recitation of the obvious, but she needed to isolate the matter at hand in her own way.

"Mister Brill was willing to help and accepted the challenge. Through his diligence, a system came about that collected people's Essence as they entered. It eliminated the need for individual Journeys and arbitrary outcomes. It kept Essence in The Commons, where it belongs, and stored it in an orderly, predictable, and efficient manner."

"Correct. And the challenge?"

"To continue executing Mister Brill's vision of maximizing growth and minimizing expenditure."

He waited for her to demonstrate the tiniest sign that she'd thought things through on her own and reached a deeper understanding of their predicament. Instead, her dumb silence indicated she was finished speaking. He considered sewing her mouth closed himself, then and there. "You've increased the Brucker woman's dosage?"

"To the point where distraction is no longer a factor. She concentrates on her work."

"How do you know?"

"She hasn't sought out Charlene Moseley since the bump-up. And then there's her little boy." She frowned, as if enduring a cramp. "She doesn't discuss him. At all."

"Is that a concern?"

"Maybe. Yes. Before, she would talk about him when asked. Now it's as if she doesn't even want to think of him. He's alone all day. I think there are some sort of educational tapes she leaves him to listen to—she's mentioned them—but I don't know what they are or where she obtained them." She looked to Truitt for some level of sympathy. "Sir, he's her son."

"I don't care."

"Sir?"

He let the question hang on her idiot face. If she truly sought understanding, perhaps fear might be of assistance. "What does one damaged little monster of a child matter so long as his mother performs in the fashion in which we need her to perform?" He leaned on the desk, elbows nudging it hard enough for the water in the iris's vase to register the disturbance.

She watched the water shudder.

"I will explain this in the simplest of terms, and then I should never have to do so again," he said. "Throw your manual out. It's propaganda. Dogma. It will not serve you. There is no morality to what we do. Mister Brill is a thief who steals what rightly belongs to the universe. He victimizes and we help him, lest we become victims ourselves. Essence is not easily taken, stored, or used. We expend a great amount of effort to control it. Some theories hold that Essence is sentient—that it remembers how The Commons used to be and wishes to return to that state. I don't believe that, but I do think that it's like water. If you allow it to do so, it will leak and promote corrosion, rot, and all of the associated issues. Mister Brill sees it as data. Its representation matters little to me, so long as it is ours to command."

He looked around June's office. Its walls were bare, but he was quite certain that if she kept it long enough, they'd soon sport motivational posters and a calendar featuring monthly photos of chicks and other baby beasts paired with adorable captions. He would see the situation ameliorated long before that.

"Someone from that bus is attracting a great deal of Essence and wreaking havoc on our efficiency quotients," he said. "It's showing up in every measure we use, and Mister Brill is not pleased because it places him in a situation more precarious than he would prefer. We have everyone from that drop zone in hand except the boy, and we'll have him soon enough. Meanwhile, Annie Brucker is our best hope for smoothing out these little waves. You, in turn, are our best hope for controlling her."

He stood and grabbed the edge of June's desk with both hands, tipping it up and letting it fall with a bang. The vase toppled over, spilling water across an open ledger before rolling off the desk and hitting the floor with a wet crash.

"One more matter for you to understand," he said. "If I go to The Fen, you'll be devoured by that warehouse long before I get there. Yet that's not the chief reason for ensuring that the Brucker woman succeeds in restoring our influence. Whatever Mister Brill does with us, we'd both better pray he retains his power. Because while we're not technically on a Journey to decide our fate, The Commons remains a place of judgment. We're the bad guys. Do you really think that's gone unnoticed?"

He shook a sliver of vase from the toe of his shoe. Then he left, closing the door behind him, leaving June Medill to spend some time alone with her new understanding.

SEVENTEEN

....

EVERYBODY WOULD
IF THEY COULD

The mummy's name was Ken, and the monk's was Po. They sat with Paul, Porter, and Rain on the benches of two moss-covered picnic tables in a cookout area that was down a side road from the main freeway, hidden behind a grove of elm trees. After the breakfast brawl and the standoff with the deputy, Porter was careful about the visibility of their stops.

Paul told Porter he trusted Ken and Po with the truth, so the Envoy went with his Journeyman's choice. The two of them wanted in.

"You should know what you're signing up for," Porter said. "Helping us could win you some powerful enemies."

Po signed, and Ken interpreted. "Mine is the warrior's option," the mummy said for the monk. "I do not choose my battle. It chooses me."

"And you?"

"Po and I speak as one on this. His decision is mine."

The monk signed again. "Brill is foe to all," Ken said, adding, "My sentiments as well. Your Journey is ours, Paul."

"Miss Rain?" said Porter.

"I'm easy." She'd disassembled her shotgun and was nearly finished with its cleaning.

"This will not be."

She shrugged and began to reassemble the weapon with remarkable speed and efficiency.

"Why did those guys attack you?" Paul asked the mummy.

Rain snapped the last pieces into place and looked at Paul as if she'd just reviewed the nominees for Stupid Question of the Year and named him the winner.

"What? They called Po a scrap," he said. "What does that mean?"

Po signed, but Ken looked to Porter for clearance. Everyone sought the Envoy's permission before telling Paul anything. It got on his nerves.

"Hate has made a home in The Commons, as it has in all realms, Paul," Ken said. "Here, those from your world are seen as real, so they are called bona fides. Those born of imagination and left behind by their creators are referred to as scraps by some. We prefer to be called mythicals."

Rain pulled out a red-and-gold box of candy with the word "Gifu" in black on its label, offering one to Paul.

He ignored her.

She shook the box at him. "They're licorice."

He hated licorice, but she was trying to stop him from crossing some unseen line in asking too much about bona fides and mythicals. Clearly, it was a sensitive topic. The transition from boy to man, Pop Mike once told him, was recognizing that when a woman is trying to shut you up, you should consider it. Strongly.

"The Akashic Field, Paul." Now Porter was attempting a rescue, too. "Some people believe that the Akashic Field is everywhere—that it's a sort of hard drive for everything that's ever been, which might explain how the mythicals can exist apart from their creators. That wasn't always the case, but it is now. And the word 'scrap' is a pejorative. Don't use it."

"If it wasn't always that way, why did it change? Why are so many still around?"

Paul had hit upon something. Porter hesitated. "I don't know."

That did it. "What do you mean? Isn't it your job to know?"

"Paul," said Rain.

"No. You don't get it. I'm fine on my own. But somebody's always telling me where to live, how to live. Now my life might be over, and they still are. Your credit card doesn't work. You don't know why stuff is the way it is. Why should I listen to you about anything?"

"Because I know more than you do, and we can only hope it's enough."

"What if it's not?"

"Then Brill will take you as he's taken nearly everyone else—and the rest of us will be disposed of."

The stark candor of that curbed Paul's ire.

"The Commons is broken," Porter said. "More accurately, its purpose—to judge and determine whether its charges move backward or forward, and where they go if it's the latter—is no longer operative. Brill must hold and control what he's captured, and he is always adding to it. Always. So he gets stronger, but the Essence that gives him his strength grows more difficult to monitor and contain. While he concentrates on that, the situation out here is chaos."

Paul picked up a stick and began to break it into pieces. In New York, if he fought with Pop Mike or anyone else in the New Beginnings leadership, the worst that might happen was a loss of privileges. In The Commons, he didn't know the rules. And Porter was admitting that he didn't, either. He used to, but not now.

"For far too long, I did nothing but sit in my office and wait," Porter said as Paul reduced the stick to bits. "The Commons changed during my last Journeys. While I idled, it warped further. I was surprised when my card didn't work, true. And I will not pretend to know how bad it is out here."

"Bad," Ken said. "The bona fides who have managed to escape Brill remain free only because it's more profitable for him to acquire Essence at the drop zones. That is where people are at their weakest, and it's easier to harvest them there than it is to hunt down those who elude him. But because there are no more Journeys, the escapees have nowhere to go. It's only a matter of time before his attention turns to them."

"What about the mythicals?" Paul asked.

"The Essence of a mythical is not as convenient for Brill to claim, but it's there should he decide to do so."

"He will," Rain said. "He wants it all."

The pieces of the stick were too small for Paul to break anymore. He threw them against the ground to see if they would bounce. They did, but not the way he wanted. They ricocheted off the dirt at unpredictable angles, refusing to attain any height. "Why? Why keep taking when he can't even handle what he already has?"

"Because if he doesn't, and the system returns to working the way it should, he'll be judged. So he must ensure that such a judgment never happens," Porter said. "Once he started, he committed to seeing it through."

"It's no longer about the power or what he can do with it," said Ken. "His interest in that part probably stopped long ago. The only way he can justify his own choices now is to insist that anyone else would conduct themselves as he has, given the opportunity—but he is in this position because he is more strategic and more capable than they are."

"The bad guys never think they're bad," Porter said. "Or that they're worse than anyone else, at least."

"So Miss Gower had it wrong," Rain said, wiping her gun down.

Porter raised an eyebrow.

"My second-grade teacher. She told us people like Brill don't think about what would happen if everybody did that. But he assumes everybody would if they could. So he has to beat them to it."

That earned her a dark laugh from Porter.

"What if I'm not the one he's after?" Paul said. "What if it was someone else on the bus, and we keep sneaking around, and I never find out what my Journey's supposed to be?" Po watched him. Paul recalled how the monk acted after touching his shoulder.

"Paul," Porter began. He stopped when Po looked up at the sky.

They all heard it—a rhythmic thrumming. The whoosh-roar of something coming fast. Then a vehicle-sized blossom of orange flame nearby.

The explosion knocked Paul to the ground. He struggled to his feet, but staying upright took effort. A high ringing in his ears, a brutal hearing test, blocked all other sound. To his right, a chassis and four wheels were all that remained of the van, and those were on fire.

Black-clad Ravagers streamed through the trees. Paul tried to yell to Rain, who picked herself up off

MICHAEL ALAN PECK

the ground, to ask if she was all right. But he couldn't hear his own words. He hurried to her.

The Ravagers closed in. The chopper that destroyed the van drew nearer. Paul could see its moving blades, but all he heard was his ears' whining complaint.

He was no combat expert—but he knew a lopsided fight when he saw one. The helicopter dropped to the ground fifty yards away. His hearing began to return.

Rain pumped her shotgun. It wouldn't be any good against the Ravagers until they got in close.

A soldier took aim at Ken and fired several rounds into the big mummy, who winced with the impact but held his ground.

Porter held his staff out, as if in surrender. Po stood by, fists at his sides, assessing.

The Envoy flicked his staff, and the soldiers' rifles were gone. That was all the monk needed. As one of the Ravagers reached for his sidearm, only to find his holster empty, Po leapt and delivered a kick to the man's face that snapped his head sideways. The Ravager hit the dirt and moved no more.

Two others rushed the monk, one with a truncheon, the other with a combat knife. The first got a forearm to the face-plate for his troubles, while his partner caught an elbow to the mid-section, below his body armor. Po twisted the second soldier's arm, breaking his shoulder, then threw him for a loop onto his back.

Two troopers went for Ken. The mummy grabbed each by the back of the vest and lifted them into the air. He smashed them into each other, face to face, like human cymbals. Again. Again. He dropped them. They stayed dropped.

The numbers worked against them. More Ravagers climbed out of the chopper, one drawing a bead on Po. Porter whirled his stick, and the new arrivals were disarmed. But the effort cost the Envoy, who caught himself with his staff as his legs failed him.

Another Ravager took aim at Porter. Rain shot him. His visor shattered, and he fell, clutching his face.

Paul was out of his league compared to both enemy and friend. He felt ill.

Rain caught the attention of the helicopter's door gunner, who swiveled around toward her. Paul looked to Ken and Po for help, but they were fully engaged in their own fights.

Porter struggled to raise his staff as Rain fired at the door gunner. A pellet load, useless at a distance. She pumped another into the chamber and fired again. It was the wrong ammo for the job.

The gunner sighted in. She was going to die.

Paul's nausea became a full-on panic that churned its way up and out. He tried to shout but couldn't form words.

It was as if it was happening to other people, the situation registering from all points-of-view. Through Rain's eyes, Paul was nearly overcome by terror. He knew Porter's fatigue, Po's rage, and Ken's resigned approach to the violence. He even picked up on the cold aim of the door gunner and the other Ravagers, but those inputs were distant, veiled.

He heard his own cry as something drawn from all of them there, louder than the whir of the Black Hawk. It came through him.

A tree shot up out of the ground, under the chopper, where none had been before. It pierced the machine's belly as it grew, eviscerating it, tearing it apart in a gout of fire.

That, too, felt like it came through Paul—not there one second, destroying the chopper and towering over them the next.

The helicopter went from fearsome weapon to a cascade of burning steel, blades whining off in all directions. The wheels, guns, and other pieces plummeted through the branches, leaves rasping against them before they thudded to the ground.

The tree swayed. What remained of the chopper carcass rocked near its top, speared by branches. Paul gaped up at it, as did Rain. Ken and Po glanced around them for their enemies, who were no longer there. Then they, too, looked up.

"My God, boy," Porter said, still leaning on his staff. "My God."

All of the Ravagers were gone. A wheel fell out of the tree and bounced off the turf in front of them. It landed on its side and settled down in a floppy spin, a penny on a table. That was followed by a segment of rotor blade, which pierced the dirt and stood straight up—a flag marking the site of a miracle.

"What have you done?" said Porter.

The Envoy, Rain, Ken, and Po all turned to see Paul anew.

Paul had no answer.

EIGHTEEN

....

MERCY TRIUMPHS
OVER JUDGMENT

To a wounded vet, painkillers were the perfect illustration of a negative-feedback loop. Forget thermostats or anything high-school science teachers had to say about the concept. Good ol' agony was the best instructor.

You took your meds until the hurting subsided. You stopped. When the nerves caught fire again, back to it.

Sigh, cry, repeat.

That was the way it was supposed to work, anyway. Annie's job complicated things. When the knee hurt, the pinkies dosage rose. That meant less pain, but more fog, which slowed her down at the office. And poor numbers got the attention of June Medill.

Annie had expected a cut in medication and an increase in misery for productivity's sake, but June had surprised her. She'd doubled the dose.

After that, the pinkies had surprised her. They'd stopped working.

Now Annie was sure her negative feedback had gone positive on her, which was not good. The more pinkies she downed, the more her knee throbbed. And while that made it harder to concentrate, there was no denying she was able to work faster. Her pal the nautilus and those little bastards in the school of fish responded more quickly, provided clearer answers.

More disturbing were the dreams and her memories of them. Before, no matter how difficult her life—from physical therapy to being the single mother of a special-needs son and trying to make do on one income—she'd never doubted herself.

That had changed.

With the pain and clarity came the feeling that her dreams of the New York apartment were not just the bedtime wanderings of her imagination. Perception had tipped up into a handstand. Now the dreams were what she desired, her current reality the nightmare.

And Zach, who she'd hardly thought of all this time. She recalled feeding him and putting him to bed, but not talking to him or spending any real time with him. The clearest picture she had of him was from this morning—at the mirror, hand raised.

Why? And why hadn't she cared before now? Those were questions for when she got home.

There was another to be answered first.

"ARE YOU CUTTING my meds so I work faster?"

Annie stood in the doorway to June Medill's office. She expected a sizable helping of umbrage for her insubordination, but the squat little woman merely looked her up and down.

"Shut the door."

Annie did.

"Sit."

Annie did that, too, as curious now about June's lack of anger as she was about the pinkies' weakness.

"I can't answer your questions directly because that will expose me."

This was not going the way Annie had expected. It was almost enough to make her forget about why she'd come in the first place.

"You must hurry. There isn't time," June said. "Everything is moving. I didn't realize that until I started digging. But you're not asking the right questions."

"Did you order lower-dosage pills of my medication?"

June looked down at Annie's knee. "How does a lower level of medication make you feel? Sharper?"

"So that's a yes?"

"Did I tell you I have a degree in information science? Or that the point of information science is formulating the right query? Have I mentioned that at first, I thought that was why I was chosen for this job, but then I realized it was because of my proximity to you? My adjacency?"

Annie settled back in her chair to consider how to proceed. She knew June was giving her an opening, but didn't understand quite what it was—or why.

"Shouldn't you ask more questions?" June said. "Did you know that this trick of trying to give you information in question form won't work for long, if it's working at all—that they'll still figure out that I'm helping you? Do you agree that my plan for taking you somewhere outside to talk wouldn't have worked, and that I'm compromised already, so we might as well just talk right here?"

Annie understood. But she still wasn't sure what she needed to know first, much less how to ask in a way that June could answer.

"Did I mention you don't have much time?" June said. "Do you know what another good thing to think about might be? What made you suddenly have the willpower to come in and confront me?"

Her knee throbbed in answer. "Why wasn't it okay for me to talk to Charlene?"

"Do you think that maybe that wouldn't be a bad start if we had longer to talk, but you should be wondering about why Charlene was revealed to you in the first place? Who showed her to you? Why?" June fidgeted in her chair and brushed something from her skirt, but Annie couldn't see what it was. "This isn't working very well, is it?"

"Where's Charlene?"

"Did you know that lead-acid batteries were invented by a Frenchman? Have you ever seen one big enough to hold a person, or people, or entire worlds? Do you know how difficult it is to decide whether or not to sacrifice one person for the greater good of all, especially when it's you? Or what it's like to wonder if you're just doing it to save yourself?"

"Why are you telling me this?"

"Did you know I'm not revealing anything, that I'm just asking you questions?" June slid to one side of her chair, avoiding something. A thread of webbing stretched from her blazer to the desk. "After you asked if I ordered your meds cut, and I asked you if you felt sharper, did it occur to you that those things might be related?"

At the edge of Annie's vision, something scuttled across the floor and up June's leg. June didn't move, but it was clear she wouldn't be able to maintain that level of discipline much longer. The sight roused a familiar dread for Annie—one she'd forgotten until now.

"Do you think we've got time for one more question?" June said.

"Why are you doing this?"

"Do you know the quote, 'Mercy triumphs over judgment'? Where it comes from?"

Annie did not.

"Never mind," June said. "Where's Zach?"

"At home."

"Is he?"

ANNIE USED the bannister to haul herself up the apartment steps, letting her good knee do the lifting to quiet the pain. It didn't work. She didn't care.

Her company smartphone vibrated. She had a text message. She didn't care.

She made it to the top of the stairs. Zach's bedroom door was closed. In her New York dreams, she never allowed that. With that thought came the feeling yet again—stronger now—that those dreams were anything but.

Another buzz, another text.

Annie grabbed the doorknob and tried to turn it. It resisted, as if someone were holding it on the other side. "Zach?"

Now it turned easily, and she pushed the door open. He was right where she'd last seen him—at the mirror, hand up, tape recorder on the floor beside him.

"What are you up to, Zach?" She almost called him "buddy," but that was a false nickname, and she couldn't recall why she'd ever started using it. She never would again.

He didn't move when she sat on the floor and edged closer to look into the mirror with him. Maybe she'd see what he saw.

The phone buzzed again. She took it out of her pocket and put it on the carpet next to her so that the vibration wouldn't distract her. He gazed into the glass, arm aloft. She stared along with him. All she saw was her own reflection.

Annie was about to lower his arm for him when the phone buzzed yet again, dancing in the carpet's low pile. She glanced at the screen. All of the texts were from June Medill, and all bore the same subject line: "They're coming. They're coming. They're coming." A neat little stack of alarm.

She unlocked the phone and replied. Who was coming? The answer was instantaneous: "Leave now. Not the door. The way he told you."

The way who told her? She followed Zach's gaze into the mirror again and saw what she'd been looking at all along.

Only her own reflection. His was missing.

She reached out to touch him. Why hadn't she done that until now? What was wrong with her? Her fingers found nothing. He disappeared altogether.

Annie fought her way to her feet and went looking. He wasn't in her room.

Down the steps. Nor was he on the first floor.

She hauled herself up to the second floor again, breath hard to come by, desperation speeding her along. "Zach!"

Outside, cars pulled up fast and loud in the street. Doors slammed. She hadn't locked the front door.

She returned to Zach's bedroom. Nothing but his tape recorder and her phone, which buzzed with another text. "The way he told you."

Men's voices and running footsteps from the walk out front. She shut the bedroom door. That would gain her the same second it took to close it.

"Why should I trust you?" she thumbed back.

An instant reply. "Mercy triumphs over judgment."

Downstairs, the front door smacked against the foyer wall. "Miss Brucker?" A male voice, trying not to scare her. Failing.

The way who told her? Zach? She tried to pick up the tape recorder, but it, too, disappeared. Obscenities ran laps around the inside of her head. He'd played the tape for her. She'd heard nothing.

Another pinkie wall crumbled.

No. She had heard. Part of her had, anyway. Because she did know the way. She'd known ever since he hit play; it had just been obscured—kept from her.

Someone jiggled the bedroom doorknob from the other side. "Miss Brucker?" Again. "Here!" the man yelled.

Annie knew the way.

The bedroom door boomed with a kick. It shouldn't have held. It did. But it wouldn't for long.

The way. She looked deep into the mirror, deep into her own eyes.

Time slowed. Another kick and the crack of wood.

A tunnel of pupils. Annie stepped into the glass, just as Zach had told her to. No resistance. The mirror-image bedroom door stood open, and she hurried to it.

Two sounds in succession. The door in the bedroom behind her gave way with a bang, like a shot. Then the glass wall of the mirror she'd just entered shattered, closing her off in this backward version of her son's room.

There would be no return. Nor would there be one for Zach when she found him.

And she would find him.

NINETEEN

·····························

THE ONLY SOUND
IN THE ROOM

Mr. Brill summoned Truitt to his bedroom antechamber in the post-witching-hour darkness. Nothing good happened at that time of night, when daylight was merely a hope, not a promise.

"How?" The big man, clad in a custom-made silk kimono, was at his secondary desk—a smaller, more personal affair—working his way through a series of floating-screen readouts. His face was impassive, which was worse than when he was visibly angry. He'd gone past the displeasure phase—had decided how he would proceed.

Through the open double doors of the bedroom behind him, an unseen woman tried to muffle her weeping in the dark. Carol Laird.

"Which circumstance are we discussing, sir?"

There were two bad situations from which to choose. The corner of Mr. Brill's mouth twitched. "Pick."

"The Envoy, Porter, has discovered new capabilities in the boy? Trained him in their use?"

Mr. Brill shook his head, swept two screens aside, and drew another in. "He's discovered something, all right. But so have we, goddammit. And he doesn't know what he's got there."

"Perhaps the boy has an instinct for it."

Mr. Brill dismissed a screen with a swipe of his hand. "I had a feeling about that bus." He did the same with the second, which vanished. Now the room was lit only by a series of dim wall sconces. "Update on the Brucker woman and her son?"

The big man had said the Brucker woman's name aloud. That was a change. He was paying closer attention than he'd first let on.

"We are following some leads," Truitt said.

"Leads as in, you don't know anything? You've figured out how she got away? Where she's gone? What?"

"Leads, sir."

Truitt felt the weight of the predator stare settling on him in the near-darkness.

In the bedroom, Carol Laird cried, unable to control herself. The anguish was almost too much for Truitt, who'd thought his empathy long gone. That revelation was unwelcome at the moment.

"She doesn't let men get close," Mr. Brill said. "Something in her past. I wasn't listening. But, oh, did I get close."

The stifled sobs were the only sound in the room. Truitt was reminded of the saying—he couldn't remember whose it was—about how when one person begins to cry, someone else has stopped somewhere. He doubted that. There was always room for more tears.

"Our rabbit surprised me," the big man said. "It's one thing to have a hunch about him, but quite another to lose an entire squad because he has a talent with Essence."

"Yes, sir."

"Well, I'm a man of surprises myself."

The statement emerged wetly, words shoved through fluid. Truitt knew what was under way. He was grateful for the low light, which would prevent him from seeing it in detail.

Mr. Brill opened his mouth. Too wide. His face went slack. Black, oily tears sprouted from his eyes. Within moments, a stream of greasy ink was running down his cheeks.

It flowed from his nose as well, and when he opened his mouth wider still, like a hinge failing, it came pouring from that. Sable mercury, it pooled in his lap and ran over his thighs, leaving no trace or stain on the silk.

He leaned forward to vomit, a purging from deep in his gut. A puddle grew beneath him.

The noise became a collective moan of dread. A gathering of victims.

Free of its host, the pool rushed across the floor at Truitt. He prepared himself, but it split and went around him on either side. Then it rejoined behind him and made several circuits around his feet before sliding into the space between him and Mr. Brill.

A shadow form rose up from the oily liquid and became corporeal. It squatted there, toad-like, monstrous, pulling air into new lungs. Its breath was phlegm and trespass.

"Surprise," said Mr. Brill, his voice clear again.

With the speed of the hunter, the creature rushed the bedroom, where Carol Laird had quieted down. Maybe instinct had stopped her tears. Maybe she'd recognized that something even more savage than Mr. Brill was among them and hoped to remain beneath notice.

"A Shade, sir?" Truitt tried to keep his tone level.

"The boy has my attention."

An intake of breath from the bedroom. Carol Laird's gasp became a shriek. Then suffering. Grief.

The Shade's breathing grew in its intensity, bubbling. A series of inhalations sounded almost like laughter, enjoyment of what was being done to the woman.

Mr. Brill watched Truitt for a reaction. Truitt gave his all to barring any emotion from his face.

"Do you know that I never had any intention of helping her brother?" Mr. Brill said. He expected no answer.

Carol's scream died. Truitt would have been relieved, but the whimper that followed was far worse.

It was cut short by a final inhalation.

"I never even asked her his name." Mr. Brill crossed the room to the bedroom's entrance and peered into the darkness. "Look at the bright side, Truitt. You don't have to clean up."

He went in and shut the door.

Truitt didn't allow himself to leave until he felt reasonably certain nothing was coming back out again—coming after him.

For this night, at least.

IN THE WAREHOUSE, Truitt made his way down the rows of the inverted charges from the bus. All were completely encased in off-white chrysalises, the work here complete.

The weavers remained all around the space. His footsteps sent them scuttling off under the carpet of webbing.

At the end of the last row, they were still working on the most recent arrival. Truitt recognized her still, though her eyes and lips were threaded closed.

He wanted to tell her that what happened to Carol Laird was at least partly her fault, but she was beyond hearing. "Such is your mercy?" he said anyway.

Truitt stayed until June Medill's face could no longer be seen.

TWENTY

....

THE STORIES YOU TELL

They walked until nightfall, silent for stretches, sometimes breaking up into clusters strung out in a line. Small conversations moved their feet.

Rain walked ahead with Ken. While Porter was Paul's guide, the mummy had assigned himself the task of watching over her.

The same fatigue bearing down on Paul weighed on Rain, too, but it was difficult to spot. Paul had known hard street girls; Rain operated on another level entirely.

At one point, Porter dropped back so far that Paul grew concerned and stopped to wait for him. Po motioned Paul onward.

Paul wanted to know what Porter was up to. In the fading light, he thought he'd seen a faint glow emanating from the gray man's hands. But by the time the Envoy was with them again, Paul was too wiped out to bother with it.

Once it was dark, they got lucky and found the remains of a hunting cabin that had collapsed in on itself years before. Next to it was a bonfire pit, complete with a stack of old firewood. Many of the logs were rotten, but the ones on top were still fit for burning.

Paul thought it risky to let everyone and everything in the night know they were there. But as the campfire warmed its way into him, he didn't care about that, either.

Ken's trench coat, hat, and glasses lay on the ground beside him. In the firelight, the battle holes in his wrappings mended themselves.

"Where do we hide?" Paul said.

"We keep moving," said Porter. "Brill won't risk a repeat of our little skirmish without a fresh strategy. Not after what you did."

"What did I do?"

Porter stared into the fire along with the others.

No one was in a hurry to hazard a guess, so Paul answered his own question. "I killed them."

Po signed. Ken nodded. "Not in the manner you think," the mummy said. "That is not the way of it."

"I yelled. They died."

Po's fingers were a blur. "There's a line of thought you'll find in many belief systems that no one ever truly dies. Your Essence shifts from one reality to another. Does it remain intact? Are you a single entity, or do you scatter, with elements of you going into other lives? It is not known."

Ken shook his head at something else Po signed. The monk continued, and the mummy nodded again. Porter watched them both, content to let someone else do the explaining.

Rain grabbed one of the smaller logs from the wood pile and fed the fire. The flames jumped, as did the shadows in Ken's eyes.

"In this view, there is no death. It is all one Journey," he said. "The truth of that is a matter of debate, but there is no doubt that Brill found a way to arrest the Essence here—the flow from the world of the living to whatever lies beyond."

Po watched Paul for a reaction. When the monk seemed satisfied that he was keeping up, he continued.

"One theory holds that Brill is only able to do this because the Nistarim have abandoned us." Ken paused. "That is Po's theory," he said, speaking for himself. "I don't subscribe to that."

"Nor do I," said Porter.

"What are Nistarim?"

Po looked to Porter.

"The Tzadikim Nistarim are the righteous ones—the hidden," the Envoy said. "They're also called the Lamed Vav. The oldest religious reference that you would know comes from Jewish mysticism, but there are other, more ancient religions that hold the same belief: thirty-six individuals who cradle the existence of humankind in their hands. Their goodness is said to justify the existence of man to God."

"They are holy, and no one knows who they are," Ken said. "They themselves don't know. If they were to know, then they would not be one of the Thirty-Six. I do not pretend to make sense of this. I've never been able to convince myself that any of the story could be true." The blur of Po's fingers widened into a fan. "Po and I do not agree here."

"Either way," said Porter, "whether Brill's come to power because the force meant to stop him is asleep on the job or not, he's done it."

"How did he get so powerful?" Paul said.

"It's too long a tale for tonight, but he exploited the trust of the system. He has his own innate power, and no one's sure where that comes from, but he also gained the trust of the souls coming through here to get him started. His kind cannot gain power without the consent of his victims. To maintain that power, he must keep those victims under control. One theory holds that even though Brill has prevented Journeys from occurring, one's actions here contribute to his or her judgment and fate all the same—Brill's as well—which is why it's so important to him to stay in power and thus delay the process for himself."

"Where do the Ravagers come from?"

"Many of the Ravagers served in their past lives as soldiers or upholders of the law. Once Brill had enough Essence and influence, he was able to bend their sense of duty to his will. Like any group of warriors, the Ravagers include some who haven't a bit of noble spirit in them. But most have had their best intentions used against them."

"So I didn't kill them?"

"You cannot kill them," Ken said. "You've merely sent them beyond Brill's reach. They may have gone on to the next step in their fate. Or Brill's influence may hold their Essence here, committed to nothing, until his influence is no more. Regardless, you've liberated them from his service and, I believe, helped by preventing them from entering it again."

"But if you can make that help hurt a little, I won't cry," Rain said, tossing a stick into the fire. "I have my history." They waited for her to elaborate, but she merely continued to deliver more wood to its fiery end.

"The Essence doesn't want to feed Brill's power, as I've told you," Porter said, watching Rain. "It desires its own way, as water seeks the sea. Brill has mastered it, but when you sent the Essence of the Ravagers into that seed and made it a tree, you tapped into it, too."

Po signed. "Or perhaps it chose you," Ken said.

Paul wasn't prepared to discuss what having such strength for himself might mean. He'd always survived as someone without any power, without any influence. "What about the bona fides versus the mythicals? How does that work?"

"To us, there is no distinction," Ken said. Po nodded. "There's a saying in your world that you are the stories you tell yourselves. We are the stories you tell, too. Whether we are born when you do so, or we already exist and connect to you at the telling, it matters little. For now, we are tied to those who dreamt of us, and we come to The Commons with them. With Brill's controls in place, we, too, are held here."

"I still don't understand why he doesn't come after you."

"He hunts the easy game," Rain said. She'd begun to disassemble and clean her gun again.

Paul found himself turning his ring. Why did he and Rain make each other so jumpy?

"How do you say I hate you in sign?" she asked Po. When he demonstrated, she watched with a devotion that made Paul look away.

"How about I love you?" Paul said. He didn't know why. Maybe just for balance.

Po showed them that, too.

"Not so different, are they?" Porter said. "Do you think Mr. Brill believes them to be one and the same?"

Paul reached across Rain for more firewood, and his sleeve rode up his arm.

"Whoa," she said. His forearm bore a deep, ugly bruise running half its length. "Does that hurt?"

Porter came over for a closer look. "From the fight?"

"The accident. It's just the one."

"You shouldn't have any." Porter gently prodded the bruise. "You didn't answer Rain's question. Does it hurt?"

Paul shook his head.

The Envoy pressed hard in the center of the bruise, but there was no pain. He laid the head of his staff against the bruise and shut his eyes.

"Ouch."

"So I thought." As the others moved in to see, Porter ran his fingers over the bruise, searching. "One of these things is not like the other. Where have I heard that before?" He pulled a small penknife from his pocket, opened it, and laid the edge of the blade against the bruise's border. Then he dug in.

"Ow!"

"Sorry. That should be the worst of it." He pinched at the edge of the bruise. "Paul, my ability to move things rests on knowing them—their positions, but also their nature. I can often sense when something is not as it should be."

His tone was the same one the New Beginnings nurse used to distract little kids right before she doused a cut with antiseptic. Sure enough, he twisted the bruise and pulled.

Paul hissed as the entire thing ripped from his arm. It felt like losing a layer of skin and sounded like duct tape being pulled off the roll. He yanked his arm away. "What the hell?"

The gray man ignored him, grim now as he held the bruise to the firelight. The glow of the flames through the translucent membrane revealed fine veins within. It pulsed, hanging between Porter's two fingers.

"What is it?" Rain said.

He held it closer to the heat. It squealed and tried to curl away.

Rain recoiled. Paul rubbed the raw skin of his arm, making sure no residue was left.

"A peeper slug," Porter said. "Brill's eyes and ears. It attached itself somewhere along the way. He's been tracking us." He threw the bruise into the center of the fire.

It cried out as it sizzled into oblivion. The shrill screams finally ceased as Paul spit on his hand and rubbed his arm harder, ignoring the sting.

Porter said nothing. He stared into the flames where the slug had gone in, thinking.

....

TWENTY-ONE

A SMART BOY. A BRAVE BOY.

Tape Recorder Zach, the voice on the machine's tiny spinning wheels, told Zach what he needed to be.

A smart boy. A brave boy.

Zach was scared now, and Zach's mother wasn't here to tell him what to do. He had only the tapes—the tapes and himself.

He'd done nothing but walk since stepping into the mirror. And it didn't seem like anyone was following him. That was the reason he'd been picked, Tape Recorder Zach said. Something about how he was beneath the notice of the angry man in the suit and the white-haired man who worked for him. How he didn't see the fake world they put in front of everyone else—the world everyone else believed was real.

Zach was somewhere to the side of the angry man—in the corners and in the margins. They had a hard time fooling him and tracking him. That was why he was needed.

The angry man scared Zach. Zach's mother sometimes said that being scared was all in his head. Tape Recorder Zach didn't say anything like that. Zach thought that Tape Recorder Zach didn't want to lie to him.

The angry man in the suit was someone to be afraid of.

Tape Recorder Zach didn't mention the white-haired man who worked for the angry man, but Zach suspected he might be even scarier. There was something more to him—something down deep and hiding.

A smart boy. A brave boy.

The more Zach believed the voice in the tape recorder, the more that voice didn't sound like his. It became the voice of Zach's mother.

He thought that the farther he walked and the more he listened, the less the tape recorder worried about whether or not he trusted it. They were friends.

The shift from his own voice to the voice of Zach's mother was to get him used to the truth. The tape recorder was a stranger, and that stranger was his only guide. He'd been told over and over not to trust strangers. Now he had no choice.

Zach walked straight ahead, as the tape recorder told him to. The hallway looked just like the one in the apartment, only a lot longer.

He passed doors much like the doors to his bedroom and Zach's mother's room. They appeared over and over, and he knew that he could easily open them to see what was inside.

The voice told him to keep walking.

It meant it.

Whoever was inside those rooms wanted him to join them. The voice that used to be Zach's and was now Zach's mother's didn't even want him looking at the doors. The voice kept talking so he wouldn't forget to keep going. It spoke to him to keep the voices in the rooms from talking.

The hallway went on and on. Zach did as he was told. He walked.

Finally, the hallway ended at a red metal door with a square window. The window was small and made of thick glass with wires in it. The door had a big handle with a thumb button that was almost too high for Zach to reach. The button was impossible for him to move, though he tried very hard.

Zach's mother's voice said something to the door that was too soft for Zach to understand. Or maybe he wasn't supposed to hear it.

When he tried one more time, the thumb button clicked down. The door opened.

On the other side, steps descended into the dark. Zach couldn't see anything, and he was afraid to go in.

Zach's mother said something again. Lights in the stairwell ceiling turned on. They weren't very bright, but they were enough for him to see where he was going.

A smart boy. A brave boy.

He grabbed the metal railing and started down. He wanted to know how far he was going, so he counted. The problem was that he could only go as high as ten. He had to start over before he even got to the bottom of the first bunch. So he decided to count bunches of steps, but again he had to stop at ten and start over.

After his first set of ten, Zach heard a baby crying from somewhere up above. Then the lights went out, and he was in the dark.

The tape recorder said something. The lights flickered but went out again.

Zach held his hand up in front of his face and moved it toward him until he touched his nose. He couldn't see it.

Someone in the dark took his hand. The skin was as cold as Zach's mother's when she took him for a walk on pot-roast days, but it wasn't as big as hers.

It was the hand of another child.

Zach tried to pull away, but the hand wouldn't let go. The voice of Zach's mother told him he needed to go faster. Now she sounded scared, too.

A stairway door opened and closed in the blackness way up above. It clunked as heavily as the door Zach had come through, but it sounded like it was much higher than Zach's door.

The cold hand pulled him downward. Hard.

He hurried.

Zach counted groups of ten until he lost count. The fronts of his legs burned with the effort. The hand pulled harder.

He tripped and pitched forward into the dark but managed to grab the railing. The hand holding his kept him from falling. It was very strong and squeezed hard enough to hurt. He hung there for a second, then found his feet again.

Someone was coming down the stairs far above in big, wet thuds. Zach wasn't moving fast enough.

The hand holding his pulled, and he nearly fell again.

The tape-recorder voice started talking. Then many small, icy hands picked Zach up and carried him down.

It was too dark for him to tell how fast they were going, but it was faster than he could have gone on his own. Much faster. Like falling.

A feeling came to him, as if someone put it in his head. It came from the hands holding him—hands of cold, hard children he couldn't see.

The cold children were afraid, too, but not for themselves. They had already faced whatever was coming for him. They hadn't been fast enough, and now they couldn't leave.

They were scared for Zach. They were afraid they would be too slow again. They wanted to save him because they couldn't be saved themselves.

Zach was sad for the cold, lost children.

In the dark, he heard some of them stumble, but he never worried about falling himself. There were always more hands to catch him and hold him.

There were so many hands that the children of the dark weren't descending the steps themselves anymore. They were passing him along.

He rolled over and over across their hands. Down.

Dizzy, he felt sick. And still the wet, heavy steps above drew closer.

Zach understood why there were more hands and more children now. This was where whatever was coming after him had caught many of them—near the bottom.

They'd almost made it out. They'd been so close. Just not close enough.

It was all he could do to hang onto the tape recorder.

He was lowered to the ground, the hands so gentle that he didn't realize he was on his feet until he almost tumbled over.

The lights came back on. He wavered in front of another thick metal door with wired glass. It spun, as did the floor and walls. He was woozy from all of the rolling.

Zach put his hand on the door's thumb button, knowing what would happen. The button wouldn't budge.

The footsteps drew closer—sodden, like clods of watered earth. With each step, soft things skittered down the steps ahead of the feet and dropped down through the space in the staircase's center to the floor near him. He didn't look to see what the dropping things were. He knew they'd be wriggling.

Zach pushed with his thumb as hard as he could. His own yelp of distress surprised him. He was such a quiet boy—a smart boy, a brave boy—but not now.

Then the button went down. It was easy to move the door. He pushed.

The steps above grew closer still. The skittering of the falling things grew louder.

The door opened. The smell of warm, wet air greeted him—the air after a thunderstorm on a heavy summer evening. He stepped outside into nighttime.

His sense of relief didn't last long. The lights in the stairwell behind him went out as the damp slap of the footsteps sounded from only a few floors above.

He tried to push the door closed. It wouldn't move.

A smart boy. A brave boy.

Zach pushed as hard as he could. It would not move.

Harder. It would not move.

He looked up. A folding steel closer at the door's top was locked into place, out of reach.

The voice on the tape recorder, the voice of Zach's mother, began talking again. He still couldn't understand her.

He didn't care. He wanted the door closed. So did she, and that scared him even more.

The footsteps drew nearer. His breathing echoed in his ears as he gave the wide-open door his all. He heard no such strain from whatever was hurrying down the stairs.

He began to cry—a rare thing for him.

The tape-recorder voice, the voice of Zach's mother, was panicky. The door wouldn't move. The steps were nearly upon him.

He thought about running, but knew he'd be caught. It had to be the door.

Another yelp. His tears splashed the back of his hand—one, then more. They ran down the skin there. The slapping steps reached the bottom of the stairs. His tears reached the door handle, wetting it.

The door closed fast—so fast that it almost ripped his thumbnail off. It boomed shut just as something huge launched itself from the other side.

The impact on the door was hard and loud. On the tape, Zach's mother gasped.

Zach stepped back.

It hit again, and the door bowed outward with the power of whatever was trying to break it down. But it held.

The voice of Zach's mother told Zach to turn around, away from the thing that wanted him. He obeyed, just as he'd listened when it told him not to open any of the hallway doors.

It was quiet, but not a good quiet. A tickle traveled up the back of his neck.

Something was looking out at him through the door's wired-glass window. To look back and see what it was would be bad—would give it power.

Zach's mother's voice said to hurry. The tears on the door handle would dry soon.

Zach walked away. Fast.

A smart boy. A brave boy.

Smart enough and brave enough to never look back.

....

TWENTY-TWO

NONE MORE THAN YOU

Their group was getting good at the important things: fighting, traveling in silence, waiting.

At a shelter by the side of the road, Porter decided they should get on the next bus that came along. Faster progress was worth the risk of being spotted and recognized, he said.

So they killed time to make it. Porter stood in the middle of the road, gazing into the distance, as if trying to will a bus into existence. Po meditated on a nearby bench, Ken beside him. Paul and Rain shared a hillside a short distance away.

After sitting completely still for an hour, Po hopped off the bench and joined Porter. He looked down the road, then turned to sign at Ken.

"A bus is coming," the mummy told the Envoy.

"I don't see it," said Porter. "Do you?" he asked Po.

"He can hear it," Ken said.

"Po can hear?" Paul asked Rain. He kept his voice lower than he might have only a moment before.

"Better than we do, according to Ken."

"He doesn't talk."

"He's a mythical. He was created for some old seventies kung-fu movies. Ken says he can only speak the way he was dubbed in English—in this cheesy stereotype. He hates it. It's undignified. So he signs."

The bus rumbled into view. Paul stood, swept dry grass from his pants, and shouldered his pack.

"Paul?" Rain said. "Thank you."

"For what?"

"For what you did in the fight."

"I had no control. I killed people."

"You heard Porter. You freed those Ravagers—and you saved us." She stood, too, grabbing her pack and shotgun.

"I'm afraid," he said.

"That you won't be able to do it again?"

"That I won't be able to control it. And it'll be one of you next time."

"I don't think so." She reached out to place her hand on his chest, her palm over his heart. "Porter. Ken. Po. Me. Why are we with you when we know it will bring Brill down on us?" She spread her fingers. "Because we believe."

Then she walked down the hill, leaving Paul to ask himself if he believed, too.

And if so, in what?

THE BUS WAS of the yellow school variety, which Paul recognized from the days he'd chosen to attend. Those days were rare—just numerous enough to keep him from getting kicked out of the foster home of the day or out of New Beginnings.

A battered rear-engine model with a flat front, the bus boasted the usual safety features: no seat belts and rubber padding as hard as the steel it covered. He almost felt nostalgic, making his way to the back with the others while Porter paid the driver.

Their fellow passengers were the usual Commons types, meaning that they were highly unusual. Three men were composed of melting ice. A bride and groom were holograms projected by a small unit sitting next to them. Two seats' worth of little girls in black had identical shag cuts and eyes that were glowing sapphires in their petite skulls.

Ken and Po led the way to the rear, where they realized that the bus was full, and they'd have to stand in the aisle. As they approached the rear gate, however, the bus stretched to accommodate them, creating two new rows of vacant seats.

On the way back, they passed a portly man whose days-old facial growth, dirty hat, and stained coat weren't an adequate warning for the odor that assaulted them once they got close.

He looked Rain up and down without any attempt at subtlety. She pretended not to notice, but when she was right at his ear, she adjusted her hold on her shotgun and casually swung it to the side, forcing him to duck.

"Spare a bill for a fellow who's down?" the man asked Paul.

Paul acted as if he hadn't heard the question. Rain waited for him to take a window seat and then sat next to him. It occurred to Paul that she might want room to maneuver the gun again—just in case.

Porter finished paying and made his way back to them.

"Spare a bill for a fellow who's down?" the dirty man asked as he passed.

"Sorry."

"Why not? You can always jump more out of some poor sucker's wallet."

The Envoy stopped to face him.

"Hiya, Porter." The man proudly flashed his sorry dental state.

"Hello, Leery." Porter's tone was flat.

They all paid attention to the dirty man now. He returned the favor, studying each of them before settling on Paul.

"What are you doing here?" Porter asked him.

"Not Envoying. That's for certain. And I'll bet right about now, you're wishing you weren't, either."

"My last Journey was back when dates still counted. You know that."

"And I haven't had a smoke today." Leery spat on the floor of the bus. It disappeared with a hiss. "You know who this is?" he asked Paul. "Hardest-working Envoy in The Commons. The only working Envoy in The Commons. Mister Persister. Never give up, even if it means other people get killed."

Paul looked to Porter for his lead. The Envoy had ice in his eyes as he weighed his options.

Po stared at the dirty man as if he'd already decided how to proceed. Whatever it was, it would mean picking more teeth off his robe.

"Thing is," Leery said, turning in his seat toward Paul, "he'd better be persistent, 'cause if I'm hearing things, then Brill is, too." He leaned forward. "And persistence might not be enough for an old man who's out of practice and out of his mind if he thinks he's what he used to be."

"That's enough, Leery."

"Oh, come on, Porter. We go back. You and your staff, me and my lid." He grabbed his rotting hat and straightened it, nearly separating the crown from the brim in the process. "Back when it was still alive. You don't have to listen to me, of course. It's just talk." He lowered his stubbly chin until his eyes just barely peered out at Paul from under his hat and flashed a black grin. "Thing is, now it's *talk*."

AT THE BOTTOM of the exit ramp, the bus turned and entered a roadhouse parking lot. Only one of the lot's four pole lamps worked, and the bulb in that one didn't have much time left.

Leery struggled down the steps into the murk, cursing the bus for refusing to lower itself the way it had for others. The steps tilted down abruptly, spilling him out onto the pavement. He picked himself up and cursed even harder as the doors shut behind him.

The bus pulled away. Leery watched the windows pass until the one with Porter's stripling came into view. He whacked the glass.

Even though the effort nearly threw him off his feet again, he enjoyed a laugh at how startled the boy looked. "Good luck, kid!" he said. "We all need it—but none more than you!"

In the bus's rear-door window, Porter regarded him with an expression of pity. The breeze of the departing bus pulled the hat from Leery's head. He caught it, but the brim tore almost all the way off.

The cell phone in Leery's pocket trilled. Not his phone, but the one he'd been given—the one with the ringtone that sounded like wrath and couldn't be changed.

"Yeah?" he said with a bravado he didn't feel. "Yes. But you already knew that. Well, you know where I am, so you know where they are. That squares us, doesn't it?"

The call dropped. He threw the phone to the ground and stomped on it. It broke with a wet crunch, like a fat roach, and spattered his shoes and pant cuffs with dark eggs and ichor.

Leery spewed profanity for the umpteenth time that day. Inky liquid sprung from the phone and formed a puddle, which stopped him from stomping it again. Too much blood for something so small.

He retreated from the puddle and headed for the bar.

AN HOUR LATER, the bus approached a wall of spotlight beams that crossed the highway. Behind the trucks holding the lights, three Black Hawks blocked the road, the gap between two of them just large enough for one vehicle to pass through at a time.

The bus rolled up to the checkpoint, which was manned by a squad of Ravagers. Three of them boarded, the latter two covering the passengers with their assault rifles while the first walked the aisle. He took a visual inventory of the riders, eyes unseen behind his face-plate.

Porter lay stretched out across a seat in the back—alone, sweating, shivering. Rain, in Leery's old seat now, gave the Ravager a disinterested glance as he headed for the Envoy.

Ken, Po, and Paul were gone.

"Hey!" Rain said to the soldier as he was about to prod Porter with his baton. "Could you do something about the old man? He's been like that since he got on. What if it's catching? We don't know it's not, right?"

The Ravager decided not to poke him after all. He watched him hug himself, the hollow of Porter's throat running with sweat.

"Hey, seriously?" Rain said.

Long minutes later, the Ravagers left the bus, the driver closing the door behind them. Two other soldiers waved the bus on.

Inside, Porter sat up, hunched and shaking harder than ever. He flicked his staff, and Ken, Po, and Paul reappeared in their seats.

Rain stood to lay a hand on his shoulder. He'd done it.

He looked up at her, tried to smile, and passed out.

WELL AFTER MIDNIGHT, Leery left the roadhouse with the help of the bartender and some patrons who didn't appreciate his observations on bona fides and scraps. One of the men and his family had evaded Brill and the Ravagers for two decades. His wife had zebra stripes and a tail, and the man's assistance consisted of opening the door before the others jettisoned the former Envoy out into the night.

Leery had long ago made peace with indignities, whether self-imposed or introduced by others. Thus, when his shadow grew larger on the asphalt in the rectangle of light cast by the doorway, and he found yet again that he didn't bounce very well, he took none of it personally. He simply peeled himself off the ground and set about finding a quiet spot in which to pass out.

Another shadow crossed his, broad and thick. Some rival drunk.

He made his unsteady way around the side of the tavern to where there wasn't as much light. No need to let the competition get the best bed first.

Behind him, someone sniffed, testing the air—a large man from the sound of it—and Leery knew he had him beat. Anyone who balked at the smell of garbage didn't deserve a place to sleep.

He turned to sneer at his fellow vagrant. No one was there.

Rounding the corner, he grabbed at the building for support and missed. He fell into a corral of trash cans, knocking a few lids off and catching a coat of fragrant slime on his arm.

The sniffing again. Closer.

A shadow on the wall—a moving shadow.

The trash cans toppled in a symphony of rattling metal and splitting bags. Someone big jumped him from behind.

Leery tumbled into a pile of garbage bags, breaking one open with his face. The weight on his back couldn't have been just one guy.

He couldn't breathe, but whoever was on top of him had no such problem. The panting in his ears filled his skull.

His insides became acid, burning their way out through his spine. He screamed, but the trash muffled it. Then he regretted squandering that breath. The weight prevented him from getting any of it back.

Leery's life bled out.

His uncle, showing him how to row a boat. That neighbor girl who watched him when his parents went out—the nice one. Her name was gone before he could come up with it.

He found the wind to scream into the garbage again. Then his throat closed, and he shriveled like an empty bag, its wet insides stuck together.

Whatever was on his back liked it.

His father tried to help him fly the kite he'd gotten as a giveaway. There was no wind.

He watched a school filmstrip about building your own ant farm.

His sister counted dead ants in a slow ticking of numbers. It was vital to her to get the tally right.

The counting stopped.

....

TWENTY-THREE

DEAD LEAVES AND MOTHS

L eaving the broken mirror of the bedroom behind, Annie followed the directions given by her memory of the tape recordings. Which worked fine until she ignored the advice it repeated most often: to keep passing the doors.

Just as the hallway she walked for hours was a repeating copy of the hall in the apartment she'd escaped, every door here looked like that hall's bedroom doors. And something behind those doors—a whole collection of somethings—wanted her to open one. Needed it.

The voice in the remembered tape recordings— a woman's voice that sounded familiar, though a hair or two removed from one she could name— kept urging her to hurry. Breaking the mirror risked exposing those who'd helped her, the voice said, and her pursuers would repair and use it in short order if they thought they had a shot at catching her.

When she asked who'd taken a risk for her, she got no answer. The memory voice was an audio tour, not a living guide.

Whoever or whatever wanted Annie to try a door rotated through an array of lures. It knew which buttons to push. From behind the doors came distress calls from military radios, the whimpering of a frightened dog, Stars of the Lid's "Requiem for Dying Mothers," and the aroma of her mom's sauerbraten.

All of which contributed to her falling for the meanest trick the doors could muster. She had to give them credit for the way they played her.

After softening her up with the other bait and getting her into a state, they stopped for a while and let what she'd heard do its work. The silent time allowed her thoughts to return to Zach. How many times had she left him staring at the mirror, alone in the dark, or on his own for entire days? Why was it so easy for a pill to turn her not just into a bad mother, but into a woman who wasn't a mother at all?

What came from down the hall was skillfully timed. Zach crying. Her boy in pain.

It might have been easier had she not already known the sound, rare as it was. But that would have meant that her son had never grabbed the pot of boiling pasta, had never squeezed her hand with a man's strength in the E.R.

She rushed the door, a chipped but ornate beauty of heavy wood. The recorded-memory voice urged her to ignore what she heard. Easy for the voice to say—it wasn't the voice's son crying out.

The cut-glass knob turned, but the door was stuck, swollen as if on a humid day. Annie hit it with her shoulder while the voice in her head dropped all decorum and audio-tour pretense, shouting that it was a lie, it was a lie, it was a lie.

On the third hit, the stuck door gave in, and she launched herself into the room. She tried to catch herself with her good leg.

There was no floor. She fell a good foot and a half before hitting a hard surface below.

She turned her head and saved herself a broken nose as she crash-landed, but smacked the side of her skull on solid stone. Skyrockets launched, filling her vision.

Annie stayed where she was until the pain in her head subsided enough for the throb in her knee to reclaim its throne. Somewhere nearby,

Zach's crying became his laughter. It morphed into the malign chuckle of an adult, then faded.

She picked herself up off the dirty marble floor, checking the inside of her mouth with her tongue. The memory voice was gone, cut off as soon as she fell through the door. She suspected it wouldn't be back, and she could only hope that her chances of finding Zach hadn't departed with it.

The room was a second-floor ballroom or dining room in a long-ago abandoned mansion of some sort. Many a party beyond the former owners' imagining had been held in the space in their absence, judging by the charred branches and crushed beer cans spilling from a large fireplace.

Warm summer air wafted in from holes where the windows used to be. Through them was an adjacent wing, windows also missing, its walls draped with ivy.

Beyond that, the overgrown grounds stretched. Statues guarded a murky garden pool through the trees. It was a view from a skull's interior.

The wall she'd fallen out of blocked any hope of return to the hall. A life-sized painting of a door—a closed and formidable-looking thing—now hung in the real one's place. The ornate frame of the work had seen better days, but the painting itself was in even worse shape. Its canvas was stained, the paint flaked off in voids the diameter of a cymbal. Below it, outlined in missing plaster, was the ghost of one or two steps that had been removed. Had whatever force tricked her into the room taken them away as she opened the door? Given the laugh she'd heard, she couldn't rule out such nastiness.

There were several doorways into adjoining rooms—and no clear indication as to which she should choose. She opted for the right-hand one and wandered through what looked to be a servants' prep room for the ballroom, complete with a hole in the wall where a dumbwaiter could be pulled up.

She decided against investigating the hole. Inside, its cables were stretched taut, as if something heavy hung from them. She wanted to believe that was just the weight of the dumbwaiter, but the clotted smell of rotten meat—the cavity's horrid breath—made her fear otherwise.

A door led out into a hall that wasn't the same one she'd entered from. It looked similar but felt like another place altogether.

A series of what at first appeared to be identical paintings lined the walls. As Annie passed them, however, the differences became clear. Each was the same landscape—a black hillside, empty but for a building so tiny in the distance that its details couldn't be made out beyond the dark square it presented against the plum sky of dusk.

In succession, the works were like still frames in a film. A lone figure holding a lantern emerged from the building, as if someone had heard her and was coming out to investigate.

With every painting Annie passed, more figures emerged to join the first. They ventured down the hillside, lurching toward her in each—dark silhouettes whose faces couldn't be made out in the glow of the contained flames dangling from their fists.

When she stepped back, the process didn't reverse itself. The figures were now closer in the earlier frames, too.

The paintings brought no odor of threat with them the way the dumbwaiter had. But when she picked up the pace to pass them, the figures responded in kind, matching her haste. Their details and faces remained in shadows no matter how close they got or how much of the light from their lanterns filled the frames.

She got a move-on.

From the hallway behind came the tinkle of breaking glass and the splash of liquid. Then a rush of air—fire catching. The sounds repeated and got closer, coming up the hall to catch her. She smelled smoke.

A wave of warmth accompanied the breaking lanterns. Now the paintings featured the dark figures against a backdrop of spreading flames.

She moved faster.

The hallway stretched on. More breaking glass, along with the splashing of lantern oil and the whoosh of ignition. The paintings ahead were nothing but fire and dark figures frozen in it, their arms raised.

The hall began to fill with a gray-white haze of smoke. It grew warmer. She coughed, and the air burned when she drew it in.

Finally, she reached a cross corridor. The smoke made it difficult to breathe and even harder to see. She hacked, tears rolling down her face. Decision time. She turned right.

A flash of light and heat from behind. The hallway she'd just left exhaled a blast of smoke and flame, like a dragon that was a second or two off its game.

The paint on the walls back there began to bubble and peel away from the plaster beneath. The heat rose to the point of pain.

Ahead, through the haze, the hallway broadened out into a circular area with at least six doorways, all of them dark. On the floor, someone had spray-painted an arrow pointing toward one.

She made for it quickly, her coughing getting worse with the heat. She couldn't see what awaited her in the door's blackness, but she didn't have time to worry about that.

Her next step was nearly her last.

Coming through the door, she found only air. She grabbed the doorjamb and caught herself. A dank odor rose up from the cool dark below. An elevator shaft.

She pulled herself back from the abyss and checked the hall floor behind her. Now the out arrow pointed toward a different door. A child giggled somewhere in the smoke.

The temperature rose. Tears and sweat met and mingled.

The other dark doorways beckoned. The glow of the fire marching its way up the hall toward her served only to turn the smoke white, impeding her vision further.

Which door? If she assumed the one the arrow now indicated was an obvious hazard and chose from the remaining four at random, she had a twenty-five percent chance of picking the safe one. Assuming any of them were.

She settled on the second door from the right.

The phone in her pocket vibrated.

She held the screen up close in the smoke, struggling to read the text against the backlight. "Stairs left," it said. What if whoever was moving the painted arrow was now in control of her phone?

Coughing hard now, she chose to reject that notion. She ventured into the smoke all the way to the left of the six doors, reaching out ahead of her with her toes. Nothing but floor.

She wondered if it really was June Medill sending her the texts and if June still wanted to help her—if she ever really had. The answer didn't matter. She had to trust whoever it was.

The heat seared her back, and it was anyone's guess as to which might go up first, her clothing or her hair. Hacking louder, she dropped to hands and knees, hoping to find better air down low.

A large "W" was set into a black-and-gold crest in the floor in an intricate tile pattern. She felt her way along, crawling, and was beginning to think she'd been tricked again when she reached a drop-off with a rounded edge—a step.

Sure enough, there was another beneath it.

She worked her way sideways down the steps, taking it slow to feel her way around broken bottles and other sharp-edged hazards beyond identification. Either the parties here had spanned several floors, or the stairways served as dumpsters. Most likely both.

At the bottom, she seized up when she found nothing but wall to the front and sides. Then she realized she was on a landing and needed to hook around.

Up above, paintings sizzled as they went up, one by one. Good. They deserved it.

Two landings later, the smoke was gone. She got to her feet in total darkness and brought up the flashlight app on her phone.

She was in a basement, surrounded by stacks of even more paintings. These were covered in dusty drop cloths. She let them be.

Her phone buzzed.

"Straight through to the doors," the screen said. "Don't dawdle. You're not alone."

She didn't.

At the far end of the basement, stone steps strewn with filth led to a pair of overhead wooden doors. Those were barred with a heavy piece of wood jammed into the doors' rusty holders—jammed so tight that she wasn't sure she'd be able to move it.

A dry, low cough came from the blackness behind her, followed by the dragging rustle of shifting weight. Someone or something was rousing itself.

A number of good, hard yanks brought God-knows-what raining down into her hair and collar, but she was amply motivated by the sounds of her unseen roommate.

She worked the big piece of wood free. Her knee complained. Her lower back joined in.

With a few pushes, she was able to heave one of the heavy doors up and over. It landed with a rotten thud. A sky full of stars greeted her.

Another cough from behind and more dragging—closer now—propelled her up the steps and into the night. She struggled with the weight of the door again, but was able to heft it back over and closed. It slammed shut, belching out dead leaves and moths.

For good measure, she grabbed a rusty chain lying nearby, looped it through the doors' big steel pull-rings a few times, and knotted it as well as she could. The doors didn't move.

Whatever was down there wasn't trying to follow. For now.

She thumbed her phone's screen, its light illuminating her hands, which were now brown with oxidation. "Thank you, June," she typed, her dirty pads making an impressionist work of the glass.

The reply came in short order. "Not June."

A brief stomach-squeeze of fear. Maybe she'd followed the directions of someone who meant her harm or who, at best, was toying with her.

The screen refreshed. "Char."

TWENTY-FOUR

···

THE DINUHOS TREE

"They killed in bookends," Porter told Paul. He had trouble lifting his head from the seat back. Ken wanted him to rest, but the Envoy needed to talk after the encounter with Leery. "Death in the beginning, death at the end. What came in between was the lion's share of the Corps' disappearance. Many quit after the first slaughter, but not all of us. We had heart."

The bus had rolled straight through the night and into morning. Daylight brought a carnival of billboards for roadside attractions.

Porter paused, gathering strength. A faded sign for a sasquatch farm failed to make it clear whether the creatures worked the land or were grown on it. Another, partly hidden by vines, advised travelers that they shouldn't miss the dragon egg that was as big as a car. Not far down the road sat the foundations of three charred structures. Had the egg hatched, or did mama come looking for it?

Po, in particular, seemed interested in the signs. He read each carefully.

"Brill promised efficiency, and no one thought enough about what that meant," Porter said. "Why wait for the Envoys to lead Journeys on a one-on-one basis? He made sense to some—not to us, but to those who didn't question him the way they should have. The Envoys let him build his strength because we thought he was too preposterous to be taken seriously. Then it was because we were afraid. In the end, there was no fighting him. He made examples of the best of us, and that scared most of the rest away from the job. Then he and the Ravager death squads picked off those who wouldn't leave."

"Why did Leery say his hat used to be alive?" Paul asked.

"He meant the abilities it gave him, but Leery was never one for detail." Porter closed his eyes and kept them shut. "The power comes from the person, not the object," he said, just as Paul thought he was dozing again. "The object is a focal point—a tool. My staff is only more than that in my hands. For a time, like Leery, my power was gone. I was just a lonely man at a desk. I think that's why Brill never bothered with me. He didn't know I was there. And when my talent was needed, it returned."

"How did you know you had it back?"

"I didn't. I'd had false alarms over the years—feeling it when it wasn't there, like a phantom limb. I didn't know I'd be able to get to you until I did. Up to that point, it was like taking an umbrella with no idea whether it would open. I was never so happy"—his voice began to fade—"than when I realized it was back."

With that, his breath slowed and deepened. He was sound asleep.

"Essence chooses him," Ken said, watching Porter's chest rise and fall. "It returned to a good man."

"Essence gives him his powers?"

"It gives all of us everything. Power, life, lightning, fire. Essence makes a heart beat, keeps fear alive, falls as water, burns a forest in the dark, ignites an idea."

"You're saying it's all the same thing."

They passed a billboard that had no words on it, just a simple image like a wood-cut stamp: a tree with a door in its trunk. Below the tree was the number five.

Seeing that, Po signed excitedly to Ken.

Ken nodded to his friend. "Essence fuels it all. Real, imagined. It's Essence."

Farther down the road, another tree billboard had the number one beneath it. Others on the bus pointed and woke their napping friends.

Two rows up, a woman with a long bandage tied around her eyes turned toward the billboard as the bus passed it. "Would you look at that?" she said. "The Dinuhos Tree."

THE DRIVER EXITED the highway without any prodding, eager as any of his passengers to see the tree. He pulled into an expansive parking lot and opened the door. The bus emptied out.

Po signed to Ken.

"They don't know that," the mummy replied.

The tree had been well represented by its billboard rendition. Bereft of grandeur, it was squat, with a thick, knobby trunk and widespread branches, like something from a board game or a book of Brothers Grimm tales.

"Ficus religiosa," said Porter. The sight seemed to invigorate him.

Chain-draped poles bordered a plank walkway leading to the tree. The approach was just wide enough for a single-file line and just long enough to hold the bus's queue of riders.

The burned-in letters of a fissured wooden sign identified the attraction as the Dinuhos Tree. A smaller sign behind it read: "Give. Receive."

The line crept along. Each passenger stepped up alone to open a small, arched door in the base of the tree that looked to be made of the same wood as the Dinuhos itself. In fact, the door didn't appear to be an addition so much as an anomaly in the trunk that the tree allowed to be opened.

Paul took a closer look at the sign and the planks under his feet. The walkway ran all the way up to the tree, touching it, while a raised stretch of roots under the ground connected the sign to it as well. The planks and the sign were living extensions of the Dinuhos.

When it was time for those in line to take their turn, they placed an offering inside the little door, closed it, and waited. Then they opened it again to see what the tree gave them in return.

Not everyone liked what they got. Some received nothing and walked away griping or cursing. One man, whose feet would have fit someone five times his size, kicked the tree in frustration, to no effect.

The woman with the cloth over her eyes didn't show anyone what she gave or received. But she strode with purpose back to the bus, a grin on her face and tears spilling from beneath her bandage.

The driver gave up his keys and got them back, only cleaner and shinier, with a new silver fob. He took that as a sign that he should keep his job, he said.

By the time Paul drew close to the Dinuhos, several people had opened the door to find their own offering inside. Several complained that those who went first had used up the tree's generosity.

"The kindness received is that given," Ken told Rain and Paul.

When their turns came, Porter, Ken, and Po stepped out of the line. The Envoy said he was on the job. Ken explained that he and Po had no offerings and no wants.

Rain stepped up for her turn, pausing to think. Paul started to ask her what was wrong. Porter silenced him with a gentle hand to the shoulder.

"Five minutes!" the bus driver shouted.

Biting her lip, Rain took a scarred and dirty coin from her pocket. She held it with her fingertips—careful, as if it were a hornet—and put it inside the tree. She closed the door, opened it again, and claimed her gift.

It was a single shotgun shell, which she held up to the light of the sky to examine, half-smiling. She pocketed it and walked back to stand by Ken and Po.

Paul wanted to ask her about the exchange, but Porter nudged him forward for his turn. Once he was at the door, Paul had no idea what to offer. His mother's ring? No way.

It came to him. He reached into his pocket and scooped out the cat's-eye marble Zach had insisted he take when they met in Port Authority. He placed it in the tree and shut the door. "Give it back," he said.

He pictured the kid in his mind, pushing aside the vision of the small form dead in the hillside snow, imagining instead the surprised little boy finding his marble again. He concentrated until he remembered to breathe, then opened the door and looked inside. A flat piece of laminated safety glass sat in the marble's place.

Paul took the glass, careful not to cut himself, and examined it. It was from the window of his seat on the bus. Scratched into it was the tag that had glowed red: "IMUURS."

Vertigo struck him; his vision blurred, and he breathed deep to clear his head. His hands closed into fists, his mother's ring clicking against the piece of glass.

The ring grew hot—too hot, burning. He opened his fist to drop the searing glass, but it was gone, its work complete. The sizzling ring felt like it was melting into his finger, and he tried to yank it off.

At the edge of Paul's foggy vision, Porter moved in to help. Po stopped the Envoy—an easy task, given Porter's weakened state.

The burning ring held fast. Then, just as abruptly as it arrived, the heat faded.

Paul pulled the ring off. His finger no longer hurt. There wasn't even a mark on it.

That was not true of the ring, which now wasn't even warm. He turned it in the sunlight. Engraved on the inside, in serifed capital letters, was the tag from the window.

TWENTY-FIVE

....

JERRY'S RECORDS

A smart boy. A brave boy.

Zach hugged the tape recorder to his chest, even when he wasn't listening to it. He'd refused to do that with the stuffed bear, the stuffed rabbit, or the stuffed monkey Zach's mother had given him, though she'd tried so hard to show him how. But the tape recorder made him feel less scared in a way the animals never could.

He knew now that what he'd whispered into the recorder while sitting in front of the mirror may have been in his voice, but it didn't come from him. He wasn't sure who it came from, just as he couldn't say why Zach's mother thought of that apartment as home while they were there.

Zach suspected it was because she swallowed so much of the pink medicine, which made her sick. That made him sad—but not as sad as it used to.

Along with the voice of Zach's mother came thoughts that weren't in the recorded words, but instead flew between them. Those thoughts told him not to worry: Zach's mother wasn't taking the pink medicine anymore.

As he walked, some in-between words also came in the voice of another woman—a stranger. They were so faint that they sounded like whispers, and Zach couldn't hear what the words said. But he knew that was because the woman wasn't yet close enough, and that he was going toward her.

Zach's mother's voice was no longer saying only the things he himself had recorded. She was also repeating what the in-between woman said.

Zach walked along a wide road with a dotted yellow line in the middle. Empty stores and restaurants stood on either side. There wouldn't be cars coming. The weeds, grass, and bushes growing out of the big cracks in the road meant they couldn't—and didn't—use it anymore.

Still, he'd always been told to stay out of the street. So he walked on the sidewalk when there was one and balanced on the curb when there wasn't.

He stopped at every corner. He'd never been allowed to cross the street on his own, but that didn't matter now.

The traffic lights at the corners were broken and dark, staring at him with big blind eyes. But he was very careful just the same.

Where Zach was going wasn't safe. He had no control over that, so he used the control he did have. He looked both ways.

Eyes watched him from the empty stores and restaurants. Sometimes the sun hit the windows a certain way, and he could see people's heads behind the glass. Other times he could see that they weren't people at all.

He didn't look long enough to see what they were. That would be a mistake.

Zach never stopped moving. Having Zach's mother's voice with him kept the watchers away, but that wouldn't work with all of them.

If he didn't go fast enough—if they decided to come after him to see who and what he was—it wouldn't matter how loud he turned the tape recorder up. It wouldn't save him.

So he walked.

His feet began to hurt. Then they stopped. Then they hurt. Then they stopped again. A spot near his big toe grew hot.

Zach's mother's voice and the whispering woman had told him to watch for a certain sign, and finally, he saw it. On top of a tall pole sat a ball with spikes coming out of it.

Zach couldn't make the letters on the sign into a word, but he recognized their lines, which hung off of the pole inside big squares, one above the other, like alphabet blocks. R-A-A-Z-A-B was the order, starting at the bottom and going up. That was where he was going.

Behind the sign was a giant parking lot with the same kinds of cracks and plants as the street. There were cars in the lot.

Zach could tell the cars had been sitting there a long time. Their windshields were very dirty, and some were cracked. And just as he'd had the feeling people were watching him from the buildings, he sensed that not all the cars were empty.

In the center of the parking lot was a big, flat building that was only one floor high. It looked like a huge supermarket, though Zach knew it wasn't that.

Its front windows were giant rectangles of orange, red, and green. Zach couldn't see through them. On top of the building were the letters from the pole, but now they read from left to right: B-A-Z-A-A-R.

He didn't know that word.

A section of the parking lot was a chained-off Christmas-tree cemetery. It was full of brown tree skeletons with no needles on them. Next to the skeletons were circle frames holding rotten wreaths with dirty bows that had once been red. Now they were pinkish-brown.

Zach walked around the cemetery. It didn't feel good to think about walking through it.

At the front of the building was a row of doors. In the window of one of the doors was an old piece of paper with a picture of a smiling man on it. "Today," it said above the man, though it didn't say what his name was. Everyone must have already known.

Zach's mother's voice told him not to touch the door, but instead to turn and walk around to the side of the building. Her voice was almost as faint as the whispering woman's now, and Zach feared she was leaving him.

Making his way around the trees and wreaths again, Zach heard one of the front doors near where he'd been standing push open from the inside. He didn't need to look to know there was no one there. The door had opened because someone wanted him to use it, but it had tried too late to fool him.

He walked for a long time to get to the corner of the building. The building was a lot bigger than he'd thought, probably because it was getting darker, and it was harder to see. He hoped that Zach's mother's voice wouldn't go away with the light.

Around the side, Zach had more walking to do before he got to a smaller set of doors. There were more signs. One had a big pretzel on it, but seeing it didn't make Zach hungry. He hadn't been hungry at all since the bus trip in the snow.

On the other sign was a picture of a big black circle with another circle inside it and a hole inside of that. Zach wasn't sure what that was. It looked like a target, but he didn't think it was. There was also a picture of the tapes that went into the machine he carried.

On the sign were stacked groups of letters that spelled R-E-C-O-R-D-S and J-E-R-R-Y-S. He didn't know those words, either.

The doors were metal, heavy, and orange. Zach grabbed the handle of one and tried to push yet another thumb button down. He knew it wasn't going to move, just like all the others. It didn't.

Zach's mother's voice talked fast, but Zach couldn't hear what she was saying.

He used both thumbs. It didn't work.

Zach thought of Zach's mother—the real one, not the tape version—and what she might say to do. She usually told him to use his big-boy powers, which meant doing it on his own instead of waiting for her to do it for him. He hit the stop button on the recorder because Zach's mother's voice couldn't help him here.

He knew that he couldn't go anywhere else without going into the building. It was getting darker, so he needed to get in. It wouldn't be safe outside.

He looked around the parking lot. Nearby were a rock, a piece of wood with metal on the end of it, and an X-shaped tool hanging from the wheel of a car. He went over and grabbed the end of the X-tool. It was stuck.

He pulled hard with both hands. It came free, but he fell over when it did. He got up and carried the tool back to the door.

Zach tried to decide where to hit the thumb button with the tool. He didn't want to break it. He tried the thumb buttons on the other doors. None of them moved, either.

He was back to figuring out which button to hit and where to hit it when he remembered the big-boy power he hadn't tried yet. It was the one he never used—not because he couldn't, but because everyone told him he had to.

"Please," Zach told the doors. His voice disturbed the air around him. He'd forgotten what it sounded like.

When he again pushed the button on the first door he'd tried, he opened it with only one thumb. It moved easily.

Inside was a wide hallway with a cement floor. Metal gates protected storefronts on both sides of him. It looked like a cross between the New York streets Zach's mother sometimes walked him down at night when everything was closed and one of the malls they used to go to.

This place was older than the malls, like the place by the ocean that Zach and Zach's mother went to when she'd wanted to show him the ringing and beeping games last summer. It had the same light-up tubes buzzing overhead. It even had the same wooden walls—the kind with the straight black lines you could run your fingernail up and down.

He didn't do that to these walls. They looked like they'd be bad to touch.

Zach didn't linger in front of the dark stores with the closed gates. He couldn't see what was in them because the lights were off inside and not all of the overhead hallway tubes worked. He saw comic books and magazines in one store with working tubes, walls made of keys in another, and a big racetrack full of silent little cars on a table in a third.

Zach's mother's voice talked to him, even though the play button wasn't pressed down. That made no sense. But neither did the fact that the recorder played without any batteries in it. He had checked, and the battery place was empty except for white and green powder and dried brown gunk.

She told him to keep moving. There were places he needed to go before other things happened, or it would be too late.

A smart boy. A brave boy.

A fast boy.

Overhead was a hanging sign with the pictures of the pretzel, the circle with the hole, and the tape that went into his machine. Zach followed the arrow on it, which pointed to the ceiling. It meant he should go straight, not up.

The lights buzzed as he walked. Zach's mother's voice was silent.

He passed side hallways. Light spilled from tubes at the far end of them, as did the sounds of laughing, talking, and songs about dancing in the moonlight and Chicago dying at night.

Those were songs for other people and other times, not him. He hoped that the people singing the songs were happy, that they were okay. He hoped that for people a lot, but no one knew it because he didn't tell them.

He came to an open gate. The sign over it had the same letters and pictures as the one out front. Zach mother's voice told him where to walk when he went into the store. He passed walls displaying the black circles with the holes in them and racks with pictures of long-haired men.

One picture had a pair of jeans with a real zipper on it. Another had a birthday cake, and another had a banana. Zach still wasn't hungry.

He turned right, then left. No one realized it, but he knew his directions.

In front of him, a wall held several rows of the kind of tapes that went into the tape recorder. They all hung in multi-pack plastic sleeves. Now Zach's mother's voice spoke to him slowly, like the real Zach's mother and the teachers at his school when they thought he didn't understand something, but it was really just that he knew it wasn't worth listening to.

Zach's mother's voice told him the rows of hanging tapes were like a board for checkers. Each tape was a square on the board. That was easy.

She said to start in square one, all the way at the top and all the way to the left. That was easy, too, though Zach's teachers thought he couldn't do it because he never wanted to do it in front of them.

The game was to count one over, one down, two over, and then three down. Zach counted very carefully.

He took the long pack from the hook it was hanging on and tore open the top. Zach's mother's voice told him he needed the fifth tape in the sleeve.

Outside the store, one of the voices he'd heard before was getting closer. Zach's mother's voice said he needed to go faster. The guard had started his rounds.

That was the first Zach heard of any guard. He counted his way down the package until he had the right tape, took it out, and replaced the one in the machine with it.

Before he could hit play, the sound of a lady crying came out of the recorder.

Not loud.

Worse than loud.

It was the crying that the real Zach's mother did when she didn't want him to hear her.

He had the wrong tape. He had to hurry.

He counted down the pack again and realized he'd gone too fast the first time because Zach's mother's voice had scared him by talking about the guard. He'd put the number-six tape in. He yanked it out and popped number five into place.

"Hello, Zach," the unknown woman, who'd been so faint on the previous tape, said from the recorder.

He pulled number five out and put the Zach's-mother's-voice tape back in so that Zach's mother's voice could tell him if he had the right one this time.

Nothing happened. The Zach's-mother's-voice tape was at its end.

He put the number-five tape in again. The unknown woman came back.

Out in the hallway, keys jingled from around the corner. Or maybe a couple of corners. Zach hoped it was a couple.

"You need to move, sweetie," the woman said. There was something about her voice that Zach knew. Something from the bus—from the boy he gave his marble to. "Go to the back of the store."

The rear door to the store stood open. Beyond it, in the warm night of the parking lot, was Zach's mother. She didn't see him because she was facing the other way, but it was her hair.

Now he hurried, running across the store. His foot caught on the edge of a loose tile, and he dropped the recorder before he got to the door.

Zach's mother was right out there. The jingling keys were closer. He kept going.

He jumped through the doorway.

And then everything went wrong.

Everything.

When he landed outside, Zach's mother was gone. He looked around for her, but she was not there.

And it was worse than that. Much worse.

There was no parking lot.

In its place was a big lake of dark water with big rocks sticking up out of it.

He turned to go back—to get the tape recorder. Dropping it had been stupid. He needed the woman on the tape.

The door was gone, too.

Behind him was nothing but more lake. He was surrounded by water, standing on a rock of his own. The rock was a little larger than the others, about the size of the rug that his bed sat on in the apartment in New York.

"A smart boy. A brave boy," the woman on the tape said in his head, but with a hiss, as if her voice were still coming from the machine.

He tried to ask her for help, but nothing came out. It was like one of his bad dreams, where he couldn't talk, even when he wanted to.

"Egress," the woman on the tape said. "Egress."

More hiss. And something that sounded like, "Mind the Moses." She said she was sorry.

Then the stop button clicked on its own, and she said nothing more.

Zach stood alone on a rock, trapped in the middle of the big water on a starless night.

TWENTY-SIX

·······································

AUSTEN'S NIGHTLIGHTS

Porter passed out in mid-step. He pitched forward, and Po caught him before he could fall on his face. Ken picked him up and carried him as if he were a child. That had been some distance back, miles after they got off the bus in the dark and watched its red taillights fade into faraway flares they could still see after the sound of its engine faded.

They left the road and walked in the direction Porter indicated, through overgrown farm fields and woods thick as a crowd, crossing streams of black along the way. Paul didn't mind getting wet. It meant putting water between him and the Ravagers. He had no idea what Brill was using to track them, nor did he know if a running creek had any effect on it. He was comforted all the same, a fox outsmarting the pursuing hounds.

Then Porter had fainted, spent after saving them from the Ravagers on the bus. Paul had doubted him before, but not now. The gray man was giving his all.

Po agreed with Porter's choice of route, signing to Ken that they were headed in the direction Paul needed to go. Paul asked where that was.

"If he knows, he won't tell me," Ken said.

"How would he know?"

"He declines to share that. He has said that in such situations, he applies the story that fits best, and Po knows many a tale. It's then a question of whether the tale of Paul ends the same as the story Po deems to be a good match. It is an art."

Paul glanced at Rain to see if she was listening. He couldn't tell. "What's my tale?"

"Only you can know for certain," Ken said. "Po is making his best guess."

They walked on, crossing a field of thigh-high grass. The moonless sky was an inverted bowl of glistening dust.

"We are the stories we tell ourselves," Porter said from the cradle of Ken's arms. Ken stopped, apparently to see if the Envoy would rather continue on his own. Porter's jaw sagged. He was out again.

"I don't get it," Paul said.

"It is an old saying to explain the Journey and the mythicals encountered along the path—both those who help and those who seek to hinder."

A warm breeze rustled the grass and the branches of a line of tall trees up ahead. A thick windbreak separated their field from the next. The land they crossed was yet another abandoned farm.

"I still don't get it," Paul said.

Rain gave him a playful whack on the shoulder. Paul hadn't realized she'd drawn so close.

"I am who I say I am—the story I tell myself—just as you are who you say you are or said you were in life," Ken explained. "Your Journey determines whether that tale is valid. You are also the stories that others tell of you. The truth of who you were, are, and will be lies somewhere among those tales."

Po signed. "The mythicals," Ken said for him, "began as the creations of others—as invented stories told of them. Yet once created, mythicals continue their tales themselves. If someone once said Po was a warrior monk, then that was all he was until he began to fashion his own story—to live. Now he is more. Now he is angry."

The monk shot Ken a look. "That last point was mine," Ken said. They entered the trees, which were woodlands, not a mere windbreak. "Simply put, you are your idea of you. And you are others' ideas of you, whether you wish to be or not."

They walked along in near-total darkness, following Ken and Po, who had no trouble seeing where they were going.

"But you can't tell me what IMUURS means," said Paul.

"No."

"What about the other thing? Unus omnibus..."

"Unus pro omnibus. Omnes pro uno. It's Latin. One for all, all for one. A more accurate translation, I believe, is, 'One among many, many among one.' All things are joined and cannot be made separate. Though Brill is trying, and he has to work very hard to do so."

"Get it?" Rain said.

"I'm not sure. I tell the story of me. Other people tell the story of me. Which is stronger?"

"That is what your Journey determines," Ken said.

"That's what Brill steals," said Rain.

"Indeed," said Ken. "Brill has convinced all under his control that their story is the story he tells of them, not that which they tell of themselves. They don't even know there is a difference. Reality is what he says it is, the power his. However, all things are one. If the many ever choose to leave him, he cannot stop them, so long as it's the power of all, acting for all, freely exercised."

"It's that strong?"

"It is all."

As they neared the far edge of the woods, the blue glow of dawn peeked through the trees. Paul was shocked by how quickly the night had gone, at the way time passed differently in The Commons. The light washed Porter's exhaustion in blue. He was a phantom, no life apparent.

"Can't we take him somewhere?"

"We are," Ken said. "Where he wishes to go—with you."

"Maybe we can just stop for a second."

Ken showed no sign of hearing. Paul planted himself in the mummy's way, hand out to halt his progress. The big mummy could easily have plowed Paul under, but he stopped.

"I just want him to be okay," Paul said. Rain and Po stopped, too. "What isn't Porter telling me, Ken?"

"He withholds what he does not know. The Commons in the open, where the Journey occurs, has changed a great deal while Porter was forced to wait. It is far more chaotic now, as he has told you. Bona fides and mythicals mix in ways that were not seen the last time he led a Journey. He is aware of this gap in his knowledge. Yet you could not be in more capable hands."

"That covers the things he can't tell me. There's more."

"Yes."

"Things he won't tell me."

"Yes." Po signed to Ken, but the mummy kept his eyes on Paul. "I am prudent, but Po and I will say what Porter will not. With your defeat of the Ravagers, you've displayed a power that we have not witnessed before, and we have seen much. Whether you'll use it again, whether you'll learn how, I do not know. But I believe your Journey could be one that upsets the current balance of power in The Commons. I believe Brill realizes this after your victory, and I believe he is worried. What worries Brill gives us hope, and we have not had that for a long time. Thus, nothing is as important as getting you to Journey's End. Not myself. Not Po, not Rain, not Porter. So we walk."

With that, the mummy got moving, as did Po. "I trust you know what I meant," Ken said to Rain as he passed her.

She nodded and waited for Paul to continue on. When he didn't, she took him by the hand and led him through the trees.

And even after he needed no leading, she held on.

THEY EMERGED from the trees to find that the blue glow was not a coming dawn at all. The sky above was still powdered with stars, but the hill in front of them was backlit by an azure corona—the source of the light.

Po ran at the hill and was swallowed by its blackness. The little monk wasn't slowed in the least by the climb. A short time later, his silhouette popped up at the top, a nub on an eclipse that exhaled the sweet smell of grass on the wind.

The others followed.

Near the zenith, they looked up to see Po leaping about like a puppy. Framed in cerulean, he signed at Ken, who squinted to read what his friend was trying to tell him.

"That cannot be," the mummy said. He climbed faster, as if Porter were now weightless.

"What?" said Paul.

At the top of the hill, Porter began to stir. Ken set him down.

The Envoy, still drained but now on his own two feet, looked down the other side of the hill at whatever was giving off the light. Despite his fatigue, he let out a cry, amazed.

Paul and Rain closed the distance and crested the hill.

The sight before them was magic in the night. The slope of the next hill was dotted with hundreds of pale blue fires set in intricate spirals that joined one another, separated, and joined again.

The entire hillside and the surrounding darkness were riddled with dancing flame.

"Wow," Rain said.

"What is it?" said Paul.

"Something I never thought I'd see," Porter replied. "Austen's Nightlights. A safe haven."

Po turned to Paul with a grin. His fingers were a blur of rapid-fire signing. Any faster, and he might well have floated over to the next hill.

"What's he saying?"

Glee crept into Ken's normally measured tone as his friend's joy became contagious. "He's saying, 'Do you see, Paul? Paul, do you see?'"

The monk's smile grew wider still. He turned and ran down the hill in a descent just shy of a controlled fall, straight at the fiery swirls, laughter trailing behind him.

PORTER REFUSED TO BE CARRIED, but Ken helped him along as the group hiked up the hill and into the blue flame.

Each fire burned in a stone brazier set on stubby legs. Rugs woven with complex whorls ran between the fires in paths of gold and crimson that morphed into other hues when stared at.

"Who's Austen?" Paul said.

"Merely a legend—I thought," said Porter. "As the story goes, he was a Journeyman whose Envoy was killed. He created this from a dream as a neutral zone to protect himself from whatever it was that attacked them."

"Did it work?"

"Unknown. For us, it will—for tonight. It'll be gone come morning, but until then, nothing else can get in now that we've laid claim to it."

Po signed to Ken. "Why is it here at all?" the mummy said for him. "Why now?"

"Any answer I give is speculation. I never believed this existed, and I've never known anyone who's seen it in person. It's said that the Nightlights come from a place of mercy." The Envoy turned to Paul. "That they're here now says something good about your Journey and you, I think." He looked at Rain. "And maybe not just you."

Rain eyed the ground shyly. In the blue glow, her hair shone like raven feathers.

Porter eased himself down onto one of the rugs, close to its fire. "Perhaps you're more than guns and monsters after all." He laid back to look up at the stars.

Ken and Po each took a rug, too, sitting down to take in the view and serenity.

Paul and Rain remained standing. "Is it safe to walk around?" Paul said.

Porter gave no answer. He was fast asleep again, but it looked to be a more peaceful rest than the state of exhaustion of just a short time before.

"This is a safe haven," Ken said.

Paul's eyes met Rain's and held. They walked off among the hillside's fires.

LYING ON A RUG by the fires at the spiral's edge, Rain sitting next to him, Paul scanned the night sky for the constellations that Pop Mike made every New Beginnings kid learn. Stars were dreams, they were told, and you couldn't aim for a dream if you didn't know its name.

He saw nothing familiar above.

Rain finished cleaning and reassembling her shotgun, facing away from Paul and the fire. She blocked her own light, but Paul suspected she could do the routine in total darkness. She'd hardly stopped moving since their arrival at the Nightlights.

"Are you all right?"

"No." She checked the gun's action. "I've never been all right."

"We can pick another fire—one closer in."

She shook her head.

"We're safe here." He thought he heard her laugh. "Porter said nothing bad can get in."

"It already has."

"Who don't you trust?" He sat up.

She stopped working. "I shouldn't be here."

"We're okay. You've got the cleanest shotgun in The Commons. And we have a kick-ass monk, a big-ass mummy, and a guy who can make us disappear if we need to. I'm not worried."

"Maybe you should be." She checked the shotgun's action again. "We don't know each other. Not how you think." Before Paul could come up with a response, she reached into her pocket and pulled out her box of candy. Shaking a couple into her palm, she offered him one.

He popped it into his mouth and immediately wished he hadn't. "Thanks."

"You don't have to be polite. I don't like them, either. If you're a licorice fan, they're the best thing ever. If you're not, they're just something to endure."

"So why eat them?"

"Exactly." She handed him the box.

He tipped the red-and-gold label toward the blue flames to see it better. "Gee-foo?"

"Sisu. It's Finnish. It's the spirit of not giving up, even when things are hopeless. You go on. No matter what."

He tried to apply that concept to dissolving the candy in his mouth as quickly as possible. "Is that me? Hopeless? Does anyone get to the end of a Journey anymore?"

"Does it matter?"

Paul worked on the Sisu, refusing to surrender. "I'm worried about Porter."

"Me, too. He didn't know what he was getting into with this assignment. Not that it would have stopped him. He's hurting. If he keeps this up"— she snapped something together, took it apart, and snapped it together once more, satisfied with the sound this time—"we'll just have to pick up the slack."

"Not you. This is on me."

She swiveled around to watch the blue flames with him. "Why were you on that bus, Paul? What was waiting for you in San Francisco? Besides Gaia."

"It's what wasn't waiting." He reached out to the fire. It was not hot. When he let it lick his palm, there was only a tingle, which brought with it a sense of things being better than they'd been before he made contact. Even the Sisu didn't taste so bad. "Reminders."

"Of?"

"Everything that told me I was nothing." He put his entire hand into the flames. His fear of honesty burned away. "My mother gave me up because she couldn't handle having a kid around. Maybe she really couldn't—I don't know—but the fact that she didn't even try doesn't make me feel like much. Then she was gone." He wanted to say everything, even if Rain wasn't willing to do the same. "I've jumped around my whole life. New Beginnings— the place I lived in New York—was the longest I stayed anywhere, but even that reminded me, 'Hey, kid—don't forget. You're nothing.'"

"Do you believe that?"

He removed his hand from the fire. It was unharmed. "I don't know."

"I'll say this again and again until you hear it. Porter's putting everything he has into this. I'm here, and so are Ken and Po. Would we do that for nothing?"

"That's the problem."

"What?"

"You all think I matter. I'm not used to it."

"Me, neither."

"You? You're"—he wrestled the word beautiful down just in time—"you count. You have an effect on people."

"Oh, absolutely. Just ask the ones I shoot."

The laugh he waited for didn't come. He saw the Ravagers disappearing because of him, and he understood. "I've lost as many fights as I've won. What does that count for, in the end?"

"Most of them? Nothing," she said. "If you're lucky, you have maybe one important fight in your life. If you're lucky."

He considered that, surrendering to the hypnosis of the flames. "Okay, what about that one?"

"That one you have to win."

DURING THE NIGHT, Paul dreamt that Porter spoke with a woman somewhere off in the dark, as far away as the Envoy could be without leaving the protection of the fires.

The woman shouldn't have been able to enter the Nightlights zone. She shouldn't even have been able to see them. But rules were ever-changing in The Commons, and more so in its dreams.

She and Porter spoke quietly, voices low. The woman remained in shadow.

In the phantasmal air, Paul smelled smoke from something other than the Nightlights. It was the ghost of far-away fire, of long ago—the memory of a burning that would not heal. The woman couldn't get close to the blue flames.

Closed lids. Asleep, aware.

Her voice was that of someone older, but it had steel in it. She and Porter had scars in common.

Their words became clear, easily heard, as if Paul were standing with the two old Envoys. Which is what they were.

"This is the job, Jonas," she said. "The work of now. The work of to be."

In the dream, there were masses of people behind the woman, just out of reach of the Nightlights, beyond the shadows cast. Their ranks stretched far off into the night.

He had no sense of their numbers. There were far too many for that. But they watched him.

The dream was of all-seeing eyes.

WHEN PAUL AWOKE in the morning, he and Rain were huddled together in the dewy grass. The rug and fire were gone.

He'd thrown an arm over her. She hugged her holstered gun.

If the fires were gone, so was their protection.

He sat up. Rain stirred.

Po stood a distance away, his back to them. Paul suspected that the monk had been facing them only moments before, keeping watch. He'd never seen him or Ken sleep.

Rain shook her hair out and tied it up in a ponytail. Paul got up and stretched, and they started back to where they'd left Porter and Ken.

"Good morning," Rain said to Po as they passed him in the empty grass, the Nightlights nowhere to be seen. The little man nodded, and Paul was struck by how well he'd learned to read the monk's expressions. Po wanted them to understand that he'd intruded only enough to ensure their safety.

Porter and Ken sat in the grass as if the rugs and fiery bowls were still there. They all exchanged good mornings. Po walked past them and stopped a few yards away, looking down the hill at an empty road snaking off into the distance below.

"I cannot believe this is the same person who demolished a dozen men in a diner," Porter said, watching him. "It's hard to think he was so angry, even though I saw the aftermath for myself."

"He is still angry," Ken said. "It does not fade. He merely distracts it when he can." He stood to follow Po's gaze down the road.

Paul looked, too, but saw nothing.

"It is diversion at best, not true calm," the mummy continued. "My real fear is that if he were left to his own devices, his fights would end only with his death or the death of his opponents. So I finish them for him, before that can happen."

"He can hear this, right?" Rain said.

"I would not trouble myself saying it if he could not. He needs to know where he must improve."

The monk turned to face them, as if preparing a rejoinder of some sort. Then they all heard what had drawn his attention.

The faint grind of an approaching engine.

PAUL'S EYES weren't nearly as good as Po's, but by the time the approaching vehicle pulled to the side of the road at the base of their hill, he could see it was an old Volkswagen microbus painted in a camouflage motif. It was the kind Pop Mike referred to as a hair-madillo whenever anyone asked the old man about the office-wall photo of his younger self, sporting shoulder-length hair and a collar-brushing beard, standing next to one.

"How are you feeling?" Ken asked Porter as two men and a woman climbed out of the van and made their way toward them in the early-morning light. The trio's camouflage fatigues and dark hair blended with the landscape to produce the effect of three disembodied faces in buoyant ascent.

"Like a kitten at four a.m., and the world's my owner's toe," the Envoy said, stretching dramatically for effect. He appeared to be refreshed, but his foot-pouncing days, if not behind him forever, were a few more nights' rest away. His cough did nothing to alter that impression.

The visitors climbed quickly. They were fit.

From the neck up, all three—who looked to be in their early thirties—were the type one would expect to see climb out of a VW bus. The men had hair past their shoulders, one with a beard to match. The woman's thicket of curly hair was held in place by a headband with beaded flowers sewn into it.

They walked with a straight-backed, stiff-shouldered gait that spoke of hours of drilling, and each had a pistol on the hip. Their shoulder patches would have been appropriate for a Marine recruiting poster had they not featured pink-and-yellow peace signs.

"Let me get this straight," said the bearded one when they were close enough for conversation. "I missed a once-in-a-lifetime chance at Austen's Nightlights because some ratty old coot got here first?"

Porter squared up to face him. Paul and Rain did the same.

Ken and Po, curiously, remained loose. Paul wasn't concerned, however; he'd seen how fast the two could fly into action when needed.

"Sad to say, yes," Porter said. "And wouldn't it just dump sand in your shorts if this old coot booted your ass up to your eyebrows?"

The bearded man locked eyes with the Envoy. "He never gets any more agreeable, does he?"

"Be serious," the woman said. "He's lost ground."

The stare-down continued for long seconds. The bearded man broke into a grin, let out a cry, and opened his arms for a hug. Porter obliged.

"Your note said you'd be in last night," the man said. "We were scared to death when you didn't show. We came looking."

"I'm sorry," Porter said. "Our party's grown, and I haven't the strength to keep jumping everyone all over The Commons. Anyway, it wouldn't be a proper Journey if I did, as you know. Didn't you receive my update?"

"Who could decrypt it?" The woman gave Porter a hug of her own. "Your key is ten generations old."

"My Corps credit card's no good. If the system's been compromised, I can't trust the official channels." He finished the trio off with a big hug for the second man. "I'm dragging. The Nightlights could not have been timed better."

A seriousness overtook the four—a group acknowledgement of a weight Paul couldn't name.

The other man broke the spell. "How were they?"

"I'd be lying if I told you they were anything less than transcendent—and you'd know it. My apologies."

"Don't be ridiculous," the woman said. "They appear to those in need. Missing them is a sign that life's going well."

Porter made a round of introductions. The bearded man was Liam and his wife was Nicolette. The other man, who was only a few inches shorter than Ken, was D.W.

They lived a few hours' drive from the Nightlights. At the speed Porter's group had been traveling, it would have been at least another two days of walking before they reached them.

"We had dinner ready," Nicolette said.

"Let's make it breakfast, then." Porter bounced his staff on the toe of his boot.

"Breakfast is long gone by now. Your group's not the only one growing. We have a lot more mouths to feed than we did last time we saw you. You'll be surprised."

"This Journey's already full of surprises," Porter said.

....

TWENTY-SEVEN

WESTON

nnie's knee marked the miles. Char helped distract her via text, explaining the way things stood from her perspective, which, she admitted, was limited. Mostly, the diversion was enough. Mostly.

June Medill had reported Char as a risk, which had tossed her back into the hordes of stored people and their Essence. It was the best thing that could have happened to her. Now Char was more deeply tapped into a key sector of the network, and while she couldn't see who was in that sector with her, it allowed her to do more for Annie than she otherwise might have.

Had June known she was setting Charlene up to go where she was needed? Had she done it on purpose? Annie thought so. Char disagreed. But help was help, and Annie said a small prayer for June Medill.

Annie had no idea where to find Zach. Having escaped the pinkies' mist, she was sharp again. With that came the knowledge that her current world was not real. Plus, as any jury of mothers would unanimously agree were she tried before them, she had abandoned her son.

That was the worst of it. The rest wasn't much better.

She was, as Charlene explained it, dead—in a place ruled by the vulture-investor version of the Devil, who used people like Annie to stay on top. She and her colleagues helped Spreadsheet Satan manage his assets while June Medill and her cohorts kept the workforce doped up on their addiction of choice.

Charlene, for her part, was back in webs, or floating in a bog, or suffering some other horror. She didn't share, and whether it was because she didn't want to tip the powers-that-be off to who she was or just that she didn't want to talk about it, Annie didn't ask. She was grateful for the assist and the presence of an old friend.

She walked a landscape left by those whose Journeys had been stolen. Some of what she traversed had, in turn, been altered by the scattered few who were still free and wandering. If you were out and about and didn't give Mr. Brill a reason to come after you—gathering in groups large enough to challenge him or to make it worth sending the Ravagers in—you could live among the mythicals and pretend everything was groovy.

All you had to do was abandon the dream of anything better and live off the leavings.

What Annie needed to remember about those leavings, Char told her repeatedly, was that many of them were challenges untaken—traps set to capture, injure, or kill. The world was loaded with monsters to battle, deadly puzzles to solve, and friends who were not friends.

She had to watch her back.

Even with that and the small matter of every step hurting like hell, she was thankful. The farther she got from Mr. Brill's nerve center, the less she worried about being pursued by his minions.

The detritus of other lives and memories was something to behold, too. A while after making her way from White Marsh Hall, as Char informed her the abandoned mansion was called, Annie found herself crossing a vast artificial moonscape complete with a lunar lander that appeared to have been designed by a second-grader with a crayon.

Past the lander, she limped into a barren plain dotted with filled-in craters.

A click from behind.

Annie turned to see a sheet-metal moon man pop up out of an open pit, bullseye targets on forehead and chest, a bubble-tipped rifle aimed her way. She stared at him. He stared back.

As if disappointed, he sank back down into the crater, which closed over him. A scratchy recorded laugh came from somewhere in the sky above.

That happened four more times. It was a life-sized shooting game that mocked her whenever she missed the opportunity to nail a target, which was often.

After that came a roller coaster made of rotten ivy-covered timbers, and then a haunted boat ride—its trough dry and strewn with trash, its cave mouth dark and vacant. She passed that cave as fast as she was able. No telling what called it home now.

A rebel underground was fully operational in Mr. Brill's empire, Char told her. It existed on multiple levels—sparks weak in isolation, but a flame of hope when united.

The most at-risk members were those closest to Mr. Brill, the ones in his office. They played key roles as direct parts of his operation, but they couldn't be relied upon because they were also the most likely to be caught.

Details of the rebellion were distributed. Char knew what she needed to know and nothing more. If Mr. Brill intercepted Char's texts—possible, even with the encryption chops of Char's compatriots— he'd have but a fraction of the picture.

Annie figured that Mr. Brill had never had kids or pets. Anyone with a five-year-old or a beagle could tell you: attempt to control life however you like, but even little victories cost you big—and you never succeed completely.

Life did what it wanted, and that's what Mr. Brill's stored energy—the stolen humanity, with its love, fears, and dreams—aimed to do. It wanted out.

Mr. Brill's comatose charges dreamt, and in those dreams found others with the same visions. They tapped into the massed Essence to communicate and guide, albeit with stealth and care. Mr. Brill could shut it all down—but only if he knew about it.

Charlene related this in text after text, and Annie took it in line by line. The fact that she'd read it all meant she'd been walking forever. And when she checked her battery and realized she'd need to save her juice for when it really counted, she turned her phone off.

Past the amusement park was an empty shopping mall done up in an amusement-park theme. The faux-marble pillars outside the dead department stores featured vintage-esque signs for a place called Wonderland. Annie passed a banner featuring cane-bearing gents and parasol-carrying women gunning down moon men. The mall was inspired by the old park she'd just crossed.

People once had fun for its own sake. Then fun became shopping with a fun veneer. Such a place was without a spirit long before Mr. Brill came to take it.

After the mall came a narrow, cracked road with the remnants of a double-yellow line running down its center. Annie soon reached an intersection where the pavement ahead was torn up for construction, broken into large chunks of decaying asphalt. She had no choice but to turn left onto an even narrower road, identified by a rust-abbreviated sign as "ntier."

Her little boy was out here. On his own.

"Bad parent" was too kind a term for her level of failure. Avenging Annie, Char used to call her when she was hell-bent on fixing someone's mistake, but Char knew enough to leave it alone when Annie was tackling one of her own.

At the end of the road, she did her lopsided lope through a gravel parking lot filled with the oxidized corpses of a dozen school buses. They rested on squashed tires that lent them a cockeyed, lazy composure. The question of the name on the partial sign was answered by the neatly painted letters on the side of each: Frontier Day Camp.

She continued down a gravel road, past an assortment of storage sheds and two hulking converted barns. The place had been a farm before it was a camp.

The roll-up door to one of the barns was open. Inside, generations of kids and counselors had marked their time at Frontier in thick, bright paint. Diane did so in broad aqua strokes in '68. Mush followed in coral with an even wider brush in '72. Skeeter left word in hunter green a year later.

The road took her along an overgrown athletic field and a ring of painted turquoise boulders placed around a fire pit. It ran off into a treed-in patch just past a swimming pool that the years had turned into an algae-crusted petri dish. The hurricane fence surrounding it was no longer any sort of barrier, but no kid would get near that water, given the stink and the likelihood of snapping turtles the size of rider-mowers beneath the slime. And there weren't any children around anyway.

She damn near missed the Black Hawk.

Annie only happened to look back because she wanted to see how far she'd come. Spotting the helicopter across the athletic field with the sun in her eyes, the machine's paint job camouflaging it against the trees, was a matter of not-to-be-hoped-for-twice luck.

She hit the deck. They'd all watched the propaganda videos of the Ravagers running live-fire exercises in the choppers. June Medill had followed Truitt's orders to the letter and made the data-diggers watch the footage to remind them of who they worked for—and what kind of strength backed him. It wasn't unheard of for the Black Hawks and their Ravagers to hunt down staffers like her who decided the job was no longer a fit.

You didn't resign. Mr. Brill retired you. Everyone knew that.

Limping along, how long had she been exposed to those in the Black Hawk or to the troopers who might be deployed around the field? There was a chance that they weren't looking for her—that they were on some unrelated mission. But she knew how tightly Mr. Brill managed resources—all expenditures were about ROI, and she'd taken a lot of know-how with her.

She remained flat on her stomach on the crushed stone, waiting to hear the sound of boots on gravel or feel the prod of a rifle barrel in the back. Between wondering how she'd be able to make her way out of range and worrying over her lack of progress toward Zach, it only felt like a month or two.

She'd been dumb-lucky all along, or maybe Truitt and the boys were just toying with her to see where she'd go. She prepared herself for the inevitable crackle of a nearby radio or a truncheon upside the skull.

What she didn't count on was what she got— the rapid-fire knock of a far-off woodpecker, the trill of a cicada, and long silences. No arrest. No boots swishing through the knee-high grass of the overgrown field. Nothing.

She didn't feel safe enough to stand and survey the area. So she fired up her phone to see if Char knew how many units were operating in the area or, that being too much to ask, something as simple as where the hell she was.

The phone greeted her with zero bars, zero signal. Yet an answer awaited her: "Your ride's here."

AFTER A SUFFICIENT AMOUNT of time in combat, Annie lost the ability to wake up in the morning without the fear that someone out there might want her dead.

Developing that level of foreboding required two shots. The first had to be close, the next nearer still. With the second one came the realization that the shooter was trying to leave you bleeding in the dirt and was, in fact, methodically sighting in to ensure that you soon would be.

It dawned on you that some people's plans involved stopping your heart. After that, you no longer saw the world as a place that by default desired you to be in it.

Everything took on a muted tone of vigilance. Beware the unseen who sees.

So Annie decided against strolling across the field to the chopper, shouting out greetings and asking the Ravagers what kind of MRE desserts they might like to trade. She advanced with care— poised for the static rising up the spine that would have her kissing the ground, frantic, weighing her next move on the way down.

Closing in, she saw, heard, and felt nothing. That didn't soothe her in the least. If the chopper was her way onward—and she noted that Charlene had never said where it would take her—who was supposed to fly the thing?

She saw who wasn't supposed to when she drew close enough to spot the toes of two polished black boots through the open side hatch. Those boots didn't move, and she knew that no matter how sneaky she'd been, she'd made enough noise for whoever was inside to hear her.

Her days as a trained warrior slipping unheard over the sand were long gone. She was a freaked-out mom who had no practice advancing through tall grass in a hot situation. Yet whoever was in those boots didn't budge when she snapped a stick beneath her heel.

Because there wasn't anyone in them. The uniform draped over the seat was empty, too, as if the person who'd worn it had been spirited away or turned to powder, like the unnamed grayscale soldiers in late-night alien-invasion movies. The helicopter's only inhabitant was a dead pilot whose arms dangled at his sides, fingernails a half-inch shy of scraping the cockpit floor.

Annie entertained the notion that maybe Char knew what she was talking about—that maybe the helicopter represented no threat. In which case, the worst part of the situation was that there were no living fliers to be seen.

She worked her way around the Black Hawk and peered into the cockpit at the slumped body of the pilot. He looked like he'd fallen asleep, his bones jellied while he dreamt of someplace better.

He was pitched forward in his harness, his helmet's ebony face-plate an electrical storm of cracks. Blood crusted his pants and seat. Maybe he'd had a hard landing against the control panel, had broken his neck. Whatever had befallen him, he wasn't taking her anywhere.

Wait—what was she doing?

A man was dead, Ravager or no, and she thought only of what he couldn't do for her? Maybe the pinkies weren't entirely gone from her system.

How many pilots had she known during her deployment? Could she remember their names now? Where had her caring gone?

Ravagers had no identification on their black uniforms. Brill thought of them as just another asset, and he exploited their sense of duty to command them. They wore no dog tags. They had no identities. So there was nothing to call the dead man unless she gave him a name of her own.

The only one that came to her was that of a ghostly soldier from TV-watching years gone by. Weston. The pilot would be Chief Warrant Officer Weston, a name that was better than none at all.

"I'm sorry, Weston," she told the dead man. "I wish there were more I could do for you."

Weston showed no gratitude. But he wore an M9 in a holster. However she moved on from this place—whether by air as Char indicated or at her own limping pace—it would be a good idea to arm herself.

She surveyed the scene behind her yet again. She saw no signs of life across the field. There was no helpful pilot on his or her way to whisk her off into the sky and carry her to Zach.

The Commons was built on dream and memory, but Brill owned most of both. The Annies of The Commons didn't receive deliverance from thin air.

A breeze kicked up, rustling the tall grass in the sun. The warmth of the sound in contrast to her predicament brought a small stab of despair. The real world was giant enough. This one, for all she knew, was even larger.

Zach was out there in it, and she didn't know where. The promise of a ride to him—if indeed that was what Char meant, and if indeed it really was Char texting her—was a heartless prank.

The grass swayed. The leaves in the nearby trees whispered. They said that Annie was stuck with a dead pilot.

What she heard next ran counter to that. She hadn't been doped up enough to forget the sound of a Beretta slide pulling and returning to chamber a round.

She faced the cockpit again. What registered first was the intense blue of CWO Weston's right eye, now seen easily as he glared through his shattered visor.

The next thing was the terrible void of the barrel's nose. She couldn't help but stare into it—and at the former dead man who aimed it.

TWENTY-EIGHT

....

A STRANGELOVE FETISH

The hair-madillo, as it turned out, was a far cry from its underpowered Type Two forebear. It was electric, armored, and quick.

Nicolette drove, and the ride was so smooth that Paul didn't realize how fast they were going until he checked the speedometer. The needle was nestled comfortably at 125. These hippies liked their tech.

After a half-hour ride that would've taken twice that in a lesser vehicle, they left the highway. A series of ever-narrowing roads carried them past overgrown fields, abandoned houses, and imploded barns. Emaciated cattle, their hides taut like shrink-wrapped calaveras, were penned in by wire fences of barbs and rust. D.W. explained that the landscape had been shaped by one Journeyman's memories of childhood farm foreclosures and the misery and decline that followed.

Several more turns put them on a pitted road winding through woods of primeval density. The surfaces were more pothole than pavement, but again, Paul wouldn't have known had he not looked at the asphalt ahead. The microbus absorbed the terrain's abuse with ease and handled curves like it was traveling a track designed just for it.

As they approached a house-sized pile of rocks and rubble, a hole of light up ahead indicated they'd soon be leaving the trees. Nicolette let up on the gas, and Liam thumbed a password into his smartphone.

The front of the pile lifted up—a gate revealing a hidden garage. Nicolette cut the bus to the opposite side of the road and backed in.

"Neat," Porter said as they climbed out. "I don't remember this."

"We keep plenty busy with mods and projects," D.W. said. "We don't want to announce our presence to anyone passing through."

"Who would that be?"

"Ravagers, mostly. They already know about us, of course, but they have no idea how we've grown."

"And how have you grown?"

D.W. chuckled as the gate dropped behind him. The garage was a pile of rocks again. Water even burbled up from between two of the larger stones, completing the deception.

They walked out of the woods and across a field to a downcast one-room cabin that looked as if it could be flattened by a sneeze. After the impressive illusion of the garage, Paul expected to step into a high-tech palace, but the interior matched the outside. A couple of old chairs whose glue had long since departed flanked a neglected fireplace and a table that hadn't seen level in decades, if ever.

Paul tried to keep the surprise off his face. Rain surveyed the room with a practiced stoicism. Ken and Po, similarly, betrayed nothing.

Nicolette seemed touched by the group's attempt at manners.

Liam pressed his palm against a portion of the wall over the fireplace. The wood glowed green under his hand. A section of the rough plank floor opened with a hydraulic hiss, exposing a steel stairway lit by indigo LEDs.

"Come on down," Nicolette said. "You'll love what we've done in the basement."

MR. BRILL SAT SLUMPED in his desk chair, eyes closed and head back, as if dozing. Truitt knew better. The big man was hard at work in the guise of the Shade, lids fluttering as he guided the shadow beast. He merged more completely with it, his breathing deeper.

The monitors floating around Mr. Brill displayed what the monster saw. It traveled through thick woods, outpaced by the microbus driven by the Envoy's friends.

Two sources tracked the movements of the Envoy and Journeyman. The first was the visual input from the Shade. The second was a data stream available only to Mr. Brill. He'd shared nothing about it with Truitt.

The Shade rested. Sheltered from the morning sun by the trees, it studied the tiny cabin as the pathetic structure slowly lost its struggle against gravity in the adjacent field.

Rhythmic blades announced the approach of a Ravager helicopter overhead. Mr. Brill stirred in his trance.

When the beat of the chopper's rotor was loudest, the Shade rushed the cabin. The ground around it remained in shadow as it kept pace with the Black Hawk above. It stayed beneath the machine as it buzzed the sad little hut, safe from the sun's damaging rays.

The beast plowed into the cabin door, smashing it open. Mr. Brill grunted with the effort. The barrier had been more solid than it looked.

The Shade entered, panting, Mr. Brill breathing with it. A look around revealed a dirty little space that appeared to be unoccupied.

But Mr. Brill had chosen to focus on it. Mr. Brill did nothing without a reason, and that reason was always profit.

THE STAIRS DESCENDED ten long flights beneath the surface. At the bottom, Liam led them through three heavy access hatches as thick as Paul's arm was long, each of which required a breath scan from him before opening. They entered a tunnel hallway large enough to accommodate foot and vehicle traffic together and passed both as they progressed deeper into what looked to be a military complex.

The people in the tunnels were dressed in uniforms identical to those worn by their three hosts. All sported headbands and beads—the women with hair past their shoulders, the men with equally long hair, many with beards as well.

Some carried clipboards, like counselors headed off to teach campers the proper care of an automatic weapon. Others had laptops. All were armed.

It was some operation. Even the usually guarded Rain appeared to be impressed as she watched the hippie soldiers and their firepower.

They stopped at an elevator, and she caught the eye of a passing soldier who looked to be about her age. The guy smiled. She held his gaze for a long second before looking away.

Paul's face grew hot.

D.W. came to his rescue without knowing it by choosing that moment to start telling them about the complex. "We take credit for finding it, not building it. All this came from one Journeyman, a five-star general with a Strangelove fetish. Believe it or not, as much as we've grown, we only use part of the place. There are miles of tunnels and hundreds of missile silos. Frankly, we barely maintain security in our little sector as it is. We'd never be able to cover even a fraction of the thing."

Porter watched hippies pass as Nicolette stopped the group at a pair of brushed-steel elevator doors and pressed her palm to an adjacent reader pad. "All bona fides," he said. "Brill leaves you alone?"

"Ravagers probe our defenses, but they ease up if we don't fight back hard enough to make them suspect what's down here," Liam said. "The bona fides who've been hiding out up there all this time find their way here once they're told about us. We'd love to rescue the new people, too, but we can't afford to go to war."

"Yet," Nicolette added as the elevator arrived. "We can't yet."

THE SHADE SUCKED WET WIND, and Mr. Brill matched it breath for breath. Spinning in place, the monster scanned the cabin's interior. As it turned, ropes of black drool flew, splattering the walls, telling Mr. Brill all he needed to know about the space.

Truitt had to look away from the screen before he grew sick from the motion.

After too long a time for Truitt's taste, the spinning ceased. The beast's gaze focused on a spot in the middle of the floor. It hopped over to it, its breathing ragged and excited, and looked down at a patch of planks that, to Truitt's eye, were no different from its neighbors. They were all splinters and raised nail heads.

Again, Mr. Brill knew better. A portion of the wall over the fireplace glowed blue, and the section of floor in front of the Shade rose up, exposing a hatchway beneath.

Mr. Brill smiled again.

THE TRIP DOWN should have felt like jumping off a skyscraper, given how fast they plummeted, but there was no physical sensation of it. The chief indication of the elevator's speed was a digital readout indicating the number of feet passing. Paul tried to watch it, but the display made him feel queasy.

Next to the readout was an old military insignia that had been redone in rainbow colors. Dancing bears flanked it, and larger versions of the same peace signs that were on the hippie-soldier uniforms graced the doors.

"Your tax dollars at work," D.W. said. "Masada, only down deep, not up high."

A loud rumble shook the elevator as it reached bottom and came to a halt.

"Masada didn't end well, did it?" Nicolette said.

"Depends on whose side you were on," said Liam.

Paul didn't know what Masada was, but he liked neither the shaking nor the hippies' tone.

The doors slid open. Another tremor traveled through the car and the tunnel beyond. Several hippie soldiers ran by as Liam led the way out.

They hurried down the hall, Nicolette taking them through multiple steel-doored checkpoints with palm scanners. Within minutes, they entered a cathedral-sized control room carved out of the bedrock. Teams of hippie soldiers manned consoles facing a bank of screens that displayed views of the base's hallways and the ground above.

Three soldiers—two men and a woman—watched a bank of monitors offering a range of exterior views. All showed Ravager helicopters, trucks, and ground troops moving through the woods and converging on a set of massive doors set into a hillside.

Another impact from above made its way down to the room.

"Heavyweights at the gates, more at the silo lids," the woman said. "They're hitting the farther reaches with bunker busters. We'll hold for a while, but they'll be inside sooner or later if they're serious about it."

"How many?" D.W. said.

"Too many. More than usual—a lot more."

D.W. watched the Ravagers stream across the fields. He turned to Paul, then Porter. "The rumors got here ahead of you," he told the Envoy. "And the Nightlights. It all adds up to something. But what?"

"Unknown," Porter said. "We're on the road to find out."

Another explosion. A nearby console buzzed with the hit.

D.W. came to a decision. "The railroad."

Nicolette gave him a look.

"You have a better idea?" he said.

She didn't. Nor did her friends.

"Nobody's been down there for two years," Liam said. "It's charged?"

"The systems would let us know if it weren't," said D.W.

It was clear that Nicolette didn't agree with the call. She eyed Liam for support.

"I'll take them," he said.

Paul hoped it wasn't significant that Liam wouldn't look at Nicolette when he spoke. Or that she, in turn, wouldn't face them.

THEY RAN DOWN CORRIDORS, passing hippie soldiers headed the opposite way. Porter's breathing came hard, but each bomb that hit above only spurred them to go faster.

Liam stopped to load a small bag with homemade nutrition bars, bottles of water, and other provisions. They rushed through several dim meeting rooms and a gym, then down another long hallway.

Paul weighed the situation on the run. The hippies were in a hardened complex built to withstand a full-on assault. Yet they assumed their defenses would be breached. That spoke to the respect they had for the Ravager forces—and to how badly Brill wanted to find him.

As D.W. said, it all added up to something. How would Paul handle whatever that was?

They hurried through a staging room the size of an aircraft hangar. Table after table held plants that resembled those seen on every anti-drug poster made since the 1950s. Grow lamps lit them from above, and irrigation tubes hung from the ceiling.

Rain shot Liam a questioning glance.

"Hemp," he said as he stopped them at a hatch in the floor. He jammed a key into a heavy padlock holding a series of interlocking bars in place. It took a little jiggling—and a lot of language that would have earned him hours in the New Beginnings cool-off room—before the lock opened. The bar mechanism, rusted into place, required a number of boot-heel stomps before following suit.

The hatch groaned as Liam hauled it up. Clumps of accumulated muck dropped from its edges as he locked it into its open position. A set of steel steps—half staircase, half ladder—led down into black.

THE MURDER WAS PERSONAL. Truitt saw everything through the eyes of the Shade in movie-sized images on Mr. Brill's monitors, as if he were the life-taker. Surprisingly, the effect was not without its pleasure.

The security system that controlled the missile complex's elevator was no challenge for the monster. Because Mr. Brill's access to the Essence of The Commons itself was so far-reaching, little in the realm could refuse his will. It was only a matter of him taking an interest and judging the cost and effort to be worth the return.

Finding the boy was certainly that.

The elevator doors parted, revealing a long-haired young woman in military garb running past.

The Shade caught her and fed, the girl's cries such that the monitors' audio cut in and out as the system tried to compensate for the rise in pitch and volume.

The view tilted up to take in three armed soldiers rushing toward the scene of the attack. They hoped to rescue the girl, but wouldn't even be able to save themselves.

The Shade met them halfway. Mr. Brill gave a shuddering sigh.

The butchery complete, the dark beast continued down the hall, toward the sound of shouts and footsteps. Truitt found himself excited by how many there were.

Then he remembered his place.

THE LOWER TUNNEL was lit by a string of bare bulbs, though it was charitable to call it lighting in any meaningful sense. Liam led the group toward an older, smaller hatch. Atop it, water dripping from the rock ceiling had built itself a small stalagmite.

The vibration of another strike made its way down to them. The bulbs swung; the drips became dribbles.

This hatch wasn't locked. Paul considered asking Liam why they didn't worry about anyone coming up from below or errant hippies wandering down without permission. But he was going to find out regardless.

Liam pulled at a ring on the hatch, straining against a seal of water and gunk. He lifted it, and the ladder that was revealed in the dim light was gummy, damp, and old—a relic of the U.S.-Soviet arms race visited most frequently by flood and worms.

"I'd love to tell you it's not as bad as it looks," Liam said. "It's worse."

He grabbed three heavy-duty flashlights from the bag and handed them out. "There's an open-air train down there. It's ancient, but it works."

Porter, Ken, and Rain each took a light. Rain aimed hers down the ladder. The hatchway swallowed the beam, refusing to surrender its secrets to anyone who wouldn't give themselves over to it.

"The engine's a simple set-up," Liam said. "Right hand, gas. Left hand, brake. The battery's charged by a solar array up top. The tunnel ends under a complex that was never finished—miles from here. You with me?"

They nodded, accompanied by the buzz of another explosion.

"There are reasons we don't use this train. A lot of them. So move. They will hear you coming, but this is their hibernation season, and they'll be slow to wake up. Go full-out. Do not stop. Do not get off until the end. And do not think for one second that I am exaggerating." He scanned their faces to ensure the last part sunk in. "We wouldn't do this if there were any other way. Keep going, and you'll be clear before they get to you."

Liam looked at each of them again to ensure they understood the gravity of what he was saying. He stopped at Rain. "One more thing. I was going to be diplomatic, but there's no time."

Something huge hit up top, prompting heavier dribbling.

"We need to know we gave you an option, tough as it is," Liam told her. "The Ravagers want Paul, not you or the mythicals. It's Porter's job to take the crazy train. When Paul leaves, my guess is the Ravagers will break off, especially with the reception we're going to give them. It'll be too expensive for Brill to stick it out."

Another big hit. Water flowed freely.

"As a bona fide, you're a target for Brill out there. Your odds are better with us," Liam said. "Will you stay?"

A whump up above lent sound and feeling to the bomb Liam had dropped.

Rain was speechless.

"I'm sorry," Liam told Porter. "It's what we do. We have to ask."

"I understand," Porter said, watching Rain.

"It's your choice," Liam said to her. "If Paul's caught, so are you. We all want him to reach Journey's End. If he does—when he does—where can you go, assuming Brill knows your part in this?"

Rain looked to Porter, then Paul.

It was a knee in Paul's gut. The next bomb hit closer. He tried to prepare himself.

Boom.

"You decide," Rain said to Paul.

"What?"

"I'll come with you, or I'll stay here. What do you want?"

Her. More than anything he'd ever wanted. "Rain, I can't—"

Boom.

"I need to get up there," Liam said.

"Do you want me with you?" she asked as if he needed time to think it over. He already knew. He'd known since they met.

"Yes."

Boom.

"All right, then," Liam said. "Off we go. Remember. Right hand go, left hand stop."

Ken and Po hit the ladder and hurried down. Porter moved to the hatch next, stopping to shake Liam's hand.

"We'd planned a nicer trip for you," Liam said.

"I never intended to put you at risk," the Envoy replied. "We've done good business together, my friend."

"And will again. Good luck to you."

Porter started down.

Boom.

Rain took Liam's hand, one gun-toting pro to another. "Thanks for the offer."

"It stands as long as this place does."

She descended, leaving Liam and Paul.

"Oh, hey," Liam said.

Paul wasn't sure how to feel about him now. He wanted to believe Liam's offer to Rain was official, not personal. He wanted to.

The hippie soldier handed his bag to Paul. "Breakfast. Again, it was supposed to be hot. And better."

"It's fine," Paul said. He hoped that would prove to be true.

Boom.

Harder now. Louder.

Paul went down the ladder, and Liam shut the hatch above him.

THE OTHERS WAITED in the train tunnel below. The space was earthen, dark, and wet, and it didn't feel right. The cold moisture was one reason. The dankness and its odor of threat—the inside of a casket would smell like that—was another.

A string of free-hanging bulbs, many of them burned out, disappeared into the clammy distance. They provided a bit of light, revealing nothing more comforting ahead.

On the tracks sat a rusty, scum-layered mini-train with, as Liam had said, an open-air engine and cars. A filth-encrusted headlight on the engine did little to supplement the poor illumination provided by the bulbs.

Po was already at the controls, his robe smeared with the mud and grime that covered the train's every surface. Porter sat next to him.

Ken helped Paul off the ladder, which was missing its last few rungs.

Bumph.

The explosion, somewhat more muffled than those they'd heard on the next level up, dropped more mud onto the train. And them.

Somewhere nearby, a hard fall of water began. Paul followed Ken and Rain into the car behind the engine.

"Let's move before this thing becomes our tomb," Porter said.

Po squeezed the train's throttle. It responded with a loud bang. He tried again, prompting the same reply. The monk exchanged a look with Porter and massaged the handle.

Ba-bumph. The bombs were either getting bigger or penetrating more deeply.

Another squeeze. A slightly more subdued bang. One more try ended in a series of clicks and, finally, a hum from the engine.

The monk grabbed the filthy brake lever.

It didn't budge.

Ba-ba-bumph!

Mud and water rained down. A volleyball-sized rock followed. It just missed crushing Porter's skull and bounced off the hood of the engine, denting the steel and obliterating the headlight in a tinkle of glass.

MR. BRILL TWITCHED like a sleeping dog's leg as Truitt watched the monitors.

The Shade rushed past tables filled with small plants, the screen's perspective rising and dipping with the monster's off-kilter gait.

At the edge of the screen, a hippie soldier ran along an adjacent row of tables, headed back the other way. The man didn't spot the Shade in the dim light, and Mr. Brill couldn't be bothered with him now.

The monster reached out and ran its arm through the plants. They curled and died as it took their Essence, robbing them of their tiny lives.

With the boost, the Shade made faster progress.

KEN CLIMBED UP into the engine and shoved Po and Porter over. Grabbing the rust-seized brake, he put his sizable shoulders into it.

The handle snapped off.

Ba-ba-bumph.

It was as if the Ravager bombs and the broken brake were establishing a dialogue.

Cold water gushed from the ceiling, soaking them all.

THE SHADE PULLED a heavy floor hatch open as easily as it might have picked up a gum wrapper. It didn't bother with the ladder, instead dropping through the square opening to the wet floor below.

Mr. Brill made sniffing sounds as the Shade did the same on the screens. Spotting another hatch, they snorted with satisfaction. The beast cleared the distance to it with one leap.

PORTER, KEN, AND PO studied the stump of the brake lever like it might have a suggestion of its own to offer.

Rain unholstered her shotgun and laid it across her lap.

Paul wished he had something to do, too.

"Hit the gas," Porter told Po.

The monk gave the throttle a full squeeze again. The engine hummed and whined as it fought the brakes, which gave no ground.

"Everyone hang on," Porter said over the motor's protests.

Ken sized the situation up and leapt back into the car with Paul and Rain.

Porter tapped the brake stump with his staff. The lurch that followed as the brake stump fell to its lowest possible position would have given Paul and Rain a mean case of whiplash had Ken not braced their heads with his immense arm.

The train took off like a dragster, tearing free of the wires charging its battery.

Paul looked back to see the full length of cars emerge from the black space behind them. He counted eight before he faced forward again. It seemed like a better idea to watch where they were going, as if he could oversee and affect their progress.

The engine gathered speed. He couldn't see anything ahead.

They were running blind.

❖ ❖ ❖

THE SHADE LANDED in a dark tunnel.

A pair of taillights sped away from it. A railway.

The beast leapt after the lights, grabbing for the train's last car. It fell short, slipped in mud and went face-first into the muck and wooden ties of the track bed.

Mr. Brill had missed his train. Truitt kept that joke to himself.

Ba-ba-ba-bumph! The loudest explosion yet rocked the monitor's view from side to side with rim-shot timing.

The Shade righted itself as darkness descended from above, shrouding the screen completely.

Mr. Brill grunted again.

Truitt wondered if that had hurt.

PAUL TURNED TO CHECK the rear of the train again as the ceiling collapsed behind them. The lights back there went out, and the tunnel vanished.

"Drive carefully," Porter told Po. The monk continued to squeeze the throttle hard. "No brakes."

Po stared into the darkness rushing at them.

None of them could see where they were going, and they were going at full speed.

The monk eased up on the throttle.

The train didn't slow.

He let go altogether.

They continued at their nose-bleed pace.

Po looked to Porter for guidance. He received only a shrug in reply.

They hurtled toward their destination in the dripping blackness with no notion of how they would stop when they got there.

....

TWENTY-NINE

I WAS A SOLDIER, TOO

Annie had never actually seen any of the numerous guns aimed at her in her dangerous years. She'd heard bullets whine by, watched slugs send hard-packed earth flying. She'd been targeted by those too far away or too well concealed to spot. But she'd never once stared down a barrel pointed her way.

It wasn't a streak she'd wanted to end.

With passwords and security between the embedded Americans and the Iraqis less than perfect, several friends on transition teams had related the joy of the experience. Her MiTTs friend Borman told of M4s and type fifty-sixes pointed at his head for long minutes while he and the men he was advising convinced each other that they all were who they said they were.

One thing he'd had right: it didn't matter where you laid your eyes; all you saw was the hole at the gun's bad end. And the longer you looked, the bigger it got.

Annie's phone vibrated. She ignored it. If she was about to get her face shot off, she'd do so undistracted.

The next notification came with a mild electric shock—a reminder that no matter how much the phone she held resembled hers at home, it was not that phone. Here, the phone you thought you understood could electrocute you before the dead soldier had a chance to blow you away.

She chanced a glance at the screen. "READ THIS NOW," said the subject line of the newly arrived text. "NOW."

Annie opened the message. "Go to the app store and install QRBoy," it said. "He pulls the trigger in sixty seconds."

She mistyped the name of the app twice before finding it.

In a college physics course, she'd learned about Einstein's concept of time dilation, which holds that a clock at the top of a tower runs faster than the same clock at the bottom because the latter clock is closer to the mass of the earth. Similarly, one minute with a gun on you will seem like hours.

Unless you'll be shot in the head if you muff the task at hand, in which case time passes at a brisk clip.

She lost ten seconds when the phone demanded her password before allowing a new app to be installed—and a few more while she struggled to remember it.

The steadiness of Weston's aim was matched by his stare. Dead men don't blink.

The moments passed in a fluid sequence.

She installed the app.

Her phone crashed. It always did when she downloaded something new, and she was used to it, really.

She rebooted it and launched QRBoy.

The intro screen looked like it had been designed for customer loyalty or in-store coupons before some hacker in a hurry messed with it. Which was, in all likelihood, exactly what had happened.

Instructions popped up: "Type Ravager name and show him or her resulting QR code."

A gender-conscious programmer. Refreshing.

She had only the name she'd made up, so she typed that in. "Weston."

How much time did she have left, anyway?

The software generated a black-and-white square with an erratic checkerboard pattern—one of those discount codes she never remembered to use at the register. She held the phone out like a crucifix.

Weston's aim and gaze held steady. They had one another covered with the weapons at hand. His would put her on the ground with one shot—and in it, should some passer-by be kind enough to bury what the scavengers didn't want. Hers would earn her a complimentary espresso at the local Bean Machine after ten check-ins, a logo mug at twenty.

Nothing happened.

Then more nothing.

Annie got sick of the whole thing.

"Enough," she told the Ravager long minutes into the stand-off. She lowered her phone, disgusted at the game she'd been forced to play, and dropped it into her pocket. "Shoot me in the back if you like. I'm gonna go find my son."

She spun on her heel, walked away from the chopper and the pilot, and didn't look back. How far might she make it before hearing the crack of the gun? The frustrated part of her said it didn't matter. The mother part said no shot would come because Zach was out there, and he needed her. If the Ravager wasn't going to help, she would continue on her own.

One step became another. Before she knew it, she'd counted to ten. After that, she stopped keeping track.

No shot followed. Instead, the clicking of switches on the Black Hawk's console stopped her. Weston was preparing for take-off.

She watched the pilot work from a distance, astounded by both her survival and the deftness with which he went about his job. It was all routine, as if only seconds before, he hadn't been about to kill a young mother of one.

He proceeded through the Black Hawk's start-up in a collage of machine music, a concert given by vacuum cleaners and jet engines. The rotors got up to speed and overwhelmed all other sound.

Her phone vibrated again. "Your ride's here," Char's text repeated.

Annie walked back to the chopper and climbed into the cockpit next to Weston, who didn't so much as acknowledge her return. Then she waited to be airborne and hoped that the dead man who'd almost brought her quest to a bloody halt would now take her to her little boy.

IN THE AIR, Annie couldn't distinguish the terrain of The Commons from that back home. The forests and hills they flew over looked just like those she knew, the deserts identical to those she saw when flying into L.A.

But after a while came houses, shopping centers, malls, schools, and roads that were interspersed with blank-slate nature in a broken pattern that wasn't the logical flow of a map. The change was too abrupt, the terrain stuck in the process of re-shaping itself.

It was a landscape needing direction—wanting to be told what to do. From on high, it looked like it'd been waiting forever.

With the pinky haze gone, her memory of the bus was back. No longer was it hidden behind an antacid-colored shroud with the rest of her real life. That was the hard part of it—the memories of the genuine versus the false recollections manufactured by the meds, if meds were all they were.

The odd little suburban apartment she'd shared with Zach was an illusion of sorts, but the way she'd left him on his own was not. She'd have to deal with that after she found him.

Memory returned as a punishment there in the air. Night slid sideways into broken glass. Passengers screamed.

Helicopters. Soldiers. Blood. Snow. Fire. Spiders.

She stole glances at Weston. She knew what the Ravagers were and what they did, but not who or why. Having worked the data, traveling through its imagery of cracking pipes, schools of fish, and angry bees, she'd retained only the basics. Ravagers were former cops, ex-military.

"I was a soldier, too, Weston," she told the pilot, who gazed straight ahead. "Did they tell you that when they said to help me? Did Charlene let you know?" Silence. "Did they say anything about me?"

He maintained his heading.

Annie thought of all the Westons she'd met and said goodbye to—if there'd been a chance for any parting at all—in her war years. The Westons of the world wanted to mean something. The boardroom hawks and talk-radio tough guys didn't care about that.

The Westons weren't walking guns to be aimed as easily at one target as another. They followed orders. They'd chosen to do their best—wanted to leave a place better off than it was when they arrived. Those in charge didn't earn that trust—that nobility of duty.

"I'm going to find my little boy, Weston. He gave me my life back after they took the metal out of me. When I came home, I was still on the table, screaming inside, and nobody could hear it but my son. He heard, and he needed me. So I got up. Now I'm going to find Zach—and God help anyone who tries to keep him from me."

The pilot continued to stare out the windshield as if she hadn't uttered a sound. So Annie did the same. But when she looked at him again, he was watching her, meeting her gaze with his sole visible eye.

He'd heard every word.

....

THIRTY

THE SMELL OF LICORICE

M r. Brill sagged in his chair, his face turned down to his custom belt as if evaluating it. His eyes were closed, and a long string of something viscous descended from his mouth toward the buckle.

The monitor's screen was black and silent. It had been since the mud and stones rained down on the Shade—burying the monster in darkness and, from the looks of it, knocking Mr. Brill unconscious.

Truitt hadn't realized how closely tied the beast and the boss were on a physical level. He wondered what it meant for Mr. Brill—what it meant for all of them—if the Shade had been killed.

He didn't wonder for long.

With a grunt, Mr. Brill jerked his head up, eyes still closed. He wiped the saliva—if that's what it was—from his mouth with the back of his suit sleeve before it had a chance to complete its journey.

From the monitor and the office's unseen speakers came the Shade's rumbling, choleric cough as it roused itself. Mr. Brill sat up, and the Shade began to dig its way out.

Dim light from the tunnel's few bulbs soon peeked through cracks in the creature's muddy prison. It made short work of freeing itself.

THE FIRST SIDE TUNNEL the train passed was too dark to see into. But judging by the stacks of rail and timber blocking it, Paul surmised it was an incomplete branch of the line they were running on.

The next was smaller, hand-dug, and a little better lit by the functioning bulbs hanging in front of it. Inside, its walls writhed.

"Did you see that?" Paul asked Rain over the rush of air and the train's squealing wheels.

She chambered a round.

Up in the engine car, Po turned from the frozen throttle to look back past the rest of the group, to the rear of the train.

A cat-sized something fell from the tunnel ceiling and landed on Rain. The train hit a string of burned-out bulbs. Blackness enveloped them yet again as she reached over her shoulder to investigate the new weight on the holster between her shoulder blades.

After that came a lot of yelling.

Paul couldn't understand what she said but didn't need to. He reached out and grabbed a mound of wet, squirming fur, pulled it off, and held it out at arm's length. In the dark, he couldn't see a thing. Something clicked in front of his face.

The next string of working bulbs revealed his catch: a grotesque combination of rat, beetle, and shrimp. It had the body of the first, the head and pincers of the second, the thick, plated tail of the third.

And the temperament of a hornet.

Furious, the thing waved its six legs in the air, tail lashing about and pincers clasping, wet and sharp, trying to get at his wrist. Then, with a hiss, it changed tactics and went for his eyes. He flung it into the darkness.

"What the hell was that?" Rain shouted.

"I don't know! But I'm glad it's gone!"

The train passed under a patch of black in the tunnel roof. A torrent of fur, pincers, and writing pink legs poured down on them from above, filling the cars with seething shrimp-tailed rat-beetles.

Rain let out a string of curses.

In the engine, Porter did the same, matching her enthusiasm with every expletive.

THE SHADE WAS FAST—and frightfully so.

On the monitor, it chased down the train's taillights, devouring the gap with ease. Mr. Brill's breathing filled the room, laden with exertion.

When the tunnel bugs attacked the train, Truitt assumed the game was up. But the little horrors wanted nothing to do with the Shade—and for good reason. It consumed those that weren't able to get out of its way, building strength.

Mr. Brill's exhalations became part effort, part ecstasy as the Essence flowed into him. Now his quarry was within reach. He had strength to spare.

The red lights grew larger. The rat-bugs the Shade didn't grab along the way were crushed underfoot, their little deaths feeding the pursuit.

The panting from the monitor and that of Mr. Brill joined. The lights drew near.

Overeager, the Shade grabbed for the rear coupler of the last car and missed. But this time, it didn't fall. It lost a few steps and had to push to recover the lost ground.

The hordes of tunnel bugs thickened, cascading down from above and streaming from the side tunnels as the train and the Shade passed. They would be a hindrance before long, but for now, the monster feasted.

It dove for the coupler again, this time grabbing hold. Now the monitor image shook as the beast was dragged along, pummeled by railroad ties. Dreadfully strong, it held on.

The Shade pulled itself to the train, clambering up and onto the rear car, where it enjoyed a brief rest. The car was filled with rat-bugs climbing over each other in their haste to get away from it. It consumed more of them and made its way forward.

PAUL AND RAIN ripped the attacking rat-beetles from themselves and each other. Pincers pierced arm and neck.

The creatures went after hair and clothing where they couldn't find flesh. There were so many that most made do with tearing into whatever presented itself.

Paul pawed at Rain's back and tore away as many as he could. When he had a handful of wet fur, he yanked and threw. Just as often, he caught the business end and got bitten for his trouble.

She did the same for him. Her nonstop obscenities made it clear that she was just as unlucky with the parts she grabbed.

When the train passed from light to dark and back again, Paul caught bloody flashes of her. The beetle-things didn't bite deep, but they were legion.

He was no better. The two of them blinked red in the staccato of the intermittent bulbs, faces and hands strung with blood.

The train shuddered as it crushed the buildup of rat-beetles on the tracks. And still they came. Their group was getting the worst of this fight.

From deep down came a heat Paul had only felt a time or two before—in very bad beat-downs where winning wasn't possible and the price of a loss wasn't clear, but promised to be high. It took hold, burned within.

He was starting to panic.

And from the pitch of Rain's cries, he wasn't alone.

"Paul!" Porter said. The Envoy cleared beetle-things with his staff, jumping them away from the train. With each swing, the little monsters disappeared, but were soon replaced by twice the number.

There were too many.

Ken employed his long reach to pull beetle-rats from Porter. Despite his mitt-sized hands, the mummy made almost no difference. Po tried as well, his head striped in red, and fared about the same.

The train spasmed over the furry bodies and plated tails, crushing them. It shook from side to side, lifted off the rails, found steel once more.

"You have to do it again!" Porter shouted to Paul. "Now!"

Paul tried to do just that, but didn't know how he'd done it the first time. The tree that took down the chopper came from something rushing out to meet something coming in. The force of it had surprised him as much as anyone.

And he couldn't find it now.

Another rain of beetle-rats. The train lurched left, then right.

Porter swept his staff across Ken. The coat of beetle-rats clinging to the mummy melted away. "It's there, Paul! Call it!"

They hit a curve in the dark at full velocity. The car bucked, throwing Rain.

Her shotgun clattered to the floor and slid. She lunged and caught it before it could go overboard, but her momentum carried her off the edge.

Ken dove for her, driving Paul into one of the bench seats. The padded steel caught Paul in the side, knocking the wind out of him.

The beetle-things pressed their advantage.

In the strobe of the overhead bulbs, Rain dangled over nothing, shotgun in hand. Ken, prone on the car's floor, had a hold of her, but the curve and the momentum prevented him from hauling her back in.

She screamed.

The train went dark under a string of dead bulbs, then lit up weakly again under a long span of feeble incandescence.

The beetle-rats streamed over Ken to invade Rain's shirt. She was a thrashing mass of them. They even hung from her hair, trailing behind in the train's wind, pulling at her.

She screamed again.

Paul's heat became power. "Rain!"

The all-seeing perspective of the battle with the Ravagers—of the moment just before the tree pierced the Black Hawk—returned. Rain's suffering and fear. Ken's desperate attempt to help. A greater force—the strength of all and everything—telling Paul that he could change this.

A crackling in the air poured in to merge with its counterpart inside him. The result pushed outward, like fire.

They entered another dark patch. A torrent of what felt like small stones or marbles cut loose from above.

The wet fur and the biting of the pincers faded. Vanished.

In their place came the battering of thousands of hard black pellets filling the train. The tunnel filled with the smell of licorice.

On a straightaway, the train sped up, wheels smashing through the pellets in a grinding chorus. Then it began to slow once more beneath the growing hail streaming down on them from the holes in the tunnel ceiling.

The cars were swamped in cloying sweetness. Ken picked himself up, pulling Rain back into the car with him, fighting the surge of falling candy.

She clutched her shotgun, managed a laugh in the face of what she'd just endured, and spit a stray pellet into her hand. "No way," she said. "Sisu."

It took a moment for Paul to understand. "It's what came to mind," he said, half to himself.

Porter cupped his hands, which filled with hard nuggets of licorice. "This is new to me."

As if it were old hat to Paul.

SURELY, SOMEWHERE IN HIS TRANCE, Mr. Brill was outraged. The boy's act of changing the rat-bugs into black marbles or stones of some sort was sheer waste. A breach in efficiency was one of the big man's chief irritants.

It was difficult for Truitt to see the stones clearly in the monitor. However, when the Shade grabbed a handful to taste, it quickly spit them back out, along with a sizable amount of Stygian goop.

The data on the floating screens indicated that Paul Reid had transmuted the little creatures' Essence from one form to another—in this case, from living to inert, which brought a multiplier into play.

There were now more black pellets than there'd been rat-bugs, the disparity in Essence working out to something along the lines of a 500-to-one ratio. Black stones filled the train to overflowing. The boy's manipulation had reached a considerable portion of rat-bugs that hadn't made it out of the deeper lairs.

The Shade clambered over thousands upon thousands of nuggets. It was a struggle, but it had absorbed huge reserves of Essence to work with.

The monster's breathing drove it forward. Soon, Truitt could make out the silhouettes of its quarry up in the front car.

Until, at least, another black cascade obscured them once more.

Truitt allowed himself an inward smile at Mr. Brill's expense. If there were more nuggets than creatures, there was also a good deal more weight pressing down on the earthen tunnel roof.

The ceiling had just collapsed again.

THE TRAIN LABORED UP AN INCLINE, arrested by the rising tide of Sisu and its licorice bouquet. The aroma couldn't stop the train, in theory. But if any scent could entertain a reasonable hope of doing so, it'd be the sticky sweetness swaddling them now.

Po signed something to Ken. They all looked up to see a large hole expanding above as they passed under it.

The ceiling gave. Candy quickly buried the rear of the train, which slowed and came to a standstill.

Its back half was entombed in a hillside of mud and Sisu.

Paul's bites, coated in sugary sweat, itched and stung. In the meager light of the surviving bulbs, his arms and hands were netted in drying blood.

Rain, Porter, and Po looked much the same. Yet none of the bites were large or deep, and they could only hope there was no venom involved.

"I didn't do that last part," Paul told them. "The cave-in."

"No?" Porter said, running his fingers over his blood-pocked face in wonderment. "What part did you do?"

"I wanted them gone, so they were." He finished inspecting his myriad wounds. "Sisu came to mind. They had to be turned into something."

Porter surveyed the group. "Everyone all right?"

No one answered. If bloody, wet, mud-crusted, and pincer-chewed qualified, then yes, they were.

"Well, we walk from here," the Envoy said. He cast a baleful eye over the roof of the tunnel ahead. "Let's just hope the rest of this stays off our skulls."

THE BOY'S LUCK couldn't hold.

Truitt, for all his buried enjoyment at the Shade's setbacks, ultimately wanted what Mr. Brill wanted. Paul Reid needed to be brought within the fold, his apparent ability to change the flow of Essence controlled or shut down altogether.

Mr. Brill's structure of power was, simply put, a dam blocking the flow of Essence, with vents and causeways directing that energy. As Truitt had explained to June Medill, if that dam were ever opened fully or burst, with Mr. Brill's influence washed away, the judgment underlying The Commons and the justice that was its foundation would awaken.

Verdicts would be arrived at, fates locked into place. Mr. Brill and those who had done his bidding would not be viewed kindly.

Thus, the Shade needed to liberate itself.

Mr. Brill chuffed and shifted his bulk.

The Shade began to dig out.

THIRTY-ONE

....

A CLOUDED LENS

"I thought Liam said those things were hibernating." Paul's mud-stiffened pants and the complaints of his countless bites weren't doing his mood much good.

"The bombs disturbed their nap," Porter said.

The beetle-rats had taken a lot out of them. The long slog up the slope of the tunnel took more. Exhaustion settled in. Even Ken and Po slowed under the malaise of spirit as they trudged along.

After a time, Paul noticed that Porter was moving even slower than the rest of them. He'd spent a great deal of his recovered energy jumping the beetle-rats away from the train.

"How far is this silo?" the Envoy said.

"Liam did not specify," Ken said. "Several miles."

"Well, I'll endeavor to remain positive. It can't get much more unpleasant."

Po halted abruptly and turned to face the tunnel behind them.

"What?" said Ken.

A growl, like that of a wolf or something worse, echoed up the tunnel in answer. A splash followed. Another. And then a series of slapping footfalls as something big and weighty ran through the mud with a speed rivaling that of the train they'd just crashed.

Rain pulled her shotgun. Before anything else could be said, a mud-covered monster—an upright horned toad or bulldog demon the size of a bear— came straight at them.

Po engaged. It went for him at full speed, which was exactly what the monk wanted. As the dark thing charged, the monk rolled onto his back and, with hands and feet, used its mass and momentum to launch it through the wet air. It hit the tunnel wall with a low smack, dropping onto what passed for its head.

It bounced up immediately, faster than Po, who looked to be staggered by his contact with it. He got to his feet, but without his usual grace.

They fanned out around the monster, forcing it to address all directions. It, in turn, sized them up—its breath heavy but not labored. Even with the distance it had just covered, it was not tired, and its flight into the wall hadn't cost it anything.

"A Shade," Ken said. "An Essence leech."

"Brill's hand," Porter agreed.

At the utterance of the name, the Shade turned toward the Envoy. "It's been some time, Mister Brill," he told it.

The shadow beast sprang at Paul without warning. Po met it in the air with a double-foot kick that deflected it and sent it sprawling to the tunnel floor. The monk landed and tumbled, rolling to his feet. But once again, he'd lost a step or two.

The Shade came right back up.

Ba-room! Rain blasted the monster full in the face. The force knocked it back a step but otherwise didn't appear to cause any harm. "Any ideas on how to kill this thing?" she asked no one in particular.

"It prefers bona-fide Essence, as Brill does," Porter said. "But it will take anyone or anything in a pinch. It hates sunlight, which we don't have. And wooden weaponry or anything that used to be alive—again, which we don't have."

It went for Po, but Ken headed it off. He swung both fists overhead, smashing it to the ground. The blow and the following thud were such that all of them felt it.

The Shade grunted with what sounded like discomfort. Good thing the mummy was on their side.

"Anything dead—or undead," Ken said.

It was true. Like Po, the mummy was visibly shaken by his contact with the beast, but he'd hurt it noticeably more than his friend had.

Porter watched the monster rise from the floor. It panted wetly. "I'm certain you don't know or care, Mister Brill, but we've a score to settle. Many of them. Dance with me?"

It wasn't clear to Paul whether the Shade had understood the Envoy or not. Either way, it leapt at Paul instead.

Paul was no stranger to the mayhem of a good fight, but all of his experience had been against human opponents. This was another level. This was a drooling vehicle-sized mass of pissed-off evil coming through the air at him. So he did what came naturally.

He froze.

Again, Ken was there first, body-blocking it to the ground. Porter, with surprising speed of his own, flicked his staff around and caught the beast on its sloping shoulder.

The effort cost the Envoy. He gasped and dropped his stick, but succeeded in jumping away a chunk of the Shade's shoulder. It let out a bawl, which seemed to come both from it and from the walls around them. A gout of black pudding erupted from its wound.

Rain let the monster have it again, blowing it back into the wall. It pushed itself off of the mud and faced them, gripping its shoulder to stem the flow. Porter picked himself up.

They faced it in a half-moon formation, taking stock. Ken was wobbly, Po more so. Porter was upright—but was shaky and separated from his staff, which lay in the mud a short distance away. Rain was fine, but it was clear that her gun could only move the Shade, not hurt it. And while they watched, the flow from its shoulder slowed, then stopped.

"There's more of that for you, to be sure," Porter said. "Another round?" His tone was brave, but he didn't look ready to go again.

Po eyed Porter's staff.

The Shade, its healing finished, faced the Envoy. Wherever he was, Mr. Brill had accepted the challenge.

So had Paul. Whatever had held him in place a moment before was banished by the realization that his allies were all limited in what they could contribute—or were just flat-out spent.

"No," he said.

They all turned to him as he stepped forward, the monster included. A dollop of goo dropped from its mouth to the tunnel floor with a splat.

An awareness took possession of Paul. He was a part of everyone in the tunnel—where they stood, their pulses. Even the Shade had a pulse. Each breath they took, tense and tight, was his breath.

They were poised for battle, and now he knew truly why fights were so short. Nobody, human or inhuman, could maintain such a state for long.

His sense of the group's presence—of their Essence—roamed beyond them and into the soil of the tunnel. Beetle-rats deep in their warrens—ones he hadn't reached in his panic. He knew their names, though they fit no language.

The soil, too, had its name. As did the water dripping into the tunnel. The steel of the train and rails. The wooden ties that held that steel.

Everything.

If he let himself go, he'd be absorbed by those things. But he wouldn't allow that to happen. If anything, they wanted to be absorbed into him—to bend to his will.

And while it would be a mistake to give into that urge for too long, he knew that he was not helpless before Brill and his creature. Not even close.

Ken maneuvered to impose himself between Paul and the Shade. Paul knew it without looking, just as he knew that Po had moved closer to Porter's staff and was about to dive for it. He knew Rain was going to chamber a round before the sound of it reached his ears.

"Leave my friends alone," he said. "I'm here."

Porter spoke his name. Rain started to ask him what he thought he was doing. He screened them out, sent his thoughts to the tunnel. Directed it to help him.

The Shade leapt. Paul closed his eyes, blinking out what was about to hit him. He set his mind on the no-longer living.

A half-dozen thick wooden stakes rose up out of the tunnel floor in front of him, reaching forward in pointed arcs. They met the Shade at a height of a good eight feet. It impaled itself on them, long arms reaching for him.

The beast shrieked and writhed, its screams terrible to hear. Yet it continued to grab for Paul, driving itself further onto the wood, its cries louder, higher.

He knew now what the others saw in him. They were warriors all. And while he felt the Shade's screams go through them, he also sensed their respect for the strength he displayed.

Losing fights taught you to finish them when you were winning. "They had it right," he told the creature. "You do hate wood."

The screams of surprise and frustration became full-blown pain. The monster gave up reaching for him and instead attempted to lift itself off the stakes. No good—with every try, it lost its grip. It couldn't maintain contact with the wood.

Essence freely leaked from the Shade, and Paul called it to him for his own. "What else?" he said. "Oh. Right."

He didn't need to close his eyes to focus now. The tunnel was all too eager to help. With his silent guidance, its ceiling began to hollow out and up in a tube, an invisible drill boring to the surface. The dank funk around them receded as Paul turned the disappearing soil into fresh air.

The others stood and stared at the spectacle, too awestruck to speak—or maybe they were just enjoying the show. Rain took it all in. Po smiled.

The Shade began to kick, trying to loosen the stakes enough for it to get its feet on the ground and gain leverage. Paul hurried, concentration slipping a bit.

Some of the soil didn't finish its transformation to air and instead dropped onto the Shade's head as dirt. He willed the tube toward the surface.

The dark beast rocked back and forth on the stakes, its screams undulating with the motion—a blend of anger and agony.

Too late.

"Bright light," Paul said.

And there was. The tunnel went from darkness to sunlight as the hole in the tunnel roof broke through to the world above, which answered with illumination.

Burned by the rays, helpless to get away from them, the Shade wailed. It thrashed, mud flying from it—mud and layers of itself. Smoke rose as the monster began to come apart, shaken to pieces by its own struggles.

The light from above had an odd, shifting quality, as if filtered through a clouded lens. The reason was revealed a moment later as a great volume of water crashed down through the hole in a massive torrent, breaking over the Shade and the stakes that ran it through.

The water flowed over their feet and stopped as abruptly as it had arrived. The wet Shade now gave off steam as pieces of its flesh continued to fly from it.

And still it fought. Soon it was down to ebon muscle, then bone, as it shook itself apart, its cries growing dry as chalk.

Finally, it was spent. Paul had used Essence stolen from the beast to dig the hole in the roof. With its remainder, he shifted his thoughts to creation, closing his eyes again. He needed to get this right. He knew he'd succeeded when he heard Rain gasp.

He opened his eyes. The Shade's skeleton sagged on the stakes. The bones of its long fingers dangled, as if accusing the wet earth of crimes against it. Final wisps of steam rose from the frame.

Now the reward for Paul's efforts was plain to see. A spiral staircase of sturdy wood reached up into the hole in the ceiling from the floor in front of them, corkscrewing its way around the smooth clay walls to the surface above.

"I CAN'T EXPLAIN IT," Paul said as they climbed. "It's like making an idea solid."

They rose up from a deep well. Porter never seemed to have a chance to recover. Paul felt his weariness, as well as the licks that Ken and Po had taken on his behalf.

If only Paul had discovered his abilities earlier. There was no denying he had them now. If he'd gotten better with them sooner, he might have been practiced enough to keep his friends from getting hurt. As it was, they had to protect him until he was freaked out enough to do something useful.

Friends.

He'd had friends among some of the New Beginnings kids, but those relationships were more like pacts to watch each other's backs. There was little real caring. Few of them were around long enough.

In contrast, Porter stayed on as his Envoy when it might well get him killed. The others had even less reason to stick with him. But as Rain said, they did anyway.

There was nothing but downside for any of them should Paul fail. Come to think of it, even if Paul made it, Mr. Brill and the Ravagers would take it out on them. So he needed to get good at what he did.

The way up was long. Porter's hard breathing was a soundtrack to the effort, punctuated by the squish of their wet footwear on the steps. Where had the water come from?

That answer became apparent as they reached the top and gained a view of the surface world for what seemed like the first time in days. Paul's upward tunnel had pierced the center of a white concrete expanse—the floor of a rectangular pit with thick black lines painted along its floor.

There were numbers on the vertical cement walls around them and a tile border above those numbers. They stood in the deep end of an Olympic-sized swimming pool, which Paul had just drained.

"Stinking sprawl," Porter said.

Up at the shallow end, a gaggle of old ladies in one-piece swimsuits and bathing caps adorned with plastic flowers perched on the pool deck's edge, gawking at them. Paul could only guess at what they were thinking. The mole people, invading at last.

Behind the women was a one-story cinderblock pool office. On the front of it hung a whiteboard that said in neat capital letters, "Water ballet, 3 pm." Next to that, an oversized clock showed the current time: 3:05.

A sturdy-looking coach flipping pages on a clipboard hustled out of the office. "Ladies, I'm so sorry," she said, eyes on her papers. "Anita called to reschedule, and I just couldn't get her off the phone."

She shut up when faced with the waterless pool and its filthy, bloody inhabitants—one a mummy and the others looking nearly as dangerous.

Paul grew a little light-headed when he considered what he'd almost done. Had the class started on time, the pool would have drained the women down dozens of stories, right onto the Shade and the stakes.

"We regret the damage, madam," Porter offered. "If ever you were going to begin late, this was certainly the day to do so."

The class and their teacher didn't respond. Even if they didn't know about the monster and the pointy doom below, they surely saw that they'd nearly met the fate of bubbles in a bathtub.

They remained silent as Paul and the dirty, exhausted group crossed to the shallow end and mounted the steps. Around them was a collection of three-floor buildings with an adjoining restaurant, gift shop, playground, shuffleboard court, and putting green. They'd reached the Dew Drop Inn, according to a sign in the distance—a family motor lodge.

"Any vacancies?" Porter asked, cracking mud from his hat. "With showers?"

Rain shook crud from her sleeves. "And a laundry room?"

....

THIRTY-TWO

THE BATTLE OF THE DEW DROP INN

I n The Commons, as in life, a Journey was often a series of lines connecting the dots of diners. So it seemed as Porter sat in a booth with Ken and Po in the Dew Drop Inn's Pot Luck Family Restaurant.

Worn out though he was, he hadn't been able to sleep after checking into his room and cleaning up. So he'd decided on coffee with a diet-cola chaser. It was an old combo for him; his Envoy colleagues used to suggest that he drop the can into the mug for efficiency's sake.

Ken and Po, who were already there when Porter arrived, made for perfectly acceptable sounding boards for Porter's ideas on the unusual stakes of Paul Reid's Journey. It wasn't the same as talking it over with Envoys, though—and the two didn't know to make the depth-charge joke.

The mummy had a triangular peg puzzle in front of him. In the past hour or so, he'd left it with a single peg in its center—solved—numerous times. Po was well into a palace built with sugar packets and stirrers and had somehow managed a series of flying buttresses.

"I owe you two a debt for standing with us," Porter told them. "If nothing else, I thank you for not destroying this place before I've finished my coffee."

Ken nodded and loaded the puzzle with pegs. Shelley, the waitress who'd been filling them with coffee and tea while trying to sell them some scratch-crust pie, stopped by with a fresh pot.

"You sure I can't get you anything to eat?"

"No, thank you, Shelley," Ken said. "Just the check, please."

"Big guy like you?" She'd taken a shine to the mummy—not in a romantic way, but more in the fashion that women her age sometimes did when they saw the opportunity to have an experienced, non-threatening male provide them with a peek at his side's playbook.

Porter judged her to be about nineteen or twenty, but he could still see the child in her when she lingered by their table, trying to steer Ken back to the topic of her relationship. He'd tackled her questions and problems earlier, right after the dinner crowd cleared out, around cup two or three.

Shelley was older than Rain by a few years, but had the bearing and eyes of someone a decade younger. Age came not with days passed, but with the life they carried. "So you think that should be it for Cody," she said, writing out the check.

The mummy jumped a peg and removed it from the board. "If he cannot be trusted with his word, he cannot be trusted with your heart. Karaoke was important to you, and he chose to duet with—"

"Veronica."

"Veronica. Promises should not be taken lightly. He'll break more than those."

She set the check down on the table and watched him claim a couple more pegs. Her manager called to her. At the window between the kitchen and the counter, hot platters waited. "I have questions, and I usually know the answers," she said, heading for the meals. "I just need to hear someone else say it."

Porter watched her go. "I have questions, too, but only one of them counts."

Po set down the sugar packet he'd been about to place on top of a tower. Ken stopped demolishing the puzzle. "Which one?" the mummy said.

"What do you think Paul is?"

"I prefer who, not what. Mythicals tend to be sensitive to semantics."

Porter sat back in the booth. "I'm sorry if I've offended you."

"You haven't. I merely wish to be clear. Who someone is defines what they are, and the two are inseparable." Ken began jumping pegs again. "Bona fides insist on two distinct classes—two worlds: one of the real and living, one of the dead and imaginary. Straight lines in a universe squared off. As an oft-quoted mythical once said, isn't it pretty to think so? Spacetime is curved, and it is so because of what exists within it. The separations are artificial—distinctions drawn by those who insist on dominating that which is not a part of them. Except that it *is* part of them."

Three moves later, the mummy was once again left with one peg in the center. He won the game even faster when he wasn't focused on it.

"Meaning?"

"Meaning that the 'real' world and The Commons are not so far apart as many wish to believe. Meaning that Brill thinks that what he is controlling is not only apart from him but beneath him. He is mistaken. We are all a part of it—and of one another. He controls what allows itself to be controlled. Who's to say it will continue to do so?"

Ken filled the puzzle yet again and began jumping pegs even more rapidly. He did so with precision despite his huge hands. The plastic and wood never so much as clicked. "Po has a theory."

The monk studied his packet project.

"My friend believes that Paul is Tzadikim Nistarim," Ken said. "One of the Thirty-Six. And he thinks Brill knows it."

"And you?"

"I am not certain that it matters."

Po removed a wing of his sugar castle and began building up instead of out. The additional story rose into the air straight and sturdy.

"Who is the burned woman, Porter?" Ken said.

Porter stalled.

"You spoke with her at the Nightlights. The woman of a different fire." He jumped another peg. "It's our turn for an answer, is it not?"

"How long have you wanted to ask me?"

"You were also away from Paul and Rain for a time before our fight at the truck stop."

Po stopped building.

Porter smiled. *Beware the soft-spoken when secrets are kept, for they hear what the thunderers do not.* "If you truly believe that everything is everything, as the song says, then you'll understand why I can't tell you. Brill already knows more than we'd like, and it's only too easy for him to learn even more." He upended his soda, draining it, and set the can down with a silence equal to Ken's. "But know that it's in our power to begin again."

The mummy pushed the puzzle away from him.

One peg remained—dead center.

THE FIGHT WASN'T OVER.

The view of the tunnel returned to the floating monitors, and Mr. Brill sat up. The squeal of something dying pierced the silence of the office.

Mr. Brill gave a start. Then the one cry became many, and the many a wall of shrill termination.

Truitt had sat in the soundless spot for hours, waiting to see what would happen. He'd been certain that Mr. Brill would awaken—and sure that when he did, it would be very bad for devoted servant Gerald Truitt to be absent.

The boy had delivered a painful lesson to Mr. Brill and his creature. When the beast had died—or came as close as it could to dying—the last sight Truitt had witnessed through its eyes was one of sunlight and steam.

The Reid boy was even stronger than they had realized. He, his Envoy, and their little miscreant band had handed what could charitably be called an old-fashioned whupping to the big man.

Now Mr. Brill and the Shade were coming around, and the moonlight washing down through the hole in the tunnel roof revealed the cause.

A host of the rat-bug creatures had emerged from their holes to gnaw at the Shade's bones and the stakes from which the skeleton was suspended. When enough of them massed, the monster drained them.

The ones that made initial contact with the bones had no chance of escape. The others might have been able to crawl back to their dens, but they were too densely packed together and had no room to maneuver. So life was taken from them in sequence and delivered to the Shade.

On the screen, they perished and withered in the pale light. Their keening was a sure sign that the process was not painless.

The bones swathed themselves in the musculature, tissue, and shadow skin that defeat had taken from the Shade. Soon it would revive, but there was still the matter of it being impaled on the wood.

As Mr. Brill continued to gather himself, Truitt quietly stepped over to him and laid his fingers softly against the back of the big man's neck for a moment.

Mr. Brill gave another start.

For a short moment, Truitt had the sensation of his own head and hands being taken from him—of surrendered control.

A blink. Then two. He wasn't steering himself. He'd been shoved over to the passenger seat. A separate force—unseen, so much larger than him—took the wheel.

A very old power climbed up his spine, coursing through him and into Mr. Brill. Generations of blood-swathed birth and death, creation and demise. Somewhere an infant cried. Elsewhere a grown man.

Truitt was but a conduit for an energy that felt as if it might burn his very eyes out. Something, someone—or several someones—with no choice but to break cover and reveal a heretofore unseen presence. Regrettable, but necessary.

Mr. Brill twitched several times as the force went through him in turn and into the Shade. A force to overcome that which held the beast fast to the stakes.

Then the transfer was complete.

Truitt returned to his seat. Forgetting about ever having gotten up at all, he watched the screen again.

Was that a staircase?

PO LOOKED OUT THE WINDOW and slid from the booth, demolishing his palace with his sleeve in a rare display of clumsiness. He hurried past Shelley, who was making another run at them, coffee pot in hand.

Before Porter could say anything to Ken, the mummy was up and following his friend out the door.

The Envoy pulled a wad of bills from his pocket and threw them on the table. "Please excuse us," he told Shelley.

"Hey!" the waitress called after him when she saw the fat overpayment. "This isn't New York!"

THE HELICOPTERS WERE in the sky and in the room, their whup-whup-whup shaking the window glass and door. Paul thought he was awake, but realized he hadn't been when he opened his eyes.

His hair and pillow were still damp from his shower. He'd been in a deep sleep, though not for long.

The choppers were coming. Someone was pounding on his door.

"Paul!" Rain shouted through the thick wood. She hit it with something harder than her fist. "Get up!"

He pulled on his pants, opened the door, and squinted into the hall light. She had her shotgun out. The rotor beats outside grew louder still.

"They're here."

THE TRUCKS WERE CLOSE ENOUGH to be heard over the approaching choppers when Porter and Ken reached the parking lot. Po was crouched behind a maintenance van next to an old framed-glass phone booth.

Porter started to ask him where the Shade was, for he had a hunch that that was what had called the monk out here. He'd begun to suspect that Po had a way of sensing things that was beyond mere hearing. Then the beast's squat darkness rose from the dry swimming pool, vaulted the fence, and came at them.

It closed in fast, aiming for Ken in a low charge. Po launched himself from behind the van in a two-footed kick that caught the monster dead center.

The monk bounced off and landed on his feet as the Shade hit the asphalt. The monster was up instantly, bellowing.

Porter assumed that it—and, through it, Mr. Brill—had tired of these skirmishes. Porter was sick of them, too, but was at a loss as to how they might make this the last, especially when they'd all thought the previous one was.

The three of them spread out to keep the Shade from the motel. Porter raised his staff and waited for the next round.

PAUL AND RAIN PUSHED THROUGH the lobby doors and hurried out into the parking lot. Amid the cacophony of the arriving Ravagers, the fight a mere hundred yards away was a silent ballet.

The Shade charged Po. The monk flipped out of the way and kicked it in the back as it passed under him.

Paul ran toward them, unsure what he would do when he got there.

The monster went face-first into the cracked pavement and bounced to its feet.

Po stumbled as he landed.

The Shade charged him again.

Ken was there with a two-fisted blow that smashed the beast to the asphalt. It rose more slowly this time.

The mummy could hurt the Shade, but doing so took its toll. He staggered backward, and the Shade launched itself at him.

Po intercepted the monster with another kick, knocking it off course. It righted itself and landed. The monk hit the hard surface of the lot, crumpled, and stayed down.

Paul and Rain closed in, as did the choppers and trucks. Several Dew Drop Inn guests and staff members emerged to see what all the commotion was.

Porter caught the Shade down low with his staff, removing a chunk of its leg. Black blood ran like crude oil, but now it was the gray man's turn to pay for his contact with the beast. He caught himself on his staff.

Ken ran at the monster, turning his shoulder into its chest like a lineman. The Shade struck the nearby van and bounced off, the vehicle's side crumpling, and took out the adjacent phone booth. Glass exploded from both van and booth with the successive hits, showering the parking lot in sharp, clear gems.

The Shade hauled itself from the mangled frame of the phone booth. Its blood loss slowed and stopped, its leg reconstructing itself.

It turned toward Rain as she and Paul joined the fight, but Ken was too fast for it. He gripped it in a bear hug, raised it up over his head and drove it into the asphalt with enough force to send a network of fractures out from the impact's epicenter.

Everything slowed. Despite the choppers and trucks, Paul would later remember hearing nuggets of glass crunch under foot—and would wonder what might have been different if he'd acted sooner.

The Shade struggled to rise.

Ken ignored the fatigue of his prolonged contact with the beast. Staggering over to the skeleton of the phone booth, he ripped the deformed steel from the pavement.

The Shade found its wobbly legs and stood just as Ken finished crushing the frame of the ruined booth. He gathered the flattened structure and clubbed the beast hard with it. The monster was stunned long enough for the mummy to bend the metal tightly around its shadowy form in a ring and twist the ends closed, imprisoning it.

The noise of choppers and trucks was so close now that it was almost its own quiet. Paul heard Ken clearly when he spoke, though the mummy didn't raise his voice.

All else fell away.

"Paul." Ken held the Shade tight. "We are none of us substantial, none of us big. That is thrust upon us. All of us. Do you understand?"

Paul thought he did. And with that comprehension came the ache of a loss he couldn't yet identify. "Yes."

"Do you?"

"Yes." As Paul said it, he knew that his answer wasn't quite true. He didn't understand entirely. There was a difference to the mummy's tone—the quality of a decision having been reached.

Of finality.

Po recovered enough to get to his feet.

Ken said Rain's name. Then Porter's.

The Shade thrashed, attempting to free itself. The mummy reached into his pocket, pulled out his Wayfarers, and tossed them to Po.

"Goodbye, friend," Ken told the monk. "If we should meet..."

The captive Shade raged and kicked, to no avail.

Full understanding came to Paul, to Po—to all of them—too late.

Ken let go of the imprisoned Shade. He reared back for momentum and rammed both fists into the night creature, reaching for its dark heart.

The monster howled and fell over backward, taking the mummy with it. Ken screamed, his volume matching the Shade's as the beast was forced to absorb his Essence, an energy lethal to it.

He drove his arms in deeper. Po made a grab for him but was thrown backward by the exchange of forces.

The Shade's cries and Ken's became one, reached a crescendo. The two blurred into each other, wavering for a long time.

There was no send-off for the hero, no denouement to mark his noble passing. Mummy and foe simply vanished. Their fading echo became but a susurration. And then they were gone.

The air around the group pulsed with Ravager choppers, grated with the rumble of their trucks. A dozen vehicles pulled up, disgorging black-clad Ravagers in full battle gear.

Just as many Black Hawks circled the sky above.

Po, stricken, sobbed and fell to his knees on the asphalt. He collapsed into his grief, ignoring the broken glass. Chin to chest, he cradled the Wayfarers in his hands as if they were a baby bird.

The first of the Ravagers reached him and raised his rifle high, poised to slam its heavy heel into his head. The monk offered no defense.

True seeing.

Porter lifted his staff to protect Po but was unsteady.

Rain took aim at the Ravager as five or six of his fellow troopers drew down on her.

The wave of loss crested over Paul's friends, whose only sin was to sign on to his Journey hoping to help him.

"No more." His voice rose of its own volition, taking his control with it. The heat inside him hastened to meet that outside—hard and true.

Paul's words ended in a thunderclap that deafened even him. Lightning flashed.

A ball of force issued from him in all directions.

Another followed, waves rippling outward.

The Ravager about to bludgeon Po flickered out, extinguished. Those preparing to shoot Rain were next—erased as they squeezed their triggers.

Paul felt them there and gone, drawn into the tide of Essence that pulled them in as it grew. It claimed Ravagers as it went. There, not there—the trucks and the troops they carried.

The sky crackled, fissured into wrath. Lightning ripped into helicopters, eliminating them in blinding flares.

Thunder followed, then sheets of rain from what remained a blue sky. There were no clouds; the Essence Paul sent upward returned in a sunlit drenching.

More.

Downpour bouncing around him, Paul raised his arms and gave further voice to his violence. The sound joined with the Essence.

It possessed him—and he it.

Neither was in control.

A distant chopper spun to the ground in a flaming eddy. He shaped its fire into projectiles and sent them into the next wave of trucks. Ravager and vehicle alike were incinerated and added to the storm.

Porter dropped to one knee, unable to withstand the torrent. Po remained as he'd been when he'd first collapsed, removed in his mourning.

Farther away, choppers wheeled around and tried to escape. Their efforts amounted to naught.

Paul took them. He laid claim to all of them—truck, chopper, soldier—and Essence whose sources he didn't even know.

The rain fell harder. The storm grew. It wouldn't slow because Paul wouldn't allow it—nor did it wish to.

"Paul!" Rain fought her way to him through the deluge. "Stop!"

He would not.

She would have to understand that. So would Porter and Po.

Stopping was the last thing he wanted to do. He was going to make it worse.

"It's over!" She grabbed his shoulders. "You have to stop!" Shaking him now. "They're gone, Paul! It's just us!"

He summoned still more. The Dew Drop Inn trembled. The guests who'd come out to see what was happening scrambled back inside for shelter under roofs that were losing shingles to the wind.

"Stop!" She hit him, though that was only noted, not felt. "It's us!" She hit him again. And again. "It's us! It's us!"

Us. Us. Who? All of them. The travelers who'd already been through so much together.

Somehow, he heard her. He heard, he listened, and he came back—to her, to Porter, to Po.

As it had started, the storm ceased. Its rain dropped to the ground in a final layer, bouncing in one last sheet.

"It's us," Rain said with the last of her voice. She cradled his face in both her hands, fingers light.

He blinked, returning to himself. The lights and darks of his eyesight restored themselves to normalcy as he looked around at what he'd done.

Porter rose to his feet.

When they saw it was over, guests emerged once more—the bravest first, then others.

Po remained on his knees. Paul could hear the monk crying now.

The grief made a small thing of the departed fury.

TRUITT MISSED THE ENDING. After the mummy did away with Mr. Brill's Shade, the floating monitors showed naught but snow.

That was bad. They didn't go dark or switch to an alternate view. Instead, the dance of dots across the screens indicated that something wasn't just turned off—it was broken.

He was able to piece together what came after from reports sent by Ravagers as they closed in on the target before being destroyed. Those reports told the tale of Paul Reid's obliteration of an entire battalion—of the boy's backlash frying whole sectors of Mr. Brill's infrastructure.

There was no denying the truth of the thing. It was a disaster.

Mr. Brill convulsed and opened his eyes as if recovering from a nightmare—or now waking to one. He tried to form a question, but his voice failed. He leaned over, head between knees, and gulped air.

Waiting for the questions about what had just happened, Truitt formulated the answers that would keep him from joining June Medill in eternal suffering.

PAUL WOKE UP IN THE DARK of his room. For a moment, he thought he'd never left it.

He went into the bathroom and drank some water, then went to the window and pulled the curtains aside, peering out into the night.

In the parking lot, Rain sat on a curb a few yards from the kneeling Po. The monk hadn't moved from the spot where Ken had been killed.

Killed—no matter how much it hurt to say it, to admit that the gentle mummy warrior had sacrificed himself for them. Whatever the question of whether Ravagers or anyone else in The Commons could truly die, the mummy was no longer with them.

"Goodbye, friend," he'd said before taking Paul's burden on himself—a weight that had crushed him.

Ken was gone.

Paul went outside and crossed the moonlit parking lot. His storm had taken out all the pole lamps. He sat on the curb beside Rain.

She didn't look at him, instead watching Po grieve. Her eyes reflected the monk's anguish. She'd been crying.

"Look what I did," she said.

"You?"

"It was coming for me when Ken..."

"Oh, no. Come on. No way."

She began to cry again—quiet tears.

He rested his fingers on her arm. "Who was it after? Who should have stopped it? Me. I didn't finish it. I thought I did, but I didn't. And then I wasn't quick enough to realize what Ken was doing. We lost him because he was protecting me. Because everyone has to protect me."

Moving his hand along her neck, he stopped at the holster strapped across her shoulders. He'd seen it, but it hadn't registered. Her pack sat beside her. "Hey. Were you—are you leaving?"

She didn't answer.

"Rain?"

"It'll be better for you."

"No—no, no."

"I'll be okay."

"I won't." He pulled her close.

"I shouldn't be here."

He chose his words with care. "You asked what I wanted, and I told you I wanted you with me. I still do."

She remained silent, wiping her eyes.

"Let's go inside." He stood and offered her his hand. After a moment, she let herself be pulled to her feet.

Both of them watched the monk. Po wouldn't allow them to do anything for him.

"I know," Paul said. "Believe me. I know."

DAWN PUSHED ITS WAY through the crack between the curtains. Paul turned over to find that Rain was no longer with him, though the shape of her in the sheets proved she had been. He went to the window, looked out, and dressed in a hurry.

Out in the parking lot, Porter stood, pack at his side. Nearby, Rain crouched next to Po, who still hadn't budged. She spoke softly to him as Paul approached in the morning's first light.

"We're very close now," Porter told Paul. "You know that, don't you?"

"Yes."

The Envoy watched Rain coax Po to his feet. "How do you feel?"

"Washed out," Paul said. "But I'm here."

"Do you understand what you did?"

"Not with my head. With my heart, maybe."

"That's all the understanding needed."

Po looked to the crushed frame of the phone booth, lying in its own pebbled glass where Ken had made his decision and left them behind.

"How about you?" Paul said.

The gray man sighed. "I grow old ... I grow old."

Rain bent to brush glass and gravel from Po's robe and asked him something only the monk could hear. He nodded. He was coming with them.

"You're ready for Journey's End," Porter said. "Do you know that as well?"

"I think so."

"Humility is a luxury. Yes, you do. No, you don't."

"Yes."

"I'm sorry, Paul, but that distinction is important. I don't know how many jumps I have left in me. Thanks to Ken, it should be what we need." He looked around at their remaining troupe, measuring each in turn. "Are we ready?"

Paul nodded.

"Yes," said Rain.

Po straightened up, gave the site of Ken's departure one last glance, and joined them. His pride of bearing was his answer.

Porter held his staff out and beckoned each of them to put a hand on it. They did—Rain's atop Po's, Paul's on hers. The Envoy closed his eyes.

He gave the stick a turn.

PART THREE:
IMUURS

....

THIRTY-THREE

EL AEROPUERTO FANTASMAGORICO

They descended into a small airport dotted with patches of gray snow that defied the summer temperatures outside. In a place where sea creatures showed you dead friends and dead media carried you through mirrors, Annie was still surprised to see such hardy remnants of winter.

It was even more puzzling when she realized her error. As Weston took the chopper down, the snow became ashen worms—and the worms became weasels as they approached the tarmac.

When they were 100 feet above a spot near the control tower, a man-sized weasel emerged from the building. He waved his arms to clear away his smaller cousins so that the Black Hawk could touch down. The animals obeyed.

Weston babied the helicopter to the asphalt, and the weasels retreated to avoid the rotors' wash. While the Ravager powered the engines down and the blades slowed, the animals all turned to face the giant weasel, drawing themselves upright in a foot-high wall of fur around the chopper.

The large weasel wasn't a weasel. He was a man in a homemade coat of sewn-together pelts. On his forearm sat a hooded falcon, attached to him with jesses.

The blades stopped. All was silent but for the jingle of the falcon's bells as the man approached. Annie opened the door on her side and climbed out, flexing her knee.

"Howdy," the man said from beneath his fuzzy hood. "I'm Wrangler John. They told me you were on the way. Thank you for not crushing my ferrets."

Then he pulled a .44 Magnum from one of his pockets and took aim at Weston. "They didn't say anything about a black-hat, though."

"He's with me. He won't hurt you."

"Doesn't look like he'll hurt anyone." He lowered his hand-cannon and made it vanish into his pelts.

She turned to look at the pilot. The young man's head rested against his seat, face turned toward her, his visible eye blue glass. He really was gone this time.

Weston.

Annie removed his broken head gear, smoothed his hair, and closed his eyes. Sitting him up straight, she put his helmet in his lap and folded his hands over it. Then she told him goodbye.

The animals remained respectfully silent and upright, as if in salute.

"That's the damnedest thing I ever saw," Wrangler John said as she shut the Black Hawk door. "He brought you here to help—not as a prisoner or anything."

"He's the weird one? You're the weasel whisperer." It came out harsher than she'd intended, her voice hoarse with a grief she hadn't anticipated.

"Ferrets," he said. "Please."

THE AIRPORT HAD NEVER BEEN USED for its original purpose, Wrangler John explained. It was an exact replica of a real-world Spanish boondoggle built in a place no one wanted to fly to.

The ferrets parted for Annie and Wrangler John as they headed for the control tower, scores of them standing upright on either side of the path they cleared like miniature royal guardsmen. Nearby, a field was carpeted with fat rabbits munching away on emerald grass.

Wrangler John lived alone, having been hired to control the bunny and bird populations and make it safer for air traffic. Only there was no air traffic, and the ferrets and the falcon refused to kill any rabbits or birds.

Which was how he liked it. It was important for Annie to understand that he was no life-taker. His coat was made only of the pelts of animals that died of natural causes.

The ferrets kept pace with them as they walked. When they reached the tower, Wrangler John held the door for her.

A sign marked the facility as "El Aeropuerto Fantasmagorico." The letters were bordered in tufts of fur. It appeared to be a hand-crafted labor of love—an artisan-made prototype that would be mass-produced with far less care and sold at the airport gift shop. When Annie asked about that, Wrangler John brightened. He'd made the sign himself, and a shop was in the works. The target opening date had yet to be determined.

Inside, he broke the news with an apologetic tone that they'd have to use the steps to get up top rather than the elevator right in front of them. "We can't spare the battery juice," he said. "We need it to get you tapped in. That's a big pull."

Annie's pride powered her up the stairs, ache and all. She didn't get there fast, but she got there. That was pretty much the theme of her post-warrior years.

Upstairs in the main control room, an array of radar units and computers were draped in plastic tarps. Most were not even plugged in.

In the center of the space, one radar screen stood uncovered. Dark and unpowered, it was a hulk of cold, dead metal. The equipment was ancient, unlike the recently built airport that served as its home. Vintage Cold War screens, green and curved like bottle bottoms, were housed in steel thick as cast-iron skillets.

Wrangler John settled the falcon on a mews in the corner.

"Tapped into what?" Annie said.

"The field. Your friends plus a whole bunch of strangers—unknown to you and me both, which is key. They'll connect you where you need to be connected."

"What kind of strangers?"

"All kinds. Everybody. You can't really name just one."

She eyed the units as he tethered the bird and removed its hood. "How old is this radar?"

"Sonar. You need to listen, not watch."

The sonar unit was dark. "No power?"

He laughed. Taking her by the shoulders, he turned her to the windows behind them.

Out on the asphalt was a football-field-sized spread of hamster wheels the size of car tires, all of them empty. "Watch this."

He crossed the room to a battered metal desk that looked as if it had been scavenged from another era and carted in, which it most likely had. A man who wouldn't let ferret pelts go to waste would see the value in used furniture.

Wrangler John thumbed a switch on a bulky microphone with a base like a clothes iron and a head the size of a pepper mill—the kind Annie hadn't seen since helping with announcements at sleep-away camp. Feedback squealed across the grass and tarmac from speakers on the outside walls and light poles.

He waited for it to fade, clapped his hands into the mike in a staccato pattern, and flipped the switch back off. "Watch," he told her.

The lawn emptied of rabbits. They headed for the wheels, filling them in a quick and orderly fashion—thousands of them stretching to the horizon and beyond.

After a few minutes, Wrangler John turned the mike on and clapped into it again. Annie's old Morse Code training interpreted the single-word command: go.

The rabbits went, setting their wheels into motion. "Give them a sec to hop to it," he said, taking a great deal of pride in his pun. He didn't have company very often.

"You can barely hear them."

He beamed. "It's a constant oiling process. By the time I finish lubing, it's time to start over because the first ones need it again. I keep trying to come up with a more efficient way, but efficiency loses to elegance."

With a low buzz, the ceiling's racks of fluorescent lights flared. Then came a symphony of beeping as the computers awoke in red and green constellations made hazy by their plastic shrouds.

The screen in front of her came to life. A pinpoint of white in the center of its screen grew brighter and spread outward.

"We have solar, too," he said. "But it's not nearly as reliable as the bunnies. Which reminds me."

He pulled a tarp from a unit that looked even older than the others—a rolling leviathan with gun-gray sides. The metal of its cabinet appeared to have been hammered into shape by smiths, not stamped out in a factory.

He palmed a rocker switch to turn the unit on. Nothing happened.

A pop preceded a hiss that sounded more organic than electric.

The air filled with the bouquet of burnt fur. He reached into the unit's back and extricated a smoking ferret, which fled the room as soon as he set it down.

With much muttering, he got the unit up and running. The smell of scorched beast cleared from the air as the machine's hum grew. "You'll like this. You'll like this a lot."

Annie was fairly certain he was speaking to her and not the machine.

She waited a few moments, but her patience was running out. "John?"

"Wrangler John, please." He continued puttering as if the exchange completed the conversation.

"Wrangler John?"

He stopped working, surprised that she wanted more.

"What are we tapping into?"

He blinked several times, like she'd spoken a language he'd only just learned, and he needed time to translate. Then he wiped the dust from his hands onto his coat, saying something in a low voice about how hot it was.

"I'm looking for my son," she said. "What are we doing?"

"Your son?" He wiped again. She suspected there wasn't any dust left; he just needed something to do. "You're telling me it's a kid? The name sounded so grown-up when they sent it. I mean, go figure—Zach."

....

THIRTY-FOUR

THE FARMER AND
THE MONSTERS

T he splashing woke Zach. He lay on his side on the bed-sized rock he was trapped on, his ear sore against a patch of moss covering the hard stone.

It was morning. The sun beat down.

In the air above, large white birds with long bills wheeled about in wide circles. Every now and then, one would bomb down into the lake and bob back up, water draining out of the sides of its face. Sometimes the birds flapped back up into the air, disappointed. Other times, they happily swallowed whatever the water left behind.

They were catching fish. The birds had woken him up over breakfast.

Pelicans. The p-word in the book Zach's mother used when she wanted him to learn letters, even after he'd already learned them and had moved on to whole words. He couldn't read every word, but if he understood what one meant, heard someone say it, and was able to make a connection, he didn't forget it.

Pelican. P was for pelican.

Zach stood for a better look.

The pelicans dove into the water, sometimes coming up with fish, sometimes not. When they did, they took to the rocks to enjoy their meal. Sometimes they tried to take the fish from one another, but for the most part, the supply was such that they could catch what they wanted without having to steal.

The wind moved the water in little waves. However, not all of the waves were blown, and not all of them were small.

Some were made by something underneath the water—they were too fat and slow to have been made by the birds. Zach was safe on his rock, but what was large enough to make such waves?

The rocks around Zach's rock were not far. He could jump to one if he tried really hard. The pelicans stayed off of the ones nearest him. They didn't know that he wouldn't try to catch them like they caught the fish.

He tried to imagine himself trapping one in his mouth. That wouldn't work—and he wasn't hungry.

Many of the surrounding rocks sat in a circle, while others broke the pattern. If Zach stared long enough, he got dizzy from trying to figure out how it worked.

That was how he found the Farmer Says.

He turned around and around, studying the rocks until he stumbled and kicked the moss he'd tried to use as a pillow. There was something solid underneath it—something that shifted when he nudged it with his heel. It wasn't part of the stone.

Zach peeled back the sheet of moss as if he were uncovering a treasure and revealed a toy he knew. It was the one with the little man in the middle who, when his string was pulled, spun around, pointed to things, and announced what they were.

On the one in his class, the little man was a fireman who pointed to firehouse things—an engine, a ladder, a hose. On the one he saw in the store, a circus man pointed to a lion, a tiger, an elephant, and other circus animals.

This one was a farmer. He had a duck, and a pig, and a cow to point to.

He also had animals Zach had never seen on any farm. One looked like an octopus in a shell.

There was also a peacock, a weird squid thing, and a scary lizard-fish that had a head like a snake and a long mouth full of teeth, like a crocodile. Its body appeared to be part polliwog, part shark.

Zach had a hard time sounding out what the word said until he pulled the string. The little farmer went around and stopped on the lizard-fish. "Mosasaur," he said.

Mind the mosasaur. That's what the tape re-corder lady had said. Zach needed no warning. If he saw one, he'd mind it.

He pulled the string again. This time, the little farmer stopped on an open door with an e-word underneath it. "Egress," the farmer said.

A series of loud grunts. The waves in the water became choppier, slapping into one another in a panic. The grunting came from the pelicans as they pulled out of dives or flew up out of the water onto the rocks—even the rocks close to Zach.

They were more afraid of whatever was making the waves than they were of him.

A huge, scaly back broke the surface of the wa-ter—like a fat snake the size of a submarine. One giant flipper came into view and vanished beneath the surface, then another.

The pelicans weren't safe for long. One unlucky bird chose the wrong rock, which was different from the others in a terrible way.

At first, the pelican was well above the waves. Then the rock under it sank, leaving the bird bobbing and flapping in the water.

With the benefit of a few more seconds, the pelican might have gotten up into the air. But it didn't have them.

A crocodile-like snout the size of a bumper car rose up out of the water beneath and took the bird in one piece. It was gone in a squawk.

And the lizard-fish's head continued to emerge from the water.

It was that big.

"Mosasaur," said the farmer. Zach hadn't pulled his string.

The beast rolled toward Zach, one massive eye rising from the water, and looked right at him. It appeared to be grinning, but this wasn't a creature that smiled—or inspired anyone else to. It was all teeth.

"Mosasaur," the farmer repeated.

Zach wanted a bathroom. Even more, he wanted the thing to stop looking at him. He wanted it to leave.

After a long time, it did. With a watery crash, it dove.

Another grunt from farther away. A distant rock sank, depositing its pelican into the water before it could take off.

It met the same fate as the last.

The bird and the rock that betrayed it were too far away for Zach's mosasaur to have gotten over there so fast. There were more than one of the lizard-fish.

The lake was big. It could hold many big things. Many.

The farmer spun on his own again. He stopped on the door. "Egress."

This time, Zach followed the farmer's finger beyond the toy. In the distance, something rectangular jutted up a rock. A real door.

A grunt from behind was followed by splashing before it was cut off. Another rock, another pelican.

The rest of the birds got the message and launched themselves into the air.

Zach looked at the rocks nearest him and then at the door in the distance. He needed to jump from rock to rock to get to the door, but he didn't know which rock would hold him and which would drop from sight, feeding him to the monsters.

The bathroom feeling came back when the rock Zach was standing on shook, tipped slightly, and then tipped back. It wasn't enough to make him fall, but he nearly dropped the Farmer Says toy. The rock vibrated a bit, then stopped.

It was going to happen slowly, but it was going to happen.

A moment later, all of the farther-away rocks sank beneath the waves, along with some of the ones nearest him. That left only a perfect circle of them around Zach's rock, all within jumping distance.

It was a puzzle. A game. Zach had to jump to another rock before the one he was on sank.

Whenever he turned to check the position of one of the monsters, the little farmer pointed to the icon on his wheel and spoke up. "Mosasaur," he said.

And when Zach turned to face the far-off door, the little farmer spun and pointed to the picture of that. "Egress."

He couldn't decide where to jump.

The boulder he was on shook slightly.

"Mosasaur," said the little farmer. "Egress."

....

THIRTY-FIVE

THE SHRINE OF THE LOST

They appeared in a box canyon lit by a combination of daylight and a golden luminescence issued by the rock surfaces. Paul felt none of the dizzying effects of Porter's jumps now.

The morning sky was the rippling blue of a turning opal—a coruscating ceiling. It was a peace Paul didn't want to disturb, not even with the sound of his breath.

The walls were high—and filled with name plaques all the way to their tops. At the canyon's center, a reflecting pool held a mirror image of the sky, its surface pierced by a shaft of sunlight. A small stone bench sat beside it.

"What is this?" Rain's tone was subdued. She, too, was reluctant to break the stillness.

"Unto them will I give in mine house and within my walls a memorial and a name better than of sons and daughters," Porter said. "I will give them an everlasting name, that shall not be cut off." He leaned on his staff. "This is The Shrine of the Lost."

"The lost what?" Paul said.

"Souls. Journeys. Envoys who gave up along the way. The lost purpose of all those Brill has taken— and those left behind. Husbands. Wives. Children. Friends."

Po's sigh shivered off the stone. He was crying.

"My friends and I built this," Porter said. "An Envoy named Audra Farrelly invited that sunbeam in. It's never left, and that was a long time ago. As a creator, I may enter to admit the worthy who have fallen, but only then."

Porter led Po to the bench, and they sat. The Envoy closed his eyes, and the monk followed suit.

Faint voices filled the air around them, rising in volume until words could be heard. Mothers called for girls who would never come home. Whistles trilled for long-gone boys to return from the park. Ringing phones would not be answered. An old woman cried, "I'm trying!"

Lonely zephyrs.

The sunbeam heeded Porter's and Po's meditation, widening over the water to embrace them. Slivers of light broke away to highlight two of the plaques on the walls, one bright and new, the other tarnished with years.

"Khentimentiu: friend," read the first. "Honorable always, honored now."

The old plaque was much higher on the wall, but Paul could read it as if it were right in front of him. The light granted him that. "John Vincent Porter, b. 1927 - d. 1931," it said. And on the line below: "Have you news of my boy Jack?"

"My last descendant," Porter said. "No more."

"I'm sorry," said Rain, wiping away tears of her own.

"Thank you. As am I—for the heedless time that led to my own Journey long ago. Sorry that Brill has kept me and those like me from guiding others and redeeming ourselves and sorry that he's destroyed so many who'll never have the opportunity." He stood and looked up at the illuminated names. "For John, for Ken. For Paul and what he bears. For all of us."

The light faded from the plaques, which blended in with their brethren again.

"Oh, but I'm the grim one, eh?" Porter said. "There's some good fortune in the loss that carried us here. Ken's sacrifice was a gift greater than he knew."

"How so?" Paul said.

"Like Austen's Nightlights, the Shrine is not a constant place. It opens only to mark the passing of one who's earned its notice. Because of Ken, we're much nearer to our destination. This is accessible from anywhere in The Commons, which means we can go anywhere from here. It's a roundhouse—a waypoint."

Po rose, eyes dry now. He was prepared.

Paul wasn't. Leaving The Shrine was like the loss of someone dear. They weren't meant to stay, but it felt as if he'd found a thing long missing, reflected in his mother's eyes in her photo, whatever she saw when turning to look at it. Now it was being taken from him. "To where?"

Porter held out his staff in answer. They put their hands on it in the same order as before, Paul pausing to look around once more before taking hold of it.

The sunbeam twitched, and Ken's plaque glinted in response—a star passing through their group, touching all of them in turn, Po last of all.

Porter gave his staff a turn.

THEY ARRIVED IN THE CENTER of a road that crossed a sweeping playa, its asphalt bleached and fissured from years of abiding the sun's abuse. The dotted line bisecting it was nearly invisible.

It was twilight. The opal had turned again; the air was now coral and plum.

Across the expanse of the playa's sands, mammoth dunes rose from the floor, reaching toward mountains beyond. The sky over the peaks was thick with black clouds, the heavens a purple crown.

"Gaia?" Paul said.

"Journey's End," said Porter. "I'm not permitted to continue—I must send you on without me."

"Alone?"

The Envoy looked at Po, then Rain. "I don't think so."

"This is where it ends."

"No. This is where it begins."

Paul watched the rolling ink of the clouds. "Whatever it is, I'll handle it."

"Wherever would we be without the hopes of our youth?" the Envoy said sincerely.

"We'd disappear," said Rain.

Porter held his staff out, and they all grasped it in their customary order. "When you arrive, Paul, there may be no one with you. But I think one of us will be—whoever's meant to."

Paul searched the gray man's eyes for guidance.

"Whatever you face, whatever fight you find, stay true," Porter said. "You cannot go astray if you do."

"This isn't just about me, is it?"

The Envoy watched the heavens stir and weighed his answer. "What I've seen you do here reflects an ability unmatched, except by that of Brill himself. I've been out of the game, but I trust what I feel and know." The clouds tumbled in the fading light. His eyes never left them. "I believe you've tapped into the fundamental Essence of The Commons, as he does. The difference is that he's stolen it, whereas it reaches out to you. He's addicted to his power—and doesn't know that. You can serve yours without being yoked to it. That's the key to mastery. You cannot serve what you do not know, and you cannot know what you do not respect. It's chosen you, but you don't own it. Gratitude is your strength."

"*Chien li ti kwei yu yi shuay,*" Po said. All three of them started at the sound of the monk speaking. "An ant may well destroy a whole dam."

Porter eyed the monk with an even greater appreciation than before and nodded in agreement.

"Serve or misuse? That's the question. Your answer? You'll know it now."

He gave the staff's wood a twist.

PAUL AND RAIN ARRIVED, just the two of them, on another flat expanse of desert. They stood under the canopy of black clouds, separated from Porter and Po by the mountains and dunes.

All around was Gaia, a temporary city of themed camps, tents, and intricate works of art. A matchstick cathedral awaited the faithful. A graveyard of tombstones in Day-Glo blues, reds, greens, and oranges represented those who'd miss the service.

"Hey," Paul said.

"Yeah." Rain's confidence had deserted her again.

The tent camps and shelters were marked by painted-wood and neon signs. Void, Comix, Script Kitty, Pagan Rights, Atro-Fee, Body Shot, Zen-Sation. The tubes of the signs were dark, without power. The tents were empty, as if the party had only just ended, its revelers departed in haste.

Surveying it all, bathing it in a glow of lavender, cinnamon, and buttercup, was the titular Gaia herself, a fifty-foot wood-frame woman in a state of advanced pregnancy. The light from the neon tubes outlining her was the only illumination in all of Gaia.

"Paul?"

A woman's voice from behind the Comix tent.

He took off running.

"Who do you think built—" Rain said. By the time he rounded the tent corner, she was yelling his name.

Beyond Comix sat a big-top-sized tent-building: a framed-canvas carnival mansion.

He saw her. The color of her hair. She was walking away from him, down the long scarlet carpet of the tent's front entrance. Overhead, a canopy of crimson-striped canvas and ornate black fringe, small gold flags atop its peaks, sheltered her as she abandoned him.

Again.

Her hair was the red of the photo.

"Mom?"

Rain found him just as Jeanne, his mother—his *mother*—vanished into the tent's interior.

"Are you crazy?" Rain said. "You don't just take off like that."

Only minutes before, her worry would have meant everything to him. Now he had no room for it.

His mother.

"Hello, Paul."

A thin white-haired man in a business suit stood at the near end of the big tent's walk. He wouldn't step beyond its border. That wasn't permitted.

Rain took Paul's hand, her palm damp.

"Welcome," the man said. "My name is Gerald Truitt."

....

THIRTY-SIX

TIME WILL TELL

A nnie tapped into the network—and almost lost her mind.

Wrangler John's setup lacked the buffers and niceties of Mr. Brill's. There were no shields to safeguard her from the potency of the information that engulfed her when she made contact.

Just as bad was when that information realized it was hurting her. It reversed itself and withdrew, nearly yanking her consciousness right out of her head.

As a teenager, she'd jumped into a hard surf on Nantucket, the first time she'd been in the ocean in years. She'd assumed that because she'd grown bigger and stronger, she'd be able to handle whatever the water was capable of dishing out.

The first wave took her over its crest and drove her into the carved-out sand beneath the foam. Then the undertow had tried to make the lesson permanent by drawing her out to sea.

Tapping in, getting swamped by data, and having the data retreat was much the same as being body slammed by the Atlantic.

Only worse.

"I don't know the particulars," Wrangler John said.

She forced herself to keep peering into the red goggle-like thing he called a Virtual Boy, or VB. The name he used for it depended on how fast he was trying to explain one step in the process before moving to the next.

"A lot of people took on a lot of risk to get your boy to where he is," he said. "You know the drill. No single one of us knows the whole scheme, which keeps us from giving it away if The Ravagers come calling. But that means there's no one to tell you how this works. I can get you started, but you'll have to figure out where to find him. He needs help. And he needs it now."

She rolled her chair back from the VB and the table on which it sat. Half her brain remained in the red landscape. "Where is he?"

"That's what I'm trying to say. I don't know."

She looked him up and down for soft spots.

He took a step backward. "You find him, and you help him. You're the only one who can. That's all they told me. Honest."

"Who are they?"

"Everyone."

"Who is everyone? What does that mean?"

"You. Me. All of us. You have to see for yourself, or you won't believe me."

"What about Brill?"

"Him, too, which is why we have to stay on the down-low while we work. That's the risk. We all came out of safe places to do this because in the end, nothing's safe with Brill in power."

She held him in a hard stare.

"That's all I know."

"Who's in charge?"

"Good question."

She marked her spot on his body visually without lingering long enough to tell him what to protect. Targeting was a comfort.

So. The Virtual Boy. This time, the joining was more gentle, as if the force there expected her return and had adjusted for it.

"I think—" said Wrangler John.

"Shush."

The VB goggles presented a purple-on-black cartoon reef. Blocky, pixelated starfish bopped across it, dancing to a tune only they could hear.

The longer she watched, the more convincing the reef became.

Gradually, greens and yellows were introduced, then a clumsy illusion of three dimensions that slowly grew lifelike. She was immersed in an undersea realm.

The reef was real. It had been when she'd encountered it in her cubicle in Mr. Brill's offices, too—but not like this. Here, she was one with the waves washing through the structure, united with the creatures who called it home.

A blenny peeked out of its hiding spot, then disappeared when she looked at it. Parrotfish scored the coral near a colony of psychedelic shrimp.

It was absolutely beautiful. Yet she was about to pull away again and demand that Wrangler John help her find Zach when she was rudely interrupted by an inability to breathe.

She was underwater. Real water. And she wasn't a fish.

Her choked whoop was filtered by the sea around her. She sounded exactly like she would have expected someone inhaling an ocean to sound. And just as one couldn't look cool riding a merry-go-round or eating spaghetti, she was sure she came off as very silly while drowning.

Wrangler John said something and touched her shoulder.

She flapped her arm, shaking him off.

For the first time since quitting the pinkies, she wasn't aware of any pain in her knee. Mainly because she was about to black out.

The nautilus appeared. And just like that, she could breathe.

She had no hint of its approach. It went from absent to present, and then she was sucking wind like a sprinter.

It wasted no time with pleasantries, didn't wait for her to catch her breath. It began spinning into the coral, as it had when it led her to Charlene. But it moved faster now, and she didn't need to ask why.

Something was wrong. They had to hurry.

"They told me they could keep him safe for a while, but you have to take over." Wrangler John's voice bled through the salty water and foam.

She ignored him.

The nautilus twirled into a blur, and Annie, still giddy from lack of oxygen, recalled those old black-and-whites where the front page of a newspaper spun toward the screen and stopped, its headline announcing a new plot point.

Drowning was kind of a stop-the-presses thing.

The nautilus's spinning slowed. Its circle began to reveal itself as something else.

The ocean bottom disappeared. She was somewhere in the reef's middle and saw nothing in the depths until, strangely, a new seafloor rose rapidly toward her.

At first, it was a single moving layer. Soon it became a mass of shiny cones with eyes.

Squid.

Humboldt squid, which she'd never seen or heard of before. But she knew what they were called anyway. And that knowledge, newly discovered in her head, was not her own.

Someone touched her. She remembered that the someone's name was Wrangler John. She wanted to ask him if his knack for communing with mustelids and leporids extended, perhaps, to befriending carnivorous cephalopods.

Once again, she had no idea where those details were coming from.

The squid swarmed—touching, identifying, maybe trying to see if she was edible. Then they were gone.

With a brush and a tickle, the water was empty.

Or not.

What started as a hunch became certainty. A sense of vague, mammoth shapes far down, far away.

Something else was in the water with her now. Bad. Huge. Many.

The giants were a danger to her. To the reef itself.

Someone was in trouble. Prey.

She allowed her awareness to wander too close to the monsters—to their ancient consciousness, their forever mouths and teeth, their hunger. As craven as it was to think so, she was relieved that they sought someone else, not her.

The nautilus was gone.

She'd thought of it as a mere magical familiar, her guide to the data. It was so much more. It was, as Wrangler John said, everyone.

Everything.

In its place was a stunning mandala of a peacock in shifting detail and shades. Its tail feathers formed a circle that filled the disk shape the nautilus had traced. The magnificent bird's deep-seeking eyes were its center.

Eyes that saw into her. Through her. Beyond her.

Once again, she was in the presence of some-thing that, if it wished, could pull her mind from her—reduce her to a husk, a cicada shell clinging to a tree in the muggy rattle of early August.

She couldn't escape the eyes, and she couldn't look at them. To attempt it was tantamount to fac-ing a star gone nova.

There was no menace here, nothing like that of the vague giants. But it was too much. It would end her.

She stood before the eyes of the gods. "Please," she whispered.

The scrutiny ceased. The tail feathers spread further. And the bird was gone.

It took Annie long seconds to process what was revealed: a honeycomb pattern, a close-up of a pinecone seen from above. A ghost of biology class, when teachers made her and her friends go gather-ing in the woods, bringing with them inevitable dirt, mites, and other assorted insect visitors.

The pinecone, too, faded.

Revelation.

If she could have screamed into the water, she would have. It all fit.

She understood. She knew what the threat was in the vast reaches and depths.

Sunk into the reef, revealed now, was a marred clock face. She'd bought one just like it—a time-teaching toy—at a flea market at the Cathedral of Saint John the Divine, where peacocks roamed the grounds. Its flaws had matched this one chip for chip, scratch for scratch.

The toy had never delivered the lessons she'd hoped it would.

But as the clock grew translucent—as images beneath became clearer—she understood.

The massive horrors in the water. Creatures felt but not seen.

They were Brill.

And she knew now who their prey was.

Zach jumped because he couldn't stay on the sinking rock. With his eye on the far-off door—a way out, he hoped—he leapt for the rock between him and it. He held tight to the Farmer Says. Maybe it had more to tell him.

His takeoff carried him farther than he'd thought he could jump, but he didn't think about that for long. As he was about to land, the rock vanished.

He went feet-first into the waves and plunged beneath them. His world became water, and the next mistakes came one after the other.

The first was opening his eyes, only to find that he could see perfectly. That was okay in the swimming pool where Zach and Zach's mother would go in the summer so that he could practice holding his face under and blowing bubbles. It was not okay when it showed him one of the mosasaurs hurtling through the water at him—a black cave rimmed with teeth the size of knives, growing as it approached.

The next was inhaling water. His lungs fought back with bubbles that blocked the lizard-fish from his view—and reminded him that he didn't know how to swim.

The little farmer saved him. The farmer and the pelicans.

Despite the fear and choking, Zach hung onto the toy. It pulled him upward. It shouldn't have been able to, but things worked differently here.

As he rose, balls of white hit the water hard, shooting past him and down into the depths.

Zach got to the surface and coughed up water. He managed to hang onto the farmer, which kept him from sinking.

All around, pelicans dropped from the sky as fast as they could.

At first, he thought that they, too, were enemies trying to target him. But they pierced the waves a distance away—nowhere near him—and he saw what they were up to.

They didn't come back up. Not one of them. They dive-bombed the mosasaur, and the water grew choppy and red as the monster fish, distracted by food so close by, thrashed about and devoured the birds.

The pelicans were sacrificing themselves for him.

Buoying himself with the farmer, Zach made for the only rock left—the one he should have chosen. The stone he'd stood on was gone, as were the others. With the mosasaur closest to him distracted, he had a chance.

He held the little farmer out in front of him and kicked, as he'd seen kids do at the pool. He made headway. But then there were no diving pelicans left, and the mosasaur was not far.

It was forever. He kicked furiously, water splashing about behind him. The rock grew closer—but not close enough.

The mosasaur did the rest of the work. It came for him, pushing a mass of water ahead.

The wave it created picked Zach up and carried him to the rock with speed—too much speed. Right before he smacked into the side of the stone, he turned his face and struck it with his ear and chest.

Zach nearly lost his grip on the farmer, but was able to toss it up onto the rock and grab at the stone's side. His fingers, wet and soft, tore. It felt like they were being set aflame by the salt water.

He barely made it.

As he hauled himself up onto the rock, the scales of the mosasaur's green back broke the surface just beyond the stone—in front of him now. The great creature breached and dove back into the waves, foam flying in a pageant of predator anger. Another wave washed across the rock as a second monster made its presence known.

"Mosasaur," said the little farmer. Zach needed no reminding of what he faced. "Egress."

The boulder with the door on it was closer now. Zach's rock was ringed by new neighbors.

Already the subtle vibration had begun. His new safety wouldn't last.

He had to choose again, and there were no pelicans left to save him in the next round. No more mistakes allowed.

"Mosasaur," said the little farmer as one passed underneath, generating another swell. "Egress."

Zach eyed the rock directly between him and the door. That had been the wrong choice last time, but he badly wanted to try that way again. It was the straight line.

His rock trembled, signaling its impending descent.

"Egress," said the farmer.

The little man had saved his life. But Zach really wished he'd shut up.

....

THIRTY-SEVEN

THIS IS WHERE IT BEGINS

"I t's okay."

Rain didn't answer, but she gripped Paul's hand hard. It wasn't clear where her urgency came from—fear of their situation or the desire to lend him strength.

Beneath those possibilities lurked a third answer. And Paul put it aside.

Before they stepped onto the carpet, they set their packs down, planning to retrieve them on the way back out. The man who'd introduced himself as Truitt betrayed nothing with his expression, but Paul had the feeling he was amused that they assumed they'd return here.

Entering the huge tent, they found themselves in a long corridor darkened by thick canvas walls on either side. It was difficult to see those walls clearly in the gloom, but Paul felt the pressing weight of them.

Truitt walked ahead, his silhouette framed in a small square of light at the corridor's end. "Your arrival's been greatly anticipated," he said without looking back at them.

Rain squeezed harder still.

Paul suspected that Truitt was speaking to him alone. It was all he could do not to ask about Jeanne, which was probably why Rain held his hand so tightly. She didn't want him bolting again.

He wouldn't do that for the same reason he wouldn't ask Truitt where his mother had gone. It was too delicate—too precious. He didn't want to risk destroying it or scaring it away.

Paul did not like Truitt. Nor did Rain. The way she looked at the man, and he at her, spoke of a familiarity and contempt Paul needed to understand.

Yet he didn't want to. He'd shut those questions out all along—since her tattoo had caught the fly in the van, since she'd blasted Deck through the bathroom door.

Rain had layers. Everyone did. She just might have had more than most.

The light ahead promised knowledge. Jeanne, the Journey, and what his final challenge would be.

Knowledge of Rain, whom he thought he might love. He knew so little about her. He knew so little about love.

But her hand was in his, and she held on. If this was not love, it was the closest he'd ever come. And it was enough.

Jeanne was ahead. He felt her near. And this dark, beautiful girl, in a dream he feared questioning lest he kill it, might even love him back.

So he followed the man he didn't like. He prayed the man would lead him to his mother, that he would face Journey's End bravely, that he would be a match for it.

And he said not a thing.

The light at the end of the corridor was a curtain of white. When Truitt entered it, the white grew too bright to look at. Framed in the glare, he was all shadow, no features.

"There are doors we are required to pass through," Truitt said. "We are expected, and this is what is demanded of us. Much to do—"

He disappeared into the white. It sealed itself behind him, cutting off whatever he said next, dimming until it was more tolerable to look at.

Paul made for the light. Rain held on, trying to stop him. At the point where he would have had to pull her, the white brightening around him, she came along.

Her grip never let up.

They passed through into a shadowy but sumptuous hallway. Its walls were paneled in dark wood, from which sprang gas lamps with crystal globes that threw shifting patterns of fiery veins onto the ceiling. Their feet sank into thick carpet.

Paul was not impressed by money in principle, but presented with what it could buy, he was cowed just the same.

There was wealth here. Wealth and power.

At the end of the hallway stood two massive doors of old hardwood, darker than the wall panels. Such doors opened on places of import. In the flickering light of the gas lamps, figures carved into the door appeared to dance.

Truitt grasped one of a pair of filigreed knobs covered in whorls tarnished with age. Each was the size of a dinner plate. His hand was tiny against it, as Paul and Rain would be against whatever lay beyond.

The door opened too easily for its size, revealing a cozy living-room setting. Rather, it was the foyer entrance to one. They could see the room it led to in a tall antique mirror set at an angle across a marble floor.

Only one detail in the room reflected in the glass mattered to Paul. A wood-and-velvet couch faced away from the mirror. On it, her back to them, sat a red-haired woman attending to a steaming teapot.

Her.

"Don't," Rain said. "Let's go back."

Paul stepped into the foyer. Rain maintained her grip and crossed the threshold with him.

The door shut behind them, its mass venting a hiss of air from the room. Rain let go of his hand.

They'd been fooled.

The mirror was gone—and with it the room and the red-haired woman. Truitt was nowhere to be seen.

They now stood in a spacious office filled with floating screens that were all dark. In the center of it sat a large man behind an even larger desk.

His suit fit him perfectly. His smile did not.

Rain chambered a round.

Paul didn't need that clue.

He knew the man.

....

THIRTY-EIGHT

SECOND GUESS

Over the years, Annie had been called mother, data jockey, and soldier. That was the order of importance, and she'd never imagined it would ever be shuffled.

But her son now faced horrific danger, and there was only one way to see him through it. She had to be all three.

The mother needed to be controlled. If she lost her head, Zach died. So she'd use all of her training for how to remain rational under fire—her days of real bullets sent her way. The focus that had carried her from bed, to wheelchair, to crutches, to cane, to brace—and then, finally, to carrying her own weight.

The clock game's familiarity meant a connection to Zach. The rocks around him matched the positions of the numbers. The images she saw through the clock face were distorted, but the data flow told her the rest—the data and the bond between mother and child.

In the first round, Zach had chosen the direct line to the door. That was most definitely wrong. However, she couldn't determine the clock's orientation, so she didn't know what hour the correct choice represented. Where was twelve? Where was six?

The rules, as far as she had deduced from the flow of information, were these: when the second hand finished one revolution, his rock would lower him into the water with the killing giants if he was still on it.

Annie screened that part out. It profited nothing to allow it in.

Choosing the wrong rock did the same thing. But the correct rock restarted the clock, giving him another sixty seconds—and a whole new circle of options from which to choose. The point of the whole exercise was for him to reach the door—the way out.

All Annie had to do was pick the right rock and figure out how to communicate her choice to Zach. Then she had to do it again and again until he was free.

First things first. Make fast choices, and try to learn something each time. The second hand was nearly halfway around, and she had no clue which number to choose next.

Clue. The key part of the time-teaching game they'd played at home.

Three clues.

What hour did Zach jump to last round? She concentrated as hard as she could on silently asking the question.

Nothing.

She repeated it out loud.

"What?" said Wrangler John from far away.

Annie shushed him.

The clock game's hour hand clicked to one o'clock, which wasn't really much help in choosing the next one. She couldn't assume that the stone closest to the door would always be twelve, even though it had been in the last round.

Why hadn't she just asked which rock was the right choice? She'd wasted a clue.

"What was that?" Wrangler John said.

Annie waved her hand frantically in the water.

She must have done the same in the room she sat in because he shut up.

The second hand grew hideously close to completing its revolution. There was only time enough to shout a guess.

She went with what had worked last time. "One o'clock!"

"What?" said Wrangler John.

The number one turned green on the clock face, indicating her choice.

It was a horrible joke. She saw no way for her son to get the message. How could he know how the clock face was oriented? How could he know it was a clock at all?

The most horrible part, of course, was that he was a boy of five.

He didn't know how to tell time.

....

THIRTY-NINE

AN OFFER, AN ANSWER

M r. Brill had a talent shared by many a tough guy in the neighborhood around New Beginnings. He was completely at ease with silence.

He lorded that over Paul and Rain, reptilian smile on display while they awaited his words. He was a businessman, but Paul knew the street version of the game. Don't speak if you don't have to—few words, more power.

If Mr. Brill was concerned that he was unarmed while Rain held a loaded shotgun, he hid it well. He offered Paul a seat in front of his desk. There was only one, and thus no such offer for Rain.

Paul declined.

"This will be easier if you sit." Mr. Brill's voice was too loud after the peace of Gaia. "But it'll be easy all the same—for you, for me, for The Commons. All I have to say is this: congratulations."

Rain let her shotgun creep up, but a warning glance from Mr. Brill made her reconsider. She aimed it at the floor again.

Paul suspected that wouldn't last long.

"For what?" Paul said when it was apparent that Mr. Brill wouldn't speak again without a response.

"For completing your Journey—for acing your test. You knew that the Shade was my proxy."

Paul nodded.

"And you know that the Journey ends with your challenge. What you don't know is that the rules need not be so unforgiving, especially when I've changed them." He drew the moment out. "You'll ask how, but had your Envoy stayed current instead of sitting and rotting in his office, he could have told you. I am The Commons. The Commons is me, and so are its laws. Your challenge was to overcome my Shade—and through it, me."

"Why?"

"How else was I to know whether you really are what you appear to be?" He waited again. "You really aren't aware, are you?" A professionally placed laugh. "You're Nistarim, and you don't even know it."

Paul tried to buy time with silence of his own. He didn't have Mr. Brill's knack.

"The Lamed Vav," Mr. Brill continued. "I know you know. Your Envoy, slow as he was, told you about them. The fact that I know, and why I know, is another part of the story. But we'll get to that."

The big man squared his shoulders and the screens around him came to life. They were filled with horror, with abomination. Hanging bodies in webbed cocoons. Sodden people in a swamp. Wasted leavings of humanity, terrified, clinging to a cliff in a cold wind, toes out over the lip of an inadequate ledge. Ravagers truncheoned new arrivals, beat them down with rifle butts.

"The Thirty-Six Righteous Ones." Mr. Brill said. "Their power is yours, Paul. You've proven that. You couldn't manipulate the Essence of The Commons if it weren't."

"You're lying. The Nistarim can't know who they are."

Mr. Brill sighed. "I never should have killed so many Envoys. Maybe you would have gotten one with sense." He looked around at the screens, enthralled by the power that was his—the people, the Essence. "Use your head. The Nistarim lose their power as soon as they know of it? Does that add up?"

Paul was listening for the lie, but couldn't hear it. He looked to Rain for help.

She kept her cold stare on Mr. Brill.

"You were able to do what you did because of your place among the Thirty-Six, and you know I speak true. You defeated a thing of my creation—a part of me. You are what you are."

"Our friend died killing your monster," Rain said.

Mr. Brill shrugged. Ken's death was inconsequential. And he still didn't bother to look at her. "How can I tell what you are?" he said to Paul. "How have I been able to achieve what I have?" He folded his arms, and his suit rippled with the muscle beneath. "I think you know."

No. Paul didn't.

Rain tried to raise her shotgun again. She failed.

"Paul." The big man smirked. "You're Nistarim."

She tried one more time. Nothing.

"Only here's the thing." Mr. Brill's face was once again that of a pleased carnivore. "So am I."

HER SON'S LIFE depended on a little plastic man in overalls. The farmer spun and pointed with an enthusiastic, "Egress!"

Zach wasted no time. He jumped.

Annie saw his foot leave the rock, but her mind was on the dragon fish. She knew it was properly called a mosasaur, but a child's name made it seem just that much less deadly—and only just. The monsters could easily breach the waves and pluck Zach from the air. She'd seen videos of flying great whites. That didn't seem to be in the rules here, thank God.

He landed with a yelp. It was Annie who'd made the sound. The rock was real. She'd chosen correctly.

The second hand wouldn't stop to throw her a party, and she had no idea why one o'clock had been the right answer again. There was no safety here.

With that knowledge came even more knowledge, an expanded awareness well beyond hers. The knowledge of the nautilus.

There were other things in the water, which wasn't water at all. It was Essence expressed.

When Annie let down her guard, it came together. The water, The Commons, shared borders with other realms—with the "real" world that she came from and beyond.

Infinity was an inadequate term. Essence was so much bigger than Brill and The Commons. It was too much for her mind to hold. To remain tapped in, she had to keep the information that didn't fit the current situation at bay.

One notion moved forward to present itself. The water monsters were not all alike. There was one far below—much larger and blackberry-colored in contrast to the greenish-brown of the others. It remained in the deep, blocking her out completely. Whether it was Brill himself or merely a servant there to rule the others, she didn't know. It was walled off, and that scared the hell out of her.

The hand had nearly completed its revolution. She was almost out of time again, and she had no more an idea of what to choose than she'd had before. Clocks showed no mercy.

She used the second of her three clues to ask for the number. She said it out loud, her training keeping the quaver from her voice in case Zach could hear. With just one clue left now, the clock's two glowed green.

"POWER IS NOT ABOUT MORALS—not about ethics," Mr. Brill said. "It's about wisdom. It's wise to use it, stupid not to. Power has no right or wrong. It's yours, or it's not." He nodded with satisfaction.

"And it's ours, Paul. We are Nistarim—two of the Thirty-Six."

The big man stood, relaxed, as if talking to friends. Rain, of course, would have had him staring down a barrel by now if he'd let her.

Despite the many questions still to be asked, though, Paul knew this: Mr. Brill was no friend.

"I'll put this to you and let you mull it over," Mr. Brill continued. "Consider that you and I share a power—an astounding ability possessed by only thirty-four others. Who are they? I don't know. I don't care. By myself, I have harnessed the power of The Commons. Imagine what two of us might do together."

The earlier silence had been unnerving. This was worse.

"One more thing. What was your Journey?" Mr. Brill didn't wait for Paul to admit that he had no idea. "What if the challenge was the Journey itself, to prove that you are what so many before you appeared to be, but weren't—a fellow Nistar? All you'd have to do now to decide your fate is agree to change the world—all of the worlds—with me. Think of it."

He sat back down. Even in his chair, he remained above them. The smile returned.

If Paul put his feelings aside, what Mr. Brill said had a logic to it. But he was wrong. Power and the decision to use it were absolutely a question of morality. Pop Mike had taught him that.

Yet Mr. Brill was right in the sense that it was about wisdom, too. Combining Paul's morality and Mr. Brill's experience might work. The power obeyed both of them. Could Paul influence Mr. Brill—apply a fairness to Mr. Brill's domain?

Maybe fighting the Mr. Brills, blazing it out with them, was not the way to go. That was their game. Lose, and you squander your chance to make a difference. Win, and you become like them for your victory. So how was that better? If Paul were to ask Mr. Brill whether he could make a promise and honor it, the answer might tell him all he needed to know.

"Don't." Rain never took her eyes off Mr. Brill. "You'll be done before you start. He can't take it from you. Don't give it to him."

Mr. Brill's face betrayed nothing. But his eyes darkened, deepened.

"Ask yourself one thing if you don't ask anything else," she said. "He tried to kill you. He tried to kill all of us. Without Ken, he might have done it. But he failed. Why?"

Paul could feel the shadow rising up in the big man.

"He's afraid of you. He can't beat you without your help. And everything he puts into fighting you makes it harder to keep the Essence he's stolen under his control. So how about asking him something? Ask him to show you where your new home will be after he's suckered you."

Paul heard what she said. It rang true. But it also led to other more pressing questions: How did Rain know that Mr. Brill would put him anywhere? How did she know what it was to cut a deal with him?

With a speed that rivaled Po's, Mr. Brill backhanded the air in front of him, as if ridding it of a pest. Without his hand getting anywhere near Rain, he smacked her with sickening force. She flew one way, her gun another.

Mr. Brill turned to Paul.

FORTY

....

UNUS PRO OMNIBUS

Z ach landed on a patch of algae slime and almost slid off the number-two rock. Somehow, he managed to catch himself.

That was the brutal rule set of this game. Annie could buy information but not guarantees. After her last clue was gone, either she figured out the logic behind the sequence—and she prayed there was one—or she continued guessing with one-in-twelve odds, a ninety-two percent chance on every attempt that she'd point her son toward his death.

The second hand continued its revolution. Was it speeding up, or was it the terror that made it seem that way? How much time had she just wasted wondering that?

The Humboldt squid returned. In ones and twos at first. Then the layer of them grew in the surrounding water, swirling at the edge of her vision, plucking at her thoughts.

They amused themselves by trying to distract her. And when she reached out with her mind to push them away, one responded.

With a slip of its clawed tentacle, it reached into her, the Essence of its brethren coming with it. She stifled the urge to cry out, afraid that Wrangler John might break the connection if she did.

It wasn't an attack. There was no pain. It was a bonding, not a piercing, and it brought the consciousness of lives uncounted with it. The squid throttled back for her sake, just as the reef had. They were trying to help.

She was down to one clue. She let them.

Her mind bloomed into dream. Charlene on the table. Annie had no sense of herself on the table next to her, as she had been when the doctors, via the protocol of triage, had abandoned Char to her fate. Here, the light remained in her friend's eyes.

"That's an order," Charlene told her.

Neither Annie nor Char had been much for chain-of-command. Char was carrying out the routine they used whenever they needed to violate a rule. One would order the other to do the forbidden thing, creating an excuse to cross the line. It was never delivered with serious intent, but Charlene wasn't kidding now.

"What is?"

"The order," Char said.

The second hand drew near. The hand. The monsters. The immense mosasaur so far below—dwarfing the others, blue now when it had been purple. And the doctors who let Charlene Moseley die because triage determined the order.

Annie would have to use her last clue. One, two, three clues in order. The deadline approached, the point of doom after two right answers—one, two.

In order. The order.

"Three," Annie said.

The little farmer spun and pointed. "Egress," he said.

Zach got whatever running start he could on the too-small stone and leapt.

The Humboldt's tentacle flexed. Data flowed. For no reason Annie could discern, with her little boy in the air, death below, and the decision made, she thought of the skinny boy on the bus.

Paul.

IT ALWAYS CAME down to a fight.

Paul used to think that only happened in his world—the world of kids with nothing but taking if you won and losing if you lost. Later, he learned that it was the same everywhere.

Some fights had rules that were broken once they got going, but most had none from the start. Paul was used to that, just as he was accustomed to the luck of it. Sometimes you had it on your side, and sometimes it was with the other guy. And you needed to appreciate it when you caught a break.

Paul's break came right after Mr. Brill leapt over the desk and presented himself, daring Paul to take a swing at him. Paul missed, distances being deceptive in the office. But he was nearly as grateful as he was surprised when he pulled off the same no-contact trick Mr. Brill had used against Rain. The big man went sailing back across the space.

Rain struggled to her hands and knees, shaking her head to clear it. Paul hurried over to her.

From behind them, Mr. Brill laughed.

A moment later, the office became a vast, empty warehouse with an endless expanse of concrete floor. He gave them just long enough for the change to register before he introduced another.

The portion of the floor beneath Paul, as well as the surrounding area, became a thin sheet of glass, which shattered under his weight. He plummeted

for long seconds into a shaft as deep as a well before hitting sand at the bottom of it. The impact
knocked the wind out of him. Broken glass bit into
his palms as he pushed himself upright.

Sand began to pour down onto him from above.

Mr. Brill was going to bury him.

He made the mistake of looking up as he got to
his feet. Grit coated his eyes and the inside of his
mouth, but not before he spied the stamp-sized
square of the pit's opening far above.

The sand around his legs rose, encasing them,
squeezing.

Soon enough, it was to his waist.

IT WASN'T AS EASY as one-two-three. It couldn't be.
Yet Zach landed safely on the next stone, and the
second hand made its way onward with stomach-
fluttering speed.

It seemed simple enough. The order had held
for three moves in a row, so Annie should have felt
pretty good about four being next.

But it couldn't be that easy.

The Humboldt were restless. The tentacle
pushed deeper into her consciousness, turning as it
did so.

She was swamped with knowledge that was of no use to her at the moment. Paul was on the outer reaches of her thinking. Charlene remained, but Annie couldn't focus enough to ask her friend for help in choosing.

Doubt was at its worst in a hot situation. You questioned yourself when you needed to make decisive moves. It was a problem of will.

Force it. Proceed.

Well, you couldn't. Because the time you hammered the questions down and out of sight might be the time it was critical to ask them.

The answer was in Char's eyes. And Annie couldn't read it.

The hand was nearly at its zenith. She decided to go with four.

But Char.

Her last clue.

She used it. The correct choice glowed green on the clock face.

"Five!"

"What?" said Wrangler John.

WITHIN A FEW YEARS after his mother's death, Paul had been in more scraps and beat-downs than he could recall—had faced kids he couldn't name. He'd lost some and come out of others in better shape than his opponents.

But that wasn't always the same as winning.

He watched people from regular homes on the bus and on the street. He wondered what the world might be like if they were all forced to learn what it meant to come out on top without victory because you'd had too much taken away before getting there.

Paul hadn't been in a really serious bang-up until a few days before Christmas the year he turned twelve. He'd made his way through a variety of shelters, an on-and-off official human bouncing from state to state, and was living in a Connecticut foster home with another system kid, a fifteen-year-old named Martha.

Martha was the protector no boy had ever been for him. A beauty with sandy curls, a model's smile, a contagious cheer, and leaf-green eyes, Martha was a better fighter than most guys.

She'd proven it again just a month earlier, when a wrestler from the nearby private school was looking for his ex-girlfriend and found her at Martha's bus stop. He got ugly. Martha intervened. The wrestler escalated.

Martha won—and won big. The story made the local paper, and the wrestler went looking for her for payback, as did several of his friends.

They found her when she and Paul were carrying donated gifts from a sporting-goods store to the shelter they'd lived in before their foster placement. They saw him and his three buddies across the ball field, but they didn't want to leave the gifts and probably couldn't have outrun their pursuers anyway.

Had they known what was coming, they would have tried.

Connecticut surprised Paul with two life-learnings. One was that beautifully groomed public space was seldom visited by adults and thus was an anything-goes zone, however awful that anything might be. So long as those doing the anything had the right name and family income, it could get really, really bad. The other was that privileged kids were quicker to go for blood and were more vicious than the meanest people Paul went up against in the shelters.

Martha had humiliated the wrestler. She'd disrespected the caste.

Paul happened to be with her—and tried to help.

Too bad for him.

Martha, for all her prowess, was outnumbered.

Too bad for Martha.

She carried a stack of wrapped gift boxes, which occupied both hands. Paul had a couple of bags and an aluminum bat with a bow around it.

The last thing he saw clearly was that bow coming for his head. After that, his left eye wouldn't work. He was on the ground, facing away from the action, and the fight was mostly sounds.

Martha caught someone in the balls with a kick. Only that would prompt the noise made by whoever she got.

Then it went all bad for her. Fists landed.

Paul managed to pick himself up off the pitcher's mound after hearing elastic give way with a snap. Fabric tore. Martha was a girl, and that could be used against her.

"What's in the box, Martha?" the wrestler kept asking after he'd booted the gifts aside. "What's in the box?"

The sounds got worse.

Paul couldn't say for sure what was in most of the boxes, but he knew what the bottom one held—a chain-and-lock combo destined for a group-home kid whose bike would never have been stolen again, had it been delivered. It never made it there.

What stopped Paul from foolishly going for the bat was that he'd just been hit with it. It was hollow—too light. He was already on his feet, so it obviously wasn't the tool for the job.

"What's in the box?" they said. Something else ripped.

Paul made it to the dropped gifts while the wrestler and his pals were otherwise occupied. They made jokes about bases.

Grabbing the bat, Paul flung it away as hard as he could so that they wouldn't have a weapon. It clipped the top of the backstop on its way over it, ringing out with an aluminum peal.

One of them looked up from what he was doing. Paul went for him first.

He didn't recall what happened next. The doctor's report said he'd suffered a concussion.

The paperwork for the wrestler and his friends was longer, more detailed. It included months of follow-up visits for each of them. The police said that Paul stopped swinging the chain-lock only when it grew so slick that it flew from his hands. He didn't remember telling them that.

When he was sent out-of-state and arrived at New Beginnings, Pop Mike told him he'd only avoided the juvenile court system because the wrestler's parents didn't want their son's name in the news anymore. They feared that when the rounds of surgery and physical therapy were done, the notoriety might force even his dad's alma mater to turn him away come application time.

Paul never saw Martha again.

He didn't know why such memories flowed when things in The Commons were at their worst. But as the sand poured down over his hair and into his eyes—it was chest-high now, and breathing required effort—the way up was one of complete clarity.

"Didn't I tell you?" Mr. Brill shouted at Rain, far above. That would make sense later.

Paul knew what to do. The sand heard him, listened, obeyed.

It was time to show Mr. Brill what was in the box.

NO MORE CLUES. A lifetime of training couldn't have stopped Annie from focusing on that. Two, three, five lifetimes.

No.

No begging or praying would freeze the second hand. It really was moving faster. She was certain of it.

One, two, three, five. That and three clues had kept her little boy alive. She took no pride in his survival, congratulated herself not at all. She did not know what to do next. And for her failing, he would be the one who paid.

She had never been good at puzzle games. Didn't have the patience for them. On the base, choosing between the puzzlers and the first-person shooters on the ancient PC they'd salvaged, she went for boy games such as *Quake* or *Starcraft*, not the head-beating *7th Guest* or *Myst*.

Big mistake, but how was she to know? No one told her she needed to practice so she could keep her kid from being eaten alive after she'd already gotten him killed because she could only afford a bus and not a plane.

The hand marched on. She was out of goddamn clues. One, two, three, five. A sum? Eleven felt wrong.

First letters? O-t-t-f. Ottf.

In a memory class she took once, digits corresponded to consonants. If only she could remember what those were. Such a silly thing to know, she'd thought. Letters for numbers. When would she ever use that?

"One, two, three, five," she said aloud to herself, like that might shake something loose. The hand whizzed past the halfway mark. It never tired.

She repeated it. Maybe Wrangler John had something to offer. "John?" Her voice cracked.

Nothing.

Zach stood on the rock, looking to the farmer for guidance. The little man remained pointed at five, his previous answer.

Such a small boy. Such an adult way about him. He'd always had that, which made his disability all the more cruel—as if he understood exactly what he was missing, what was passing him by, and remained stoic in the face of that loss.

The hand raced ever forward. Of course it did. That was its job. It worked with the dragon fish against her son, who stood alone on a wet rock and stared at a stupid toy, waiting for it to save him.

Not it.

Her.

Waiting for his mother to save him. And Mom was out of ideas.

She would lose him, and she would watch it happen. Watch it. Know it. If she tried hard enough, if she begged, would they let her go with him?

As if on cue, the huge mosasaur that had stayed deep and away from the others turned to face up, toward Zach. It had ignored him until this point.

It was orange now, a safety-bright leviathan. Yet Annie still had difficulty sensing it. Even with the Humboldt connection and the mass of knowledge they delivered, it was shadowy territory to her.

The monster shifted its orientation again. Like a bubble released from beneath it, a nugget of information rose up, as if the mosasaur had let its guard down and allowed the wee fact to escape.

With that, she knew.

The orange mosasaur remained apart from the rest because it was trapped down there. No reason for the confinement was attached to the data. It simply wasn't able to approach the surface.

Well, that was some comfort, anyway—one less water dragon to worry about. Could it drown, given time? She hoped so.

The hand. "One, two, three, five," she said again. "John."

"Liberace?" he offered, distant as ever—farther, maybe. "You need another one."

Another what? Annie was going to forfeit Zach. Her boy—her world. And she depended on a man who communed with weasels for an answer. And all he had to contribute was a rhinestone grand and a candelabra.

Useless. No help. I wish my brother George was here.

Rhinestones. Sequins. Spangles. Ornamentation. Color. Peacock. Pinecone.

How did they fit together? Had anyone said they did?

Pinecone. Sequins.

What was the sequence?

Pinecone. Sequence.

No. Not Liberace. That just rhymed with what Wrangler John had really said.

Pinecone. Sequence. Another one.

She ran the numbers. One, one, two, three, five. Yes, and yes again.

She'd always aced Bio. How had she missed that until now?

If ever she failed her son, it would not be here.

Eight, you soggy, stinking lizards. Choke on crazy eight.

THE SAND FILLED THE PIT beneath Paul's feet, raising him up. He didn't ask now—he and the grains were of each other. The faster he wanted them to come, the more swiftly they did. He flew on the deserts of legend, a storm in his own right.

At the surface, Mr. Brill stood over Rain, who was still on her hands and knees. He knew Paul was there. Paul could sense it.

The sand carried Paul up above the floor until he stood atop a mound so large that it erased all traces of the pit and the broken glass. Rivulets of sand spilled down its sides.

Mr. Brill faced him, beaming with something akin to pride—the abusive father whose son just showed he could take a punch. "You won't disappoint me." He dismissed Rain with a wave. "Not like this one."

He flicked something from his lapel. It became a bullet of fire that headed for Paul, fist-sized and growing.

The sand beneath Paul spread out flat, lowering him to the floor. The fireball passed over his head.

Mr. Brill liked that. Thus far, it was only a game for him. He enjoyed a huge advantage in experience.

The fiery missile boomeranged. Heat from behind announced its return.

Paul let it strike him dead-center in the back. He welcomed the flames, didn't turn them aside. They bathed him, burning away his doubts, his hesitation.

He burned, but was not harmed. The fire faded to trickles of yellow and orange—the final streams of a volcano coming to rest—then died altogether.

"Good," said Mr. Brill. "You learn faster than I did. I kept trying to talk to it, but it doesn't want that. It wants you to rule it."

The floor around Paul and Rain disappeared, leaving each of them on top of a rough sandstone tower, harsh winds beating about them. Paul's toes were perfectly aligned with the edge of the abyss— a drop of a hundred stories.

The walls of the space around their towers were those of skyscrapers at night, studded and winking with windows lit from within. Silhouettes of faces looked out from the glow of their rooms— sightless, featureless in their bright coronas.

Rain struggled to rise. Something was burning somewhere. Sirens keened far below.

The pillars began to crumble. Fragments trickled past windows filled with those who didn't know or care, those who peered out into the night at something worse than falling stone.

They were the passengers from the bus, the dead from the snowy hillside. They were those who came into The Commons alone or arrived in tragedies large and small. Crimes. Wars. Or maybe those who kissed loved ones goodnight and never greeted them in the light of morning. Robbed of their Journeys. Denied their challenges, their destinations, their fates.

"They're mine." Mr. Brill let the weight of that settle in. "We are chosen. We are more than them. They feed a greater good—us. I know you know. I feel that knowledge like I feel them. We all had the same chances, the same opportunities. Yet they do not command, and we do. The Thirty-Six. The Nistarim."

Paul could hear Rain's breathing. It was steady. She was playing possum, waiting for an opening. "You take your power from the people it belongs to," he said. "You weren't chosen by anyone."

Mr. Brill's smile never faded. "There's some truth to that. But do you know how I came to be here? I'm but one of thirty-six. I couldn't just grab everything. It was handed to me freely. Souls who weren't willing to risk failing in their Journeys, to meet a fate that wasn't to their liking. They came to me for an easier way—frightened, wanting from me what they wouldn't do themselves."

"Why the Ravagers, then? Why force people if they wanted your help?"

"They didn't all know enough to want it. Just like the Envoys. I gave them the option of working with me. They refused. I can't be bothered with convincing everyone. Now the Envoys are gone, and there would be chaos if I didn't take my duties seriously. Do you know the volume of Essence entering The Commons every day? Every night? Do you know what it would mean if I abdicated?"

Paul gazed down at the dark faces in the windows. Would they have given up willingly? Were their Journeys too hard?

"Consider this, Paul. Can I allow you to move on from here when your strength added to mine would mean levels of control I only dream of? You know I can't. You know I won't. So the answer is yours to give. Accept who you are—or forfeit it."

Paul already knew his answer. Mr. Brill would, too.

A pit opened up behind the big man. Then it grew deeper.

FORTY-ONE

....

OMNES PRO UNO

With the answer came the shame of how long it had taken her to figure it out.

Fibonacci. The numbers of nature. How had she not gotten it earlier, given all she'd seen since leaving Mr. Brill's offices?

Brill's power was industry and artifice. True might—a city leveled by the shifting of the earth, the heat of a star, lightning—was of the natural world. The Humboldt knew, as did she. And with that, she and Zach might yet make it through this thing.

Through to what, though? That was a whole other question, but Annie only had to consider the next jump for now. Trying to solve big-picture riddles would put her up against the weirdness of the entire package. Then the faults in her mental armor would widen and spread.

In the Fibonacci sequence, each number was the sum of the two preceding it. One plus one was two; one plus two was three; two and three made five, and three and five got you to eight—the most recent correct choice.

"Thirteen." Wrangler John was an echo trying its best to help, as if Annie were incapable of simple addition. But she couldn't stay annoyed at the man. He and Liberace were the heroes here.

Still, there were only twelve numbers on the clock face. There was no thirteen.

Her familiar foes climbed through the ropes and into the ring. Ladies and gentlemen, wrestling fans, in this corner, the terrible twosome of Doubt and Fear. We can only hope the refs have checked their tights for foreign objects.

Doubt and Fear. The very opponents she'd been trained to overcome.

And who had trained her? Uncle Sam and the U.S. Army, who kept everything and everyone punctual. If you're late, don't bother showing up.

What did they train her with? Scrupulous scheduling. Tenacious time-tracking. Not in twelve-hour increments, but on the tried-and-true twenty-four–hour clock.

Thirteen-hundred hours.

She didn't even have to say it out loud.

PAUL ANSWERED MR. BRILL'S OFFER as hard as he could.

He willed a pit into being, silently driving it a hundred stories down into the floor behind the big man, who didn't seem to notice. The potential energy of all that compacted stone left Paul shaking with the effort it required to contain it.

But he had no intention of keeping it there. He released the compressed Essence under the floor in front of Mr. Brill.

The floor ruptured. A column of earth and rock shot up into the air, rumbling as the released Essence fueled its momentum.

At forty feet up, Paul brought the pillar back down in a curve, a striking snake headed straight at Mr. Brill. It smashed into him, pile-driving him down into the pit behind him.

The Essence buried Mr. Brill mineshaft-deep, its reverberations sending cracks out across the floor in a star pattern as it filled the pit to the surface. It wanted to regain its form, coalesce into something static, so Paul worked with that.

Within moments, the last of the rocky thunder faded. There was no evidence of the hole or Mr. Brill—only smooth floor.

"Nice." Rain was on her feet on her tower, shotgun in hand. She was unsteady, but her ability to stand at all was a testament to her strength. The source of that and the other assorted ways in which she wasn't quite like most other girls was a topic for conversations Paul intended to have. "How far down?"

"Far enough. I hope." The tower under Paul and its surrounding windowed walls became floor again. Rain's, too. They started toward each other.

A whip-like sound from beneath his feet was a declaration that the fight wasn't over.

Barbed cable sprung from the floor to wrap around his ankles, tripping him. Another rose up behind to bind his wrists.

It hurt, which wasn't necessary. That attention to detail told him he'd succeeded, at least, in making Mr. Brill angry.

The cables reached upward and, finding a purchase in heights unseen, hauled him up off the floor. Joining behind his back, they held him suspended, hog-tied, and then constricted, barbs piercing his clothes and skin.

A javelin, brown with rust, sprouted from the floor. Its sharp tip stopped just below Paul's stomach, nudging the hanging edge of his shirt aside.

Rain took a step forward.

Paul dropped a sickening inch, stopping with a jerk. Now he could feel the javelin point kissing the inside of his navel. Another step would impale him.

She retreated.

The cable holding him aloft began to unravel itself. He rotated slowly over the spear, its point his axis, as if in a breeze.

"Now," said Mr. Brill.

The spin brought Paul around to see the big man standing below. His demeanor and clothing were unchanged, as if Paul's attack had never occurred. "You have strength. Maybe even more than me, given the time to develop it, and I hope you appreciate my candor. But I will not grant you that time."

Below the javelin's tip, angled steel thorns sprouted and blossomed down the shaft to the floor. Flecks of oxidation fell like snow.

"Do I hear a yes?" Mr. Brill said.

Paul laughed the way any group-home kid did in the face of a threat, be it expulsion or a beat-down. Defiance and spite. Pride was pride.

The cable sang out in a sharp series of pings, and Paul shivered with the vibrations. Strands ruptured in turn, one after another.

Mr. Brill had started a timer of sorts. All three of them knew what would happen when the count-down ended.

"Now there's the strength of will you showed my Shade."

"The Shade was you," Paul said as Mr. Brill rotated into view again. "And Ken sent you home with his fists in your heart."

"Ken." The big man spat the name out. "A scrap. A freak missed by no one."

Paul's anger was an audible crackle. The cable and javelin evaporated, and he dropped, landing on his feet. Lightning burned the air around Mr. Brill, bathing him in white and hurling him to the floor in a burst of sparks.

The fury hurt when it expressed itself. Fabric tore in Paul's mind. He reached into a fallen gift box for its chain and lock.

"You still think—" Mr. Brill began, his voice a struggle. The electricity became solid. A coffin encased the big man in steel. Only his head and neck were visible. "Mere theater."

It was anything but. The end of the box irised into a sharp ring that sealed itself against Mr. Brill's throat, cutting into the soft skin there.

In his mind, Paul whirled the lock around in an arc, like bolas. He walked over to Mr. Brill and looked down at him on the floor, toes stopping just shy of his head. "You need to know something. This isn't just my Journey."

Mr. Brill tried to laugh. The edge against his neck bit deeper. Dots of red bloomed on the steel.

"I'm freeing them—all of them. The people on the bus. Everyone."

The big man exhibited the same confidence he'd shown all along. A touch more blood appeared at the razor iris's edge.

"Rain gets to move on," Paul said. "It's her Journey, too. She's earned it."

The red circle did nothing to check Mr. Brill's mirth. "Oh, she's earned something. Only not what you think. Her deal's been made already."

"Paul." Rain's voice lacked its strength.

"With me," said Mr. Brill.

There it was. The suspicion that Paul hadn't wanted to recognize. Why she'd tried to leave. Why she'd seemed to be familiar with Gerald Truitt. By the fire of the Nightlights, she'd warned him that something bad had made its way in with them.

"Look what I did," she'd told him in the Dew Drop Inn parking lot.

Rain's face wore the truth of it. For a moment, she looked as if she might have something—anything—to say. But there was nothing.

A shadow crossed her arm, under her jacket sleeve. It emerged, dark and fast, dropped to the floor, and scuttled over to Mr. Brill.

It was too fast for Paul to see clearly, but he didn't have to. The spider tattoo.

With that, the coffin was empty. Mr. Brill stood behind Rain now, neck healed, his hands on her— and on her with familiarity.

She didn't move to stop him. Her eyes searched Paul's, but she allowed Mr. Brill to touch her and gave up trying to speak.

"Paul Reid," said Mr. Brill. "Meet Rain. I don't believe you know her. I don't believe you know her at all."

THE LITTLE FARMER pointed to 1300 hours. Zach made the leap to the safe rock with ease.

Annie relaxed the tiniest little bit. He was one jump away from the stone with the door on it.

This far in, the game was almost too simple. The only remaining time in the sequence that could be expressed on a twenty-four–hour clock was 2100, which was the nine under current circumstances. Zach was once again surrounded by stones, but one of them was the rock with the door. It was at nine o'clock—right in front of him.

Why did she assume it would remain that simple?

It didn't.

The stones around Zach's disappeared, including the one with the door.

Annie cried out as if she'd been struck. Wrangler John put a hand on her shoulder. She pulled away from him. Hard.

All of the rocks were gone. All of them.

Now there were only mosasaurs in the water with her son and the stone under him. Huge, cold, voracious monsters.

Hic sunt dracones.

She felt them—not physically, but as a bond with something you wanted to run from. She'd heard the term "lizard brain" many a time, but she'd never understood it until now.

They didn't focus on Zach. They didn't have to. They knew where he was. And he was within reach.

They didn't even think of one another. Not as competition. They were one, all part of Mr. Brill. When Zach hit the water, they'd feed as a single entity.

And the largest one. Trapped on the bottom, shifting hues. It had been the color of a tangerine, but it was changing again.

It darkened to the color of blood-orange flesh. And it remained directly beneath the stone Zach perched on.

The other mosasaurs paid little attention to her son.

The big one thought of nothing but.

The second hand sped along. Zach, true to form, betrayed no emotion as he watched the little farmer for a sign. But there was none to give.

The stones were gone. The game was over. The hand would finish its trip. Zach's stone would sink.

It was only when there was once again almost no time left that Annie came up with a final desperate move.

"Nine!" she shouted, and immediately wished she hadn't. The last thing Zach would see as his stone sank was the little farmer pointing to the open sea.

Dutiful to the end, the little man spun. And pointed.

Annie had to push Wrangler John's hand away again.

Stupid. So stupid. Nobody had said the rock would sink. What if it didn't? What if it was a safe haven after all, and Zach left it because of her?

The farmer pointed at the door icon, though now there was no door there.

That way was nothing. That way was monsters.

Her son looked out on the empty water. He turned the toy to and fro. The little man rolled with the motion—consistent, turning and shifting to point in the chosen direction.

The second hand reached its zenith.

Annie stopped breathing.

The stone held steady.

Hope bloomed anew. The rock would not sink. Zach would be fine.

His expression changed. Annie knew that look.

He took a step back. And launched himself.

Over the water. Into the abyss.

ZACH SKINNED HIS KNEES landing on the rock, which appeared in time to keep him from the monsters. He also scraped his knuckles hanging onto the little farmer, his fingers grinding into the stone as he went down.

The little farmer was valuable still. He trusted it, although that trust didn't guarantee everything would work out. The spinning man was part of something bigger. He'd told himself that on the tape recorder before stepping into the mirror.

Zach missed Zach's mother. She was looking for him. He wanted to tell her he'd see her soon, but that would be a lie. They had to do what was needed first, all of them—Zach, Zach's mother, the boy from the bus, and the boy's friends, who Zach couldn't see and didn't know.

What he did know was this: even all of them together weren't enough to beat the man in the suit and the white-haired man from the spider room.

They needed the help that was trying to reach them. Which was why Zach listened to the little farmer, Tape Recorder Zach, and the ladies, all of whom had to reach the people they wanted to help without the man in the suit and the white-haired man finding out.

For that, they needed Zach.

He stood and faced the egress, which was just a plain wooden door. A closed one.

His jeans stuck to his scraped knees. Little flaps of skin hung from his fingers where the stone had dug into them, and there was sand under the flaps. His fingers were numb from hitting the rock, but they'd sting soon—and bleed. And other parts of him were sore from previous impact. This was a painful game.

Zach waited for the red to seep out from the flaps. When it did, he carefully took the piece of paper with the words from the bus out of his pocket. It was wet and close to falling apart. He dabbed at the blood. It hurt, but he had to do it.

The little farmer pointed to a picture on the dial that looked like a piece of candy in a wrapper with twisted ends. When Zach tilted the toy, the little man shifted, pointing to the spot on the rock where Zach's fingers had mashed when he landed.

Zach wasn't happy with the little farmer. He'd tricked Zach. But the little man was showing him something important.

There was a hole in the rock, and it was filled with the same sand that was stuck under Zach's flaps. He'd knocked a bit away when he landed, revealing something shiny buried there. Had Zach not hit the way he did, he'd have missed the shiny thing.

He scooped the sand away until a little eye peeked out at him. His marble. It had returned to him, and now he'd take it the rest of the way.

Zach blotted a little more blood onto the crayon writing because he wanted to be sure. It soaked into the wet paper and spread in threads, like red lightning, like the tie-dyed shirts he and Zach's mother made—the shirts with the circle signs with the triangles in them.

The same circle signs from the uniform of the girl soldier who was gone because of the other monster: not one of the ones under the water, but one related to them—the dark one. Gone along with the crying lady and the big wrapped man.

Zach couldn't say for sure how he knew these things. Maybe he'd heard them talked about in the hiss of the tapes and only understood them now. Maybe they'd traveled to him across the water or through the spinning of the little farmer.

The important thing was remembering to listen. Most people forgot that part.

It was sad, what happened to the women and the big wrapped man. Zach would do this for them and for all of the others whose names he didn't and couldn't know.

The piece of paper was starting to tear because of the water, so Zach had to be even more careful with it. He wrapped it around the marble and twisted its ends, just like in the drawing on the Farmer Says.

Nothing happened. He twisted a little harder and hoped. The wet paper caught fire.

Zach's hand burned. He nearly dropped the marble, but his trust saw him through. He closed his hand around the heat and hung on tight.

It hurt bad. Really bad.

At last, the flames died. Zach opened his hand. Smoke rose from his palm in the sea breeze.

The paper was gone. Its letters had been etched into the marble's glass by the heat, carved there in small white capitals: UNUS PRO OMNIBUS. OMNES PRO UNO.

The tape recorder hadn't told Zach what would happen next, but he knew—and he wished someone else could do it for him. There was no one. He faced the door.

In his hand, the last of the smoke clung to the marble's surface, as if painted on in clouds. When he didn't look directly at the marble, when it was at the edge of his seeing, it was a tiny world of greens, blues, grays, and whites—a globe. When he looked straight at it again, it was only glass and letters.

It was enough.

A smart boy. A brave boy. Zach raised the marble, its white words facing the door, and rapped on the wood three times with it.

A push came from deep down in the water—unseen but sensed like the other knowledge. There. It created its own current, free now.

The door opened easily. On the other side was the rest of the rock.

He stepped into the doorway. The little farmer, tucked under his arm, whirred around.

Halfway through, the little man stopped on the picture of the dragon fish, which was now as red as the blood from Zach's fingers. "Mosasaur."

The door and stone vanished. Zach stepped through into nothing. He fell forward, the water rushing up toward him, the little farmer tucked under his arm, the cat's-eye marble clutched in his fist.

The dragon fish hurtled up from deep down on the bottom, so much larger than the others, its mouth a cave. It, like the picture on the toy, was as red as blood.

The monster swallowed him whole.

·····································

FORTY-TWO

A LITTLE BREEZE,
LIKE A BREATH

On Mr. Brill's screens, a wall of vines, each as thick as a leg, stretched hundreds of feet into the air. Trapped in the growth, only their faces visible, were thousands of captives who slept with eyes open.

Their slumber was dark and restless. Paul's growing ability to tap in as much as he dared told him so. The victims were all too aware of what Mr. Brill was doing to them, but it came to them in dreams of incursion.

Smaller vines invaded their skin, their mouths, their eyes. Wherever there was a way in, the plants found or made them, siphoning Essence.

Charges, Mr. Brill called them—and one was missing. Her space was an open pocket in the vines—body-sized, a pillaged womb.

"There's always one who wants to live just a lit- tle more than the rest," Mr. Brill said. "That whole I-couldn't-care-less act is a lie. Just like she is. I heard her begging to serve without even listening for it. She was more desperate. She had the need. Just like you, Paul." His hands moved on her. "A beautiful girl and a spider tattoo. A little obvious, but she caught me a fly." And moved again. "Buzz, buzz."

Mr. Brill's words bit deep, like hooks.

"I tried to leave," Rain told Paul. He wanted so badly to speak, but nothing would come. "Twice. Over the tunnel, I told you to choose. I thought you knew. I gave you a chance."

"Did you want to leave?" Paul said.

"No. But I tried again when I knew I was the one who got Ken killed."

Mr. Brill shone with accomplishment. "That peeper-slug bruise? I have those scattered all throughout The Commons. That one attached when you got your new clothes. But it was a decoy. I knew the Envoy would find it, and he never thought to look for another. Her eyes? My eyes. Her ears? Mine."

"The Nightlights," Paul said, ignoring Mr. Brill. "The motel."

"No." Her eyes stayed on him. "The fires kept him out, and so did I at the motel, after Ken—"

At the mummy's name, her voice broke. She took a slow, shivering breath. "I love you."

"Love," Mr. Brill said. "Nobody loves anyone, Paul. Learn that now. The question isn't what she sells. It's how much—and for how much."

She wheeled around, flipped her shotgun straight up under Mr. Brill's chin, and pulled the trigger. It was so loud, so close, that Paul's ears quit. So did several of the screens.

Mr. Brill let out a runny bellow and fell backward, a scarlet mess from the necktie up. Paul nearly retched.

By the time she fired again, his face was healed. Her shot transformed into water droplets bouncing from his chest like rain on a tarp. "Our deal?" he said.

"Shot."

Her gun glowed red-hot, and she was forced to drop it. The floor of the space became water, and Rain and the fallen gun plunged beneath its surface.

Paul and Mr. Brill remained standing atop it.

"The Commons is mine," Mr. Brill told Paul. "Until you know yourself, I'm stronger, and you need time to gain that knowledge." The surface of the water hardened into glass, sealing Rain beneath. "Time she does not have."

She maintained her steely calm. Her palms pressed hard against the underside of the clear floor, their skin flat and white as she looked up at Paul.

"Did you hear her take a breath?" Mr. Brill tapped his foot once, twice. "I didn't."

Her eyes betrayed her. Fear.

"Let her up," Paul said.

"Our deal's over. You heard her. Now there's room for one with you."

"Let her up."

The floor turned obsidian.

"It's easier if you don't look," Mr. Brill said.

The thumping from beneath the black floor matched that of Paul's heart, beat for beat.

WRANGLER JOHN, hearing Annie's scream, tried to pull her away from the Virtual Boy. She clawed at his hands, and her nails claimed skin. He let go.

He was on her side and was only trying to help, but she'd apologize later. Her son had been taken from her.

Again.

The interruption pulled her from the water, returning her to the purple-on-black pixels of the reef. A moment later, she was sucked back in with a force that stole her breath.

There, again, was the nautilus. The nautilus became the Humboldt, and the Humboldt reached into her mind once more—and none too gently. End-game approached. Her comfort would not be a consideration.

Annie joined with the millions of squid and adjusted as fast as she could. Another data dump.

She was a part of it. So was Zach. They all were, always had been. And they were in danger. At risk.

The Essence was The Commons and its inhabitants. It was alive, and it wanted out. It hadn't sat still all this time. It had fought Mr. Brill.

When direct attacks failed, the captive Essence and that which wasn't under Mr. Brill's sway retreated to their corners to plan a way out. They became a network of roots that, with nothing but time, sought cracks in his infrastructure. Bit by furtive bit, they undermined his foundation.

It had begun lifetimes before, in small moves passing beneath his notice—like a mammoth theme park with far-reaching tunnels and subterranean rooms for characters to travel in, unnoticed by the customer. What if the corporation lost track of the older passages, fell out of touch with its staff, grew too confident to detect rebellion in the forgotten reaches?

Underground railroads literal and figurative. Discarded landscapes from the unfinished Journeys of Mr. Brill's usurpation. The lowliest of the bona fides who were never captured and the mythicals whom Mr. Brill didn't deign to consider setting the stage for his overthrow.

The hopeless kept the faith.

Annie with her inside connections. Zach with a mind that moved beyond the normal spectrum. Paul with an ability to rival Mr. Brill's. He was one of the Thirty-Six: young, good-hearted, and—given the right help—just strong enough to overcome the gap in experience. Symbols and icons that might rule the day if put into motion without a hitch.

No small feat, but it was all they had. One shot.

Annie reached a place of calm. Her son had been taken by a creature of the rebellion, not of Mr. Brill. Solving the puzzle had allowed it to act.

Zach had made it across a deadly landscape of traps lying in wait, the guidance of many seeing him through. They were all his Envoys, and he was where he needed to be.

So was Annie.

So was Paul.

The hope of the hopeless.

ZACH WOKE UP in the apartment with the mirrored doors. He was back where he started, in his bed.

All for nothing. Undone.

The pain told him the truth. Scraped hands, something hard in his back. He dug beneath him for it—the etched marble.

On the night table sat the Farmer Says.

It had happened. It was happening still.

He was sore. He hurt all over, and his clothes were torn and stiff. But he climbed out of bed, clutching the marble, and picked up the Farmer Says despite the hurting.

All travel was a circle. It looped in on itself and took you, if not back to where you started, then close to it. It was up to you to continue.

So he tested this apartment. He went to the closed bedroom door and put his hand on the knob. He would find Zach's mother and ask her. She was near.

He stepped out into the hall. When he closed the door behind him, it was a hall no longer.

Zach stood on the beach of a huge blue lake. The door behind him was gone as soon as he let go of it, replaced by a wood-plank walkway that climbed up and over a dune. Beyond that was a forest.

A woman sat in a chair at the water's edge, facing the lake. She had red hair like Zach's mother, but Zach could see only the back of her head.

Squeezing the marble, he tried to decide what to do. He pulled the string of the Farmer Says. Nothing happened.

"Hello, Zach," the lady said.

He walked down to her because there was no other choice, and because she knew his name. It took longer than it should have.

Zach didn't want to get too close to the water, but he had to approach the woman. As he drew nearer, his reluctance found its reason.

There was something in the water. Many somethings. He didn't know what they were, but they scared him.

The woman had put the fear into him. She wanted to keep him safe.

When Zach finally got to the woman, he walked around to her front, his back to the lake so that he wouldn't have to see it. Her face was pretty, though something told him she'd had no face at all until he got close enough for her to need one. Yet her smile was friendly.

Not kind. Friendly.

"It's wisest to not look," she told him. "And less scary."

Her chair was woven plastic bands on metal tubes. Green on white, with dark spots from the basement storage, just like the one Zach's mother used when they went to see Fourth of July fireworks.

Zach knew her. She was the woman from the picture. Paul's mother.

A voice in Zach's head—Tape Recorder Zach—told him that the woman wore the face she needed for the situation at hand. If another one had made her job easier, she'd wear that.

"You have something I need," she said. "Something you've come a long way to give me. We're very proud of you, Zach. You've done just what we required you to do."

She reached out and gently tapped the hand that gripped the little farmer. His pain was gone, his scrapes healed.

The lady who wasn't Paul's mother glanced down at the fist that held the marble, but didn't want him to catch her at it. She put both her hands out, palms up.

"Now," she said. "It's important—very important—that you choose one of my hands and put what you've brought me into it. You can think about it if you want. We have time. But you must choose on your own."

Zach ignored her hands. Instead, he looked into her eyes. Despite what she'd said about having time, she was in a hurry.

He made his decision and held the marble out. He would drop it into her right hand.

At least, he thought it was her right. That always confused him, what to call people's hands when their right was his left. Probably Not Paul's Mother stopped smiling, then brought the grin back again—hard, as if recovering from a mistake.

It happened quickly.

Zach dropped the marble—and realized two things. She'd said he was doing just what they required him to do, not what was needed. And she'd said it was important that he choose a hand to put the marble into, which wasn't the same thing as saying there were right and wrong choices.

It was only important that he choose to give it to her.

It was a trick.

What he did next wasn't possible. But he did it anyway. Because possible wouldn't stay still.

He caught the marble as it fell, reclaiming it with the same fingers that had just let go of it. He was faster than Not Paul's Mother, grabbing it again before she could.

Her smile began to fade. He didn't wait for it to finish.

He wheeled around, winding up with the turn. Then he threw the marble as far out into the lake as he could.

Not Paul's Mother screamed. She no longer sounded like a woman. Or even human.

The marble arced out over the calm flat of the lake. It flew faster and farther than Zach had ever thrown anything in his life—farther than he was able to.

When it was about to splash down, a delicate arm of water—a slender woman's arm, like that of a young mother—reached up from a circle of ripples and caught it. Droplets sprayed from the hand as the marble was captured, and the arm pulled it beneath the surface.

As the arm sank out of view, it seemed for a moment that it had become a mass of tentacles, like those of an octopus.

Or a squid.

The lake returned to stillness. The scream behind him died.

A little breeze, like a breath, rose off the water. It brushed past Zach's face—a caress—and was gone with a sigh.

That sigh was one of old, deep worry—released and done away with at last.

....

FORTY-THREE

THE BETTER ANGELS OF OUR NATURE

Mr. Brill held back. It was more enjoyable for him to watch Paul suffer as Rain slowly drowned. The growing bond between Paul and Mr. Brill transmitted the big man's odious pleasure in staticky bursts, like a radio station just coming into range.

Paul concentrated on removing the solid layer that sealed Rain underneath it, but his opponent relented only enough for it to shift back from opaqueness to transparency.

His shock at what was revealed fed Mr. Brill's joy even further.

The water under the steel-hard surface was thick with fat squid. They were so numerous that Paul first thought it was a sea of brains and eyes pressed against the underside.

Rain was lost in them, nowhere to be seen.

Paul knelt and placed his hands on the hard surface, trying to will it away.

Mr. Brill's amusement grew.

The squid responded, and Paul saw them for what they were. They were Humboldt. *Dosidicus gigas. Diablo rojo.*

They were everything. Paul knew. So did Mr. Brill, who willed the surface to darken again, commanding the squid to retreat.

The surface remained clear. The Humboldt shifted beneath it, rippling in a wave toward Paul's hands.

Mr. Brill swept his arm through the air, the force of the move smashing into Paul. But Paul didn't break contact.

Again.

And again still.

Paul felt like his insides had broken loose.

What's in the box?

The blows rained down with the force of an aluminum bat on a long-ago field.

With the cruelty of boots in an alley.

A girl cried.

The heat around Paul's eye tunneled into a deep ache, accompanied by a fissure from his shoulder on down. His ankle shrieked.

It all rolled across and through. Doing nothing to protect himself cost him dearly.

He withstood. Endured. Held. And that was a change in his favor.

The Humboldt were the difference.

Paul felt Mr. Brill's fear sprout. Only a little. But still—afraid.

The big man couldn't push the squid back with fury alone. He lashed out further, accomplished nothing.

The Humboldt delivered their strength to Paul from the depths of the water.

Mr. Brill slammed him again. He crumpled, then raised himself back up to his knees. His joints were hinges. Their pins were being hammered out.

But he held on. And Mr. Brill's desperation grew.

The foundations of The Commons trembled with the violence. Mr. Brill poured everything he had into the attack, putting worlds at risk.

Mr. Brill was still too strong to overcome straight-on unless the Humboldt were able to finish what they'd started. If they couldn't, Paul would fall.

"Okay," Paul said, half-turning to his opponent, who was poised to deliver a shot that might have broken him. "I give."

The words did no more than fall out of him.

"What?" Mr. Brill's question had no trust or belief in it.

"Let her up. I'll do what you want."

Mr. Brill weighed the truth of that. "Step back. Cut yourself off from them."

Paul kept his hands where they were.

Mr. Brill watched him. The reprieve wouldn't last much longer.

It was enough.

Down below, a gap appeared in the Humboldt, racing toward Paul. A white hand—Rain's—with something dark and small clutched in it, the Humboldt her vessel.

It all happened at once.

Paul once again focused on breaking the barrier.

Mr. Brill saw he was stalling and struck him again, but fear cost the big man control. His blow missed Paul and slammed into the hard surface over the water, flexing it. It bounced back into flatness.

Rain came through.

The thing she held smacked the underside of the barrier with a crack loud enough to split worlds.

The water's surface shattered, blowing upward in a spray of shards.

Paul and Mr. Brill were both knocked flat. The gale that followed kept them that way for long moments.

The wind died.

All was quiet but for the sound of faint dripping.

Rain coughed, learning to breathe again.

Mr. Brill sprung to his feet.

Paul stood more slowly.

She was mere yards away, facedown at the water's edge, raggedly sucking in air.

Paul started toward her.

"No," she managed.

Mr. Brill's attack would resume. They both knew it. But she was as fast as she'd ever been, mustering enough strength to flip the dark stone to Paul.

It all slowed down.

He reached out and caught the little sphere. It clacked against his mother's ring with the force and weight of something much larger. The mass of lives. Of destiny.

He nearly dropped it, but held on and opened his fist to see what her hard-won gift was.

There in his palm, against his ring, was a blood-red marble with words etched into it.

He didn't even need to read them. He knew what they said. What they meant.

As did Mr. Brill.

They waited for it to happen.

It didn't.

Rain coughed again.

The water was still and flat once more, the Humboldt gone. Their part was done, the marble heavy in Paul's palm.

Nothing happened.

Mr. Brill laughed.

HE'D DONE IT. Zach was gone from her awareness but was out of danger for the time being. Even if she didn't know where he was, it was enough. Her son had done it.

The rest was up to a skinny kid who, though powerful beyond his age and size, was not equal to the task on his own. No one was. That was the whole point of the Thirty-Six. It was the numbers.

There were only two of the Thirty-Six in The Commons. The others were out of play for reasons ranging from not knowing who they were or being too far away to matter to not yet being in existence, though the very idea of them was enough to keep the number whole. That was as much as she was able to understand, and even that could fry her if she let too much of it in.

If her limited knowledge of the power was enough to nearly wipe her mind, then the power itself would burn Paul out of existence. That was why the numbers here were wrong.

The unbound Essence, which had waited and planned for so long, was desperate to unite itself with the shackled part held by Mr. Brill. And like too much juice focused on a portion of the grid in a surge, it would destroy the slight boy if he accepted it all, no matter his good intentions.

Annie was the final piece of the circuit. Zach had delivered the power to Paul, but it required direction in order to be of any use. It needed her guidance.

Yet from everything she could see, she was being asked to kill a teenage boy in order to put things back the way they should be. Or, to be more precise, to allow him to kill himself.

Paul wouldn't survive.

She couldn't do it.

"It's not your choice," Wrangler John said. His voice was well inside her head now, and it was delivered in an ancient tongue. Hebrew, Aramaic, or something even older than those—the word of wave on rock, breeze through leaves, moon in grass.

His hand grasped her shoulder. She let it stay there. "It will do it anyway," he said. "With you, it happens the way we need it to, though there still aren't any guarantees. Without you, the kid stands alone."

"I can't have this on me."

"It's not. It's much bigger. You know that."

The question of what might happen to Zach if she backed out now flashed through her mind, but this decision felt separate from him. His part in this was done. "No," she said.

The hand left her shoulder.

Silence.

She waited for him to try to convince her again. He didn't. Maybe he knew it'd be pointless.

Click.

Her vision went dark.

The vast knowledge of The Commons. The Nistarim. The universes beyond.

It all winked out. Everything. And she didn't need any extra brain power to understand why. She got it on her own.

Wrangler John had killed the Virtual Boy's power. Cut her off. Just like that. Plan B.

Annie and her consciousness reached a fork in the road and chose different directions.

She fainted dead away.

"IT DIDN'T WORK." Mr. Brill's laughter brimmed with triumph. "None of it." He now knew everything done to get the marble into Paul's hand.

"Paul," Rain said. She was not who he'd known up until now—or who he'd thought he'd known. The marble had done nothing; she was scared. "Paul."

He knew her fear—its evolution—just as he knew what Mr. Brill knew. There was truth in what Mr. Brill had said; he and Paul were of a kind.

Rain had done what she had because she'd been afraid—because that was what she had to do at the time. She then tried to help where she could, and she tried to leave. In the end, she'd just hoped that it would work out.

Only it hadn't. Mr. Brill was right. It was all for nothing.

The big man winked. Rain's shotgun leapt into the air and flew at her. She'd recovered enough to catch it.

Their cards had been played. It was futile. Mr. Brill would win this fight, and he was going to have fun doing it. That meant giving Rain her gun back. And he just kept laughing.

Paul read the marble's words. What had failed?

Rain chambered a round, but it took the last of her strength. It was all she could do to keep it pointed in Mr. Brill's direction.

He, in turn, merely watched, beaming. He was having a fine time.

The etched writing: Unus pro omnibus, omnes pro uno. The graffiti on the bus seat, which Zach had scrawled on the page from Paul's notebook years before, seemingly.

It all came together. No scream required. No tree, no storm. All together.

Paul understood. The Latin needed no translation. Nor did the rest: IMUURS.

The marble heated up in his hand. It hurt. The fire spread to his mother's ring, just as it had at the Dinuhos Tree. He closed his hand tightly, flesh against searing metal. It hurt. He squeezed. His distress brought an even broader smile to Mr. Brill's face.

Then the pain receded. Paul opened his hand. The marble was once again the cat's-eye Zach had given him in the Port Authority basement.

He knew without looking. The graffiti Latin from the marble had joined the letters from the glass on the inside of his ring. There was no mystery here.

It began. Energy rivered into him. There would be an end. All for one, one for all.

Mr. Brill's eyes narrowed. Rain brightened as she sensed the fundamental shift.

"You don't understand," Paul told Mr. Brill. "You never have."

The power came faster—through his heart, along his spine. Up, down, into all of him, setting his mind alight. The nature of his eyesight changed. Edges glowed. Rain, Mr. Brill, everything lit from within. And still it came.

Rain appeared to take strength from the overflow. She kept her shotgun trained on Mr. Brill, but spared a glance for Paul, concerned.

"It isn't yours," Paul said. "It's not mine. We're just borrowing it."

"What are you—?"

Paul cut him off. "It isn't knowing you're one of the Thirty-Six that stops you from being one. It's using it for yourself—thinking you deserve it more than those we serve." It was too much. And only a sliver of what was to come had entered him.

"Didn't you wonder why controlling it was so hard? Don't you think that's been tried? Truth will out."

Mr. Brill was about to attack again.

"It belongs to all, and we belong to it. I-M-U-U-R-S." Paul took even more of it in. "I am you. You are us."

It was going to rip him apart.

Rain lowered her gun.

"You can't own what you're a part of," he told Mr. Brill. "I'll show you."

Fast as ever, instincts sharp as concertina wire, Rain hit the deck.

It didn't come from Paul. It came through him. The humility of knowing he was only a vessel was why it worked—a willingness to let it go that made him stronger than the likes of Mr. Brill.

The power reached that of the storm that had taken the Ravagers at the Dew Drop Inn. Then it surpassed it.

An impossible gale, wind made solid, hit him. He remained on his feet—didn't budge. It focused on his center, joining what he held within. He raised his hands, palms out, before him. The movement was not his; it was the will of The Commons and all beyond it.

He felt himself torn at first, but then it shifted. It was a joining—him with all.

Paul and Mr. Brill stood with Rain in the office, a place of thievery and malice. Yet the two Nistarim also stood on a plane all their own, a nothingness of light and not-light, sensed and unseen.

Mr. Brill lashed out across the distance. The blow would have destroyed Paul only moments before, but it never reached him.

Paul had joined with The Commons and its brother and sister worlds. He was one of the Thirty-Six. Nistarim. Lamed Vav. He completed the group.

And Mr. Brill was no longer of them.

Paul unleashed their ferocity. It flowed through his mother's ring and then from his whole being—arms, eyes, mouth. It hit Mr. Brill as fist, wave, torrent—it washed him away.

Mr. Brill fought his way back using all of the Essence he'd stolen and controlled. For a time, he succeeded. But he was pitted against too much. Paul could not have let up if he'd wanted to—and he did not want to.

The fury came. The entirety of it raged at Mr. Brill, who was nothing against the whole of existence itself. Paul understood what Annie and Zach had done for him. He knew now. Annie needn't have worried, needn't have tried to hold it back for his sake.

The storm knew where it wanted to go—where it needed to—and it joined with what Mr. Brill stole. It cast off its chains after so, so long.

Mr. Brill glowed white. It was the same light that had come at Paul through the windshield of the bus, the unchecked might of rightful order reclaimed. The big man was hurled from the ground he stood on. Pieces of him tore away and were lost. He began to scream.

Thief. Raider. Taker. His pain became terror and grief; he could not contain it. Not him—not even him. That which he'd forced to bend worked twofold toward his ruination. It joined the invading Essence with a hatred hot against Paul's skin. And still it came.

It was forever, worlds here and gone, everything and everyone. Its time had come.

The storm ended with the cry of a raw throat. The last of it, Mr. Brill's screams falling away, came as a fading breath from Paul himself. It was spent. As was he.

With the snap of a second passed, Paul and Mr. Brill joined Rain back in the vast office.

Paul had nothing left. Strangely, Mr. Brill looked only mildly worse for wear—intact, uninjured, just a bit faded.

Yet Paul sensed a change in him. Something was missing—had been taken. Which didn't mean he wasn't dangerous. Paul knew he had a lethal move or two left.

The big man did the only thing the Mr. Brills of the world know how to do—assail. With a nod, he willed a crack to open in the floor and sent it Paul's way, widening it as it approached.

Despite his exhaustion, Paul stopped the crack, closing it with an effort that traveled right back at the big man. It sealed itself as it went, but its force continued past Mr. Brill, opening again behind him, widening into a deep fissure.

Mr. Brill gathered what he had remaining and spent it on a ball of red-hot plasma that emerged from between his palms. It sizzled straight at Paul, reaching the size of a small car as it rushed toward him.

Again, Paul halted the attack. The ball hung in the air between them, hissing in yellows, oranges, and reds that undulated across it.

"I need something from you," Rain told Paul. She spoke as if they were alone. And they were, really.

"Yes." It was a difficult thing, but Paul understood. Forgiveness. She'd wronged him, but he could grant them another chance to know each other, whatever that knowing meant. He looked at her even as he kept the fiery ball suspended in the air. "Yes."

She held his gaze a moment, then smiled true—grace, strength, joy without edge.

Mr. Brill met the fate of his victims. His features faded as he fragmented—blurred and wiped away by the light from the fiery ball he himself had created. His suit hung limp from his wasting form.

"Do you know why we won?" Paul said to him. "Why we'll always win?" His opponent could not speak. "Because the exploiters are exploited in the end. I've taken nothing. It gave itself to me, and I released it."

Mr. Brill still didn't comprehend.

"No matter how much you deserve this, I feel sorry for you," Paul said. "That's the difference."

He didn't push; he simply asked the ball to go to Mr. Brill. It did.

Then came a change of heart. He stopped it just shy of destroying the former big man.

"No," Rain said. "Free us."

"We're already free. And I don't fight like that."

The ball of plasma flared, dissipating with the sibilance of water killing fire. It vanished in a supernova spray.

Mr. Brill managed one more laugh. But it was rough, desiccated. "You don't fight like that."

Paul turned to leave. After a few steps, he looked up to watch what happened next flash across the floating screens as it played out behind him.

Mr. Brill cocked his arm to deliver a blow to Paul's back. Rain raised her shotgun, nothing holding her back now. The blast roared with the power of Paul's forgiveness within it, echoing through the chamber.

Mr. Brill tumbled back into the chasm of his own making, his own blackness. He clawed at the air and was gone from sight without a sound. The abyss snapped closed like a mouth, sealing itself over him. The floor was uniform once more, healed.

"I fight like that," Rain said. She kept her gun trained on the now-unremarkable spot on the floor, ensuring that it remained that way. "You should learn."

The shotgun shell. The Dinuhos Tree's gift to her. Her wish.

"When we made our deal, he said I was buying mercy on layaway. He wouldn't tell me the final price. So I named my own." She swung the gun over her shoulder, dropping the weapon into its holster. "And paid it."

Around them, Mr. Brill's screens filled with specks of black-and-white static, noise, and snow. Their source was gone, and a brightness from outside washed the monitors out, fading them slowly like the man they'd served.

Out there, the sun ascended. With its arrival, the reign of Mr. Brill, the Nistar gone dark, came to an end.

Paul offered his hand.

Rain took it.

They went out into the light.

....

FORTY-FOUR

WHERE THE WICKED CEASE FROM TROUBLING

O n the beach, Zach studied the spot in the water where the marble had been caught and pulled down. Something had happened.

That something was big. And he'd helped.

The little farmer whirred. He watched it go. After several revolutions, it settled on the picture of the door. It said nothing, but Zach knew he'd be leaving soon.

"You're a bad boy," said the lady on the beach. She wasn't happy with the big thing that had happened. "You're a very bad boy—and you're mine now."

"No, Sheila," a woman's voice said from the Farmer Says speaker. "He's not."

It was the same voice from the number-eight tape, the woman who'd left him on the rock with the mosasaurs. Zach was mad at her. She'd led him into a trap.

"He is so," Sheila said. "Go away, Jeanne. This is my realm."

Zach turned to face the lady on the beach. She no longer looked like Paul's mother—the woman in the picture on the bus. Her face could have been anyone's. This was the real Sheila—who could be whatever the person she was trying to fool wished her to be but who was also canny enough not to push too hard. She hadn't tried to be Zach's mother, for instance. She'd never have fooled him.

"No," Jeanne said. Her voice was full, real—not what it should have sounded like coming from tiny holes in plastic. "He doesn't belong to you or to us. He's suffered enough, and he never should have been in such danger to begin with. He did what was needed—more than anyone had a right to ask of him—and now he's leaving. His mother is coming."

Mother. Zach knew now.

Jeanne. Paul's mother.

Sheila said nothing. She hadn't really believed she'd be able to keep him. He could feel that. Whatever power was hers was changing—falling back into another place, where it fit in with other strengths.

"You'll have your chance, Sheila," Jeanne said. "There's a lot of work to do. But he is not a bad boy."

She didn't need to say the rest.

A smart boy. A brave boy.

Zach was both. So he did something he almost never did. He laughed.

Then came something he absolutely never did.

"Thank you," he said.

SHE AWOKE TO WHISKERS at her nose, lips sealed against hers. A kiss. No. Fingers clamped her nose shut.

Someone forced breath into her mouth. She coughed. It stopped.

When the lips left hers, Annie said, "Okay."

And she was. She opened her eyes.

Wrangler John dropped onto his butt on the floor beside her. He crab-walked sideways a few feet as she took stock of her surroundings.

She was on the floor, on her back. The Virtual Boy stood on the table above, red glow gone, dead and dark. Its job was finished.

"I hope you know what that was," he said as she sat up and rubbed her eyes. "It wasn't—you know."

Eyes shut, she massaged her temples until the images of the Virtual Boy faded from the insides of her lids. "Where'd you learn to do that?"

"Fifty-seventh Med. Tan Son Nhut. The Original Dustoff." He watched her bring herself back the rest of the way. "I'm sorry. You were holding everything up. They told me to take you out of the loop. Last resort. I had no choice."

"I didn't know."

"You weren't breathing. Old training dies hard."

"Thank you." She pretended not to notice his embarrassment. Medics never changed. Gratitude was the worst thing you could do to them. "I'm sorry about your hand."

He shrugged and didn't bother to look at the bleeding scratches.

"What now?" she said.

"Everything's realigning. No one knows where Brill is, but he's gone. The machine's rebooting."

He started to get up as Annie rose to her feet, but remained on the floor when it was clear that she was used to compensating for her knee.

"As I said, then: what now?"

He shrugged. "We didn't think much beyond getting rid of him. Not many on our side have been around long enough to remember how it's supposed to work."

"The squid take it from here?" She waited for her head to finish clearing.

"They're multiplying and leaving. Again, nobody knows where. Wherever it is they're supposed to go. But there are way more than there were before. The rabbits and the ferrets are going, too, and I suppose I should let the bird take off. I don't know what I'll do. Make something up, I guess." He shifted position. He didn't look to be the type who was comfortable sitting on the floor. "I'm sorry."

"For what?"

"I'm a professional, but it's been a long time. And, well—do you mind if I kind of choose to look at what just happened as about ninety-eight percent mouth-to-mouth and two percent kiss?" When she said nothing, he buried his face in his knees. "Now I'm creeping you out."

She laughed. "That's the closest I've had to action since my son was conceived."

He wouldn't look at her.

She oriented herself. The door was to the left. "Speaking of which, before you blew my brains out, I feel like I got a bit of a line on where he is."

When Wrangler John didn't say anything else, Annie headed for the exit.

"Wait."

She did.

He stood and looked out the window at Weston's Black Hawk. "The Dustoff. I can fly."

Her ride was still here.

"Zach's with our people," he said. "He's a little hero, your boy. He got past Shoreline Sheila. She took down a lot of Journeymen in her time, but not him. Bright kid—a kid among kids."

"Yes," Annie said. "He is."

ON THE PLAYA, the festival was gone. Tents, booths—all absent, with no sign left to mark any of it but for the charred framework of Gaia herself, recognizable only to those who'd seen her before the flames had their say. She would collapse to the ground in the coming weeks, months, or years and be reunited with her earth.

Paul had missed his chance.

"That's another Journey," Rain told him. Her hardness had left her. She'd completed a Journey of her own.

He looked out across the playa to the high sand dunes separating them from the other side—where they'd crossed over, where they needed to go. "I guess we're walking."

LATER, THEY CRESTED A TALL DUNE, their packs a growing weight on their shoulders. The air and sky ahead wavered in the heat.

Paul had dug into his supplies and given Rain a ball cap to shield her from the sun. A wet kerchief hung down over the back of her neck.

He wore a t-shirt on his head like a proper desert nomad—or one forced to improvise. She'd only laughed at him for the first couple of miles. He loved that sound and wanted more.

Slow ups. Faster downs. All under the gaze of the withering sun. One dune was much like another, but each got harder and harder to conquer in the yellow-white rays.

They side-skidded down the slope of yet another dune.

"Aren't you going to ask?" Rain said.

The weight of the sun on Paul's head slowed the arrival of his answer. "No."

"Why not?"

They rested in a valley. There was no respite from the light, which had been such a comfort at the Shrine of the Lost but was no friend now.

"Because you didn't know me when you cut your deal. And because I'm a liar, too. When I left New Beginnings, I knew I wasn't coming back. But that's not what I told the man who wants to be my father. You can't build goodbye on a lie."

He pulled the t-shirt off his head to wring it out, but the sweat had long since evaporated. "I can't help but think that's what made all this happen— that I'd be in San Francisco now if I hadn't said that to him, and everyone would be safe." He fashioned a hat from the shirt again and started up the next dune.

"Just the one?"

He stopped to look back down at her. "What?"

She squinted up at him in the sunlight, which washed her into blinding absolution. "Just the one lie?"

He wanted to ask her how many she had to her name—and if she would cut the same deal again, given the choice.

Instead, he resumed his climb.

FINALLY, THEY TOPPED THE HIGHEST of the dunes—
the one Paul had been focusing on to keep himself
going.

Everything fell away when they saw what was
beyond it.

People. Thousands—no, millions—covering the
playa. And in the distance, past the masses, an immense columned building they all waited to enter.

A train station. The people had come for their
trips—their Journeys. And the crowd grew as Paul
and Rain watched.

"Wow," she said.

Paul and Rain went down to the people—pulled,
needed. Something had changed.

The two of them hurried, faster than they'd
moved for hours. Sand cascaded from their boots
as they descended.

At the bottom, the crowd remained focused on
the horizon but parted for the newcomers. Paul
and Rain were a rill making their way through. A
path opened, and they allowed it to lead them.

A host of faces. Men, women, boys, girls. So
many styles of dress. Hoop skirts, knickers, top
hats, and other formal wear, the garb of bygone
eras. How long had Mr. Brill held them?

At the crowd's center, the throng stepped aside to let them through. There, in a circular clearing, stood Porter and Po.

The Envoy looked up from his battered Newton and grinned broadly. Happiness wasn't at home on the gray man's face just yet, but it was settling in. He looked to have shed twenty years.

Beside him, the little monk beamed like a child who couldn't wait to show them the gift he'd made—the card he'd drawn himself.

"I said it some time ago. I'll say it now." Porter leaned on his staff more out of ceremony than necessity. "My God, boy. What have you done?"

"All these people," Paul said.

"Yes. And more arrive by the minute. The Commons is expanding. There's so much to do now that the most important Journeys in many lifetimes have come to an end."

Journeys. Plural.

It didn't seem possible for Porter's smile to grow. Yet it did. "It seems I left the office before the other assignments came in, but they've finished, too." He returned to the Newton's screen. "Paul Benjamin Reid. Ann Elizabeth Thomas Brucker. Zachary Robert Brucker."

Annie and Zach. Where were they?

Porter said Rain's full name aloud. Her real name. Paul wanted to stop there, to ask this girl so much he needed to know.

"And two more on their way to whatever awaits them," Porter said. "Gerald Truitt. James Prescott Brill." He waited for that to sink in. "Both fates determined, destinations known only to The Commons."

The Envoy surveyed the crowds of souls waiting silently to enter the station. "I've got my work cut out for me, certainly. But there's a volunteer list for the Envoy Corps that's as long as ten trains. And I've got the muscle to whip them into shape."

Po reached into the pocket of his robe. With great solemnity, he donned Ken's Wayfarers. The gravity of the duty and the memory of his friend kept an expression of grim formality on his face. Then he broke into another proud grin. Paul wished the mummy could be there to see it.

"And us?" Rain's fingers entwined with Paul's.

"Known only to The Commons." The gray man allowed a trace of the old sadness to touch his face. "That is all I can tell you, other than the most important words I have in me." He looked at each of them. "Thank you."

Po removed the sunglasses and nodded at Paul, then Rain, his gratitude joining with the Envoy's.

507

It was all going away so fast.

"I won't forget," Paul said to Rain.

She took his other hand and gave him a soft kiss. It ran all the way through him. "I won't, either."

But they did.

....

FORTY-FIVE

AND THE WEARY
ARE AT REST

H e dreamt of walking in a desert. A man gripped his elbow and spoke softly to him. The man was close, but his voice came from a distance. It was difficult to hear him.

In the way dreams go, what he knew as truth shifted. It changed because it was no longer true— or because he'd been wrong about it all along.

The man was trying to steer him toward water. Only it wasn't water. It was merely the way he needed to go.

He was thirsty—so thirsty that he couldn't swallow. The dream was a white oven.

People in the distance, behind a veil of blown sand.

A woman, older—with strong but kind eyes in a ruined face of melted seams.

A flash of a second woman. Red hair.

He fought for the word. "Mom." It wouldn't come.

Again. It wouldn't.

The older woman, sad, standing between him and the fiery hair.

Step into the photo. Impossible. Out of reach.

Passed. Past.

The man walked him onward. The sand became snow, the oven cold. Fires burned on a hillside but gave no warmth.

Icy water dripped from above, loosening crusted blood. A flourish of feathers and color.

He'd been in a fight. Worse than a fight, the man said.

At some point, they told each other goodbye.

He knew he'd see the man again. The man did, too. But not for a long time yet, with any luck.

The man let go of his arm. A tightness remained there.

Egress, someone said.

He'd thought the man was hanging onto him for support, but the man needed no help. He could stand on his own. And more. The look of him was misleading. The grayness, the walking staff.

He wanted to thank the man. But there was no man.

Paul could stand on his own, too.

And more.

PAUL FELT THE BURN OF THE IV before he saw the taped-over needle in his arm. His lids parted only with effort, as if they hadn't been asked to reveal anything in months. The tube was slung over a stainless-steel rack on wheels, with a hanging bag of something clear on the other end.

A hospital room.

Sunlight filtered through the window and IV bag, throwing a rippling pattern on the wall like the surface of an amber swimming pool. The space was filled with candy, balloons, and get-well cards—a mosaic of blue, yellow, white, green, orange, and shades in between.

He had puzzled over such colors a lifetime ago but couldn't remember where or when.

The ache in his head sloshed back and forth when he moved the tiniest bit. Some unseen demon poured generously from a cruel pitcher of misery, right into his ear.

His mouth was too sandy to move his tongue. He blinked. It hurt.

Two tabloid front pages were taped to the nearest wall. "Hell on a Hill," clamored the *Post* in white capital letters set over a photo of a mangled bus. "Prayers for Paul," proclaimed the *Daily News* above a shot of someone—not him, surely—in a bed, head encased in bandages. The figure was unrecognizable. Centered in a nest of tubes, he was flanked by enough lit-up gadgets and meters to pilot a starship.

In the picture, Pop Mike rose from a chair by the bed, reaching for the lens. Somebody wasn't supposed to be snapping photos.

The pages were faded from the sun.

Paul looked around the room. The machines were absent—as were the multitude of tubes, except for the IV.

He tried to move his feet. His ankle throbbed in response.

Across the room, a silver-haired nurse wrote on a clipboard, her back to him.

Paul thought to say something to her, but the nearest card stopped him. It boasted a pastel peacock, tail spread with pride. "Here's hoping you get your color back!" Bulgy words that left scant white space.

Someone had once said something about all-seeing eyes.

He reached for the peacock, the needle in his arm punishing him for the effort. His fingers grazed the card, and it clattered to the tile floor.

The nurse let out a yip and spun around to face him, hand on heart.

They stared at each other.

After a while, it came to him. He was smiling.

....

FORTY-SIX

TO ARRIVE WHERE
WE STARTED

The black clouds unleashed warm summer fury on the sidewalks of Hell's Kitchen. From the vantage point of the New Beginnings admissions desk a half-floor below street level, a wire-reinforced fire window showed only feet, ankles, and shins negotiating the pummeled concrete.

Paul could tell which people carried umbrellas by how their shoes moved through the rain, which rebounded off the cement as if fired from on high. Those who'd planned ahead walked. Everyone else ran like hell.

He completed an intake form for Johnny Day, a sodden fifteen-year-old just three days off the bus from Portland and two nights on the streets.

The kid stared at him.

Paul tried to ignore it but soon surrendered. "Yes."

"I knew it. You hard, right? They knocked you down but not out."

He handed Johnny the form. "Take that to the entry nurse, and try not to get it wet. Down the hall to your left." He pointed without looking. It wasn't Johnny Day's fault, but Paul really hated talking about the bus.

"She sweet?"

"Say again?"

"The nurse."

"He's all right. Cold hands."

Johnny Day waited for a follow-up, but Paul wasn't in the mood. The day was winding down, but the storm would herd more drenched admissions in before it ended.

The kid shrugged. With a barely audible "a'ight," he squeaked across the floor in the direction indicated.

Paul watched him long enough to ensure that he stopped at the correct door. A lot of the kids brought in by bad weather couldn't read and wanted to hide that, so Paul tried to give them a heads-up before they missed the prominent sign and made it obvious to everyone.

Keeping the peace at New Beginnings started with the preservation of dignity for all newbies. Those who felt bad about themselves inevitably tried to spread it to others. That's how things, hearts, and people got broken.

Johnny passed Pop Mike, who also watched him until he entered the right room. Then the old man gave Paul a status-checking raise of the eyebrows.

Paul nodded.

The thunk of the front door's steel push-bar and a splash of water announced the arrival of the intake van. The drain outside was running slow again.

A driver in a slicker so yellow it hurt dripped in, followed by a dozen newcomers in increasing degrees of soaked. "Wet ones," he said. "Laundry room unlocked?"

Paul nodded again. The new kids stepped into the receiving area, watering the donated issues of *Sports Illustrated* and *Cosmopolitan* and reducing some fallen free weeklies to mush beneath their soles.

The leading ones stopped to look around, then realized they were preventing those behind from coming in out of the downpour. Apologies circulated to a soundtrack of sneakers and pulp.

Paul worked the line with a practiced blend of care and efficiency. These kids needed to know they'd found a safe haven. They also had to understand there would be a structure and a routine they hadn't had on the street or, most likely, in the homes they'd fled.

This was payback for the years it had taken him to learn those same things—for the patience he'd required from Pop Mike. Justice had a sense of humor.

Form by form, kid by kid, all were processed and marched off to the clothing room to change into dry outfits before seeing the nurse. Rory had an eye infection and was separated out immediately. Kurt required time with a pro bono attorney. Paloma spoke no English and couldn't stop crying. Wilson seemed to think he'd been arrested.

Paul made them feel welcome. From a distance, Pop Mike watched him. By the time Paul finished, the old man had wandered off. That happened more and more lately—a good sign. He trusted Paul to work on his own.

A single drop hit the floor, surprising and loud. Paul hadn't noticed the straggler by the door.

The boy stood looking out the window, his back to Paul, a small pack thrown over slim shoulders.

He watched the rain as if weighing an exit back out into the elements.

Inside or outside wouldn't have made much difference, dryness-wise. The gray sweatshirt the kid wore, the hood pulled up to hide his face, was saturated to a dark slate. The wet cotton sagged around his head, pull-strings hydrating the hard floor.

"Just clothes or clothes-and-a-bed?"

The boy watched the scurrying feet pass at eye level but didn't reply.

"I don't mean to rush you, but if it's clothes-and-a-bed, you need to sign up in the next five minutes. After that, we can still give you something to wear, but you'll have to come back in the morning if you change your mind and want a place to stay."

Silence.

Paul tried again. "Were you the last one off?"

"I wasn't on the van."

A girl.

Making her decision, she approached the desk. By the time Paul ducked under the counter to grab another form, she'd pulled her hood down and shaken her long hair out—hair so black that Paul was sure it was just as dark when dry.

A girl with eyes as inky as her hair—and a depth there that reduced him to nothing. "Are the beds dry?" she said.

He remembered that he was supposed to answer. "As long as the roof holds. There's no guarantee of that, but yeah—dry for now. The food, too." What was he saying?

She took the form and pen he offered. He didn't trust himself to write in a steady hand, so he had her fill it out. Pretty girls and the resulting effect on him continued their tradition of knocking him off-center. He wanted to believe he was getting better at hiding it. He wasn't.

"Ray-Anne Blair?" he said, reading upside-down, trying to modulate his voice. His job was to make girls feel at home, not scare them off.

Something about her was familiar. Kids left and came back all the time, of course, and after enough intakes, they started to look alike. He hated admitting that because it made him feel callous.

But he couldn't shake the feeling of having met her before.

She handed him the form.

He was grateful to have something else to occupy his eyes. "Is this your first time with us?"

The girl took an odd red-and-gold box of candy from her pack and rattled it, checking for dryness. Satisfied, she shook a black disk into her palm. It looked like a tiny hockey puck.

The box was one of those things travelers brought home from far away when they couldn't think of anything else to buy you. "Gifu," it said in thick black lettering.

"Sisu?" She held the candy out to him.

The world tipped at a strange angle.

Bump-di-di-bump.

EPILOGUE

....

UNCLE LIGHTS-OUT

U ncle Lights-Out was not the blind man's full nickname. It was Uncle Lights-Out-Nobody-Home. But the squatter's camp neighbors who had pinned it on him thought that was too much of a mouthful.

He was unable to see—which explained the first half of his moniker—and had been for as long as he could remember. His memories were few, and he didn't trust them, so he ignored most attempts at conversation. That explained the rest.

Uncle Lights-Out didn't mind his name. He knew he wouldn't have it for long.

Nor did he mind his dodgy remembrances. They kept him from attracting attention, from raising suspicion. They provided him with cover.

Others accepted that Uncle Lights-Out was who he appeared to be because he believed it himself. In

the camp, questions were scarce. No one liked having to answer to anyone.

All of that eased his departure.

When the dog pulled him away from his tent in
the park, it acted on no command spoken or heard.
Uncle Lights-Out knew then that it was safe to put
the shield of his false memories aside.

"Where you going, Uncle?" his neighbors said.
He ignored them, allowing the dog to lead him out
of the trees, to the path.

His other thoughts, those telling him he'd soon
enjoy a very different existence, could now surface.
There was no need to keep them at bay; he wasn't
at risk any longer.

Leaving the camp, Uncle Lights-Out heard his
neighbors calling him back to claim his collection
can and its jingling coins. He didn't answer.

Uncle Lights-Out hoped they'd soon fight over
the can, though they'd probably safeguard it for his
return. He should have been grateful.

He wasn't. He would not be back.

By the second corner, Uncle Lights-Out no
longer needed the dog to tell him when the signal
changed. He couldn't see but knew.

Uncle Lights-Out did need the beast to show
him the way to his destination. And the dog served
as a distraction to anyone who might stop him, es-

pecially New York's police. He was journeying into a neighborhood that vagrants were told to avoid—told with words, told with deeds.

He was not far from the squatters' camp. Yet he rapidly moved from a place of hunger and filth to a realm of privilege and control.

Blocks from the park's southern entrance, the dog steered him off the main sidewalk and away from the passers-by, most of whom avoided looking at him. A woman dug in her purse for change, then realized he wasn't begging.

He gazed into her with his cloudy, sightless eyes. She shrank away. The time for his arrival was truly now.

Avenue of the Americas. Uncle Lights-Out and the dog approached the revolving doors of an ebon office tower, passing through the mist of a sculpture fountain.

The midday sun in the spray created a rainbow. The colors fled before the dog and Uncle Lights-Out.

So, too, did the good will of the men at the reception desk of the lobby they entered. The warmth they offered a woman in a charcoal suit bled away when they saw Uncle Lights-Out. It was a competition for which was the most offensive to them—the dog, the smell, or Uncle Lights-Out's boldness in crossing the threshold to this place.

The nearer of the two guards approached, shaking his head in refusal. Uncle Lights-Out fixed him with his gaze. The guard let him pass.

Uncle Lights-Out stepped up to the desk alone. The dog was gone, no longer necessary. Now he remembered everything.

"Are you here to see someone?" the second guard said.

"They are here to see me. I am expected."

Indeed, a man and a woman, also in charcoal suits, emerged from an elevator bank. They headed for the desk and Uncle Lights-Out, each bearing a practiced smile of welcome.

"Your name, sir?"

"Truitt," Uncle Lights-Out said. "Gerald."

Much to do. Much to rue.

JOIN THE COMMONERS

Keep up with The Commons via our email list by signing up at http://michaelalanpeck.com.

Or follow us on social media for news, updates on new releases, and more.

Facebook
http://www.facebook.com/michaelalanpeckauthor

Twitter
http://twitter.com/michaelapeck

Google+
http://plus.google.com/+MichaelPeckAuthor/

And thank you for taking the Journey with us.

ACKNOWLEDGMENTS

My friend Larry Brody says that if you want to create without collaborating, write a novel. And while he has a point, that doesn't mean you should try it without help.

Thus, I owe a hefty round of gratitude to a talented and generous group of people: Dan Fernandez for the wonderful cover and graphic design; Sarah Terez Rosenblum, Renée Bauer, and Marti McKenna for feedback and editing; Michael Visnov for character visualization; and Storystudio Chicago for getting me moving. Thank you all.

ABOUT THE AUTHOR

Michael Alan Peck tells tales big and small.
Life's magical, but it isn't always enough for a
good story. So he makes up the rest.

He grew up outside Philadelphia and has lived
in New York, L.A., and San Francisco. His
current home base is Chicago.